TOXIC

Jacqui Rose is a novelist who hails from South Yorkshire. She first came to appreciate the power of the written word when as a child she charged her classmates a packet of sherbet dips to write their essays for them. Adopted at a young age and always a daydreamer, she felt isolated growing up in a small mining v[illegible] kept her company. Jacq[illegible] whether it be screenplay[illegible]. She is the author of six bestselling novels as well as the author of two political thrillers written under a male pseudonym. She is a keen equestrian and the owner of two horses and spends most days riding.

Also by Jacqui Rose

Taken
Trapped
Dishonour
Betrayed
Avenged
Disobey

avon.

Published by AVON
A Division of HarperCollins*Publishers* Ltd
1 London Bridge Street
London SE1 9GF

www.harpercollins.co.uk

A Paperback Original 2018

2

A catalogue copy of this book is
available from the British Library.

ISBN: 978-0-00-828728-3

Typeset in Minion by Palimpsest Book Production Limited,
Falkirk, Stirlingshire
Printed and bound in the UK by
CPI Group (UK) Ltd, Croydon, CR0 4YY

This book is produced from independently certified FSC™ paper
to ensure responsible forest management.

For more information visit: www.harpercollins.co.uk/green

To AP and Boo – my joy, my heart, my soul's desire, my keepers of my peace, my freedom givers, my wingless journeymen – it's only a shame horses can't read.

The Devil asked me how I knew my way around the halls of hell. I told him I did not need a map for the darkness I know so well.

BEFORE

She could hear them now. They weren't far behind. Closing in and coming ever nearer, calling their names. She could almost feel their breath on her neck, their cloying touch on her skin, pulling her back. They needed to move but above the sound of the rain she could hear the barking dogs, louder and louder. They didn't have long. She knew that. She could feel the blood trickling down her legs and panic beginning to rise as the dark set in. And the pain, the pain was getting worse. She couldn't breathe. It was holding her. Slowing her down, making her not want to move, but she had to push through. They had to keep going. They couldn't rest, not until they were safe. Shhh, they had to be quiet. They had to be still . . . The dogs, there they were again. Nearer . . . Nearer . . . But oh God, the pain. She didn't know how long she could bare it . . . Maybe if they just stayed here. Maybe they'd be okay, but she was so cold, and the bleeding was getting heavier . . . Oh Christ, the blood. The dogs would smell the blood if she didn't cover it up.

Then, crawling out into the moonlight as the rain poured down, she saw them, they were coming. It was too late, they were coming . . .

YESTERDAY

ESSEX

In a remote scrap yard, four miles outside Saffron Waldon, Johnny Dwyer bent over the perfectly cut up lines of coke. He paused, almost in reverence, looking appreciatively at the white powder before eagerly pushing the fifty-pound note up into his nostril, hungrily sampling the new batch of cocaine he'd just shipped in.

He felt the burn at the back of his nose followed by the tingling sensation in his throat. This was the best part. The first rush which he'd spend the rest of the night trying to chase 'Can I move now, Johnny? I've got cramp in me bleedin' foot.'

Johnny stared down at the brass in disgust. Whores, they were all the same. Moaning and doing his head in. Jesus, if he'd wanted that, he would've stayed at home. He didn't know why he'd even bothered and now, now he was regretting it *big* time.

'If you know what's good for you, you'll shut the fuck up and keep still.' He bent down again, snorting another line off the hooker's stomach whilst trying, then quickly giving up on remembering her name.

'I ain't going to lie here any longer, I've got to go to the bog. I'll bleedin' piss meself otherwise.'

Whining and pulling a face she began to wriggle, spilling the coke down the side of her scrawny tattooed hip.

Johnny gnawed down on his lip. That was it. The final straw. Not only did this silly cow think it was okay to waste some decent blow, but she was now beginning to spoil his high.

Leaping towards her and pushing his hands down hard against her throat, Johnny's eyes bulged with rage.

'And I ain't going to pay for some bleedin' crackhead like you to have a piss in my bathroom, so if you wanna . . .'

'Boss?'

The door to the portacabin was flung open. Johnny scowled. 'Fuck me, what happened to knocking? Give a man a chance to put his cock away.'

Big Billy Baldwin, who stood no taller than five feet, grinned at Johnny. 'Sorry boss, but he's here. Ma told me to bring him straight to you. She said you'd know what to do. She also said "enjoy!"'

Tucking his penis back in his trousers, Johnny wiped his nose and nodded. 'Fine, bring him in . . . oh, and get her out of here.'

Happy to oblige, Billy stepped forward, grabbing hold and dragging the naked woman off the table.

'That hurt! Get off me! Oi! Who d'ya think yer manhandling? And what about me bleedin' money? I need me clothes! I've a mind to—'

The cabin door shut, muting the rest of her words.

Straightening himself up, Johnny rubbed his chin, feeling the coarse dark stubble, a throwback to his Romany genes. Sighing, he swept back his black hair as he leant forward on his chair, moodily spinning round the well-used cosh which sat in front of him on the desk.

He hadn't had the best of days; he'd heard a few things through the Essex grapevine which hadn't made him very happy. In fact, they'd positively pissed him off.

Ma had told him his wife, Bree, was acting suspiciously again, no doubt planning, thinking about leaving him as she so often did. But of course, that was just never going to happen. No one left him . . . *ever*. And if the stupid mare dared or thought she could just get up and go with the kids, then she really was braver than most men he knew.

But he'd sort it. He always did when she decided to step out of line. Though it always surprised him that she *still* hadn't learnt the lesson by now; she was his, and she was going nowhere. Yet even with all he'd taught her, every few months she'd get a bee in her bonnet about how she was going to leave, and every few months Ma would tell him about it. And then, well, he just sorted it the best way he knew how.

Rolling a spliff, Johnny thought about the other piece of information he'd heard today. The information which Ron the runt who was not only one of the biggest grasses between Essex and John o' Groats, but also one of the biggest liars – had delighted in telling him.

'It's true Johnny, I swear it is. I swear. I wouldn't lie to you. I was told by one of me sources.'

Johnny had stared at him in disbelief, but even when Billy – who'd been branding one of the horses at the time – had held a red-hot, glowing horseshoe inches away from Ron's face, the runt had sworn that his information was true. That now Reginald Reynolds, the kingpin of Essex, was dead, Vaughn Sadler and Alfie Jennings, two legendary faces of Soho, had decided to come back home. Home to Essex to set up shop and take the crown.

And if Ron *was* right? Well bollocks to that. There was simply no way he was about to let that happen. No bleedin' way at all.

On top of all that, he was now going to have to deal with Shane, one of his employees who thought it was okay to do a moonlight fucking flit and go and work somewhere else. So, before he could relax, and get on with the rest of his night, he was going to have to teach Shane a lesson. Then hopefully, things could finally get back to normal.

The door opened.

'Hello, Shane. Glad you could make it. Come on in.' Johnny cracked his knuckles, smiling as the tall, lanky young man was brought in by Billy.

Rubbing a bit of coke on his gums, Johnny's crystal-blue eyes stared coldly. 'Have I or have I not done a lot for you?'

Shane Hanlan mumbled, gazing down at the chipped, grey vinyl floor. 'Yes, boss . . . yes.'

Amusing himself, Johnny tapped the cosh on the palm of his hand, winking at Billy as he leaned towards a trembling, blanching Shane. 'I can't hear you. Speak up, son.'

'Yes, boss! Yes!'

'That's better. Now I need to ask you a question . . . Do you think I'm stupid?'

Shane's head shot up, his eyes darted around the room as his words rushed out. 'No, of course not! No way.'

'No? Then why? Why after all that me and Ma have done for you, do you do this? We train you up. Give you a job. Even welcome you into our home. For what, though? So you can throw it all back in me face and go and leave me?'

'I was going to come back. Straight up I was. Johnny, you got to believe me.'

Johnny Dwyer exploded. His handsome face turning red. He opened his mouth and bellowed as the veins in the side of his head swelled and pulsated. 'Do I look like I have mug written all over me forehead? Well, do I?'

With his whole body shaking, Shane could just about tremble out a 'No'.

'No, that's right. But you son, you have disloyalty written right through you, so much so it's coming out of your fucking arse. And now you've given me no option. I got to teach you a lesson, and it breaks me heart to do so. But what choice did you give me, hey? You should never have tried to leave.'

He paused for a moment before whispering into Shane's ear. '*I already told ya, nobody leaves Johnny*.'

Pulling back from him, Johnny Dwyer's eyes filled with tears. He lifted the cosh in the air, staring compassionately at Shane. He smiled warmly, speaking softly.

'I'm sorry, son. I really am.'

The cosh came whistling down, cracking and splitting Shane's nose in one blow, tearing the skin apart on his eyelids. The blood splattered and poured all over the portacabin walls and floor, and as Johnny brought the cosh down time and time again, Shane Hanlan dropped to the ground, screaming and writhing in agony whilst begging for his life.

Ten minutes later, covered in blood, Johnny Dwyer sat on the floor exhausted, cradling Shane in his arms.

'That's it son, it's over now. Don't you worry about a thing. You hear me? No need to cry.'

A rasping sound bubbled from Shane's mouth, his face swollen into an unrecognisable pulp.

'We'll get you cleaned up and then everything can get back to normal. And I'm *really* glad you're back, son. I thought it was time for my boy to come back to me. You'd been gone long enough. But next time, just remember, nobody ever leaves me . . . *ever*.'

As Johnny bent down to kiss Shane on his forehead, a sound of screeching tyres and blaring horns came from outside the portacabin.

Leaping up, Johnny ran out. 'What the . . .'

'Get down, boss! Get down!' Billy yelled as he dived on the floor and gunfire shots came hard and fast, cracking and speeding through the air, ricocheting off oil cans and scrap metal, and bouncing off skips in the yard.

Sprinting across in front of the portacabins, Johnny threw himself behind the pile of crashed racing cars, frantically scrambling to get to one of the numerous guns which were hidden around the yard.

'Look out!' Billy's voice soared urgently through the air.

Spinning around, Johnny saw the dazzling lights of a speeding red car coming towards him. Desperately, he scrabbled along the hard, gravelled ground, waiting for the impact to hit. But instead the car came to a screeching halt, inches away.

Johnny could smell the heat from the engine. The bumper of the car almost in contact with his face. He was pinned against the wall and all he could do was watch whilst the driver of the car, dressed in a black balaclava, jumped out, rushing round to crouch down beside him.

'Take this as a warning, Dwyer. Next time there won't be another chance.'

Reversing at speed, the driver hurled a petrol bomb towards one of the barns, sending it up into a ball of yellow and orange flames. 'You've been warned, Dwyer!'

Johnny silently watched the car drive off into the darkness. Tasting the hatred in his mouth.

'Who do ya think it was, boss?'

Johnny's face curled up into a snarl. 'I don't know, Billy, but when I find out, they're going to be dead men.'

By the side of the old watermill on the River Bourne the red car pulled up, skidding to a halt in the darkness of the night. Pulling off his balaclava as he turned off the ignition, Alfie Jennings grinned at Vaughn. 'Vaughnie, we're back. We're fucking back. Essex won't know what's hit them.'

TODAY

ESSEX

1

Bree Dwyer chewed nervously on her fingers. She felt sick and was dog-tired having been up most of the night listening to every sound and jumping at every car light which came onto the site.

She glanced up at the large white, glittery-faced clock as she stood in the kitchen of her immaculate, newly decorated static mobile home which was situated just outside the village of Ashdon, close to Shadwell Wood.

She shared her home with her husband and little Molly and Kieran, and on the odd, miserable occasion, her mother-in-law, who only lived next door.

Sighing and taking a sip of orange juice out of an Arsenal mug, Bree tried to swallow, but her mouth was too dry and too sticky, and her stomach kept alternating between painful cramps and butterflies.

She wasn't ill, she knew that. Though she wished that was all it was. No, her problem was just down to good old-fashioned nerves. Because today was the day she was *supposed* to be leaving her husband, Johnny, once and for all.

A sudden wave of nausea rushed over her, forcing her to run to the bathroom and lean over the toilet bowl as the sweet sickly water rushed into her mouth. Starting to shake and praying it wasn't the start of a panic attack, which she often suffered from. She took a deep breath, terrified at the thought of what she was about to do. A moment later, Bree Dwyer began to vomit.

Flushing the toilet, which was entirely encrusted with Swarovski crystals, Bree rinsed out her mouth, pushing her long blonde hair behind her ears. She caught sight of her reflection in the mirror, but quickly turned away. Hating what she saw. Hating seeing the look of fear in her green eyes, reminding her of a startled rabbit.

Holding onto the basin, Bree squeezed her eyes shut, took another deep breath before counting down from ten. Okay, she was ready. It was about to begin.

'Molly! Kieran! Quickly! Come on babies, we got to go.'

A few seconds later, Molly, who'd just turned six and proudly told anybody who'd listen, appeared at the bathroom door, clutching one of her stuffed giraffes.

Her long corkscrew blonde hair tumbled down in waves over her tiny, little shoulders. She spoke, sounding like someone much older than her age.

'What's the rush? Where are we going? Are the others coming?'

Bending down to hurriedly button up Molly's butterfly print blouse properly, Bree shook her head, speaking in a whisper as if there was somebody listening. 'No, darlin', they're not.'

Molly scowled. Her button nose wrinkling up. 'Why not? I want them to come.'

Nervously, Bree looked around. It seemed like her heart was pounding so hard in her chest, it was just about the only thing she could hear. 'I know sweetheart, but if they do, then they'll find out about the surprise.'

Molly's face suddenly lit up. She called in excitement, 'Kieran! Kieran! Come on, there's a surprise.'

Panicked at the volume of her daughter's voice, Bree gently shushed Molly, putting her finger over her lips. 'Shhh! We got to try to keep quiet, darlin'. We don't want anyone hearing us, do we?'

Smiling and kissing Molly on her forehead, Bree tried to push down the rising panic, attempting to ignore the thought she'd started something she couldn't finish.

'Well, what is it? What's the surprise? Is it for me?' Kieran Dwyer, although only nine, was the spitting image of his father. Both in temperament and looks. He stood at the bathroom door, grinning widely. He loved surprises.

'No, sweetheart.'

Kieran folded his arms petulantly, reminding Bree so much of Johnny. 'Then I ain't going bleedin' nowhere. Go on your own.'

Tenderly smoothing down his thick black hair, Bree looked sadly at Kieran. She loved him so much at times it ached, but with each passing day, Kieran was becoming more and more like Johnny. Idolising him and wanting to be just like his father when he 'grew up'; another reason why she had to get them away before it was too late.

Patiently, Bree spoke, crouching down to Kieran's height. 'Okay, I tell you what, how about this. If you come with me now, I'll buy you *any* game you want.'

Kieran's blue eyes darkened as he stared suspiciously at Bree. 'Any game?'

'Any. I promise. But we have to go, *now*.'

'Why?'

That was enough talk. Grabbing hold of both Kieran's and Molly's hands, Bree gently pulled the pair along the hallway. But as they neared the front door, it burst open and a tall figure, silhouetted against the bright sun, stood just inside the hallway.

'Hello, darlin'. What's all this then?'

Backing away, Bree clutched the children's hands tightly as she began to shake.

'Johnny . . . I . . . I . . .'

High-pitched laughter burst out as he clapped his hands, skipping on the spot. 'Bree falls for it every time! Funny Bree. Funny Bree.'

Bree's legs collapsed underneath her. 'Ryan! You bleedin' idiot. What you have to go and do that for?'

Ryan shrugged, looking hurt. His face crumpled as he held his head and rocked back and forth on the spot. 'I found kittens. Nice, nice kittens. Have I done bad? Has Ryan done bad? In trouble with Ma? In trouble with Ma?'

Bree stared at Ryan Dwyer, Johnny's identical twin brother. She tried to keep her voice even as she smiled at him kindly, trying to alleviate his panic. 'Shhh, Ryan. It's okay. You're not in trouble. I promise. But we have to go. Come on, hurry.'

Molly piped up. 'We're going to get a surprise.'

Ryan's eyes narrowed, looking troubled, his mind trying to comprehend. He stuttered.

'Does . . . does . . . does Johnny know? Got to tell Johnny. We tell Johnny.'

Getting up, with her legs still trembling, Bree spoke soothingly. 'Well it wouldn't be a surprise then, would it, Ryan. Look, darlin', we need to go. Come on Molly, hold my hand.'

Bree only managed to get part way down the stone white path before Ryan, who was dressed as usual in a blue Ralph Lauren tracksuit, stopped.

'Wait! Need to tell Ma!'

Bree spun round, her face strained with fear. 'No, Ryan, you don't need to do that. *Please.* It's just our secret. Remember? It will spoil the surprise.'

Ryan turned his head to the side, keeping his eyes on Bree. He rocked on his feet, looking anxious as he played with his hands. 'No, need to tell Ma. Need to tell Ma. Ma! Ma!'

'Please, Ryan, no! Don't!'

'Ma!'

The pink front door to the next mobile home was opened. 'What the bleedin' hell's all that racket for?'

Ma Dwyer stood in a blue, silk cornflower print dressing gown, tied too tightly around her bulging waistline. She rested her arms on her hips as her grossly obese body wobbled towards Bree and Ryan; the top of her legs sounding noisily as they rubbed and squelched together with sweat.

With egg yolk dried on her chin, Ma Dwyer sniffed, then burped loudly. 'This better bloody be good Ryan, otherwise I'll be giving you another brain injury.'

Holding Ryan's hand, Bree shook her head frantically. Her eyes wide with terror. 'Ryan, no. Look at me, no!'

'What she bleedin' on about? Go on, tell yer ma.'

A moment of hesitation rushed through Ryan's eyes before Ma Dwyer reached up and whacked her son hard around the head. 'I'm talking to you, you little shit.'

Ryan rubbed his head, looking so much younger than his thirty years. 'We shouldn't tell you. Can't tell Ma.'

Ma stared at Ryan. Her voice was mean and hard. 'I'm warning you son, you better tell me, unless of course you want to be in trouble. Is that what you want, Ryan? You want to be in trouble?'

Agitated, Ryan looked down, playing with his hands as he shook his head. 'No. No.'

'Then tell me!'

Blurting the words out as quickly as he could, Ryan said, 'She's off to get Johnny a surprise. A secret.'

Ma Dwyer grinned nastily. 'Is she now . . . Take the kids into the house, Ryan, I want a little word with Bree.'

'But I want to see the kittens.'

'I said take the friggin' kids inside, you dopey muppet!'

Ma Dwyer watched as Ryan skipped into the house with Molly and Kieran, who were giggling happily. She turned coldly to Bree.

'So now you can tell me all about this surprise, or maybe I should just call Johnny and ask him . . . Oh, no need . . . Look . . . Somebody's going to be taught a lesson.'

As Ma cackled, Bree swivelled round to see Johnny's black

Range Rover coming up the drive. The next minute Bree started to run, listening to the sound of Ma Dwyer's screeching voice behind her.

'Johnny! Johnny! Quick, she went that way!'

Bree Dwyer had never run so fast in her life. She could hardly get her breath as she leapt and bounded through the thick undergrowth of Shadwell Wood, feeling the bushes and branches tearing at her flesh.

She could hear Johnny behind her as she raced through the woods. Faster and faster she went, stumbling down ditches, scrambling and falling as her shoe caught in the twisted shrubs. She slipped on the wet leaves and her nails scraped at the mud as she tried to get her footing, as she slid back down the hill.

She could taste her tears and her own fear and her chest began to tighten. She was too afraid to look behind her, but she knew Johnny was there. Closing in. Coming to get her.

'Don't run from me, Bree! There's nowhere to go!'

Johnny's voice seemed to engulf the whole of the area; echoing through the trees, echoing through the branches. Her legs were aching now, but she continued to run, her thin trousers covered in blood. She headed towards a small, gravelled track aiming for the copse on the other side.

'Bree! Bree!'

She glanced back, then she heard a roar. A screech. The sudden slamming of brakes.

'Look where you're going, you dozy mare! I could've killed you.'

She spun round, feeling the car on her leg as she leant her hands on the hot bonnet. Panting.

Blinking.

Staring at the driver. A moment of slight recognition passed between them before Bree began to run.

'Hey, come back! You alright, love?'

Limping, she leant against a tree, trying to get her breath. She had no idea where she was, and even though the woods were close to where she lived, she'd never ventured into them on her own.

Setting off again along an overgrown path, Bree heard the cracking of twigs but before she had time to turn around, heavy, rough hands grabbed her. She screamed as she was pulled down into the undergrowth. Feeling Johnny's breath against her neck.

She froze as he sat behind her, putting his hands round her waist, drawing her in between his legs. Kissing her on her neck whilst stroking her hair.

He spoke quietly. A dangerous lull in his voice. 'What did you think you were doing, Bree?'

Her words were breathless with fear. 'Nothing.'

'You was going to leave me, weren't you?'

She shook her head quickly. 'I wasn't, I swear, Johnny.'

Slightly too hard, he nibbled the lobe of her ear, making Bree flinch. 'I don't believe you, baby.'

Bree shivered, feeling like she had a thousand ants crawling underneath her skin. 'All I wanted to do was just take the kids out. I was going to get you a surprise.'

He shrieked into her ear, causing the nesting starlings to fly out of the trees and into the sky. 'Liar!'

'*Please*, Johnny.'

'You know what I have to do now Bree, don't you? I have to teach you a lesson.'

Bree couldn't control her shaking, her body went into spasms, and she didn't know if it was just the wet earth or if she'd wet herself in fear.

'And why do I, Bree? Why do I have to teach you a lesson?'

Bree stayed silent as her whole body trembled.

'I said, why do I? Say it! Say it, Bree!'

Crying and gasping for air, Bree Dwyer closed her eyes, only just managing to speak.

'Because nobody *ever* leaves Johnny.'

2

'Wakey, wakey! Come on my handsome darlin's, what's all this? The day has started and you two pieces of lump are still in bed.'

Lola Harding cackled loudly as she energetically opened the curtains in the garishly decorated silver and velvet master bedroom of Janine Jennings' large mansion just outside the straggling village of Wimbish in Essex.

'Do me a favour! Bloody hell, Lola! Turn it in. Are you trying to kill me?'

'No one died of a bit of sunshine, hey Janine?'

Leaning against the bedroom door, Janine Jennings sniffed as she bit into her fifth chocolate biscuit of the morning. 'Don't know why yer bothering, my husband has always been a lazy bastard.'

Alfie Jennings sat straight up. 'Ex-husband.'

Janine guffawed with laughter. Her gold necklaces jangling with her. 'You see, that's the way to get him out of bed; remind him of our nuptials. Come on Vaughnie, take them covers off yer head. What's wrong with you two? You asked me to wake you up.'

Alfie groaned. 'Not this bloody early. And if I'd known me and Vaughnie had to share a bed when you said we could stay, I wouldn't have bothered.'

Janine scowled. 'Beggars can't be choosers and anyway it's only temporary, ain't it?' She paused before adding, 'I thought you were supposed to be picking up Franny today.'

Alfie's smile was tight as he tried not to let his anger overwhelm him as he thought of Franny. Franny Doyle, the woman he'd given his heart to. So strong, so beautiful, so clever, so fearless yet with a vulnerability which had made him fall in love with her, no matter how much he had tried to stop himself. But he had, and he'd fallen hard.

The daughter of one of the most notorious gangsters, he'd met Franny in Soho but after a while they'd decided to leave and go and live in Spain; there was nothing in the West End for them anymore. The place had changed beyond recognition. There was no more making money. Gangsters and faces had moved out. Tourists and foreigners, druggies and coffee shops had moved in. The council had clamped down, going into overdrive on any illegal activity, something they would've once turned a blind eye to or at least he could've paid them off. So, Spain had been their ideal.

He'd even given up the business for her after she'd become tired of seeing how many people it hurt. And he'd been happy to go semi-legitimate, or as happy as he could've been. But now, *now* was entirely different and happy certainly wasn't a word which came to mind.

He stared at Janine and then at Vaughn. He shrugged, trying his best to sound unruffled.

'There's been a slight change of plan.'

Vaughn's words shot out. 'What the hell are you talking about?'

'Look, calm down, nothing's wrong. Franny's on her way, she's just been a bit delayed, that's all.'

Incensed, Vaughn got out of bed, throwing the duvet in Alfie's face. He walked across to the crushed velvet window seat and lit up a cigarette, inhaling it hard.

'That's all? She's got two million quid of our money which, let me remind you, is all the money we've got in the world, and you expect me to be calm?'

Alfie got up from the mattress, pulling on his red sweat top over his muscular body, much to Lola's dismay; albeit she was nearing seventy, she still had an admiring eye for a handsome man.

Then, lying through his teeth, Alfie said, 'It's just a little hiccup. Apparently when Franny got on the boat there were a lot of coast guards and police about at Puerto Banús and Puerto de la Bajadilla doing a routine sweep of all the private vessels, so she thought it was best to wait until everything's quietened down before they set off. She knows what she's doing.'

'That's what I'm afraid of. Franny knows *exactly* what she's doing.'

Alfie stared at Vaughn, hoping the anger he felt towards Franny didn't show on his face. Hoping he didn't give anything away. Not yet anyway.

When they'd left for Spain, both he and Vaughn – who he'd known since he was a teenager – had invested in property. Clubs and restaurants initially, then finally a resort just south of Torremolinos, but then – and maybe it was his own fault for not keeping an eye on the legitimate businesses as he had done the illegitimate ones – the developer had gone bankrupt before the place had been finished, heading off to Mexico with their money, leaving unpaid workers and contractors as well as him and Vaughn out of pocket. The bank had closed in and they'd been left with not much change from fuck all.

But just when they'd started to worry, Reginald Reynolds, Essex kingpin, number one face and an old trusted friend of them both, had got in contact wanting to sell his bookmaker business, which not only incorporated the best legal pitches at racetracks like Cheltenham and Newmarket, but also the monopoly on the systematic illegal betting market in the East of England. And of course, they'd jumped at the chance. It was not only the reason they'd been looking for to come back home to Essex, it was a licence to print money. And all for just two million big ones.

It was a deal that couldn't be missed and once they'd shaken on it, Reggie had put the word around that he and Vaughn were going to be his successors when he retired, which not surprisingly hadn't gone down well with a lot of people.

They hadn't known at the time, but Reginald hadn't been retiring but had been fighting cancer, and was just putting his affairs in order for his family before it was too late. Two weeks after the details had been sorted, his widow, Reenie had been in touch letting them know Reginald was dead.

Vaughn had sold his house and Alfie had sold his villa, getting the money they needed together. Obviously, the likes of Reggie and his family only dealt in cash and certainly no transfers through any bank, so it was decided that they would travel to England first and Franny would follow with the cash on the boat of an old associate of theirs, later. Easy. Or it was supposed to have been.

'Fuck's sake, what's with all the paranoia? Just leave it, okay?'

Alfie turned around but felt Vaughn's grip on his arm. 'Listen, until I have me money in me hand, I ain't going to leave anything. You hear me?'

'Get yer hands off me.' Alfie shoved Vaughn, who fell back into Lola, then, just managing to keep his balance, Vaughn sprang at Alfie, grabbing hold of his top. With his face red, he hissed his warning.

'I've already lost nearly everything because you didn't keep your eye on the ball with that developer, pretending everything was fine. So, I'm telling you now Alfie, if anything's happened to me money, I'm going to hold *you* responsible. And I'll come for you. You understand me?'

'Don't threaten me, Vaughn, unless you want to be a dead man walking.'

Scrabbling between them, Lola tried to pull the men apart. She appealed to Vaughn. 'This is Franny we're talking about. She ain't going to rip you off, is she? None of this is Alfie's fault. I know you've had it tough these last few months, but see sense, Vaughn.'

'Have you forgotten that Franny is the daughter of Patrick Doyle, one of the biggest gangsters there was?'

'No, but . . .'

'But nothing Lola. The apple don't fall far from the tree, does it?'

Lola, not enjoying hearing Vaughn saying anything negative about her friend, put her hands on her hips as she stood in front of him. 'Vaughn Sadler, have you ever, in all the time that you've known Franny, had any reason not to trust her?'

'No, but . . .'

'*But nothing*, right back at you. If Franny says she's been delayed, then she's been delayed. It's going to be fine.'

Vaughn, unable to help himself, snapped at Lola. 'In less than a month's time we are supposed to be finalising the deal with Reginald Reynolds' widow to buy his pitches, pay off who needs to be paid off to get the bookies' licences, as well as recruit and pay a trusted team of men that we can have around us. Tell me Lola, how the fuck are we supposed to do that now? More to the point, how are you expecting me to keep calm when some bird is floating round the Costa with two million big ones in her back pocket?'

'Vaughn, love—'

'No, Lola! Hear me out. Reginald did us a favour by putting us first in line for his business. Everybody wanted it, and you know that. Once we get it up and running – *if we do* – it'll mean we won't have to think about money again, but now, thanks to this muppet, there's a chance we could lose this opportunity.'

Alfie glared at Vaughn. 'Stop winding yourself up, mate. It'll be fine.'

'Will it? It better be, because I've risked everything on this. Sold everything I had right under me missus' nose and because of that, she's gone and left me. That money is all I've got.'

'It ain't only yours.'

'No, but it wasn't me who gave the money to Franny, was it?'

Alfie, always one to be hot headed, said, 'Look, so she's delayed, it's no biggie. You're acting like someone's robbed your fucking grave. And as for Casey, maybe you should've been more honest with your missus, perhaps that way she might not have done a runner, or maybe it was just her excuse.'

Vaughn went to swing at Alfie but pulled back as Lola stepped in his way. She smiled at him, hating seeing them argue. 'Vaughn, lovie, please. Alf's right, you're getting yourself worked up over nothing. Franny will be here soon, and as for Casey, she'll come round and see sense. Once she understands you did it for your future, she'll be fine about it. I'll have a word with her if it helps. Look, how about instead of all this arguing, which ain't going to do any of us any good, why don't I make you all some breakfast?'

The resounding cry of '*no*' was heard round the room as everyone present remembered the days of Lola's café, which she'd run in Soho for years. Her breakfasts had been infamous.

Lola shrugged. 'Then at least kiss and make up. Come on, Vaughn. Alf, how about you?'

Neither of the men moved and Lola sighed. She'd known and loved Alfie and Vaughn for as long as she could remember, meeting them in Soho back in the day. In all that time she'd never known the two men have so few options, but then, they may never have come back to England otherwise. She hid a small smile. Every cloud.

Vaughn, ignoring Lola's plea for reconciliation, spoke to Alfie, his voice full of hostility.

'And what are we supposed to do for money until Franny comes? What are we supposed to tell Reginald's widow?'

'We tell her nothing because there's *nothing* to tell. And in the meantime, we stick to our plan. We let everybody know we're back and we mean business. Essex is ours for the taking.'

'Just the two of us?'

'Yeah, because they won't know that, will they. We give it large like we always did. And in a couple of days Franny will be here, and then we'll have the money to recruit some of the people who used to work for us. It'll be sweet.'

Vaughn looked at Alfie. 'Okay, but I'm telling you, Franny needs to be here by the end of the week.'

Janine, who'd been unusually quiet, piped up. 'And you've got here. You can both stay here with me.'

'See, there's an offer no man can resist.' As he said it, Alfie rolled his eyes causing Janine to let out a screech.

'I saw that! Did you see that, Lola? Bleedin' fucking cheek. I don't know why I bother. You should be thanking me, Alfie. You should be grateful.'

'Grateful! I'd be more grateful to an arse full of piles.'

Seething, Janine turned to Lola. 'I knew this was a bad idea. I should never have listened to you. I'm a mug. That's what me mates said when I told them I was going to let you stay. They said, Janine. You. Are. A. Mug.'

Lola pushed Janine and Vaughn gently out of the door. She smiled at Alfie. 'Why don't you get dressed and come downstairs for a nice cup of tea.'

'Thanks Lola, I'll be there in a minute.'

'And Alfie, it's good to have you back . . . I missed ya. Both of ya.'

Hearing the others heading downstairs, Alfie pulled out his phone. He stared at the text from Franny.

Please don't be angry Alfie, but something's come up. It's probably better if you don't know what. But trust me when I say, I wish it could be different. I won't be coming to England. One day you'll understand why I've done this. If it's any consolation, I do love you. F.

Dialling Franny's number, it switched straight onto voicemail. Speaking quietly Alfie hissed through his teeth. 'Franny, it's me. You better start picking up the fucking phone, you hear me? Just pick up the fucking phone. I want my money.'

He clicked off the call before hurling the phone against the wall, wondering which was greater, his broken heart or his anger.

3

Stepping out of his silver Audi Q5, which had seen better days, Eddie Styler lit a cigarette, admiring as he always did the mock-Tudor cladding he'd had fitted last year on the large, five-bedroom property on the private gated estate, just south of Emerson Park, Essex.

The place was a far cry from the run-down council block in South London he'd been born and brought up in, where drug addicts shot up on stairwells and anyone passing who cared to used the lobby as a giant urinal.

Unlike his childhood home, which he'd been ashamed of, number 25 Colney Close impressed, making him the envy of his family, most of whom still resided in the same shit hole they were born in and no doubt would be carried out in a box from.

It'd been the double garage feature of the house which had excited him, and within minutes of seeing the place, he'd put in an offer, well over the asking price, much to his wife, Sandra's disgust. But then, when wasn't the moany cow disgusted at him for one thing or another? And God, didn't she just like to remind him how it was *her* money and not *his* that had bought the place.

But they were married, so by rights that made it his whether she liked it or not. To *have* and to hold. For *richer*, for poorer. His home. His castle.

Irritated at the thought of her, Eddie gritted his teeth too hard, causing the white filling that'd cost him near on three hundred quid last week, start to throb, making his present mood considerably worse.

Stomping towards the house and having inhaled deeply on the cigarette, which made his green eyes water, Eddie opened the front door, being hit immediately by the nauseating smell of Sandra's constantly burning vanilla and honeysuckle scented candle, causing his eyes to water some more.

He clenched his fists feeling the stress catapult through him. How long he'd resented Sandra he didn't know. Maybe it was the moment he'd said 'I do' and had lifted her wedding veil to see her dark, cold beady eyes staring at him as she chewed down on a piece of gum. But no matter when it was, Eddie knew he resented her now . . . *hated* the stupid cow now.

They'd made an odd-looking couple; her at six foot three – all pale skin and jutting bones – and him, barely five foot tall of rounded Greek heritage. But it hadn't mattered, because money had been the reason he'd got together with her in the first place, desperate to escape the poverty of his life, and Sandra, with her flashy car and expensive shoes, had been his ticket out. Well, that's what he'd thought she was. But rather than having money at his fingertips as he'd imagined, she'd held onto her bank accounts tightly like they were a life raft.

Despite her, over the years he'd tried to make a name for himself, wheeling and dealing, using old contacts and being the middleman for the Mr Bigs, but each time he'd thought he was making a reputation, each time he could smell success, each time he thought he could finally leave Sandra, someone or something came along to squeeze the balls out of whatever deal he was trying to make and he'd be left with nothing at all.

But a few years ago, things had started to look up. He'd got the call from Reginald Reynolds, the number one face in Essex, who made the Kray twins look like something out of a children's storybook.

And he'd worked hard for Reginald. Becoming his right-hand man. Setting up the beatings, the tortures, the paybacks, the deals, and with Reginald Reynolds' men behind him, his own name had become synonymous with fear. There wasn't a man alive who'd say no to him. He could run up debts at casinos, debts with pimps, he had money at his fingertips. That was, of course, before Reginald Reynolds had popped his clogs at a very inconvenient time.

At first though, he'd been pleased that Reginald had finally snuffed it, assuming he was going to take the Essex crown. But after discovering from Reggie's widow, Reenie, that rather than him – after all his loyalty – being the natural successor to his empire, he'd arranged that the scumbags, Alfie Jennings and Vaughn Sadler, were going to take over, he'd gone to the cemetery in Chigwell and pissed on Reginald's grave.

But there was one thing that Reginald hadn't managed to finalise before he'd died. A deal which only he really knew about. And once he'd pulled it off, things were going to be different. What he had lined up would change everything and no one was going to mess this up. And unlike all the other times, there was no question *he* wasn't going to pull it off. Because everything was riding on it. *Everything.*

Even though Reginald had left some outstanding money to pay on the goods, thankfully he was able to find some cash himself by forging Sandra's name on a remortgage application, getting the readies transferred into a bank account she didn't know about, which had given him enough to finalise the deal of all deals, and all without any of Reggie's men or family knowing about it. And the beautiful thing was, even if Sandra *did* eventually find out about the loan, it wouldn't matter because they'd literally be rolling in it. Or rather *he* would. And then? Well then, it'd be adios Sandra.

Tiptoeing along the dark, oak wooden hallway to the cupboard under the stairs, he glanced up towards the bedroom, pausing and checking for any sound. He opened the stair cupboard door, quickly rummaging in the large box of tools he never used, and pulled out a half empty bottle of whiskey. The screw top couldn't come off fast enough for Eddie and he knocked it back in one; wincing at the burn.

Content and preoccupied in his thoughts, Eddie absentmindedly stepped backwards, knocking over one of Sandra's glass candle holders, shattering shards of glass all over the dark wooden floor.

'Bollocks!'

Sighing and feeling the effect of the alcohol, Eddie heard Sandra, her voice grating through the silence of the darkness.

'Eddie, is that you? What time is it? Eddie! What the bleedin' hell are you doing?'

Walking up the stairs, Eddie thought it best to knock a couple of hours off, knowing that his wife would start to complain and ask a dozen questions about where he'd been if she knew the real time.

Gritting his teeth, he gave a saccharine reply. 'It's one o'clock, teddy bear. Go back to sleep.'

Immediately, the bedside light flicked on, and Sandra, sleepy eyed and messy haired, stared at him accusingly. 'How the fuck am I supposed to sleep when you're banging about like a brass band?'

Knowing it was best not to reply, Eddie undressed and slipped into bed, feeling the cold as if the sheets were made of a thin layer of ice. He shivered as he lay on the very edge of the super king size bed, which was mostly taken up by Sandra and all her cushions.

'Is Barrie in okay?'

In no mood to go on an early morning hunt for the cat he hated – who perpetually seemed to have a supercilious smugness on his face – and having seen him wandering down the street yesterday morning and not since, Eddie answered casually, pushing down the sense of loathing towards Sandra that immersed his whole being.

'He's curled up on the sofa . . .'

'Have you been drinking?'

Too quickly, Eddie shook his head and answered, 'No.'

For the next few minutes Sandra continued to stare, looking for a giveaway tell-tale sign as Eddie Styler smiled reassuringly at his wife, trying to push down his hatred, thinking as he so often did how like her brother, Alfie Jennings, she looked.

4

Great Dunmow, like so many other small market towns across Essex, was surrounded by picturesque countryside and as Alfie Jennings drove through the rural location, sitting on the River Chelmer, once home to the Romans, his mind thought back to yesterday. To the woman in the woods. She'd looked terrified, running away from something or someone, but she'd dashed away before he'd had a chance to speak to her. He was certain he knew her from somewhere, he was sure of it, her face looked so familiar, but he couldn't quite place her. It would come back to him, he was certain.

Driving past the small shops and museum on the winding, pretty high street, Alfie turned left, flicking his cigarette out of the window as he tried not to let himself think about Franny. He couldn't get his head around the text. He didn't know what he was supposed to think. But what he did know was he needed to sort out the shit she'd landed him in.

Pulling up his Range Rover by a large thatched yellow house, set by a private lake and standing in several acres of pristine grounds, Alfie got out, resisting the temptation to call Franny again. That could wait. He didn't want to wind himself up any more than he had to because if he wasn't careful, he was going to lose it. Big time.

Trying to crick the tension out of his neck as he pressed the buzzer on the gates, Alfie waited, the heavy rain trickling down the back of his coat.

Eventually he heard a man's voice crackling through the intercom, speaking in the broadest of Yorkshire accents. 'Hey up Alfie, you look like you could do with a brolly.'

Alfie looked up to the CCTV camera, his face curled up in a snarl. 'Just let me fucking in.'

He heard laughter as the electric gates duly swung open but before Alfie could get to the house, a large man with a protruding forehead and a Bryllcreamed sweep over, came around the corner armed with two golfing umbrellas.

'Here take this, we'll go into the garden and talk.'

Alfie stared at Lloyd Page. Lloyd had come down from Sheffield fifteen years ago to become one of the biggest drug traffickers in the East of England, as well as one of the boldest swindlers around. The man wouldn't lose any sleep over robbing food from his own baby's mouth if it meant him getting a few more quid.

'I ain't partial to country walks, Lloyd. I'd rather talk here.'

Lloyd belched loudly, sending the smell of pickled onions into Alfie's face. 'Suit yourself. You've always been a stubborn bastard.'

Alfie narrowed his eyes, gazing coldly and evenly at Lloyd. 'I'm not here to do niceties, I'm here to find out if there's anything going on.'

With the umbrella in one hand and a cigar in the other, Lloyd smirked, holding Alfie's gaze.

'This is what I couldn't understand on the phone when you called. You see, I was under the impression that you were supposed to take over Reginald Reynolds' crown. You and Vaughnie were supposed to be the next Kingpins, the whole of the East thought that, yet here you are, begging me for a touch.'

'I ain't begging no one.'

'No?'

'No.'

Lloyd shrugged. 'I don't believe you Alf, I think something's not quite right. I reckon you're a bit desperate, otherwise why would you be here without your sidekick? Funny that.'

Alfie stepped in close to Lloyd. 'Do I look like I'm laughing? And you don't need to worry about the ins and outs of my business. All you need to know is that I need a job, and quick. And you also need to keep your mouth shut about me being here.'

'And why would I do that? I think a lot of people would want to know, don't you?'

'Because, Lloyd, you ain't stupid and you like your life too much. You and me, we go back a long way, which means I know everything that you've done. I know everyone that you've turned over, everyone you've ripped off. Wasn't it only a couple of years ago you pulled one over on the Peterson brothers. Robbed over a ton of heroin right from under their noses. To this day, Smithy Peterson and his brothers want to know who it was. And rumour has it, they like burying people alive.'

'You wouldn't snake?'

'Oh, I would, Lloyd. I'll do what I have to. I'll take no prisoners, son.'

Lloyd's face turned into a picture of anger. 'It's quiet at the moment, there isn't anything much about.'

'Then unquieten it, because I need something.'

Sighing, Lloyd said, 'Look, there might be a shipment of coke coming through in the next few days. It'll be on a lorry and I was hoping to get my fingers on it. I'm speaking to my sources at the moment. It's not certain yet, but it sounds like it could be an easy job.'

Alfie stared out towards the immaculate landscaped garden. Jacking lorries of coke was a young man's game, often a mug's game, and it certainly didn't help that it was Lloyd Page he'd be working through. He was, as Vaughn had always described him, an idiot of the biggest kind. But then, it seemed like it might be his only option if he couldn't sort out the problem with Franny.

Not that jacking a lorry full of blow would give them the money they needed, but it was a start.

'Then I'll have that.'

'Alf, come on, I needed that myself . . .'

'I said, I'll have that.'

'But it might not even happen.'

'So, you better make sure it does.'

5

Bree Dwyer felt her husband's breath before she saw him in the dark of their cream-walled bedroom. Her body ached and the ropes tied round her hands and ankles cut deeply into her, burning and rubbing. The dried blood from her nose sat in crusty lumps above her mouth, and with the air of a priest, Johnny smiled warmly, kissing Bree calmly on her head before untying her from the wicker chair that had dug and scraped into the back of her bare legs.

He looked at her, his head cocked to one side. 'Well?'

Licking her torn lip and flinching, Bree knew exactly what was expected of her. 'I'm sorry, Johnny.'

He leaned in, the overpowering aroma of his sickly-sweet aftershave rushing up Bree's nose.

'And?'

'And I ain't ever going to try to leave you again, because . . .'

She faltered, feeling nauseous.

'Because?'

'. . . because no one leaves Johnny.'

A wide grin spread across Johnny's wind-tanned face. He laughed, pleased with himself.

'So you've learned your lesson this time, darlin'?'

Bree willed herself not to vomit there and then. Whatever she did, Bree Dwyer knew there was no way she could be sick in front of Johnny. Panicked, her eyes filled with tears as she desperately tried to swallow down the bile that rushed with force into her mouth.

Johnny's eyes darkened. 'I asked you a question.'

The door suddenly flung open, making Bree jump, and giving her the distraction she needed to alleviate the nausea.

There, standing in the doorway, was Ma Dwyer; oedema-swollen ankles and feet pushed tightly into stained, pink fluffy slippers and dressed as usual in her thigh-length silk dressing gown.

Looking contemptuously at Bree, Ma pulled out her nasal pump spray, keenly squirting it up into her left nostril. 'What's going on, baby?'

Johnny circled his fingers inside the thin, pale yellow cotton dress Bree was wearing. 'I'm just waiting for an answer, ain't I, Bree?'

Bree nodded, her eyes darting from Ma to Johnny.

Ma Dwyer frowned. 'Well we ain't got time for you two to get all lovey-dovey and kiss and make up. We gotta be somewhere. You best get moving, Johnny. Eddie Styler don't like to be stood up . . . Oh, bleedin' hell, here comes Noddy.'

Ma crossed her arms across her enormous, braless breasts as she watched her other son, Ryan, come nervously into the bedroom.

Ryan Dwyer turned to his mother. 'Ma?'

'Shut it!' And with that, Ma Dwyer marched out of the room.

Giving a last, cutting glance to Bree, Johnny headed for the door whilst snarling instructions to his brother. 'Make sure she don't go anywhere, Ryan. You understand me?'

And not waiting for an answer, Johnny hurried away.

Ryan, spectacularly identical to Johnny, looked at Bree. She smiled at him tenderly as he touched her bruised, swollen face. His damaged brain trying to understand.

'Johnny's angry with Bree. You should never leave Johnny. Trouble. Ma says there'll be trouble.'

'I know, sweetheart, I know.'

Bree went to the door, looking down the hall before closing it quietly. Pressing her body against it, she turned back to look at Ryan, her eyes filled with tears.

'But one day Ryan, we will. We'll leave here for good, and you'll be free, and then sweetheart, we'll have no more trouble.'

It was dark and the private traveller site was quiet apart from the sound of the dog barking on Willoughby's farm, some way off in the distance. As Kieran sat under the bushes – a place where he often slept – watching Ma Dwyer waddle down the path in her silk dressing gown, forcefully sniffing the white bottled, nasal plastic pump spray she always carried, he dug his fingers into his leg; drawing blood, feeling the pain and enjoying it.

The steel blade he held in his other hand caught the light of the moon. He smirked, glimpsing the reflection of his mouth, then, quietly humming, Kieran Dwyer began to cut.

6

'Pick up, for God's sake! I don't know how many bleedin' messages I've left but you can't keep ignoring me. For fuck's sake Franny, why are you doing this to me, darlin'? Just call me and let's sort this out. I get that you could be mad at me. Maybe I didn't give you as much attention as I should've done, or maybe you think I don't tell you that I love you enough. But I do love ya, from the minute I knew ya, I started falling for ya. But Jesus, Fran, whatever it is I've done, don't take it out on our future. Vaughn's future. You want me to come and find you, Franny? Is that what you want, darlin'? To show you I care? Cos I do, but I just haven't got time for these *fucking* games at the moment! Franny!'

Alfie took the phone away from his mouth, taking in deep breaths of air to calm himself down. He tried again. 'Look baby, I know you'll get these messages so *please*, just call me. I need to get me hands on the money. Sort this deal out with Reenie Reynolds before it goes tits up. I'm trying to be patient here girl, but you won't answer any of me calls, so what am I supposed to do? I feel like a muppet talking to this machine so for fuck's sake, talk to me! Yes, I've made mistakes, probably lots, but surely it can't be two million pounds' worth of mistakes! Franny! You do realise if you were anyone else, I'd hunt you down and put a bullet in your fucking head . . . but I can't do that can I? Cos I love ya. I fucking love ya . . . Franny!' He shouted down the phone before slamming it hard on the white kitchen table.

'Alfie?'

He turned, startled. 'Lola, I never saw you.'

She looked at him strangely. 'What's going on?'

'Nothing.'

Lola came to sit down next to him and took his hand gently. 'Don't give me that darlin', I spent half me life playing people, so I know when someone's telling me a Jackanory.'

'Look, it's okay.'

'It ain't, is it, though? You look like you haven't had any kip and you probably haven't eaten either. Here, have some of this.' Lola picked up the jug of porridge, pouring it into one of the breakfast bowls on the table. It slopped heavily in.

'Eat up, love.'

Alfie Jennings knew there were some things in life he couldn't do; hurting a kid, mugging a person, knocking his missus about, to name but a few. And now as he stared at the lumpy, water-logged, powder-clogged porridge, eating it was one more thing to add to the list of the things he could never do.

'Come on Alf, eat up or you'll be a bag of bones.'

Alfie raised his eyebrows at Lola. He gave her a crooked smile. 'More like I'll be a bag of bones if I eat it. I'll be bleedin' six foot under. The state of it, girl.'

Lola Harding, an ex-Tom turned café owner who meant the world to Alfie, cackled heartily; happier than she'd been for a long time.

Feeling the varicose veins in her legs begin to throb, her expression became serious.

'What's going on, Alf? What's happening with Franny? You missing her, is that it?'

He didn't want to talk about Franny, mainly because it hurt, but it hurt more knowing he didn't know why she was doing this or maybe he did.

Franny had been good for him. She'd made him grow up. Taking none of his bullshit or his womanising ways and he'd liked it. He'd liked the fact that when they'd got to Spain he'd slowed down and no longer had to look over his shoulder, but after a while, slowing down felt like a death sentence. A long, slow, agonising one and maybe she'd known that.

He'd tried to fight it. He really had. Tried to ignore the nagging feeling that something wasn't right. But no matter how much he'd tried to be what Franny had wanted him to be, he just couldn't do it. How could he? After all, he was Alfie Jennings, the boy from the East End, where poverty had lingered in the air and a black eye came quicker than a cup of tea. The boy who'd spent much of his childhood waiting outside the various brothels in Soho for his alcoholic, bullying father to cop off with the endless toothless Toms. The boy whose friends were the pimps, gangsters, bouncers and club owners of Soho. The boy whose brother, Connor, had died on a robbery gone wrong. And the boy who'd wept as he'd held his dead mother's hand all night when he'd found her in the outhouse, covered in blood, still clutching the shears she'd stabbed herself with after life had become too much. And it was those moments that had made the boy become a man.

He'd become driven, determined and ruthless. Deciding life owed him but he didn't owe anything to life. He hadn't cared who he'd hurt; eliminating anyone who'd got in the way of him achieving his goal – to become one of the untouchables. A face. Someone no one could hurt again.

And that's how he'd lived, and he'd been happy. But then he'd met Franny and all that changed. He'd done what he vowed he'd never do. He'd fallen in love. Given it all up and moved away.

It was perfect, or it had been until happy became restless, so when Reggie Reynolds had got in touch he'd jumped at it, arranging to come back to England to get back in the game as soon as he could. He loved the life he was born into. It was part of who he was. But in all that time, he realised he'd never asked Franny how she felt. Never asked her if it was okay with *her* if they came back. So maybe, just maybe, this was her way of payback. Two million pounds' worth of payback. Oh yes, Franny Doyle had a lot to answer for.

Angry at the thought of her, he clenched his fist, before leaning in to kiss Lola on her cheek. 'I'm where I need to be, but I need to tell you something about the money, and you need to swear you won't tell the others.'

7

Surrounded by marshes and wide-open wheat fields near the grassy sea wall just outside Bradwell on the Dengie Peninsula of East Essex, Eddie Styler spat the last bit of curried chicken out of the car window, landing it at the feet of Johnny and Ma Dwyer.

He picked out the piece of cardamom pod stuck in his back tooth as he got out of his hired Porsche Cayenne. It was important to keep up appearances. He no longer had Reginald's men to stand behind, and word was slowly getting out that he'd lost it, that he was no longer a name to be reckoned with. But he had to put up a front. He needed to pull off this deal no matter what. And Ma and Johnny were the perfect people to do it.

Hobbling across to the pair – the skin on the back of his feet had been rubbed off by his new Gucci loafers – Eddie looked at his watch. They were late. And late in his books equated to a lack of respect.

Eddie stared at Ma and Johnny, his squat rounded body dwarfed by Johnny's tall frame and Ma's wide girth. He enjoyed seeing the unease in their eyes. The fear which for the past few years had come hand in hand with his name. If only Sandra looked at him like that, but the only thing he ever saw in her eyes was contempt.

Pulling his thoughts away from his wife, Eddie channelled his secret humiliation and snarled at the pair, realising that neither of them knew that he no longer had any of Reginald's men at his beck and call. 'What the fuck time do you call this?'

Johnny shrugged apologetically. 'I'm sorry. I had a few domestic matters to sort out. You know how it is.'

'No, I don't, but what I do know is you're mugging me off. And I don't like it at all. Makes me think I can't rely on you and that makes me very nervous.'

Ma Dwyer piped up. She and Eddie went back a long way, and of all people he should know better than to think that. 'Look, ain't no one mugging anyone off. Johnny ain't like that, you know he's trustworthy. He's never let you down. If you've got a problem, talk to me.'

Eddie, having never liked Ma Dwyer for all the time he'd known her, nor liked the influence she had on Johnny, raised his voice. 'When I want your fucking opinion, Ma, then shoot me, cos when things become that desperate, I know it's over. But until that time, keep your mouth closed . . . The only thing I want to hear is that everything is ready. I don't want any fuck-ups, cos if there are, I warn you Johnny, it'll be your head along with your Ma's which'll be floating out to sea for the gulls to wax off.'

Smarting slightly, Johnny nodded. 'Everything's in order. Ain't nothing to worry about . . . but Eddie, and I don't mean any disrespect by this, but we were wondering when we were going to get our money, or at least part of it anyway. You know it's usually fifty per cent up front.'

Walking back to his car and feeling the chill of the sea air, Eddie stopped. Fuck. He'd hoped he might've got away without them asking. People asking questions was the last thing he needed. Then, deciding the best form of defence was attack, Eddie swivelled round, pointing his chubby finger at them as he padded towards them, putting Johnny in mind of a penguin.

'What the fuck is that supposed to mean? Are you calling me cheap? You saying I ain't good for it? Don't forget who I am. Reggie might be dead and gone, but that don't mean anything's changed. You disrespect me, you disrespect *all* of Reginald's men. One word from me and they'll have you for fucking breakfast.'

Johnny put his hands up. 'Like I say Eddie, ain't no disrespect meant. It's just that . . .'

The sound of Eddie flicking out a retractable metal baton stopped Johnny saying another word. Even he knew when it was wise to leave it.

8

Bree Dwyer reached out her hand for Kieran as she crouched on the ground. She was sore, and the bruises on her body and face had mottled her skin, turning from red to blue. 'Come on Kieran, you can't sit there all day . . . Please, darlin', come out.'

She smiled sadly as he sat under the bush, scowling and refusing to move.

'Why don't you come inside with me. We can make a cake. Watch some TV. What about playing with your sister. Molly would like that. Anything you want to do, but *please* come out.'

Looking at her coldly, Kieran kicked at the dusty ground with his feet. 'Dad said you tried to leave. He said you didn't care about us anymore.'

Bree felt the anger towards Johnny swell up inside her but she spoke warmly to Kieran.

'What? No! Sweetheart, you know I love you.'

Kieran's face screwed up in fury. 'No, you don't . . . You're a bitch! I hate you!'

'Please, don't say that. Listen to me darlin', I . . .'

'Kieran! Kieran!' Ma Dwyer's shrill voice came from inside the mobile home, carrying across the length of the site. 'Kieran! Where are you?'

'I'm coming!'

Scampering out from underneath the bush as quick as his legs would allow, Bree watched as Kieran ran without bothering to look back.

Feeling the hard ground on her knees and the heaviness in her heart, she sighed, sadness overwhelming her.

About to get up, Bree caught a glimpse of something under the bush. Glancing behind her and making sure no one was around, she reached over, stretching out her arm and scraping the skin on her elbow as it caught on a small, sharp twig.

She grabbed hold of the object, pulling it towards her, and was surprised to see it was Kieran's grey duffle bag. Quickly zipping it open, Bree frowned. Her thoughts raced back to Kieran as she stared at Molly's favourite toy giraffe, shredded and cut up into tiny pieces with a razor blade lying in what remained of the stuffing.

Confused, Bree rummaged some more. At the bottom was a rolled-up blue plastic carrier. She pulled it out, feeling something hard inside it. Immediately she placed it on the ground, taking another cautious glance around before unwrapping the bag.

A tiny yelp escaped from her lips. She stared in horror, feeling a sudden chill. Inside the bag were bones. Small little bones looking like skeletal remains. Bones wrapped up in a dirty knitted shawl that looked like it belonged to a tiny baby.

9

Janine Jennings, dressed in a luminous pink velvet tracksuit, drowned out the sound of the Jacuzzi bubbling away in the corner as she snored loudly on the cream lounger by the side of the blue tiled indoor pool.

Vaughn, lying next to her, stared up at the glass retractable roof. He sighed, irritated. 'Turn it in darlin', you sound like a bleedin' billy goat . . . Janine! Janine!'

Not getting a response, and resisting the temptation to poke her hard, Vaughn stood up, walking across to the French doors which looked out over the garden and terrace and onto the wide-open countryside beyond, surrounding the village of Wimbish. He watched the sun shining down on the sandstone paving as he thought about Casey.

He missed her. Waking up to her. Joking with her. Confiding in her. She was his best friend. Though ironically, when they'd got together, he hadn't known if it was even going to last more than a day. She had her demons, drinking to blot out her pain and he had a problem with getting close to anyone at all.

But somehow, they'd made it work, and they'd built their relationship on love and trust, which meant no lies. *Ever*. And although he wasn't entirely sure if not telling Casey about selling his house right from under her nose constituted a lie rather than just an omission, within a week of her finding out she'd got up and left, telling him she needed space to think.

So, whatever happened, he needed this deal with Reenie Reynolds to go through as quickly and as smoothly as possible, so he could explain to Casey that although he was wrong not to tell her, it'd been worth it. That risking the home they shared together hadn't been some reckless, fruitless venture, but security for their future, not to mention being able to get back to the life he'd missed.

But the problem was he couldn't get out of his mind what Alfie had said. That Casey had just used this situation as an excuse to leave him. In fact, the thought wasn't so much in his mind as eating him up inside.

'Alright Vaughnie.' Alfie, looking tense, strolled in from the main house. He stopped in front of Janine who now lay with her mouth wide open. He gave a wry smile. 'I see sleeping beauty is getting her kip, waiting for her prince, but for fuck's sake, don't kiss her, I could do with Janine not waking up for a hundred years.'

'I heard that, Alfred!'

'Yeah, well, you need to hear this too . . .' He stopped, wondering quite how to say it, quite how to make it sound as casual as possible.

Sitting up, Janine, her hair in large yellow Velcro rollers, scowled. 'You look suspicious.'

Alfie stared at her. He opened his mouth, then closed it again, then quickly said, 'There's no easy way of saying this, so I'll just come straight out with it . . . It doesn't look like Franny's coming back with the money.'

The scream from Janine was followed by a huge splash, as Vaughn ran over, catching Alfie hard on the chin with his fist before pushing him into the pool.

Spitting out a mouthful of water, Alfie yelled up at Vaughn, 'I'll sort it, okay?'

Standing above him on the side of the pool, Vaughn, his face twisted in anger, shouted back, 'How? How the fuck are you going to get two bloody quid, let alone two million?'

Janine, struggling to push herself up from the sun lounger, butted in. 'And what am I supposed to do? I rely on the money you give me and now we'll all end up on the bleedin' streets because of you!'

Pushing his hair away from his eyes, Alfie growled at Janine. 'Just shut up, Janine, I'll do a job, okay.'

Vaughn stared at Alfie. 'A job? Are you having a laugh? Just the two of us?'

'We can get a small crew then.'

'Get real Alf, cos no matter how much we say *please*, ain't nobody I know who's going to work for us for nothing.'

'Then we do it ourselves. I've already started putting me feelers out about . . .'

'Hold up, so how long have you known about Franny and the money?'

'Only a few days.'

Vaughn could hardly speak from rage. 'And you're only telling us now?'

'Well I didn't want to believe it, did I? I thought she'd come to her senses. I dunno, I thought she wouldn't do this to me.'

'Well she did and it's not just you, is it? It was two million fucking pounds of my money as well!'

'I know, and that's why I tried to line up a job to sort this shit out. I thought if we could give Reenie a down payment—'

Vaughn interrupted. 'A down payment! We ain't buying a bleedin' car you know!'

'Look, I ain't giving up without a fight. If this job comes off it's a start . . . We'll be jacking some coke from a lorry. It's not great, but it's better than nothing.'

Vaughn let out a loud, rueful laugh. 'Not great? It's a mug's game! I never came back to England to start sticking people up and maybe getting a bullet in me head.'

'But it's money Vaughn, and that's what we need. And nobody is going to get a bullet in their head. We can do this. I know we can. Look at us. This is *me*, Alfie Jennings, once Soho's number one face, and fuck me, you're Vaughn Sadler, *the* Vaughn Sadler. Come on pal, don't look like that!'

'You turned us over again! I came back home to take over a multi-million-pound business, a future for me and Casey, and you've messed that up.'

Angry himself now, Alfie shouted, 'You need to knock that idea out of your head. Your bird's well and truly flitted.'

'You bastard!'

Seething, Vaughn jumped into the pool, grabbing hold of Alfie and pushing him under the water, holding him down as Alfie splashed his arms about trying to come up for air.

'I'm going to kill you! I'm going to fucking kill you, Alf!'

Lola, who'd just walked into the pool house, yelled as she ran over, kneeling down at the side of the swimming pool. She swung at Vaughn's back, hitting him hard. 'Vaughnie, leave him alone! Let go! You're going to drown him! It ain't his fault! Stop!'

Vaughn swivelled round, glaring with contempt at Lola. 'You knew? You were in on it?'

'I weren't in on anything, but yes, I knew.'

'By heck, this is cosy, I'm missing out. Pool parties during the day, this is what they must mean about swinging in the suburbs.' Lloyd Page's voice boomed out as he stood laughing behind Lola.

Standing chest-deep in the pool with a gasping, red-faced Alfie next to him, Vaughn's expression was a picture of puzzlement and anger. 'What the fuck is he doing here?'

'I let him in,' Lola muttered, looking upset.

'I can see that, but I want to know *why*.'

'Hello to you too, Vaughn, always a pleasure, though I take it Alfie hasn't told you about our arrangement . . . about the job he begged me to give him.'

10

'What is this?'

Accusingly, Sandra stood in the hallway as Eddie opened the front door. Her tall, skinny body wrapped up in double layer of cream knitwear and jeans.

'Well go on then Eddie, I'm waiting. What have you got to say for yourself? What you playing at?'

Carefully, Eddie eased off his Gucci loafers attempting to avoid aggravating the painful blisters any more than he had to. He stared at Sandra, hating her as she held up the budget brand tin of cat food in her hand.

'They didn't have any Kitty-Kat, so I thought he'd like that.'

'How many bleedin' times have I told you, Barrie don't eat this. If I told you that you were having a bit of steak for tea and instead I put a turd on your plate, how would you like it?'

'It ain't quite the same, Sandra, and besides, he's only a cat.'

With an overhead shot, Sandra threw the tin of cat food at Eddie. 'Oh, is that how it is now.'

The tin, narrowly missing Eddie's head, smashed into the wall, leaving a large dent in the newly painted porch. He scrambled up, attempting a smile.

'Pumpkin I'm sorry, I'll go and get Barrie some food . . .'

The sound of smashing glass stopped Eddie finishing off his sentence. A loud voice came from outside.

'Eddie! Eddie! We know you're in there. We just want a word. Come on Eddie, open up!'

Eddie's face paled. He whispered to Sandra, 'Don't open the door. Come on, hurry up, let's go out the back.'

Not waiting for Sandra's reply, Eddie grabbed hold of her arm, pulling her along with him towards the kitchen.

He froze. His stomach lurching.

'Hello, Eddie. Going somewhere?'

Jason Robinson, one of the Costa del Sol's biggest faces stood in front of him, all six foot ten of muscle. His tanned, highly polished head shone proudly under the ceiling spots. 'I'm disappointed in you, Eddie. You don't come and see me. You don't answer me calls. So what am I to think, eh? Especially as you owe me some money.'

Sandra shot Eddie a look.

Jason walked forward, grinning a set of perfectly veneered teeth at her. 'Oh, hasn't he told you darlin'? Your old man owes one hell of a lot of money. You see, he liked to run up large tabs at my casinos, he also liked not to pay his bills, giving it large about Reginald Reynolds and what Reggie's men would do to us. He even got Reginald's men to put a couple of my employees in hospital to show that he meant business, didn't you Eddie? The thing is, there aren't any apron skirts to hide under anymore. Reginald's pushing up the daisies and his men don't give a fuck about you Ed, which leaves you with a major problem – me.'

Eddie stuttered his words. 'Okay . . . okay, listen, Jason, I'm good for it, or I will be. Just give me a couple of days and you'll see your money and then some.'

'Thing is, I don't believe you. And I did a bit of digging, seems like it ain't just me you owe money to. Seems like you ran up hundreds of thousands in Reggie's name, so it makes me think I won't get me money back.'

Eddie suddenly made a dash for the back door, but not before he felt a hot pain at the back of his head followed by the warmth of his own blood trickling down his neck as one of Jason's men struck him with a small steel baton.

The punches ensued, raining down on Eddie, pummelling him hard in the stomach, until he collapsed on the floor and noisily began to cough up blood, watched emotionlessly by Sandra.

Bending over Eddie, Jason pulled out his lighter. Flicking it on and off. 'A little bit of a reminder Eddie, don't fuck with me, son. You're on your own now and I'll be back very soon, and you *better* have me money, otherwise you and this house, along with your missus, will be going up in a ball of flames.'

11

'What's wrong with you? Can you just shut the hell up?' Johnny Dwyer snarled at his brother as he sat on the couch in the living room of Ma's mobile home. He rubbed his head.

'Come on Ryan, what's with the tears? You're doing me head in.'

Sobbing noisily into his hands, Ryan's whole body shook. 'Can't find them. Can't find them.'

'What can't you find?'

'Can't find them.'

Leaping up, Johnny roughly pulled his brother's hands away from his face. 'Jesus Christ, Ryan, stop crying and just tell me.'

Ryan looked up, blinking away his tears. 'Yeah? Tell Johnny?'

'Yeah. I'm your brother, ain't I? You don't keep secrets from Johnny, unless you want to be in trouble. You wanna be in trouble?'

Panicked, Ryan shook his head. '. . . the kittens. Kittens have gone.'

'What are you talking about?'

'My kittens ain't there.'

Pressing his temples to try to stop his headache, Johnny snapped. 'Then I'll get you some more, just stop fucking crying.'

'Don't want more. Want my kittens.'

Ryan burst into tears again, which sent Johnny rushing back over to where his brother sat. He grabbed Ryan by his tracksuit top, dragging him up off the sofa and pulling him across to the mirror. He yelled, the veins on his temples, bulging out. 'Look! Look! Look at you, Ryan! What do you see?'

Johnny and Ryan both stared into the mirror. Where one stopped the other one began. Even Johnny couldn't see any differences. So startlingly similar. The same piercing blue eyes. The same thick, dark hair and the same handsome, chiselled face. But as Ryan cried, Johnny snarled and suddenly the difference appeared; the cold, hard cruelty in Johnny's eyes.

'I'll tell you, shall I, Ryan? I'll tell you what I see. I see a baby and not a grown man! That's what you are Ryan, a baby!'

Ryan continued to sob as Johnny held and shook the back of his brother's neck as he talked.

'What did Ma always say to us? What did she say?'

'No crying. No crying.'

'That's right, because we're the Dwyer boys. We should *never* cry, and if one cries, Ma will make sure both of us cry, and after what you were going to do to me, I ain't never going to cry for you no more.'

12

Wrapped up in a thick towelling dressing gown with his hair still wet, Vaughn Sadler stared with loathing at Lloyd Page who sat opposite him at Janine's white kitchen table. He'd never liked the man in all the years he'd known him. He was a flash conman who happily served up heroin to kids, and certainly not someone he wanted to have dealings with. But it was beginning to dawn on him that Alfie and Franny might have given him no choice. And every fibre in his body hated them both for putting him in this position.

'By heck Lola, that was some bacon sarnie, lass. Fancy coming round my gaff to be my cook.'

Lola grinned a gummy smile, basking in praise as she scraped the burnt remnants off the large frying pan. Like a schoolgirl, she giggled. 'There's more where that came from.'

'I shouldn't. But what the heck . . . Pile it on cocker, but I'm telling you Lola, if I cack me pants, I'm blaming you.'

This remark was followed by hooting laughter, which only served to further irritate Vaughn. The man was a prize prick.

Banging his fist hard on the table, Vaughn snapped at Lola. 'When you've quite finished playing *The Great British Bake Off*, I'd appreciate it if I could talk to Lloyd in private.'

Lloyd glared at Vaughn. 'Hold up, sunshine, there's no need to talk to the lady like that. I think an apology is in order.'

Lola, feeling the tension between the two men, tried to placate. 'Oh, don't worry about it Lloyd, I'm not offended. I've known Vaughnie too long to get upset about him giving me the alligator. I'm used to him snapping. I take no notice.'

Lloyd Page's blue eyes narrowed as his jaw visibly pulsated. He cracked his gold-sovereign-covered fingers as he leant forward, narrowly missing putting his elbow in the remains of the under-done fried egg. 'You might not be offended pet, but that don't mean I'm not. Manners maketh man in my book, so unless you apologise to Lola now, believe me Vaughn, it won't be chuffing manners which'll maketh you, it'll be me.'

Vaughn leapt up, sending the dishes crashing everywhere. He grabbed hold of Lloyd's black silk shirt, hearing it rip as he bellowed over the table, his rugged handsome face screwed up in anger as his thick silver hair flopped over his eyes. 'Don't come in my fucking house and try to give out orders.'

With a supercilious smile, Lloyd spoke dangerously evenly, not raising his voice at all.

'But this ain't your house, is it? From what I understand, you and Alf are a bit desperate at the moment, aren't you? You should've seen the way he was begging me. It was shameful really.'

Still holding onto Lloyd's shirt, Vaughn hissed in his face. 'Alfie would never beg the likes of you.'

Lloyd's tone was quietly menacing. 'Are you sure about that? Desperate people do desperate things and I don't think you'd want that getting out, otherwise people will be wondering how *exactly* you and Alf are going to take over Reggie Reynolds' business . . . So that's why you should be nice to me. You *need* me, Vaughn. So let's start with you taking your hands off me, shall we?'

As Vaughn opened his mouth to tell Lloyd exactly what he thought of him, the kitchen door flung open.

The sight of Vaughn holding onto Lloyd stopped both Alfie

and Janine in their tracks, but it was Janine who ran forward first, swiping Vaughn hard across his muscular back.

'What the bleedin' hell do you think you're playing at? Let him go! We need him! Vaughn!'

Lloyd winked. 'You best do what the lady says. At least someone has a bit of sense round here, eh Janine.'

Vaughn glared at Alfie, who was now dry from his dip in the pool and with fury running through him like the North winds. 'You need to start talking, Alf. Otherwise I'm going to put him in the ground,' he growled.

'Look, Janine's right, we do need him. This job I was talking about earlier, it was from Lloyd. We could do his job.'

Vaughn shook his head vehemently. 'Oh no. No fucking way. I will not have anything to do with this fucking snake.'

Janine, munching on a king-size Mars bar, spoke angrily. 'This ain't the time to get choosy. Thanks to bleedin' Alfie, it looks like you might not have a choice.'

Lloyd shrugged his shoulders in amusement. 'That's *exactly* what I tried to tell him, Jan.'

Going for a head-butt, Vaughn lurched forward but was pulled back by Alfie as Janine squawked shrilly at him in the background. 'Vaughn, you ain't listening, just swallow yer pride for once, like all of us have to.'

Dropping hold of Lloyd, Vaughn raged. His face taking on several different shades of red. 'Alfie, you need to sort your missus out. Shut her up!'

Alfie, just as furious with Janine as Vaughn was, roared. He pointed at her, incensed. 'Ex-missus! And believe me, over the years I've tried to get her to put a sock in it, but she ain't stopped rabbiting from when I met her till now. My head's done in! But she's right, if we want to salvage this, we need to do this job.' He stopped to glare at Lloyd, trying to calm down.

13

'Give me a kiss then.'

Bree blushed, stifling a giggle. 'And if I say no?'

'Then I'll love you anyway.'

Chewing her lip, Bree thought for a moment before standing on her tiptoes, quickly landing a large, gentle kiss. 'There, happy now?'

'Won't be happy until you marry me, and don't say we're too young, say yes.'

Bree laughed but the sound of a door opening stopped her saying anything.

'You better go, Bree. She won't be happy if she finds you here.'

'I hate this.'

'I know, but once she gets to know you, she'll love you . . . just like I do. It'll take time, that's all. Just give her a chance.'

'I don't think she'll ever like me.'

'She will. I promise. Now go on, get out of here . . . I'll see you tomorrow.'

She waved goodbye, running happily towards her push bike, which she'd hidden in the bracken down by the stream. An overwhelming sense of joy came over her, something she'd never experienced before and something she'd certainly never had in her miserable childhood spent being passed from one foster home to another.

Humming quietly to herself, Bree's thoughts came to an abrupt halt. Puzzled, she looked around. Damn, it wasn't there. She must have left it further down the hill. The whole of the woods all looked the same.

She sighed, annoyed with herself for being so stupid, and quickly headed for the winding, muddy path. Although it was dusk, the track and the woods were still quite visible, but as she continued to walk, the darkness began to fall and the shadows of the trees twisted and distorted into monstrous shapes as the branches chattered and whispered in the autumn winds. She shivered.

A noise.

Another.

And Bree let out a scream as she spun round. 'Oh my god, you gave me a fright . . . Are you alright?'

There in the darkness was Ma. Her bulbous figure standing motionless. Her stare, narrow and cold.

'I warned you, Bree. I told you what would happen. You should've listened. But little bitches like you never do.'

Slowly, Bree began to back away as the wind picked up, then she started to run, heading into the dark of the woods.

It felt to Bree she was going around in circles. All the trees looked alike and all the paths seemed to be the same. Suddenly her foot caught on an ivy root, sending her forward, plunging her head first into the wet moss and mud. With her hands stinging from trying to break her fall and the rough earth digging into her skin, Bree desperately tried to keep quiet as she crawled along on her hands and knees.

A branch snapped beneath her leg, the sound resonating through the woods, and within seconds Ma Dwyer reappeared, pushing her body forcefully through the dense scrub to get to Bree, her hand reaching and grappling in the dark.

Bree began to scramble up but the mud was too wet and she found herself slipping. She turned to see Ma closing in on her, a maniacal look on her face, eyes wild and frenzied.

She screamed as she felt Ma grab her hair before she was flung backwards and dragged through the bushes. Her head felt like it was on fire, then a crippling pain exploded. Unbearable. Ripping through Bree's eye as a small branch caught and tore into her lid. She could taste the blood trickling down her cheek and into her mouth as Ma continued to drag her along.

Out from under the trees, the moon high in the night sky, Ma stared at Bree, a nasty smile on her face. Then Ma's fist came smashing down as her heavy body straddled Bree, banging her head against the ground.

'You leave my son alone! You ain't taking him from me. He's mine!'

Her mouth full of blood, Bree gave a breathless, staggered reply. 'I love him though! I love him!'

Ma let out a piercing, deafening scream. 'You can't love him, he ain't yours to love! So, you shut your dirty mouth, you just shut your dirty mouth!'

Pushing herself upright, Ma raised her foot, ready to bring it down on Bree's mouth.

'Stop, Ma! Don't!'

Ma turned to look at Johnny. 'I won't let her, Johnny. I won't let her take anyone away from me.'

Johnny walked up to Ma, he spoke gently. 'Don't do it, Ma. Don't hurt her. Bree ain't done nothin'. She ain't going to take no one away, is she?'

Ma looked down at Bree who was curled up in a ball. 'Ain't she?'

'No, she ain't . . . because nobody ever leaves Ma.'

14

'How the fuck can you lose a lorry full of horses? Who does that?' Eddie Styler raged, filling Johnny's overheated Range Rover with his seething, uncontrollable anger as they sat overlooking the deserted beach at Sandy Point, Holland Haven. He was visibly shaking and he hadn't slept one wink because every time he'd tried to close his eyes, Jason Robinson's face flashed through his mind, though it certainly hadn't helped that Sandra had insisted on grilling him like she was part of the secret police.

He hadn't eaten either, partly due to the pain in his mouth which he'd sustained from the beating, but mainly because he felt sick. Sick at the idea that if he didn't find the money to pay off the people he owed, he was a walking dead man. And not for the first time, he cursed the memory of Reginald Reynolds for leaving him with nothing after all his loyalty.

Ma sat at the back, her voice cold, a hint of amusement in it. 'Eddie, you look terrible mate, are you sure you're okay? You look like you need to see a quack.'

Hysteria coursed through Eddie. He screamed out his words as he bashed his fist on the dash over and over, in time with his words.

'And . . . Why . . . Am . . . I . . . Not . . . Okay . . . Cos . . . Of . . . You . . . Two . . . Fucks.'

Ma Dwyer leant forward from the back, putting her hand on Eddie's shoulder. 'You better calm down before you do yourself a mischief. Not only that, but you better be careful how you talk to us.'

Scrambling in his pocket, Eddie pulled out a small gun, his hand trembling as he attempted to point it at Johnny and Ma. His face going purple with fury. 'Have you forgotten who I am? Have you forgotten who you're talking to?'

Ma looked at him evenly, a small smile pulling at her lips. 'Oh no, Eddie, I know exactly who I'm talking to, but right now I just don't care.'

The gun shook in his hand as he spoke. 'You think this is a joke? Do you realise what you've done to me? Do you know what I had riding on this? You need to find my fucking lorry, cos when they come looking for me, I'll be sending them right to your door, Ma.'

'You ain't doing yourself any favours, so just put the gun down, Eddie.'

'And why should I do that? You turned me right over. Tell me Ma, were you in on it?'

She laughed nastily. 'In on what?'

Exploding again and slurring his words from the copious amounts of whiskey he'd consumed, Eddie looked on the verge of tears. 'On taking *everything* I had left in the world!'

With ease, Ma flicked the gun out of Eddie's hand. 'And that's the big problem, ain't it Eddie? You see I've been speaking to a couple of Reginald Reynolds' men, and they told me none of them are working for you anymore. Not only that, but they told me how much you liked to run up debts in Reggie's name. But now the fella's brown bread, you are out on your own and people want their money, and you ain't got it, have you? Which means you ain't got *our* money either. We want our money, Eddie.'

Eddie went into his pocket, pulling out a flick knife. 'What? Are you trying to mug me off? Your men lost me fucking lorry, so I ain't paying you nothing.'

Johnny sneered at him. 'That's not how it works, and you know it. We *still* did the job. My men *still* brought the lorry across the Channel. There were *still* risks for us. We never did anything wrong on our end, and even before this happened, you were never straight with us.'

'What am I, a fucking spirit level? I told you what you needed to know.'

Ma leant over the car seat again to squeeze Eddie's shoulder, slightly too hard for his liking. 'No, Eddie, you didn't. You never told us you didn't have any money. But now we're telling you what you need to know. If we don't get our money, Johnny here won't be held responsible for his actions. Seventy-two hours Edward, and after that, those seagulls need to be fed.'

'Alfie, you need to come and look at this.'

Alfie threw down the mucking out fork. 'Janine, whatever it is you've got to say, got to show me or bleedin' got to moan about, I don't want to know. We have been shovelling shit for the past few hours, and we have not found one bag of coke, yet who knew that a dozen or so horses could shit so much, so to say I ain't in the mood, is to put it fucking lightly.'

'Suit yourself.'

'What is that supposed to mean?'

'It means, suit yourself.'

Furious, Alfie spun round to look at her, the usually perfectly coiffed hair flopping over her face in a sweaty, hot mess.

'Fine, go on then. You win, Janine. Spit it out, tell me *exactly* what it is you have to say.'

Janine Jennings hid the biggest smile. 'I think you might like it.'

Alfie let out a roar. 'Just tell me!'

'See it for yourself.' Janine held up a small, clear plastic grip bag covered in steaming manure.

Alfie grinned. 'You found the coke.'

'No Alf, I ain't. I found the diamonds.'

'What? What are you talking about woman?'

'Diamonds, Alfred. Lots and lots of shiny diamonds.'

Lola and Janine sat at the table opposite Vaughn and Alfie in the lavishly gold decorated dining room of Janine's house. In the middle of the table sat several empty Chinese takeaway cartons along with a pile of small yet perfectly cut diamonds.

'Do you think he knows?'

Drawing his eyes away from the table, Alfie glanced at Vaughn. 'You mean Lloyd?'

'Yeah. Do you reckon he knew it wasn't coke, and just thought it was best to keep schtum?'

Picking out the last piece of chow mein from the side of one of the foil cartons, Alfie raised his eyebrows. 'But why? He only offered us the gig because he had to and let's face it, we would've taken anything.'

'Maybe, but he didn't know that.'

'Come off it Vaughnie, we were desperate. He smelled it the minute I went to see him. I nearly begged the geezer. *Nearly*.'

'So why not just be upfront with us?'

Alfie, still hungry, leaned across to Janine's plate to pinch one of her pork balls. Managing to come away with only a hard slap to his hand, he pulled a face. 'Cos there's a big difference in jacking a lorry of coke and jacking a lorry of diamonds. Perhaps when I came along he was already looking for a couple of mugs who'd be willing to take the risk, but at the same time someone who'd do the job properly. And hey presto, we come along and don't we just fit the bill.'

Vaughn nodded slowly as he thought about Lloyd. The geezer might be a prick, but he was a shrewd one. Nobody with any sense would agree to jack a lorry of diamonds on their own turf, it just wasn't worth it, and Lloyd had known that, but as Alf had said, they'd been desperate and hadn't bothered asking too many questions. They'd been slack. Too eager to get the money for Reenie Reynolds. To Lloyd it must've looked like they were a pair of puppy dogs begging for a fucking walk.

'Get him on the phone, now! Tell him we want him to come around for a little chat. Let's see what he has to say.'

Alfie looked at Vaughn dubiously. 'You sure about this?'

'No, Alf, I'm not, but what I am sure about is that nobody takes me for a mug.'

15

'So what are you telling me?' Lloyd Page stood with his henchmen in the well-manicured garden of Janine's mansion as Alf sat next to Vaughn on the chocolate rattan garden chair.

'Why don't you just come and sit down.'

'No ta, Alf. I prefer to stand. Make you nervous, does it?'

Alfie gave a cold laugh. 'Why would it? I was just being polite to me elders, age catches up on us all, thought you'd fancy a pew. You know, rest yer bones.'

With his broad Yorkshire accent dangerously icy, Lloyd held Alfie's stare. 'I'll wait till I'm dead and buried for that. Like to keep on me toes personally, Alf. Never know when you might have to do a runner . . . Anyhows, as nice as this chat is, let's get down to the nitty-gritty, shall we? I'm still in the dark here. Why the urgent phone call?'

Vaughn glanced at Alfie. Even though they had the threat of the Peterson brothers to hang over Lloyd's head, he would've felt so much better if Lloyd hadn't brought his goons. But they'd come up against worse. Much worse. And like Alf had said, when they put their minds to it, they were still a force to be reckoned with.

Alfie was still on a buzz from jacking the lorry, he got that, but what he didn't get was how he could be so calm about Franny.

Even the name wound him up. He could feel the anger towards her running around his body. The woman had turned them over and the truth was, although he was pissed with Alfie, *he* hadn't seen it coming either.

He'd known Franny and her father, Patrick Doyle, for many years, and he would've put his last pound on the fact that she wouldn't have ripped him off. Problem was she took his last pound anyway. And it was like a razor blade slicing at his skin. She'd fucked it up big time for them, and they needed to salvage the situation before it was too late.

'Christ!' All eyes turned to look at Vaughn, who had without thinking, slammed down his fist on the table, knocking over the milky tea Lola had made him earlier, sending it flying.

Lloyd scanned him darkly. 'Problem?'

'No, mate. Just a pesky insect.'

'You often do that?'

Vaughn glanced around, seeing the broken teacup on the floor. He shrugged his shoulders. 'What can I say? I hate flies.'

Silence fell and the only noise was the distant hum of the cars on the bypass.

Lloyd pushed again. 'So, come on then? What have you got for me?'

Vaughn, directing his anger at him, snapped, 'That's the fucking thing. We ain't got anything for you. There wasn't anything in the truck.'

Lloyd twisted round to look at his men, then opened his arms wide to stare at Alfie before crouching down to Vaughn's eye level and very carefully said, 'You better be fucking kidding me. I might've given you a squeeze by letting you have that job, but I was still going to get my cut, so don't think you can treat me like a mug.'

Smelling the cologne Lloyd was wearing, Vaughn curled up his nose. 'Thing is Lloyd, I'm not, and unless this was your idea of a sick joke, I want to know why, when we put our necks on the line, *you* didn't check your source properly that his information was correct. You should've known the only thing those horses were filled with was *shit*. Have you any idea how many pieces of fucking crap we went through?'

Lloyd's eyes darted everywhere. Agitated, he wagged his finger. 'No, this can't be right. You're telling me you found nothing?'

'Exactly.'

Kicking one of the rattan chairs over, Lloyd raised his voice. 'That's bullshit!'

'No Lloyd, horseshit. Lots and lots of horseshit and not much else.'

Panting, Lloyd eyeballed Vaughn and Alfie. 'I don't believe you.'

'What don't you believe?'

Lloyd bellowed, his voice becoming an octave higher as he screamed, red-faced at Vaughn. 'That the tooth fairy is real . . . What the fuck do you think I mean?'

Evenly, Vaughn said, 'Just checking.'

Lloyd took a swing at Vaughn before diving on him, tipping him backwards on the chair. Both men went down, but it was Vaughn who scrambled up first, wiping the blood off his face.

He raged at Lloyd. 'I'm telling you the truth! There was no coke! It's screwed us up as well. We were banking on being able to knock that out and get some money behind us. It ain't just you who's agged about it. Think how we feel. You ain't really lost nothin', but *we* have got a lot riding on it.'

Lloyd listened. Watched. And then slowly said, 'You're being straight up, aren't you?'

With his hands resting on his knees, and bending forward, Vaughn turned his head to look at Lloyd. 'Too right I am.'

'And what about the horses?'

'As arranged, dumped off at the sanctuary.'

'And you checked properly? The sanctuary won't suddenly find themselves knee-deep in bags of nose candy?'

'I swear on all that is precious Lloyd, there wasn't *any* coke.'

Alfie cut in. 'But maybe you knew that Lloyd, maybe you thought the lorry was transporting something else.'

As Lloyd stared at Alfie, Vaughn studied him closely, watching the genuine look of curiosity spread across his face. 'Like what, Alf?'

Alfie shrugged. 'You tell us.'

Bewilderment furrowed Lloyd's forehead. 'What the fuck are you on about?'

Vaughn glanced at Alfie, but spoke to Lloyd. 'Nothing, mate. We're all a bit pissed off, but I guess we'll just have to put this one down as the one that got away.'

16

Wednesday turned into Thursday and Bree Dwyer found herself hurriedly pushing the trolley round the small supermarket in Saffron Walden. She was trying to push the unease away, trying to forget what she saw in Kieran's bag, whilst praying that the tribute band recording of Cliff Richard's greatest hits – which was on a loop and being played throughout the store – would stop.

She checked her watch. The fourth time in less than five minutes. If she didn't get a move on the shopping list would go out the window, and she'd have to abandon the packets of crisps, burgers and iced gems, like she so often did.

Time was always her enemy. An hour and a half. That's all she had. All Johnny had given her. His present to her. Her time limit. To drive, to park, to get everything she needed, but every breath, every turn, robbed her of time.

Inanimate objects stealing those precious seconds: her purse to find the change for the carpark meter; her trainer lace needing to be tied. But she'd learnt the hard way. Over time. Throughout many beatings. She'd learnt that preparation was the key.

And so everything she did was calculated to the minute with military precision. Before she set off the money was already sorted in the glove compartment. The trainers replaced with slip-on shoes. It didn't matter if there were roadworks or traffic, because it was her job to get back. Because that was the only way. Fail to prepare, prepare to . . . well, she didn't like to think of it, to think about one of Johnny's lessons he liked to teach her.

She sighed, the grimness of the place exacerbating the sense of emptiness she felt. The half-stacked shelves. The empty aisles save an intoxicated old man. The bargain bins of processed own-brand tins. It wasn't her choice to come here, she would've rather gone to the new shopping centre further down the road, but that was at least another fifteen minutes. And that wasn't even an option.

Oh God, how she longed to run. To throw down the spaghetti hoops and run to the car. To keep on driving. Past the petrol station, past the lay-by, past the roundabout and just keep on going. But she knew. Johnny knew. She wasn't going anywhere. Not on her own. Not now. Not ever. So however tempting it was to get back in the car and never look back, she always did. She always looked back and she always returned home.

Bree glanced down at her watch again. It was getting late. She was annoyed with herself. Thinking had slowed her down, and now the line at the checkout had three people in it.

Deciding to leave the washing-up liquid, which was over in the next aisle, Bree rushed over to the till, behind the drunken man, behind a pregnant woman whose basket was filled with discount vodka and Cherryade.

Watching as the checkout man – *Steve*, according to his name badge – chewed and blew bubbles whilst trying but failing to get a packet of porridge oats to scan, Bree pushed down the sense of panic.

Indifferent to the rising impatience of the queuing customers, *Steve* excruciatingly slowly picked up a grey phone which was partly hidden under the five-pence bags. He spoke into it. His voice crackling over the store's speakers cut into a *Grazioso* version of 'The Young Ones'. 'Anyone got a price for this?'

Lacking any sign of enthusiasm, *Steve* waved the porridge oats in the air, resting his arm in his other hand as he did so.

A woman with thinning grey hair, wearing a nylon blue-checked tabard, shuffled towards the till. Speaking with a lisp owing to missing her top teeth, she sniffed, asking, 'Price for what?'

'These.'

She nodded, taking the packets of oats, and shuffled away as slowly as *Steve* had picked up the phone.

Bree, seeing that this could take some time, spoke warmly. 'Hi, I'm in a rush and I'm just wondering if there was someone else here who could go on the other till.'

Blowing another bubble, *Steve*, with cutting derision, stared at Bree. 'I don't know, let's see, shall we?' His voice dripped with sarcasm.

Steve then proceeded to get up from his swivel chair and search under the counter, before reappearing to lift up the leaflets and plastic bags on the side. He turned back to Bree, coldly. 'Doesn't look like they're there.'

'*Please*, I'm in a real hurry.'

'Look, darlin'. Everyone's in a rush, but it ain't everyone who's chewing me off about it. Only you.'

'Don't speak to her like that.'

Steve stared aggressively. 'What's it to do with you, mate?'

Alfie Jennings grinned as he stepped forward from behind Bree. 'Nothing, not a damn fucking thing, but unfortunately for you mate, I've made it my business. Problem with that . . . *Steve*?'

And as *Steve* gulped hard, unwittingly swallowing his chewing gum, he turned red before only managing a quiet voice to simply say, 'No.'

Alfie stood in the supermarket's tree-lined carpark in Saffron Walden – a medieval market town located in northwest Essex – listening but not really concentrating on the gratitude the woman was offering him. For a start, she was a sort. A proper sort. Soft pale skin, long tumbling waves, slim yet a curvaceous body . . . Oh shit. He had to stop. He was getting a boner. Not a good look in the first five minutes of speaking to her. But Christ, it'd been a while since he'd made love to a woman.

Before he'd left Spain, he hadn't seen Franny properly for at least three weeks whilst he and Vaughn got the last lot of the money together, and then when he had seen her it'd been for less than five minutes when he'd just handed the money over to her. Shit! He suddenly felt the anger rise up in him. Franny was the absolute last person he wanted to think about now. It hurt like hell. Not that he'd let on to the others how angry, how gutted he was with her, because if he did, he knew he'd end up winding himself up and no doubt arguing with Vaughn and Janine about it even more, and that was the last thing he needed.

The other reason he found himself not being able to concentrate on what this woman was saying, was the fact it'd just dawned on him that this was the woman he'd seen in the woods, looking terrified, looking like she was trying to get away – though it still hadn't come back to him how else he knew her.

'. . . so anyway, thank you so much.'

'Sorry?' Alfie shook himself out of his thoughts.

'Just thank you, I'm really grateful. Anyway, I've really got to go.'

Carrying her shopping, Bree began to jog towards her car.

A sudden thought hit Alfie. Pounding his being. 'Stop! Hold up.'

Looking at her watch, Bree, trying not to be rude, gave a tight smile as she waited.

'I know you, don't I?'

'No, I don't think so. Sorry, but I *really* have to go.'

Bree turned but was held back by Alfie as he gently grabbed her arm. 'Don't give me that.'

Confused, Bree looked worried, agitated. 'What . . . what are you talking about?'

A large grin crossed and stayed on Alfie's handsome face. 'Bree O'Neill. You were mates with my little sister. God, I remember picking you both up from school. Drove me mad. There's me, a spotty teenager wanting to give it large, but instead I've got two little kids in tow. Wasn't great for me image . . .' He stopped to laugh before saying, 'You don't remember me, do you?'

Bree stared then a small flicker of recognition turned into a shy smile. 'Alfie . . . Alfie Jennings.'

'That's right girl. It's Alfie.'

The warmth with which Alfie said this hit and ripped at Bree. Unexpectedly, she burst into tears.

Alfie, taken aback and slightly embarrassed, joked, 'Fuck me, girl, I knew I had an effect on women, but I was hoping it was more about the magnetic than the misery. Come here, you soft cow, give us a hug.'

A hug which was watched by Ma Dwyer as she sat in her car opposite.

'And did you let him touch you . . . *here?* Did he touch you here, Bree?' Johnny grabbed Bree between her legs as he whispered into her ear. Pressing his body hard against hers. She gave out a small, painful yelp.

'Did you like it, Bree? Did you ask him for more?'

'Johnny, you got to believe me. I only spoke to him for a moment.'

'Liar!' Johnny punched the wall, centimetres from Bree's head. 'Ma told me she saw you in the car park.'

Bree nodded, speaking breathlessly. 'Exactly! I only talked.'

Johnny whispered back. 'Don't lie to me. Don't make it worse.'

'I'm not.'

'What was it like, Bree?'

Terrified, Bree turned her head to the side. Her words were almost inaudible. 'Nothing happened.'

Staring at her, Johnny suddenly dropped to his knees. Sobbing as he buried and pushed his head into Bree's stomach. Wild-eyed, he gazed up at her. A ghost-like look on his face.

'How many times, Bree? Why, why, why did you do it to me? How many times did you let him fuck you?'

Bree closed her eyes, praying, trying anything she could to let her imagination protect her from what was about to follow. As Johnny began to undo his belt, she imagined the crystal-blue waters of a faraway ocean, the sparkle of the sea as she dived in. And as Johnny roughly pulled at her clothes she saw the racing dolphins. And as his hands touched her body she saw herself leaping out of the cooling ocean into the mirrored blue sky to soar over the mountains and high above the trees over the planes and fields to a place far away.

'I'll leave you to it, Johnny.' Ma Dwyer smiled at her son as she opened the door and left the room.

17

'Diamonds, all those bleedin' diamonds. Whoever those belong to ain't going to be happy.'

Putting Bree to the back of his mind, Alfie snapped. 'Fuck me, Janine, could you be anymore insightful?'

Janine sniffed. 'Don't start getting sarcastic with me, just cos you're hungry.'

'Well, I wouldn't be hungry, would I, if you'd brought me a bleedin' burger? Everyone else gets one.'

'You weren't about, were you?'

'No, because I was in the bleedin' carzey having a piss!'

Wanting to stop a row, Lola chipped in. 'These must be worth a couple of mill. Problem is, whoever they *do* belong to will come looking, and once that happens, there won't be any hiding place. It's not like the coke, with these, there's no way to knock them out without anyone getting wind. And then there's Lloyd, if he finds out, he'll think you mugged him off good and proper. There'll always be a trail and eventually Vaughnie, it'll come back to you. I'm worried. You sure you shouldn't just cut your losses and—'

Vaughn interrupted. 'Give them back?'

'Exactly. Maybe if you had people around you, but until you get some money, you won't be able to pay anybody, so it's a different ball game. Why don't you just duck out now while you can. Then once you get back on your feet you can do what you like.'

'What about Reenie though? We can't let this opportunity slip through our fingers. To own that business would put us right up there.'

Lola smiled. 'I know, darlin, but arrange to do another job. Call Franny again, go look for her, *anything* but this Vaughn. Playing with somebody else's diamonds is only going to lead to trouble. Even Lloyd didn't know about them, so whoever they do belong to, they obviously wanted to bring them into the country without anyone knowing, and now that their diamonds have disappeared, they'll come looking, they probably are already. Stay well away from this, sweetheart.'

'Hang on, hang on. Ain't no one giving them back or staying away from them,' Janine mumbled, her mouth full of a greasy cheeseburger. 'We need this, Reenie ain't going to wait, she'll sell the business to someone else and we can't let that happen.'

Lola frowned. 'Come on Janine, how can just Alfie and Vaughn take on the boys behind this. They'd be stupid to. It could be anyone. Russians. Eastern Europeans. Triads . . . Mafia.'

Janine scoffed. 'The Mafia! Do me a favour, Lola. You're talking out of your bum hole.'

'No, I bleedin' ain't. I don't trust it and like I say, even Lloyd thought it was one thing but then it turned out to be another. They don't need to be involved in this. There'll be another job out there for them.'

'Not like this there won't.'

'For starters, Janine, how are they going to get rid of them?'

Oblivious to the ketchup running down her chin, Janine haughtily said, 'Lola, they've been in the business long enough to know people.'

Lola sighed, irritated at her attitude. 'And they've been away, and people aren't happy that they're back. They'll be watching them, so any move they make will draw attention. One phone call from Vaughnie or Alf trying to sell this lot and every single crime family from here to the Costa will know about it, which *means* the people who *own* them will find out too.'

'When did they make you their bleedin' keeper?'

'And when did they make you someone that doesn't give a shit about her friends . . . Actually, don't answer that, Janine. But there's no way they should be touching them. It's like playing with fire.'

Vaughn nodded. 'Unfortunately, as much as it would be sweet and solve all our problems, I have to agree with you, Lola. We'd be mugs to go near them.'

Alfie, who'd been sitting silently, looked across and smiled at Lola. She was a cracking old bird. Fiercely loyal and always looking out for both him and Vaughn. He'd known her for years and they'd never really fallen out, mainly because he always seemed to agree with her. She spoke sense . . . but not on this. This was different and sometimes, just sometimes, the only thing to do was play with fire.

18

Janine Jennings was pacing. She was beside herself. In fact, she hadn't been this agitated since Great Aunt Ethel on her deathbed had bequeathed the Cowdray pearl necklace she'd had her eye on to her sister.

Sighing, she chewed on her nails, tasting the bitter gel polish she'd used earlier. How the hell did Vaughn think he could let this job slip through his fingers? She wasn't so worried about Alfie. He hadn't said anything, but she knew him well enough to know he'd want to do the job. He was a greedy bastard when it came to money, plus he was desperate to get back to what he knew best, to get back to the life he loved, so there was no way that Alfie would want to let this one go.

But the problem was Vaughn. If he thought he was going to impress Casey and get her back by being skint and spineless then he was mugging himself off. He didn't impress anyone. Women wanted real men. Flash cars and a bit of bling not a gutless muppet and a pub lunch with a ten-year-old Ford Focus parked outside. And come to think of it, Lola hadn't helped. What was she playing at, doing her caring Mary act? She would do well to remember it was her roof that she was living under.

Sighing again and coming to an eventual halt by the end of

her pink satin-draped bed, Janine plonked down on the mattress. She understood what Vaughn was saying about there only being the two of them. But there must be a way . . . there must be.

Staring at herself in the mirrored wardrobe, Janine bit into a Snickers bar. And then a thought came to her. Why not? What could be the harm?

Smiling to herself, Janine picked up her phone. If this didn't work. Nothing would. And at least it would put the cat among the pigeons.

Janine Jennings wasn't the only one who was pacing. Eddie Styler was treading the carpet fibres out. He was in trouble. Big time.

'Eddie! Eddie! Have you seen Barrie?'

Looking down at Barrie, who'd come to wrap his grey fluffy tail around his feet, Eddie quietly picked him up, throwing him out of the back door. 'No!'

Storming into the kitchen, her face covered in a white clay face mask and her hair tightly done up in rollers, Sandra shouted, 'Well you better go and find him then.'

Eddie gave a tight smile. He hadn't been allowed out since he'd been to see Johnny, and Sandra was not only giving him grief, but was watching his every move as well as screening his phone calls.

He stared at his wife, caked in the dried, clay mask, cracking and splitting on her face, and he couldn't help but think of the Mexican death masks. He shivered and wondered, as he so often did, how the hell he'd ever thought marrying her was a good idea.

Sandra glared at him. 'Go on then, what are you waiting for? Go and find him.'

'Whatever you say, my love.'

Narrowing her eyes, she looked at him suspiciously. 'What are you up to?'

'Nothing.'

'You better not be, otherwise it won't just be Jason Robinson you have to worry about, it'll be me.'

Eddie, not wanting Sandra to change her mind about letting him go out, edged for the door. 'I should hurry, I want to find Barrie before it gets dark.'

The coldness in Sandra's voice chilled Eddie. 'You do that Ed, but remember, this is your mess, not mine. You should pray that you can get the money you need. Get it sorted, cos I swear, I ain't going down for you, paying for you or begging for you. And when they come looking for you, I'll point them in your direction.'

Eddie, trying but not able to hold his temper, shouted, 'You're my wife, Sandra. *For better, for worse. In sickness and in health* We're in this together.'

'No Eddie, that's where you're wrong. You're on your own, *from this day forward, until death do us part.*'

19

'Open the window! Come on!'

It was pitch black on the mobile home site and Bree whispered as loudly as she felt was prudent. She looked around at every sound, ducking down behind the bushes the minute she saw any passing car. She knew she had to be cautious, the last thing she wanted was Ma appearing. She hadn't seen her for a long while. Not since the day of the woods. She'd hidden and avoided, rarely venturing up to the caravan site. Hoping that eventually the unexplained hatred Ma felt towards her would subside.

She glanced round quickly before picking up and throwing a handful of whitewashed pebbles at the window. The wind whipped and spun the small twigs and leaves.

Bree, worried her hushed tones would go unheard, raised her voice slightly.

'It's me! Open up! I need to talk to you.'

The window remained shut with no sign of life and Bree, despondent, turned to walk away.

'Hey! Psssst.'

She felt the butterflies in her stomach as she smiled, spinning back round.

'What are you doing, Bree? You shouldn't be here.'

'I know, but I couldn't wait. I need to speak to you.'

'What's so urgent it couldn't wait till Friday? Are you okay?'

Bree shook her head, as she spoke into the dark. 'Not really . . . I'm pregnant.'

There was a long pause before Bree spoke again. 'Did you hear me? I'm pregnant.'

She didn't know if it was the shadows of the night or the eeriness of the woods but the answer sounded strange. Remote and strained.

'I heard you.'

She wasn't sure what she'd expected, but she could feel herself fighting back the tears. Her words cut at the back of her throat. 'Is that all you have to say?'

'Bree, I'm sorry . . . I . . . It's just a shock, that's all.'

The silence fell again and all that could be heard was the calling of the wind to the trees with the rain hitting the leaves.

'I thought we were careful.'

The icy rain seeped its way into Bree's clothes and she shivered. 'We were, but I guess not careful enough . . . I'm sorry.'

'You don't have to say that.'

'But you're angry with me.'

'No, I'm not. I couldn't never be with you, Bree . . . I love you . . .'

'And I love you too, and that's why we've to get away if we're going to stand any kind of chance. We can't stay here.'

'I don't know.'

The impatience hit Bree's voice. 'Why? I thought this is what you wanted. You're always saying how we need to go.'

'I know, but . . . Look, maybe in a few weeks we could . . .'

'No! You've been saying that for the past couple of years. And I've waited and I've been patient, and every day I hope it's going to be the day you say "let's go". But I'm not waiting anymore. If you won't leave, fine. But I'm going. I don't want to be around here. I'm not risking it. I won't.'

'Bree, you can't go without me.'

'Then you come. Come with me. We can have this baby. Start a new life. That's what you want, ain't it?'

'You know it is, but I can't.'

Bree walked closer to the window. 'You can. You ain't a kid anymore. You can do what you like.'

'I can't Bree, you know I can't.'

'No, that's what Ma wants you to think. That's what she's told you all your life, but all you have to do is walk out of here. Come with me now.'

'But she needs me.'

Bree snapped, 'Listen to yourself, it's crazy. What she does is control you. You hate it here. The way she treats you is wrong. It always has been. You don't have to put up with it anymore. Come on.'

'But—'

'No buts. You love me and I love you. Let's start somewhere new. Somewhere no one knows us. If we stay we won't have a chance and that frightens me.'

'And Ma?'

'She'll be fine. I promise.'

And in the darkness a pact was made. 'Okay, Bree. Let's do it. I'm going to do it. I'm going to leave Ma for good.'

20

Alfie Jennings was ruminating – big time – as he sat having a sneaky cigarette in the unused stable block of Janine's mansion, the beautiful manor house outside Wimbish in the parish of Uttlesford, he never forgot he bought. Jesus, it was a hard pill to swallow and God, didn't it stick in his throat waking up on a mattress next to Vaughn each morning, knowing that the gardens and every brick, and every garish ornament had once been his. All paid for out of his pocket.

Annoyed, he sighed loudly, knowing it wasn't really that which was pissing him off. It was Franny. Always Franny. He'd tried to call her again, and again. There'd been no answer. All he'd had from her was another text simply saying *sorry*. And a whole lot of fucking good that was.

Irritated, having successfully wound himself up now, Alfie ground the cigarette butt into the concrete floor. He was sick at the idea of the Reynolds business slipping through his fingers. It was doing his head in and something had to give.

He knew Vaughn wasn't up for trying to knock out the diamonds. And although he wouldn't go all out and say that he'd lost his bottle, it was clear Vaughn had become cautious. And that was a problem, because the way he saw it, caution never won a war, or rather, it never got rid of a banging load of diamonds.

But Christ knows, it was the perfect way of getting out of the hole they were in. He got it that it could be difficult to keep it quiet and their names out of it once they were shopping the goods around. But if they got away with it? It would be game back on.

'Alright, Alfie?' Janine Jennings appeared at the stable door.

'Janine if you've come to chew me ear off, forget it. If I want to have a fag, I will. Whether it's here or in the house. Anywhere I bleedin' please, cos let's have it right, this place is mine. I paid for it. You know it and I know it, the only pity is that when I divorced you, the judge didn't see it like that.'

Taking a bite out of a Greggs iced bun, Janine shrugged. 'Once you've finished getting your Alan Whickers in a twist, maybe you'll listen to what I have to say.'

Resigned, and wanting the next few minutes to be as painless as possible, Alfie said, 'Go on then. Tell me whatever it is. Me day can't get any worse.'

'I've got a plan.'

'Actually, it's just got worse.'

'Put a cork in it and listen . . . I know how we can get Vaughnie on board with the diamonds.'

'Hold up Janine, you're jumping the gun here, darlin'. You're presuming I want to get involved. It ain't to be taken lightly. There's lots of things to consider.'

Janine pulled a face. 'Oh, don't give me that. Your ego is more precious than your dick, and fuck me, that's saying something. There's no way in the world the mighty Alfie Jennings wants to live under his ex-wife's roof any longer than he has to, or to have nothing in his pocket. Tell me I'm wrong.'

Alfie scowled as he watched Janine nibble the cherry off the top of the iced bun. 'I ain't telling you nothin' Janine, but – and it's only a but – if I did want to do the job, how could I? Seriously.

I've hardly got an army behind me, have I? Nearest I get to that is you and Lola.'

Janine winked. 'Well, that's where my plan comes into it. Leave it to me, Alfred. It'll take a few days to get it sorted, but I got it all sussed out.'

'And why does that worry me so much? Just do us all a favour, and leave it.'

Turning away, Janine blew Alfie a kiss. 'You know what they say Alf, never look a gift horse in the mouth, or in your case, what came out of its arse.'

Alfie shook his head as he listened to Janine's high-pitched laughter as she disappeared towards the house. But before he had a chance to think about what Janine might be up to, he felt the buzzing of the phone in his pocket.

Pulling it out but not recognising the number, Alfie answered cautiously, an image of Bree flashing into his mind; something that had happened often since they'd bumped into each other at the car park.

'Yeah?'

'Alfie.'

Alfie rolled his eyes, immediately recognising the voice of the male caller.

'It's me, Alf.'

'I know who it is, but what I'm wondering is, why the fuck you're calling me. What do you want?'

'I need to talk to you.'

'Well mate, right there's the difference. I don't need to talk to you.'

'*Please*, Alf.'

'Please? Oh, it's please now? That is a change from what you said the last time you saw me. Now if I recall correctly, it was more like, "cunt". "*You cunt, Alf.*"'

'Yeah, well, I might have been a bit hasty there . . . and I'm sorry about that. But I had a lot of stress at that time. Life ain't easy. You know that, Alf . . . So, come on, will you meet me?'

Lighting up another cigarette, Alfie inhaled deeply. 'Fine. Okay. When?'

'Now. I was hoping you were at the house . . . because I'm outside your gates.'

And as Alfie clicked off the phone, he wondered what it was that Eddie Styler could want to talk to him about.

21

Kieran Dwyer skipped along the edge of the fields by the ancient coppice on his dad's expansive land, which ran behind his mobile home. Ducking down by the low hedges, making sure no one could see him, he paused to get his breath.

The sun was going down and the long, wet grass had soaked the bottom of his black jeans. He'd forgotten to put on his blue-and-white-striped coat, and now he felt cold. But he didn't care. He didn't care how cold he got because he wanted to get to the far end of the woods before dark. His sister, Molly, had wanted to come, but she was six and stupid. And she would spoil it. Tell everybody about what she'd seen, because he knew that Molly couldn't ever keep a secret. And it was a secret he was going to see.

She'd been upset and started crying, but to keep her quiet he'd let her play his Xbox, something he didn't often do. But he knew it'd be worth it.

Panting as he ran happily up the hill, Kieran felt the mud soak up and over into his trainers. But he was nearly there, and if he was really quick, he could get back home without anyone noticing he'd even gone.

By the old oak tree he stopped, getting his breath again and peering around.

It was quiet, apart from the sound of the wind, and even though Kieran hadn't cared how cold he got, he was pleased the leaves from the trees sheltered him slightly from it.

Pushing through some bushes, he glanced around again. He could feel the butterflies in his tummy. This was his secret and he didn't want anyone finding out, not even Ma, who always wanted to know what he did.

At the hawthorn bush by the stream, he knelt down, squeezing his eyes shut, preparing himself for the pain from the scratching thorns as he crawled underneath it. Scrambling to the other side of the bush, Kieran came up into a clearing in the thicket. It was like his own secret garden. A place no one could see him.

He ran across to a tree on the far side, which was covered in ivy, and once again, Kieran knelt in the mud. His small fingers scrambling through a loose mound of earth which he'd placed over the hole in the tree.

With ease he pulled the earth away and put his hand inside the hole before bringing out a ragged hessian brown cloth. Then sitting cross-legged and leaning against the tree he unwrapped it and smiled.

Gazing down at the contents, his fingers gently touched the skeletal remains wrapped up in a knitted cardigan.

After a moment, Kieran carefully wrapped it up again, pushing it back into the hole in the tree. Unlike the other one he'd found, Kieran Dwyer was determined that this time, no one was going to take it away from him.

22

'So how did you know I was here?' Alfie stared at Eddie, thinking how ill he looked since the last time he'd seen him, although granted, that had been over six years ago. But it was clear age or marriage certainly wasn't treating him well. And Alfie could guess which one of the two it was.

'Your sister told me, so I thought the least I could do was come round and offer my congratulations to you and Vaughn on becoming Reginald's successors. Though I must say, I was rather surprised when I found out. I had no idea you were so close.'

Alfie glanced at Eddie, who was trying to hold a smile that didn't quite reach his eyes. He could see Eddie struggling to be anywhere close to happy for them, he could hear the resentment sticking in his throat.

Reginald had already told him that Eddie had had ambitions of grandeur. He'd also told him that he'd rather give his business away to the first stranger he came across than let Eddie Styler be in the driving seat.

Tempted but resisting rubbing salt into the wound, Alf turned the subject to his sister.

'How is Sandra? I've been meaning to get her to come round now I'm back.'

'Wonderful, as usual. You know Sandra,' Eddie said with a tight tone.

He did know Sandra. Very well. And it wasn't the way he'd describe her. But Eddie was sensible enough not to say anything different, because even though he and Sandra hadn't been as close over the past few years as they'd once been, she was still family. And there was no way he was ever going to allow anyone, especially a jumped up little prick like Eddie, to say anything about his nearest.

Flicking on the kettle in the kitchen, Alfie stared suspiciously at Eddie. 'I'm surprised Sandra didn't call me to tell me you were coming. Does she know you're here?'

'In a roundabout way.'

Alfie shook his head, already losing his patience with him. 'Don't talk in riddles, Ed. And don't bother lying to me.'

Eddie Styler, humiliated and hating every minute of having to chat small talk with Alfie, shrugged, trying to look and sound as casual as possible whilst hating his brother-in-law as much as he ever did. 'Well, she knows I've gone out.'

'Come again?'

Shuffling in his seat, Eddie, wishing he was anywhere but there, said, 'I'm looking for Barrie. I wondered if you'd seen him?'

The laughter that came out of Alfie Jennings was exactly what he'd needed, along with the bellyache from hysterics and the streaming tears of amusement that ran down his face. The same, however, could not be said of Eddie as he sat red-faced and brimming with seething hostility.

Leaning on the work surface and exhausted from laughter, his words breathless from amusement, Alfie grinned. A dazzling handsome grin. 'She's got you under proper manners, Eddie. I thought I had problems, but when I've got to pretend to the missus I'm looking for a cat, just to be allowed out, I know I've hit rock bottom.'

The roar of hilarity from Alfie was too much to bear this time for Eddie. He got up, swinging his fist and knocking the vase of flowers off the table. 'This ain't funny. None of it's funny. I'm in trouble Alf, which means so is your sister. Sandra's in trouble too.'

The laughter was silenced and Alfie stepped nearer to Eddie. His tone was dark and cold.

'I hope you're fucking kidding me Eddie, because if you've put my sister at risk because of some muppet scheme or some stupid deal gone wrong, then you'll have me to answer to.'

Arrogantly, Eddie looked up at Alf who stood well over a foot taller. 'Once upon a time I'd be bothered about that, but you're the least of my troubles. I got Jason Robinson on my back, and he's threatening us. Me *and* Sandra.'

Alfie grabbed Eddie, shaking him hard, causing his head to flick backwards and forwards.

'What the fuck have you done?'

Realising his attitude towards Alfie might've been a mistake, Eddie changed tack. 'I just owe him money, that's all.'

Alfie stared at him hard. 'How do you end up owing Jason? Of all the people.'

Sheepishly, Eddie said, 'Look, when I was working for Reggie, I may have run up a few debts but how was I supposed to know he was going to drop dead?'

'You really are something, Eddie. No wonder Reggie didn't want you to have anything to do with his business.'

Eddie smarted. 'I gave everything to that man! And the tight bastard couldn't even leave me a few quid in his will.'

'No, Eddie, what you did was go around thinking you were the dog's bollocks and spending his money like it was your own. But you've always been a ponce, ain't you?'

'Think what you like, but it ain't going to get me any closer to paying off Jason.'

'Why can't you just pay him and be done?'

'I ain't got no money. Not a penny.'

'What?'

Eddie sat down hard. His whole body slumping as he heard his own words, the reality hitting him like a herd of cattle. 'Maybe in the past, I might've spent a bit too much. I like a flutter on the horses, play a few card games, a bet here and there on the dogs, you know how it is. And there's the lifestyle, I got to keep up appearances, don't I? But then I had this pucker deal, Alf. It was sweet as. It would've solved everything. And I'm talking everything, and I put all me money into it. But then it all went Pete Tong. Let's just say never put your money in horses.'

Alfie looked at Eddie strangely. 'So, what was this deal?'

'If it's all the same to you, I'd rather not say, but I will tell you, I'm well and truly screwed.'

'Then you need to remortgage that big old house of yours, Ed. Jason Robinson isn't a man that likes to be kept waiting for his money. Go to the bank and get it sorted.'

Eddie stared at Alfie blankly.

'Oh no. No. Tell me you ain't already done that. Tell me that ain't the money you lost.'

Eddie nodded. 'What was I supposed to do? I owe a lot of people money and now I owe on the house so I can't use that. I ain't got anywhere to turn, and I'm on the clock.'

'And Sandra knows about this, does she?'

'A bit, she was there when Jason came, but she don't know about the house . . . I didn't think she needed to.'

'But that was her house, Eddie. From the money I gave her.'

Seething, Eddie's words were clipped. 'I know, and she never lets me forget it.'

Alfie glared at him. 'Be careful what you say, Ed. That's my sister you're talking about.'

'The point is, I thought I could sort it out before she was any the wiser, and I'd appreciate it if you'd keep it to yourself. I don't want her to worry . . . Look, Alf, I wouldn't normally ask you, but I'm desperate. I need you to give me some money. A few hundred thousand would sort me out. I could work it off. Work for you and Vaughn like I did Reggie.'

Coldly, Alf said, 'I can't help you, Ed.'

Full to bursting with resentment, Eddie got up from the table. He snarled. 'More like, won't. I don't know how much you're paying for the Reynolds business, but I know it won't be small change.'

Not wanting to let on to Eddie of all people that they were screwed themselves, Alfie chose his words carefully.

'Look, if I could Ed, of course I would, though it wouldn't be for you, it'd be for Sandra. But like you say, I've got Reggie's business to think of. I'm piling all me money into that, setting up and recruiting people, takes a lot of dough. If you want me to speak to Jason, I will. Maybe I can get him to give you a bit more time.'

Eddie stared at Alfie scornfully as he got up. 'The man's a psycho, he ain't gonna listen to anyone. So, thanks for nothin', *mate*. I'll make sure I remember this, just you wait!'

As Eddie stormed off, Alfie picked up the phone. Eddie was right, Jason was a psycho. And if there was ever a good reason to sell the diamonds, it was this. He had to help Sandra no matter what.

'Hey, it's me. Your big brother. I think we need to talk.'

23

Sneaking out of the bedroom with his clothes under his arm, Eddie Styler tiptoed down the stairs. He'd had to wait until Sandra had gone to sleep, which had taken well over an hour, in addition to a couple of sleeping pills slipped into her tea.

But now the deep, grunting snores reassured him that only a freight train steaming through the room would wake her up.

In the hallway, Eddie grabbed hold of Barrie, shoving him in the cat carrier, coming away with only a small scratch to his right hand. He would show Sandra not to treat him like dirt, let her feel what it was like to lose something precious. She cared more about the damn cat than she did him. Well, he was sick of it, and like Alfie, she was going to pay, one way or another.

Giving a quick glance back up the stairs and feeling satisfied with himself, Eddie picked up his car keys in one hand and a caged Barrie in the other.

Outside in his car, Eddie went into the driver's glove compartment, pulling out the cheap bottle of whiskey he'd purchased earlier. Unscrewing the top quickly, he took several long gulps before putting his foot on the accelerator and driving off into the moonlit night.

* * *

Alfie Jennings was wide awake. But not just because of the rain lashing on the window sounding like someone was outside throwing buckets of water at the glass. Nor was it because of Vaughn's rumbling snores. How any bird could lie next to him, he didn't know. But he did know what held him awake . . . Bree. He couldn't get her off his mind. Her face. The way she'd looked and sounded.

He'd wanted to ask her why she'd been running through the woods that day, looking terrified, looking like someone was after her. But it hadn't felt right, and it wasn't any of his business either. He'd also wanted to ask why she'd looked so nervous when they were talking. But he hadn't and now he wished he had. Because he wanted to know that she was alright.

Bree had been the first time he'd cared about someone other than family. But not in the romantic way. She was just a kid; a friend of his sister's.

Each day when he'd picked Sandra up from school – because her mother had been too busy in bed with some punter and the father they shared had been a violent deadbeat – Bree had always been hanging around. Nobody to pick her up. Nobody to care for her. Not wanting to go home to the abusive foster family she'd been placed with. And even though back in the day he'd been selfish and ruthless, his heart had gone out to her. Recognising something in her that was so like him.

So, he let her tag along. She'd been shy at first, blushing each and every time he spoke to her. But over time she'd opened up. Stopped looking at him from underneath her fringe and eventually she'd begun to smile. And he'd begun to care.

He'd been as protective over her as he had his sister. Caring for her, feeding her, even buying her clothes. But then one day she'd just disappeared. No warning. No communication. Nothing. And he'd been devastated. It'd broken his heart. The loss of Bree affected him as his mother had affected him when she'd taken her own life.

Eventually he'd tracked Bree down to a foster home and after making sure she was alright, he'd got Sandra to keep in touch with her. And they had done, for a while. But over the years Sandra had got on with her life and he'd been too busy ducking and diving, making a name for himself, to see what had really mattered.

The last time he'd heard about her was through the rumour mill. She'd got herself hitched to some guy in Essex. And oddly, when he'd heard, he'd worried. Because Bree was special. Kind. But worse, she was vulnerable. Desperate to be loved and cared for. But his worry hadn't lasted long because he'd just got on with his life, not giving her a second thought. Until now that was. Because now he couldn't get Bree out of his head.

24

Dripping wet, Eddie Styler stood in front of Johnny and Ma Dwyer. He shivered, cold and drenched after trudging half a mile across a large, deep, muddy field to avoid the two loose Rottweilers at the gates of Johnny's mobile site, near the village of Ashdon.

Looking longingly at the hot tea, brought in by Johnny's nervous-looking wife, Eddie sighed, licking his lips. No wonder Johnny was so protective of his woman. Her boat race was bruised with a big old shiner, along with a swollen lip, but underneath he could see what a sort she was. He wouldn't kick her out of bed any day of the week, certainly not with that body.

As Bree walked out of the room, Eddie brought his thoughts back to the matter at hand. He smiled and in return was greeted by a hostile stare from Johnny.

'See something you like, Eddie?'

Not realising he'd been so obvious in his lustful admiration and knowing Johnny's vicious reputation when it came to any man even glancing at Bree, Eddie's eyes quickly darted around, then smiled again, feigning innocence.

'Yes actually, I was thinking how nice that tea looks and whether it'd rude to ask for one.'

'That better be all you was having a butcher's at.'

Eddie shrugged whilst Ma's slurps filled the room. 'What else?'

Johnny leant forward on his elbows. 'Don't push it, Ed . . . Anyway, I suppose you're here to give me our money.'

It took everything Eddie had not to explode into anger. The man had some front. He'd lost his lorry, his horses, but more importantly the geezer had lost his diamonds, yet he still had his finger up his arse about being paid. But now wasn't the right time to show any kind of resentment because that would come. And when it did, Johnny Dwyer and his big fat ma wouldn't know what had hit them.

'No, not really.'

Ma growled. 'Are you taking the Michael? You come here unannounced in the middle of the bleedin' night and you ain't got the greens. You better have a seriously good explanation.'

'I got a proposition for you.'

Johnny's handsome face darkened. 'No, Ed. That's not how it works, mate.'

Eddie's temper got the better of him as it always did. 'Not so bleedin' long ago it was me who was telling you two what to do . . .' He trailed off, trying to catch his rage. '. . . Sorry. I'm sorry about that, Johnny. I'm under a lot of pressure. No hard feelings.'

'That all depends, don't it?'

'Jesus, Johnny, you ain't making this easy for me . . . Look, the reason why I'm here is because I need you to go all out to find me lorry or rather the *goods* in it,' Eddie said tightly.

Contemptuously, Johnny shook his head 'Not this again, Ed. You sound like you're on a loop. You ain't paid us, so we ain't going to do anything for you, and you must have proper lost it if you think there'll be anything left of the coke. Whoever jacked the lorry will have banged it out quick. Maybe taken it up north or across to Cardiff. But either way, the whole batch will have been nostriled by the sniff heads by now.'

Eddie looked at Ma, who scowled. He turned away quickly to look at Johnny before taking a deep breath, then hesitantly said, 'It wasn't coke though.'

Ma leant forward. 'Come again.'

There was a pause as Eddie worked up the courage to repeat it. 'It wasn't coke . . . It was diamonds.'

The silence strangled the air and the tension was palpable. Then without a moment's hesitation, Johnny stood up and brought back his fist, slamming it hard into Eddie's stomach, which sent him sprawling on the floor. And as Eddie curled up in a ball, coughing out phlegm, Johnny pulled out a cosh from his pocket, smashing it down across his skull.

Eddie screamed as the blood splattered across the room.

'Stop! Johnny! Stop! I'm sorry!'

With his eyes wild, Johnny brought back his foot, kicking Eddie over and over.

'You piece of shit! You was going to pull a fast one over us! Paying us to bring a lorry of coke when all along it was stones! You know that would've cost you more. Our cut would've been bigger, because the risk to my men was greater, and if they'd been caught, the time they'd have to serve would've been longer. You know you have to pay for all that, Ed, you know how it works, but you wanted to skank your way out of it.'

His mouth full of blood, Eddie gasped. 'No! No, I didn't, I swear. I would've paid you properly when I got them. I just didn't want to tell no one. You got to believe me!'

Stopping for a rest, Johnny stared down at Eddie. 'Why?'

'Cos, you got to see it from my point of view. The only reason I never told you was because the less that people knew the better. Everything depended on it. I didn't want to risk anything going wrong. But ain't that fucking ironic . . . But I would've told ya. It was all planned out. Your men were supposed to drive the lorry to my lot. After that I was going to knock out the diamonds to one of my contacts who would've paid good money. Then I would've given you your money. And like you say, it was going to be a bigger cut to what I said.'

'That's crap Eddie, and you know it.'

'Think what you like. That was how it was going to be and to show you how much I meant it, I'm willing to give you ten per cent of those diamonds.'

It was the second time in less than twenty-four hours someone had laughed in Eddie Styler's face, a fact which didn't go unnoticed by him and a fact which made him seethe.

'Eddie, you're lying on me front room floor having just had the shit kicked out of you and you're *willing* to give me ten percent of diamonds which you haven't actually got! You fuckin' muppet.'

Ma, now on her second cup of tea and sniffing the white bottled, nasal plastic pump spray she always carried, smirked. 'You'll have to do better than that, Eddie.'

Johnny sneered back. 'What do you reckon, Ma?'

'I say that Eddie needs us more than we need him. I heard that Jason Robinson is on a countdown to when he next comes and visits you. It ain't looking good, Ed.'

Holding out a hand to Eddie – whose face was covered in blood from the gash to his skull – Johnny said, 'And now we know about them, what would stop me going out there and finding the people who've got the diamonds meself? Cutting you right out of the picture.'

Taking the tissue Ma had passed him, Eddie gently wiped his head, wincing at the pain. 'You could find them, but what then? Who you going to sell them to? You need contacts Johnny, because you deal in coke, trafficking drugs and stolen goods, not diamonds. Big difference.'

'Why don't you get Reggie's men to help you?'

'You know why. I owe them, I've borrowed a lot of money from a lot of people, and it ain't like they work on a no win, no fee basis, is it? They want their money straight up front and it's the same story all over. I owe too much money, ain't no one touching me with any poxy bargepole. But what I can do, is get rid of the diamonds quickly; something you might find harder than you think. And the problem is the longer you hold onto them trying to get rid, the more likely it is that some big face will hear about them, then come sniffing around and will be only too happy to put a bullet in your head for them.'

Ma yawned widely with a line of spit attached from her bottom to her top lip. 'Save us the Jackanory, Ed. We'll do it, but I'm looking for a sixty-forty share in our favour.'

'How am I supposed to pay anyone if that's what I'm getting?'

Ma craned forward. 'Eddie, listen to me, this ain't fucking *Dragons' Den* you know. Take it or leave it.'

After a long pause, Eddie said bitterly, 'I ain't got any other option, looks like I'll have to take it then, don't it?'

Johnny winked. 'Then we have a deal. But Eddie, just out of interest, how much are we talking about? What are those rocks actually worth?'

'About three million big ones.'

25

'Oh my God, stop! What are you doing? Stop! Please! Leave him alone!'

Bree pulled at Ma Dwyer's hand as she raised it in the air, bringing a whip cracking down on her son. 'He ain't going anywhere!'

Begging, with tears streaming down her face, Bree screamed.

'Please! This isn't his fault, it's mine! It was my idea. Please let go . . . Look he's bleeding. Please, stop.'

Standing, shadowed in the darkness of the small opening in the woods, Ma cracked down the whip again, her huge body pushing Bree aside, sending her stumbling forward into the mud.

Bree watched in horror feeling helpless. They'd planned to get away, planned to be together, and Ma – somehow knowing of their plans – had followed, taking them unawares.

Standing over her son as he tried to scramble away, Ma, not caring to listen to his cries nor hear his terror, snarled at Bree. 'He ain't going anywhere. If you want to go and have that baby, go on, but he's staying here.'

'Why are you doing this? He can do what he likes, he's old enough.'

Ma's face was red, vicious with anger as she held onto her semi-unconscious son. She shook him like he was a rag doll. 'This is your fault. You should've stayed away.'

Drenched and crying, her pregnant stomach protruding, Bree dropped onto her knees, her hands sinking into the sodden earth.

'Please leave him alone!'

'Then go, and let us be.'

Bree shook her head. 'I love him though. I can't just walk away.'

Ma stopped to look at Bree. She put down the whip and stepped towards her, and Bree just for a moment thought she could see a tiny smile.

'You're learning Bree, you're learning that nobody leaves Ma.'

26

In Emerson Park, Eddie Styler watched with disgust as Sandra clipped her long toenails, which flew across the kitchen floor with such force he could've been forgiven for thinking they'd been fired out of a cannon.

'Do you have to do that in here?'

Sandra gazed darkly. 'You saying I can't clip my toenails in me own house now?'

'It's *our* house, Sandra.'

Getting up and walking across to where Eddie sat with a swollen, battered face, Sandra proceeded to poke the metal nail clippers into his chest.

'Is that right?'

'We're married.'

'Oh, and don't I bleedin' well know it. I married you when I was sixteen and we've been married seventeen years, so by that reckoning, if I'd murdered you, I'd have done less time. But never mind all that, what I want to know is where's Barrie?'

As Sandra poked him again, Eddie shrugged, enjoying the memory of dumping Barrie at the side of the road. 'I haven't seen him.'

'Then you best go and find him, and don't bother coming back until you have.'

About to say something, Eddie's mouth was left hanging open as a loud crash followed and the backdoor was broken down. Sandra ran out of the kitchen, leaving Eddie frozen to the spot. And standing with his men, looking like a lion who'd spotted his prey, was Jason Robinson.

'Hello, Eddie. How's it going?'

Stepping over the broken glass, Jason walked into the kitchen. With his perma-tan leathering his skin, he grinned widely at a shaking Eddie Styler. 'I hope you've got my money, sunshine, because time's up . . . and before you think about it, don't bother trying to leg it. I've got men outside who'd be only too happy to stop you.'

Eddie's forehead prickled with sweat. His eyes darted round. Pupils dilating with terror.

'I . . . I . . . Look, I ain't got your money.'

Jason nodded his head towards one of his men, who stepped closer to Eddie, grabbing him and packing a hard punch to the face, sending Eddie careering into the stainless-steel oven.

Deciding his best bet was to stay lying down, Eddie pleaded with Jason, who picked up one of the heavy kitchen chairs, ready to smash it over him. 'No! Please, wait. Hold on! Hear me out. I got a deal for you.'

'It's a bit late for that.'

Fervently, Eddie shook his head. 'It's never too late for three million pounds' worth of diamonds.'

'What?'

Eddie, ignoring the shocked look of amazement on Jason's face, continued to plead his case, speaking quickly. 'I got these diamonds, you see, but the lorry got proper mugged. But if you can wait, I'm going to get them back, we can cut it down the middle. We can do a two-way split. Fifty-fifty. Let me tell you about it, before you make up your mind.'

And as he began to recount a *version* of the story he wanted Jason to hear, even though he'd failed miserably at school, Eddie Styler understood that between Johnny's sixty percent and Jason's proposed fifty, the math just didn't add up. And as he lay staring at the kitchen ceiling next to a scattering of large toenail clippings, Eddie knew that if he wanted to avoid being fed to the seagulls, somehow he'd have to come up with a plan B – and fast.

On the other side of the kitchen door, Sandra Styler listened in amazement. She had no idea. No idea at all that her low-life, lying, scheming husband, had been dealing in that kind of money. But now she did, the question was what she was going to do about it.

27

Bree Dwyer sat with Kieran's duffle bag on the floor of her silver and velvet bedroom. She could see Ma pottering about the caravan site with the dogs and Johnny was out at a business meeting, which meant for the next few minutes at least she was confident no one would walk in.

She sat staring at the blue plastic bag she'd found in Kieran's bag, not wanting to open it but at the same time needing to know more. What she'd seen in his bag had chilled her.

Had it not been for the shawl, she might have put it down to a dead animal. But she couldn't ignore what it was.

The thought alone made her panic because what was she supposed to do? What was she even supposed to think? She had no one to talk to about it but she had so many questions. And Kieran, had he seen inside the bag? And if so, did he know what it was?

She was scared but what if she was just being stupid and it turned out to be nothing . . . perhaps it was. Perhaps it was just her imagination running overtime. But what about the shawl? She kept coming back to that. Maybe it was someone's idea of a joke and they'd dressed up an animal carcass . . . But nobody would do that. Would they?

But if she went to the police what would she say? And how could she go anyway? She wouldn't be able to steal the time and besides, Ma was following her, and now she'd seen her with Alfie . . . Alfie. She stopped, her breath catching in her chest as she thought of him, which she hadn't done since the car park. Since she hadn't allowed herself since the car park.

He'd been her everything when she was a kid. He'd saved her. He'd been her protector. So kind. So strong. So funny. The only person who'd ever cared about her. And she'd loved him, how she'd loved him, how she'd clung onto his hand when he'd picked her and Sandra up from the school gates. She'd never wanted to let go.

But she'd had to when they'd ripped her away and taken her to another foster home. And although she'd tried to hang onto it, the despair of her daily life had caused Alfie's face to fade from her memory like a ghost of the past. Until one day he'd come and found her, wanting to know if she was fine, and the love she saw in his face had filled her with warmth again. With hope. With the strength she'd needed to get through.

And as Bree Dwyer watched Ma through the window she realised that maybe that was her answer. Maybe Alfie Jennings would save her again.

28

It was dark and the sound of the banger racing cars filled the air as Johnny, Ma and Eddie stood above the two naked men tied tightly to wooden chairs in the small portacabin behind the track on their land.

Johnny, patting the blood-covered cosh in the palm of his hand and dripping with sweat, spoke in a dangerously low tone. 'So, let's try again, shall we? Did you or did you not have something to do with the lorry doing a magic trick?'

Jeff Rogers, a long-time employee of Johnny and Ma, his mouth full of blood and a three inch, deep cut across his forehead, shook his head. 'Johnny, you know me. There's no way I would do something like that. I ain't muggy. I'd never betray you.'

Johnny pulled a face, his tone loaded with derision. 'You see Jeff, that's what I thought, but I've had me trust pissed on before.'

Eddie Styler winked at Johnny, enjoying the feeling of power again. It'd been a rough few days but if he played this right with Ma and Johnny, and was careful, maybe, just maybe, things might work out as he'd planned. He watched with joy as Johnny traced the cosh across Jeff's face whilst he stuttered his reply.

'But . . . but that ain't me! I've never turned you over.'

'But there's always a first time for everything, ain't there?'

Jeff's face was tight with fear, tears beginning to turn his eyes glassy. '*Please.*'

Ma chuckled. 'Tears, Jeff? Johnny and Ryan used to get in trouble for tears, I used to teach them a lesson, but it made them strong, made them into who they are now. Looks like you need to be taught a lesson, Jeff.'

She drove her foot between Jeff's legs, kicking him hard in the testicles. 'I need to know that your loyalties lie in the right place, Jeff. That you had nothing to do with the lorry going walkabouts. Is that what you're saying? That you had nothing to do with it?'

Unable to speak from the pain, Jeff attempted to nod as Ma sat back down and continued to bite into her sandwich as Johnny turned his attention to the other driver, who sat shivering from a mixture of terror and cold.

'What about you? You going to tell me you weren't in on it as well? You do understand that I'll find out one way or another.'

The other driver, his bald head glistening with large beads of sweat and streaks of blood, squinted up at Johnny. His voice was more confident than Jeff's had been. 'Jon-Jon, you and me go back such a long way. I'm insulted. I weren't in on it, that's the God's honest truth. And unless Jeff was doing a De Niro, I don't think he was in on it neither. He weren't acting when they pulled us up and put a gun in his boat race. He was proper bricking it. I swear.'

'Yeah, but you could just be giving some right old baloney. How do I know you're not in this together?'

'You don't. So, crack on with what you're going to do with me, but it won't change the truth.'

Johnny drew back the cosh, then smacked it hard against the driver's ear, causing it to explode with blood. The driver screamed, his body shuddering with pain.

Smiling, Johnny said, 'Cocky bastard, ain't ya? But for some reason, and call me a mug, I actually believe you . . . So, come on. What do you remember? There must've been something. An accent? The way they walked? What about their height. Were they tall? Small . . . For fuck's sake I'm talking to you.'

The driver moaned in agony. Johnny raised his eyebrows, letting out a long sigh. 'Oh do me a favour mate, cut the wailing bitch act, cos you're beginning to piss me right off.'

'There . . . there . . . there was something.'

Johnny turned to look at Mick. 'What?'

Mumbling through his swollen lip and knocked out front tooth, Mick repeated what he'd said. 'There was something, I . . . I just remembered.'

'Go on.'

'A name.'

Johnny burst into laughter. 'Turn it in.'

'I swear.'

'Maybe you're hearing isn't as good as it once was. Maybe being a low-down piece of shit has an effect on the old King Lears.'

'I don't think so, I know what I heard.'

'Go on then.'

'Andy. He said *Andy*.'

Johnny sniffed, then spat on the floor. 'Don't mean nothing, and besides, no one does names. They were probably just taking the piss out of you, and like a muppet you fell for it.'

Tired, Johnny sighed and shook his head at Ma, before he headed for the door. He'd had enough. He'd come back later, but he needed to have a word with one of the racing drivers before he left, and it looked like he was going to draw a blank with Jeff and Mick at the moment. Though it was abundantly clear they hadn't been involved in jacking the lorry, although he'd already suspected that before, it was still good to keep them on their toes. A session like this was always good, especially as it kept his mind off Bree.

'Wait! Wait, Johnny! I remembered wrong, it wasn't Andy . . . It was *Alfie* . . . The fella said Alfie.'

29

'That can't be right.'

'I'm telling you Vaughnie, it is. Alf, I heard it with me own two ears.'

Alfie and Vaughn sat listening to Sandra in the overheated kitchen as Lola and Janine made a pile of cheese and pickle sandwiches.

'I don't know anything more about it, apart from he wanted this Jason Robinson to help him score the diamonds back.'

Alfie stared at his sister. A thousand thoughts running through his mind. 'Does he know that you heard him?'

'I don't think so. And as much as he's a prick, usually he knows whatever goes on I won't grass on him.'

'Until now.'

'Yeah, but until now I didn't think he had his fingers near that kind of money.'

Alfie took a bite out of a sandwich. He grinned. 'So, you'll grass on him if the price is right?'

'After what you told me Alf, I'd grass him out for a flymo strimmer. How he has the front to look at me knowing he's spent all me money, I'll never know. Problem is though, where the fuck are these diamonds?'

Alfie glanced towards Vaughn. He shrugged. 'Who knows, Sandra. They could be anywhere.'

'Yeah, but they're *my* diamonds and I want them back. I'm sick of Essex, I need a bit of Marbs. I don't care about the house. If I can get me hands on these stones, the bank can take it. I want sunshine all year round. That will suit me right down, thanks very much, but I need me diamonds to do it. So what do you say, Alfie? Vaughn?'

'What are you on about?'

Sandra threw her arms up into the air. 'I'm on about getting my big brother to help me get the gems back. I ain't asking for free either. I'll give you ten per cent.'

Janine Jennings scowled. 'Hang on a minute Sandra, that ain't right. Ten per cent is just a sniff of a cockerel's arse.'

Sandra Styler looked at Janine in disgust. Her ex-sister-in-law had always got on her wick.

'You've always been a greedy bleeder, Janine, and you've got a cheek to talk about a cockerel's arse when you took our Alfie here for everything he's got. My brother wouldn't be in this mess in the first place if it wasn't for you.'

Janine saw red. 'Me? Do me a favour! Your brother wouldn't be in this mess if he'd stuck with me, but instead he wanted to go off and shag every pussy between here and Middle-earth. I'm surprised he didn't come back with a hobbit on his bleedin' dick... So no, it ain't my fault, it's his, and Alfie is not going to go looking for Eddie's diamonds just to be mugged off for ten per cent.'

Raising his voice, Alfie shouted over the two of them. 'Just shut it, Janine. What's wrong with you? This is none of your business.'

He stared hard at his ex-wife. He wasn't sure what the hell she was trying to do. Janine knew full well they had the diamonds in their possession, so for her to be arguing over getting a certain percentage was crazy. He'd have to have a serious word with her later.

Alfie turned back to his sister and shook his head. 'Sorry, Sandra. No can do.'

Sandra's eyes darkened over. 'Fine. How about twenty per cent then?'

'Don't be silly. It ain't about the money, girl. It's about the manpower. There's only me and Vaughnie. It'll be too big a job to try to get rid of them without the whole of gangland thinking they can have a piece of the action. I'm sorry . . . But Sandra, I swear, when I sort this deal out with Reenie, I won't see you go short. After all, we're family.'

'Janine Jennings, what the fuck was that all about?' Alfie roared, red-faced, as Vaughn and Lola watched on as if it were a spectator sport.

Standing in the games room after saying goodbye to Sandra, Janine, with her hands on her hips, shouted just as loud. 'It was about saving your bacon as well as yours, Vaughnie. You two must be losing it. How do you know that Eddie ain't sent her?'

'Cos she's my sister.'

'When did that make any difference. Ain't you heard of Cain and bleedin' Abel?'

Alfie lit up a cigarette. 'Sandra ain't like that. I told her all about Eddie's money problems, so it's him who she's got a beef with not me.'

'But hold on, look what you're doing. You're deceiving her by not telling her that *you've* got the diamonds, so why should she be any different? Why wouldn't she mug you over and pretend she's an innocent party but all along she's got Eddie's back?'

'She wouldn't, I just know.' But as Alfie said it, he knew what Janine was saying was true. He wasn't being honest, so why on earth should he expect somebody else to be.

'Whether you want to admit it or not Alfred, you and your sister ain't been close for a long time, which means you can't trust her. Not now anyway. I ain't saying never, but believe me darlin', it's better she thinks you don't have a clue about those diamonds than her to be suspicious. We don't want this deal going wrong.'

Vaughn, who until this moment had kept out of it, looked baffled. 'I thought we agreed that we were leaving those diamonds well alone, and that we were going to look for something else as well as try to get in touch with Franny. So you need to start talking and tell me what deal you're talking about.'

Janine snapped at Vaughn. 'It's the deal where you take your finger out of your arse and see that selling them rocks is the only option you've got. Alfie agrees, don't you, Alf?'

Nose to nose, Alfie leant towards Janine. 'Anyone told you that you got a big fucking mouth?'

A loud knocking on the door stopped Janine saying anything else and she walked out of the room, leaving Alfie and Vaughn staring at each other in hostility. A moment later she popped her head round the door. 'Say hello to my visitor, everyone. Let me introduce you to your new partner in crime.'

Alfie stared in disbelief. 'Now this is a fucking joke.'

There standing larger than life was Frankie Taylor, an old friend and associate of Alfie and Vaughn's they'd known for years, growing up and working in Soho together. The three of them were always a tight crew, always had each other's backs, but of course, like everyone, they'd had their moments of hating the very sight of each other. Still, the long, rich history they had ultimately bonded them together.

'Hello gentlemen. I must say when Janine called and asked me to come over and help you boys out, I was a little surprised, but then she told me just what had happened.'

Annoyed, and butting egos, Vaughn shook his head. 'You've had a wasted trip, Frank. We're fine, we can do without your help.'

'I don't think so. I mean, when I heard about what Franny had done . . .'

'Why did you tell him?'

Frankie smiled at Vaughn. 'She had to, didn't you Janine?'

Vaughn looked at him, puzzled. 'What are you talking about?'

'I'm talking about me money. Didn't Alfie tell you?'

Vaughn glared at Alfie. He almost couldn't bear to hear anything else. Anything else that Alfie had done behind his back. Slowly he said, 'Tell me what?'

Frankie shook his head, amusement in his voice. 'Alfie, Alfie, Alfie. You were born ducking and diving. How can you not tell him?'

Alfie snapped. 'Because you were supposed to be a silent fucking partner, that's why.'

The rage Vaughn felt had become a familiar sensation as of late. 'Hold up, what are you talking about, Frank?'

'The two million Franny took. Some of that was *my* money. Alfie didn't have what he needed, so he asked me to go in with him. Which means, you and me are business partners, Vaughnie. I've always fancied running a betting empire. Now all we need to do is sell them diamonds so we can make it happen, cos now, I ain't going to be silent anymore. In fact, you are not only going to hear me, you're going to feel me right up your fucking arse until we get our money back and sort this shit out.'

As was his habit, Eddie Styler was pacing. He was raging. He was furious. He was seething. But most of all he was out for revenge. Alfie. Alfie. Alfie. The name played like a sick tune in his head. The drivers, Jeff and Mick, hadn't known or heard anything else, but his gut was saying it was him. It *had* to be Jennings because there was only one Alfie that could screw up his life so badly, who could take everything he had and come and shit on it in immeasurable proportions.

There was no way it was a coincidence that a few weeks after Alfie and Vaughn turned up on home turf, a lorry got jacked and his life went down the carzey.

He didn't think that Alfie had known that it was *his* lorry, *his* goods before he'd gone out and ambushed it, but what he did think was he was one big joke to Alfie Jennings.

He couldn't believe he'd gone around to Janine's gaff, pleading and begging Alfie to help. When all along it'd been Alfie himself who'd mugged off the diamonds. And Alfie and Vaughn must've laughed about it. Seeing him as some funny cunt. Seeing him as no better than what they'd find on the bottom of their shoe. Well, he'd show them, especially Alfie. Because this time it was *personal*. Alfie had stepped over the mark and he was sick of people seeing him as a pushover. He was sick of every Tom, Dick and prick taking the piss out of him when not too long ago they wouldn't have even been brave enough to look him in the eye.

He sighed, then checking Sandra wasn't about, Eddie went into his closet, pushing his expensive tailored suits aside to get to the back of the large wardrobe to the hidden drawer. Pulling out a half-bottle of whiskey, Eddie took a large, bitter gulp before carefully putting it back and pulling out a small loaded hand gun. Oh yes, if Alfie wanted a joke, then he'd make sure he got one. Alfie Jennings would soon be laughing on the other side of his face.

30

In the remote countryside of north-west Essex, Johnny Dwyer sat at the dining room table in his mobile home with Ma serving him up a large bowl of beef and vegetable casserole. The smell of it irritated Johnny. Everything at that moment irritated Johnny, because he had Alfie on his mind.

That name had been coming up too much lately for his liking. He, like Eddie, was certain that the only Alfie it could've been was *Jennings*. Alfie fucking Jennings.

He'd always known of Alfie, and although he'd only had dealings with him via other people, a lot of the big jobs they'd done in the past, and a lot of the coke they'd supplied or bought, had Alfie's name written all over it. Alfie Jennings, the number one face. Mr Big . . . Fuck! Johnny threw the bowl of casserole hard against the wall.

'What the bleedin' hell do you think you're doing?'

Johnny stared at his mother, his eyes dark and full of hatred. 'Shut up, Ma. The last thing I need is you in me head.'

Ma wiped away the small piece of carrot that had been precariously balancing on her lip for the last couple of minutes. She pointed at the thick brown gravy covering and slowly creeping down the wall. 'And who's going to clear this up?'

Absentmindedly, Johnny answered, 'What? . . . Oh for fuck's sake, get Bree to do it.'

Bree.

Bree.

Bree.

That little whore.

He pressed the palm of his hand into his throbbing eye. The slag was laughing at him behind his back. With him. *His* Bree and Alfie, thinking he was one big joke.

'Bitch!' Johnny shouted as he overturned the table, sending plates and food and cutlery flying everywhere. All he could see was them together. Alfie's hands over *his* woman. His dick inside *his* woman.

'Oh fuck! Oh fuck!'

Ma yelled back, 'What on earth is going on with you?'

Wide-eyed, Johnny didn't answer. She was probably thinking about him right now. Breathing hard he lifted his shirt, exposing the top of his jeans. He ripped out his belt from the loops. Well he would show her. God would he just.

Ma squawked again, 'What is the matter? You best calm down, son. I don't want me casserole plastered everywhere.'

Speaking through his teeth, Johnny snarled, 'I told you to shut it! Now get out of me way.'

'Where are you going! Johnny! Johnny!'

Johnny ran down the corridor in a blind rage, white noise filling his head. He swung open the lounge door.

'Get out, kids! Now!'

Kieran and Molly gazed up at their father before running out of the room as Bree, who'd been sitting on the floor playing clap hands with Ryan, looked up at Johnny, terrified.

He walked slowly towards her, swinging the belt he held in his hand. 'You can stay there, Ryan. You need to watch this. Because Bree's going to be in trouble. Big trouble.'

Bree began to scramble back, her legs moving quickly underneath her. 'What's going on? Johnny, what's wrong with you?'

'Ain't nothing wrong with me, it's what's wrong with you. What is it that makes you such a whore, Bree?'

Pushing herself into the corner, Bree's eyes darted to Ryan then to Ma, then back to Johnny, fear dripping in the beads of sweat. 'Please, I don't understand.'

Playing with one of his new kittens, Ryan stared at Johnny, his head tipping to one side as he rocked back and forth. 'Leave. Johnny leave. Johnny should leave. Johnny leave.'

'Shhh Ryan, no!' Bree scrambled towards Ryan, trying to comfort him. Before she could get to him, Johnny grabbed hold of her hair, yanking it as hard as he could. She screamed, trying to pull his hand away whilst he lashed the belt across her back.

'Leave. Johnny leave. Johnny should leave.'

Spitting his words, Johnny bellowed at Ryan. 'Shut up, you muppet, unless you want some of this as well!'

Dropping Bree's hair, Johnny turned towards his twin brother, raising the belt above his head ready to whip it down on him, but as he did so, Bree leapt forward, throwing herself between Ryan and the belt.

'Don't touch him! Don't you touch him!'

The leather belt hit hard and quick. Cracking across Bree's face, cutting her cheek like a knife on silk. Johnny roared, bending down to pick up Bree, fury running through him as her blood ran down.

'I'm going to kill you!'

'Stop, Johnny!' Ma's voice was firm and loud as she stood behind her son.

Raging, Johnny yelled at his mother. 'Stop? I ain't going to stop this time.'

'I said, stop!'

Johnny shook his head. 'It's a bit too late to start fucking caring about her now.'

Ma stepped closer to Johnny. 'I don't. I couldn't care less about her. It's you I care for. I ain't going to lose any sleep if you killed her, but why do it son, when we could use her to our advantage.'

'What are you talking about?'

'I'm talking about getting Bree to help us serve up Alfie. She told us they go back a long way, right? Well, we could get her to find out where the diamonds are. It sounds like he trusts her, and he don't know that *your* men were driving the lorry, and neither does he know that we know about *him*. So, he won't suspect nothing, and once we know where they are, not only will we get the diamonds, we can get rid of Jennings once and for all.'

'I won't do it! I won't!'

Ma spun round to Bree, booted her hard in the sides before leaning forward, grabbing her face in her hand, squeezing it hard. 'You'll do as I say.'

Bree's voice was full of panic. 'I can't! I can't!'

Nastily, Ma squeezed Bree's face even harder, and snarled back at her. 'Oh, you can Bree, and you will.'

Johnny looked at Bree then back at his mother. 'We can't trust her.'

Ma smiled at her son. 'Come here, boy.'

Looking like a child, Johnny walked over to his mother, leaning his head on her shoulder as the energy drained out of him.

'That's it Johnny, Ma will make it better. I'll sort it like I always do.'

'I need the noise to stop in me head.'

'Shhh, baby, I know.'

Johnny rubbed his temples. 'Why won't it stop, Ma?'

'Hey, hey . . . Don't you cry son, don't you *dare* cry. You know what I said about crying. That's it son, that's it. Ma's here. Ma will give you kisses and make it better. You're worrying too much, and there's no need to.'

'Ain't there?'

'You know there ain't cos I'll sort it . . . Listen, what have I always told ya, hey? If you rob a bank, I'll get you the gun. If you get caught, I'll do the bird. If you kill someone, I'll buy you the spade and help you bury them. I'm here for you; always. Ma ain't going nowhere, so don't you worry. I'll make sure Bree does it, because if she don't, then Ryan here, who she seems so fond of, will be the one to get it . . . That's right Bree, make your choice. If you don't do what we say, Ryan's going to get hurt. The way we like to do it. So, if I were you I'd do the right thing, otherwise he'll be in *trouble*, big painful trouble, all before you can say Alfie Jennings.'

31

Bree wandered into the small shop just off the Market Place in Saffron Walden. She came here quite often. She was too tired to go any further and although she couldn't afford to buy anything, she was happy enough just to browse, looking at all the baby clothes. So tiny. So pretty.

There were cream silk booties that looked like they were made for a doll, and terry towelling trousers that were so small she couldn't imagine they'd ever fit a baby.

'Can I help you?' The tall, dark-haired shop assistant came over to Bree, and she smiled warmly.

'No thank you. I'm just looking.'

'When are you due?'

'Not for a couple of months yet.'

'Boy or girl?'

Bree shrugged. 'I don't know.'

'You prefer a surprise?'

'Something like that.'

'Okay then, shout if you need me.' The assistant, spotting a couple walking into the shop and seeing the chance of a commission, closed down the conversation quickly as she hurried off.

Bree sighed, heading for the door. She felt so tired she could hardly put one foot in front of the other. She didn't know why. Ma, who'd offered her an olive branch since the day in the woods, had told her it was probably just her hormones running wild, but most days she just wanted to sleep. At least Ma had been kind, driving her wherever she needed to go and letting her sleep most afternoons.

She stopped suddenly, her thoughts fading away. Touching her stomach, she glanced across at the assistant who was in mid flow, discussing the merits of fleece blankets.

She looked down at the beautiful, yellow cardigan and smiled. It was so small and so delicate, with white flower-shaped buttons and a satin hem. She looked at the price tag. Too much for her to afford. But it was pretty . . . So pretty and she wanted it so much.

Then quickly, without really thinking, Bree slipped the cardigan into her bag before hurriedly leaving the shop.

32

Frankie Taylor sat in the stables with the lights turned out. He could see Janine in the kitchen from where he was. He smiled, she certainly was one of a kind. He'd known her for a long time, so long he couldn't remember not knowing her.

They'd met in Soho. Him and Vaughn, Alfie and Janine and, of course, Lola. Life in Soho had been different back then. Easier in some ways, when faces were faces and pimps were pimps. And Toms, well, they were just Toms.

Everyone had their place, and it suited him. He'd been a number one face, making his money in strip clubs and peep shows. And Alfie and Vaughn had wheeled and dealed and were names to be reckoned with. And it'd been a good living for them all. A damn good one. But over the years things changed and life had certainly become harder; the place he once felt a connection to, a place where he belonged, had become a place he no longer wanted to be.

So, eventually, he'd packed up with his missus, Gypsy, and moved away, leaving his son to run the businesses. And he had run them, alright. Run them right into the ground. And the millions he once had stashed away, ran too.

Yes, he was luckier than others. He had his gaff in Marbella, he still had his missus in tow, and for all intents and purposes he was still close to his son. And, of course, then there was the baby, the apple of his eye, his granddaughter. The one thing he didn't have though, was *lots* of money. And it was the first time in years. And he didn't like it, not one little bit, so when Alfie had asked him to go in with them it was a chance not to be missed.

When Janine had called, telling him what Franny had done, he'd thought it was a wind-up but after an hour on the phone he'd realised she was straight up. Alfie had told her that he'd invested some money, so it made sense that she had called, and it was a good job she had because knowing Alfie like he did, he would've left telling him until it was too late. And like both Vaughn and Alfie, he was eager to get back in the game. He missed it, but he missed the money more. He wasn't interested in just getting by. Who wanted just to get by? Certainly not him and certainly not Gypsy. There was no way either of them was going to go from Royal Beluga caviar to Richway Supermarket beans.

Standing up and stretching, his blue Savile Row suit fitting rather too tightly from overindulging on plates of tapas and red wine, Frankie sighed, his handsome sun-kissed face grimacing at the feel of the sunburn on his back. He wished Gypsy had come with him. She gave him stability, the love he'd always craved. The friendship and intimacy he would never swap.

They'd been married for years, since she'd been a teenager, and he'd been a good husband; not faithful, but Christ, what man was, and what woman really expected that? But good he had been. And he loved her. Cared for her and protected her. And although he'd cheated, he'd never thought of being with anybody else.

About to light a cigarette, Frankie froze. A noise coming from behind the stables made him crouch down, his attention drawn towards the darkened corner of the garden. Something or somebody was there.

Crawling forward and hiding behind the stable door, Frankie peered closer, trying to make out the silhouette of a person he thought he could see. But the rain continued to fall, blurring the vision of the trees and the garden, giving Frankie pause. Making him think it wasn't a person at all.

He stood up, peering into the dark. Then, deciding it was nothing, he turned back to walk towards the house, but almost immediately Frankie stopped. There was the noise. He was sure of it. He listened again. Straining to hear through the rain.

Slowly, Frankie edged along the wall, keeping himself as far back as possible. The noise had stopped, but he could still feel it . . . He knew there was somebody there.

Cautiously, he stooped down, running and making his way to the house, the lights in the kitchen now turned out.

Adrenaline rushed through Frankie's veins. He quickly ran across to the pine tree, pushing his body against the trunk. He craned his head round, squinting through the storm, and behind the bushes, Frankie was sure someone was moving.

Taking a deep breath, he glanced across to the house. He couldn't see Janine in the kitchen anymore but he knew he needed to get to the others to raise the alarm. The problem was that between where he hid and the back door there was a wide-open space, making him an easy target. But perhaps if he got close enough, maybe he could make a dash for it.

Creeping forward, he heard a branch snap, but before he had a chance to turn around and react, Frankie Taylor felt the cold end of a gun at the back of his head.

'Hello, Alfie! It's payback time.'

Frankie heard the click of the trigger as he was pushed down on the ground onto his knees. His heart raced, frantic, his eyes darted around for something. For *anything.*

'Say your goodbyes, Alf.'

Frankie leapt to the side, grabbing a piece of wood by the pine tree. He swung it round as the gun went off. He felt a sharp pain in his shoulder followed by a burn. Gritting his teeth and trying to ignore the pain, he swung with the wood again.

In the darkness, the gun flew out of the masked attacker's hand and Frankie, seeing this was his chance, threw himself towards it, scrambling, desperate to grab the weapon.

As he grappled in the darkness, Frankie felt an arm clamping around his head and the point of a blade held against his throat as his head was yanked back.

'I'll break your fucking neck here and now, Alfie.'

'. . . Oi! . . . Oi! . . . Who's out there! . . . Oi, stop!'

The lights came on and the sound of a gun and a shout from Vaughn followed, causing the assailant to release his grip and slip back into the shadows.

Frankie closed his eyes in relief, listening to the words of Janine

'Bleedin' hell, you alright, Frank? Frank!'

Frankie Taylor pushed himself up, mud and blood covering him. He looked at Janine, wiping the dirt from his face. He gave a wry, pained smile.

'I think I've been shot, girl, but I've had worse days.'

Running over, Alfie bent down. 'Jesus, Frank. Did you see who it was?'

Frankie shook his head. 'No, but it weren't me they were after. It was you, Alf. And let me tell you something, that was no threat. They were out to *kill* you.'

Vaughn Sadler stood in the bedroom doorway looking in on Frankie. He was patched up and fast asleep. Thankfully the bullet had only skimmed his shoulder. A flesh wound. But Frankie had been lucky. Really lucky. A couple of inches more to the right, he could've been brown bread.

That was the problem right there. It wasn't a question of being scared – he hadn't lost his bottle – but the game of selling and dealing with knocked-off diamonds took no prisoners; didn't matter if you were young or old, if your number was up, then bingo. And he just wasn't interested in that, life had become too precious. He'd wanted to run an empire, not push up any daisies.

Yes, he missed the old life, the charge, the buzz, but he didn't need to be on the front line to get that.

Though in truth, he hadn't been interested in being on the front line for a while. It had always been a means to an end for him. Even before he'd left for Spain, he'd turned his back on the Soho life. Unlike a lot of the men he worked with, hurting people had never been in his nature, and although violence had been the order of the day, the taste for it had left him years before, the day his best mate – Alfie's brother – Connor, had died in his arms when a job went wrong.

It still hurt to think about it, and the guilt over Connor Jennings' death lived with him every day. He and Alfie never spoke about it, but he'd taken it hard, and it was a long time before Alfie managed to get his life back on track. Eventually, as the years passed, the haunted look in Alfie's eyes disappeared, but he knew the pain, although hidden away, was still there.

Yes, they needed to get the money together to sort out the mess as soon as they could, and of course he didn't want to have to tell Casey that he'd lost everything, especially when he was going to try to win her back, but what he didn't need was to watch anyone close to him dying or getting hurt. And the problem was that his gut told him if he got involved in this diamond job, he'd probably end up seeing both.

33

Johnny Dwyer sat at the breakfast table, staring at Eddie Styler. His irritation was rising and it didn't help the boiled eggs his ma had made him that morning were repeating on him. Letting out a smelly burp, he spoke to Eddie, who seemed unusually quiet.

'I'm going to use Bree to set Alfie up.'

'Bree?'

Snapping at Eddie, Johnny's tone was aggressive. 'That's what I fucking said, ain't it?'

'Yeah, but I don't understand.'

'Ed, listen to me, I ain't in the best of moods today. I've got a lot of noise in me head. It's all over the place, can't seem to think straight, so I'd advise you not to piss me off.'

Eddie swallowed hard, slightly louder than he anticipated, as Ma, who'd been sitting in the corner eating a charred piece of toast and Marmite, looked up to glare at him.

'I might be being a bit of a muppet here, but I don't get it. I'm sorry.'

Massaging his forehead, desperate to stop what seemed like a constant banging in his head, Johnny muttered, 'Look, Bree and Alfie go back a long way and not many people know Bree.'

'So?'

'So, she don't get out a lot, and only those nearest to me know her name, what she looks like or even the fact that she's married to me. So, Alfie ain't going to smell a rat, she'll just be another bird who he once knew. She'll be able to give him any old crap and he'll lap it up.'

Eddie looked interested. 'How do they know each other?'

'Oh, for fuck's sake, I don't know and I don't care. Do I look like a bleedin' genealogist?'

'A what?'

With Eddie's voice going through his head like a wailing siren, Johnny growled at him. 'Shut up, Ed, you're doing my nut in. Anyway, what I do know is I'm going to get Bree to find out if Alfie really has the diamonds, and if he does, where they are.'

Eddie took a sip of the tepid tea in front of him and immediately wished he hadn't. 'How she's going to do that?'

'Use your imagination.'

Speaking out loud what he was supposed to be only thinking, Eddie said, 'Lucky bastard.'

'What did you say?'

Putting his hand over his mouth, Eddie watched Johnny's eyes darken and a throbbing vein appeared, running down the centre of his forehead.

'I . . . I . . .'

Abruptly, Johnny stood up, grabbing the butter-covered toast knife off the table. He leapt at Eddie, pushing the blunt blade against his eye. His words spat out. 'I said, what did you say?'

'I . . .'

Johnny screamed. 'Say it!'

Thinking quickly as the pain in his eye shot through his entire body, Eddie stammered, 'I only meant . . . I mean . . . I said, he's lucky . . . But only because . . . Because it's better than you going to pay him a visit . . . I meant, he's lucky, cos having Bree go speak to him is preferable to you. So he's a lucky bastard that he's got off so easily.'

Exhausted by the noise in his head, Johnny threw down the toast knife on the table. He stared at Eddie, who held his hand over his eye. 'Is that right, Ed?'

Feeling quite smug at getting away with it, Eddie nodded, causing a sharp pain to rush through his eye. 'Yeah, that's right.'

Going to sit back down, Johnny cricked his neck from side to side, trying to release the constant tension as he held a cold stare with Eddie. 'What we don't want, Ed, is Alfie and his muppets thinking we're onto them. So, we keep everything as normal. We don't say nothin'. We don't do nothin'. I know your old woman is related but you said they weren't close. Right?'

'Yeah, he ain't bothered with her properly for a long time. Besides, she don't really know anything much . . . Though when I got meself in this mess, I asked him for a favour.'

'You what?'

'No, don't worry, this was before we knew he had the diamonds. Anyway, I told him I was in trouble with a couple of people which meant Sandra was in trouble. The geezer just looked at me as if I was a floating turd.'

Ma piped up. 'Well there you go, that says it all about him. How can family mean nothing? He deserves everything he's going to get.'

Eddie agreed. 'Yeah, and it's only a shame that I couldn't . . .' He trailed off, realising what he was about to say.

Johnny looked at him strangely. 'Couldn't what, Ed?'

Breathing hard and trying to hold his gaze steady, the half a bottle of whiskey he'd drunk earlier not helping, Eddie shrugged. 'Dunno.'

Johnny leant forward, picking up the knife again, and slowly he began to tap it on the table, louder and louder. Over and over.

'Eddie, I'm waiting. If you've got something to say, you better spit it out. What is it you couldn't do?'

'Okay, look. I paid Alfie a visit last night. But don't worry he never saw me . . . I was just pissed off. I don't like to be made a fool of and—'

Johnny interrupted. 'What was the last thing I said to you the other day?'

Panicking, Eddie said the first thing that came into his mind. 'That . . . that you had to go home for your tea?'

Johnny moved so fast that it was only when Eddie landed backwards on the floor did he realise what had happened.

Sitting on top of him, Johnny grabbed Eddie's top, their faces inches away from each other. He shook Eddie hard, his face turning a deep shade of red. 'Do you want me to kill you, Ed? Cos it's beginning to look that way. You're becoming a liability and it feels like it's one big joke to you.'

Eddie screamed back. 'It ain't a joke! None of it's a fucking joke. I've lost everything and if you must know, I hate him! I fuckin' hate Alfie Jennings! I want him to pay.'

Without warning, Eddie began to cry. Deep, loud, racking sobs. Letting go, Johnny got off him, sitting cross-legged on the floor next to him. He looked up at Ma, who pulled a face, then stared back at Eddie. Wiping his tears for him with the back of his sleeve, Johnny leant forward, whispering in Eddie's ear.

'Maybe I misjudged you, mate. I didn't know you felt so deeply about him. But don't you worry, Johnny's here and I'll make sure he pays. He'll pay so much, the whole of Essex will hear him scream.'

34

'Good morning, how is the wounded soldier?'

'Fucked.'

Lola Harding cackled loudly as Frankie Taylor walked into the kitchen. 'You don't look too clever I have to admit.'

'I'll survive, darlin'.'

'Not if you're going to eat her breakfast you won't.'

'Shut up, Alf. Ignore him. He remembers my breakfasts well, don't you, Frank.'

Alfie grinned. 'And that's why he's afraid. Never mind the bleedin' bullet, it's the breakfast you have to dodge.'

Lola Harding scowled at Alfie at the same time as Janine walked into the kitchen. 'Well, let's ask Janine then, shall we?'

'Ask me what?'

'About me breakfasts. I've never seen you have a problem with them.'

'That's right, you've never seen it cos I've been too busy locked away in the bathroom, shitting it down the carzey.'

The whole of the room erupted into laughter, and even Lola who wanted to feel angry couldn't. This is what she had missed over the past couple of years. This was her family. The only real family she'd known and loved.

In the past it'd felt like her life was a car crash. Her mother had introduced her to a pimp and put her on the game at thirteen to support her father's drug habit and a year later she was not only a fully-fledged brass, but also a fully-fledged addict.

She'd had kids and, although she'd tried really hard to be better than her own mother, she'd let them down and the torment of that stayed with her each day. They'd all been taken away from her and put into care, and as adults they wouldn't give her the time of day. She didn't blame them, not one little bit. When they were little, instead of birthday parties and presents they'd got to watch one violent pimp after another beating up on her. She only hoped one day they might come looking for her and then she'd be able to tell them she was sorry.

Although it was too late for her kids, she'd managed to change and with it, so had life. Eventually she'd been able to save up to buy and run a small café in Soho; perhaps the only thing she'd ever done that she could say she was proud of.

She loved her life and the friends she'd made in Soho and when they'd left, it felt like a bereavement. The same grief she'd suffered when her kids had gone, and only a short while after everybody had packed up and gone the café she'd loved so much had become too much for her to run. So, then her time had been spent in the small flat which soared high above the city, not speaking to a soul.

They'd been painful days but then she'd bumped into Janine, who she knew well, but hadn't ever been particularly close to. They'd had a cup of tea, a chat and reminisced about how things used to be, and by the end of the day, Janine had asked her to come and stay.

And she'd never looked back. Not once. And although to most people Janine Jennings was a loud-mouthed, busybodying cow, to her, Janine was her cockney angel who saved her from a life of crippling loneliness and despair. But that didn't mean she wouldn't give her what for.

'Janine bleedin' Jennings, take that back!'

'Lola, I wish I could but I can't take it back, cos it's true.'

'That ain't fair.'

'Fair! Fair! I'll tell you what's not fair, my burning arsehole after I've had one of your scotch eggs.'

Alfie winked at her but quickly turned his attention to Vaughn and Frankie. 'We need to talk. Sort out what we're doing. Sort out what the fuck happened last night.'

Frankie shrugged then immediately regretted it as the pain fired through his shoulder.

'Well, that's why I'm here, so we can sort out these diamonds and get on with the original plan with Reenie. Then after that, once things are in order, I'm going to look for Franny. That bird has a lot to answer for.'

Alfie shuffled, not knowing whether he should defend her or not because, let's face it, there wasn't a real lot to defend. Deciding it was best to say nothing about her, Alfie chose to talk business instead.

'Problem is, it looks like they're onto us now, which is a big problem. We'll have to move sharpish.'

Vaughn, still irritated Alfie had once again gone behind his back by bringing in Frank said, 'You lot are assuming that this is going ahead. I don't agree to it. It's a joke, only last night someone was looking to blow yer head off. This is bigger than we are. We need to back out now before it's too late.'

Alfie looked at Vaughn. 'Ain't no one backing out. Now Frankie's here, we got a better chance to sort this out.'

Vaughn answered scornfully. 'Are you having a bubble? He wasn't even here a whole day, and our hero of the hour gets bleedin' shot. Ain't looking good for the rest of the movie.'

'At least he came. At least Frankie hasn't left his bollocks in Spain.'

Vaughn leant forward. He spoke in a low tone. 'Think what you like, Alf. I won't take your bait.'

'It ain't bait, Vaughnie, but maybe I'm wrong, maybe I'm giving you too much credit and it wasn't Spain where you left your bollocks, maybe it was in the warehouse that day with Connor.'

Vaughn leapt at Alfie, grabbing and throwing him against the wall as Janine and Lola began to yell. Alfie came back with a swinging fist, catching Vaughn on the side of his head, sending him clattering backwards to land on the kitchen table. He pummelled his fist into Vaughn's face, drawing blood, and as he did, Vaughn stretched out his hand to the side, his fingers feeling for the bread bin, and with a mighty effort he grabbed it before slamming it down on Alfie's head.

The clang of the bin reverberated in the room and as Alfie stumbled backwards, Janine shouted, 'Stop! Stop! Listen, that's the bell! Someone's at the gates . . . I said *stop*!'

The two men pulled apart and Vaughn pushed Alfie aside, panting hard, his lip dripping with blood. 'You want me to answer?'

'No, it's fine.'

Opening the kitchen door, Janine gave Alfie a hard stare as she left the room and went to the hallway intercom. Picking it up, she peered closely at the CCTV, not recognising the person at the gates.

'Hello, can I help you?'

Listening to the caller, Janine nodded, then said, 'Okay, hold on . . . Alfie! Alfie! It's for you. It's somebody called Bree.'

35

Bree lay in her bed. Pillows plumped up and the curtains drawn. She felt so tired. All she wanted to do was sleep until it was time to give birth. The pregnancy had hit her hard. Not so much the sickness, she'd hardly had any of that, but the tiredness. Crippling and debilitating.

She'd never imagined pregnancy would be like this. Not hers anyway. She'd always thought she'd be glowing with happiness and feeling the best she ever had. Instead, she could hardly get up and walk the small distance from the bedroom to the bathroom. And if it hadn't been for Ma, she didn't know what she would've done.

'Bree! Bree! Wake up.'

A small smile appeared on Bree's face as she heard his voice. 'Do I have to? I'm too tired.'

'Bree, I'm being serious . . . Come on!'

Slowly, Bree opened her eyes. Her lids felt so heavy and all she wanted to do was close them again. 'There, is that better . . .' She trailed off, her head falling forward.

'Stay awake, Bree.'

'Sorry. Why don't you come and sit down on the bed?'

'It's too dark in here. I'll open the curtains.'

'No! Please don't.'

His voice was urgent. 'Bree, I'm worried about you, you've got to get up. It's not good for you.'

'I'll be fine soon. Ma said this is the worst part of the pregnancy for a lot of people. Before you know it, I'll be up and dancing.'

I don't know why you won't go to a doctor.'

'I got Ma. That's just as good.'

'She was a nurse, Bree, and a long time ago at that. She ain't a doctor. So please, for me, go and see someone.'

Bree shook her head. 'You know I can't. They'll take one look at me and want to take my baby. I know what they're like. Even Ma said that was a possibility. I got no money, no job, no real home, no family and I was brought up in care. Not exactly ideal. Social services will make up their mind about me the minute they see my notes.'

'No, they won't Bree, because for a start you ain't on your own, you've got me.'

Bree looked at Ryan Dwyer. Her first and only love.

From the moment she'd set her eyes on him, he'd been her everything. She'd never looked at anyone else, never been with anyone else and she'd never felt like she did now. The nearest she'd ever come to it was when she'd been just a kid and she'd fallen for her best mate's brother, Alfie. But she'd been young then and this was different.

And yes, she had Ryan, but he was gentle, fragile, broken from his life and no one would've looked at him and seen what she did. All they'd see was a traveller, someone invisible, rough round the edges; a man who wasn't suited to be a father. She knew only too well they wouldn't give him a chance . . . or her.

'Look, nearer the time I'll have to go, won't I? But for now, it's best this way and Ma's looking after me so well. Stop worrying, Ryan.'

The effort of speaking made Bree close her eyes again. She felt Ryan come and sit next to her on the bed before feeling the gentle kiss on her lips. Giving a crooked smile, she lifted one eyelid and spoke in a whisper. 'Thank you. That was nice. Have I told you I love you?'

'Have I told you that I *love you!' Ryan paused. Frowning. 'And that's why we have to go. We have to leave here. Remember our plans? You were right, Bree. We've got to get away from this place and start a fresh life on our own.'*

Bree moved her hand to touch Ryan's gently. 'We will, but not now . . . After the baby comes.'

'Bree, please listen to me, we need to leave here and as soon as possible.'

'Can't you see the girl's exhausted?'

Ryan jumped, startled, his face paling as he saw Ma standing in the doorway holding a tray. 'Instead of spending your time whispering sweet nothings in her ear, Ryan, maybe you could try getting her to eat. She'll waste away. It ain't good not to eat when you're pregnant. I should know . . . Bree, here, I've made some dinner.'

Smiling gratefully, Bree shook her head. 'I'm not hungry. I'll eat it later.'

'No, you'll eat some now. Come on, just try a little bit.'

Bree looked down at the plate of fish, mash and carrots. She pulled a face. 'I can't.'

Pushing Ryan out of the way, Ma sat down hard on the bed. 'Fine, as long as you promise to eat it later, but at least have something to drink. Here you go, drink up.'

'No, really, I don't want it.'

Ma sighed. 'Bree darlin', you'll make yourself ill. Listen to Ma, I know best. Ain't that right, son?'

Ryan shrugged. His demeanour shrouded in sadness. 'I dunno Ma, do you?'

Attempting to push away the drink Ma was holding, Bree slid further down into the bed. 'Please, I really can't.'

'I ain't going nowhere until you drink it. You young lady, need to start listening to me or I'll take you to the doctor, and I know that's not what you want, and I certainly don't want that for you either, because we both know what they'll do. Especially as you're not looking after yourself. So, make your choice, girly.'

'Fine . . . I'll drink it . . . It smells disgusting.'

'Iron tablets always do. I remember when I was pregnant with Ryan and Johnny, I had to hold me nose to drink it, but it stopped me being anaemic which is where you're heading if you're not careful . . . That's it. Well done. See, it won't be that bad. Right, I'll pop my head in later to make sure you're alright . . . Come on son, let her sleep. She needs her rest.'

'I'll be out in a minute.'

As Ma left the room, Ryan whispered into her ear. 'Bree, Bree, you've got to listen to me, listen . . . I'm telling you, we've got to get away from here before it's too late.'

36

Alfie stood grinning at Bree as if a shy schoolboy. They stood looking at each other in the hallway of Janine's house. He, handsome and strong, towering above her, and she, beautiful and delicate, looking up to him.

'It's so good to see you. You look lovely by the way.' Alfie Jennings could've bitten his tongue. Not only did he think he sounded like a proper cheeseball, but he could see the bruises on her face. And not only did he not want to think about where and how she got them, he didn't want her to feel self-conscious.

'You don't look bad yourself.' Bree Dwyer could've bitten her tongue. Not only did she think she sounded like a bit of a bimbo, but she could see the delight on his face. And not only did she not want to think about what she was trying to do and what would happen if she didn't, but she didn't want to hurt him.

He blushed. She blushed. The hallway fell silent.

Pulling himself together, Alfie said, 'I've been thinking about you.'

'Have you? Me too.'

'Yeah?'

'Yeah.'

The hallway fell silent again.

Bree tried to pull herself together. 'I hope you don't mind me popping in like this. I wasn't going to at first. But I think I was a little rude when I saw you in the car park. I was in a hurry. Always am. Anyway, like I say, I hope you don't mind.'

'No!' Shit, he sounded too eager. Clearing his throat, Alfie sniffed, trying the casual approach. 'No, Jesus, course not. It's nice to see you, gal . . . How did you know I was here? It's meant to be a little bit of a secret.'

'Is it?'

'Yeah, stupid really.'

Bree smiled, a genuine warmth coming into her eyes. 'Why? Why's it a secret?'

'How shall I put it? I'm not always the most popular of blokes and a lot of people aren't too happy that I've come back to claim me crown . . .' He stopped to grin before laughing and saying, 'Surprise you that, don't it? How the whole world doesn't love me. I don't know. Seriously though, when I got back from Spain a little while ago, there were a few rumblings. The usual stuff. Anyway, as you see I ain't changed much since we were young, I'm still ducking and diving for me sins.'

Bree felt her body tense up, uncomfortable with trying to set a bait. 'Is that why you're back? To duck and dive.'

Alfie looked at her and laughed. 'You always were one for questions. Anyway, believe it or not, I hate talking about meself. Tell me about you. What have you been up to? Where've you been, girl? . . . Come on, let's go in the garden to talk.'

As Alfie turned to walk towards the conservatory, Bree wanted to run. Everything inside her wanted to head out the door and not come back. But then she pictured Ryan. Beautiful, sweet Ryan and she heard Ma's words. *Make your choice. If you don't do what we say, Ryan's going to get hurt, the way we like to do it.* And with those words ringing in her ears, Bree took a deep breath and ran to catch up with Alfie.

* * *

A few hours later, after Bree had gone, Vaughn walked up to Alfie who was sitting having a cigarette in the stables, reflecting how good it was to catch up with Bree.

'Who was that?' Vaughn asked as he lit up a cigar, taking in the smoke and the cold air.

'An old friend. We go way back.'

'How did she know where to find you?'

Taking a deep drag of his cigarette, Alfie looked down at the burning tip and then across to Vaughn. He frowned, and speaking quietly – and more to himself – he said, 'You know what, I don't know, she didn't say.'

37

Kieran Dwyer checked behind him as he skipped through the woods. He was excited because today was the first day that he'd used the wooden box he'd made and painted with his dad. It was heavy to carry, but he knew it was going to be worth it, and as long as he kept stopping to have a rest, he'd be able to get it up to the top wood before dark. He'd found a new hiding place, better than before. A place no one would be able to see his special find.

He enjoyed having this secret that nobody else knew about. It made him feel special, made him feel older because he knew it was mainly grown-ups who had all the secrets and whispered and spoke in corners.

As the rain started to fall, Kieran began to get worried. The bright yellow and red rainbow he'd painted on the side was beginning to run, mixing and trickling with the rain.

Hurriedly, he put the box on the ground, taking his coat off to cover and protect it from the storm. The arms and hood of his blue jacket barely covered the picture of the tree he'd done, but at least it'd stop his rainbow from ruining.

It'd taken him three whole days to paint it and his dad had told him it was the best rainbow he'd ever seen. But he needed to be quick, he wanted to get his box to safety.

'What's that?'

Kieran froze.

He swivelled round, his face twisted in anger. His sister, Molly, stood behind one of the large pine trees, kicking the wet moss at her feet with a big gappy smile.

'Go away! Go away!'

Molly's face wrinkled up. She wanted her brother to be pleased to see her, not cross. He was always cross. 'I'm going to tell Dad!'

Kieran shouted, disappointment and fury encasing his words in equal measures. 'Tell him what?'

'That you're not letting me play.'

'Snitch!'

Molly's lip quivered. 'I'm not a snitch . . . If I don't tell him, can I play? *Please*, Kieran.'

'No, go away!'

'Why?'

'Cos you're stupid and you're only six.'

'I'm telling!'

Kieran's eyes filled up with frustrated tears, his features taut with anger. 'I hate you! I hate you! You always spoil things!'

Picking up his painted box, Kieran ran. 'Go away! Go away! Don't follow me!'

'Kieran! Kieran! Come back! Kieran, I'm telling Dad!'

Kieran Dwyer ran as fast as his legs could take him. He pushed his head down, fighting against the storm as he carried the box under his arm. He could still hear Molly calling, running after him. He didn't know why she couldn't leave him alone. He didn't know why she couldn't . . . His thoughts were cut off as he tumbled forward, crashing into the bushes.

As he hit the hard, wet ground, Kieran heard a loud crack. There to the left of him, along with his secret wrapped up in the brown ragged cloth, were the broken bits of his brightly painted box.

'Nooooooo!' he cried out, his voice captured and muted by the wind. How could he hide his secret now that his box was broken? How could he make sure nobody found it? She'd ruined it. Molly had ruined everything.

With his hair stuck to his head and fury saturating him as if it were water, Kieran grabbed hold of a piece of his broken box. Clutching the wood in his hand, he scrambled up, his eyes narrowed in rage and he began to run back the way he came. Faster and faster he went. Down the muddy path, down the hill and towards the woods by the stream.

'Molly! Molly!' he called her, the piece of wood hidden behind his back. 'Molly, where are you? Come out and play!'

Molly Dwyer sat by the stream. She was cold and wet; it was getting dark and she wanted to go home. But she didn't know which way was home. If the sunshine had been out then she would know, but she didn't really like the dark because she knew that's where monsters lived. And she wished she hadn't followed Kieran. He was mean and he'd left her all alone.

'Molly! Molly! Where are you?'

That was her name! She could hear Kieran calling her name!

'Kieran! Kieran! I'm here!' The rain ran into her mouth and Molly, happy now, giggled as she called again. 'Kieran! Look, I got bubbles.'

Kieran stood a few feet in front of his sister, tapping the piece of wood behind his back. And Molly opened her mouth, hoping to catch some more rain.

'You do it, Kieran! It feels funny!'

Kieran pulled the wood from behind his back, gripping it tightly. He walked towards his sister, his face rigid with anger.

'What's that? Kieran, what's that?'

'I hate you! You ruin everything!'

Still holding the wood in his hand, Kieran ran towards Molly. She screamed and tried to retreat but as she did, she stumbled backwards, her arms flailing about as she tried to save herself from falling. 'Kieran! Help me! Kieran!'

Instinctively, Kieran ran forward to try to grab his sister but his hands slipped and his arms weren't long enough to reach. The current took Molly and the stream rushed and whirled over her face.

'Help me, Kieran!'

Even though it wasn't deep, Kieran hesitated a moment, looking at the dark, swirling water.

He waded in, the water cold and icy.

'I'm coming, Molly . . . I'm sorry! Molly, I'm coming!'

But before Kieran could get to her, a large branch bounced and bobbed along, hitting Molly with savagery, smashing into her head and taking her underneath the rushing water.

'Molly! No!'

Kieran scrambled out of the stream, running down the bank as Molly was carried along. Running ahead of his sister, Kieran decided to clamber down the bank again, slipping into the water as he did. He clung onto a branch, edging out, reaching and stretching his arm to grab her.

Clutching hold of her collar, Kieran hauled Molly towards the bank. He heaved and pulled, tugging with all his might whilst trying to get a foothold on the muddy bank.

Managing to get her far enough out of the stream to lay her down safely, Kieran looked around, suddenly realising the part of the bank they were on was far too steep to drag her up on his own.

Despairing, he glanced around, wondering what to do. Abruptly, he turned his gaze back to the large pine trees. He squinted. There in the shadows he could see someone watching, but he couldn't make out who.

'Help me! Help!'

The person stood motionless behind the bushes, behind the trees, just watching in the darkness of the storm-filled night. Perhaps they couldn't hear him. Perhaps they couldn't see him. He shouted louder, waving his hand.

'Please, I need your help!'

A groan from Molly made him turn away and look down. He could see her head was bleeding and panicked. Kieran Dwyer began to run.

His legs once again speeding underneath him. Faster and faster, using the tree trunks for balance as he bounded between them, skidding and scrambling towards home.

Nearing the caravan site, he could see his dad down by the chicken coop.

'Dad! Dad! It's Molly. She's hurt.'

'What?'

'Dad, come on. She fell in the water but I can't get her up the bank.'

Kieran ran and Johnny, throwing down the feed, began to follow, running towards the stream.

'She's there! Look!'

Johnny nodded, scrambling down the bank to scoop his daughter up with ease. He shouted after Kieran. 'Where are you going?'

'I'll be back in a minute!'

'Kieran! Hold up, son!'

Ignoring and not waiting for his father, Kieran ran as fast as he could. He needed to get back to his box before his secret got soaked in the rain.

Slowing down, Kieran saw where he had fallen, the broken pieces of brightly painted wood still scattered around. Suddenly alarmed, he looked around, throwing himself on his knees, his hands quickly searched through the mud. It wasn't there . . . His secret wasn't there . . . It had gone. Somebody had taken his secret.

A sudden noise caused Kieran to spin around, and there in the darkness he could just about make out the silhouette of the person watching him again. A moment later they disappeared into the shadows of the night.

38

'What were you doing? Why weren't you looking out for them? She could've drowned. And who's fault would that be then, hey? Come on, Bree, who's fault?' Johnny raged as he paced the bathroom floor, pointing at Bree.

Her voice trembled. 'It would have been mine, Johnny.'

He ran up to her as she knelt on the bathroom floor, crouching down to her level and, nose to nose with Bree, he hissed his words. 'That's right, Bree. *Yours*. How do you think Molly felt, hey? How do you think she felt when she fell in the water?'

'I . . . I . . .'

'What? You don't know? I'll show you, shall I?'

With great strength, Johnny grabbed Bree by her hair, pulling and dragging her across the tiled floor. He lifted her up before dunking her into a bathtub full to the brim with water. Pushing her head down with his foot as she struggled and flailed about, Johnny bellowed.

'How does that feel, Bree?'

She scraped at his legs as she fought for oxygen, her chest feeling like it was going to explode whilst her lungs gave off a burning sensation and Johnny continued to shout. 'You ain't fit to be a mother, Bree. Our little girl could've drowned. What were you doing, Bree? Were you thinking of him? Were you thinking of Alfie?'

He pulled her head up from the bath, and immediately Bree gasped in a large mouthful of air, coughing and spluttering as Johnny shook her hard. 'Is that what you were doing? Thinking of other men?'

Wheezing and red-faced, Bree managed to shake her head.

'I don't believe you!' Johnny screamed as he pushed her head back under the water with one hand and roughly began to pull up her skirt with the other. 'You're mine, Bree! Always will be. Always.'

'Daddy?' Molly Dwyer stood at the bathroom door, eyes wide.

Johnny turned, letting go of Bree who slumped back, shaking, in the bath. His demeanour changing as he smiled at his daughter.

'Get back to bed, baby. Go on, you need to rest. You gave us a fright tonight. I'll come through in a minute, but I just need to teach Mummy a lesson. She's a very bad mummy, ain't she? For letting Molly fall in the river.'

Little Molly Dwyer looked confused as she glanced over at Bree who tried her best to smile at her daughter as Johnny stood and held onto her hair.

'But it wasn't Mummy. She wasn't there.'

'That's the point darlin', she wasn't there, cos she was too busy thinking of other people when she should've been looking out for you. Now go on, do as I say.'

'But . . .'

'Molly, do as your daddy says.' Ma Dwyer – who'd been watching the proceedings from the corner of the bathroom, sitting on a white wicker chair – spoke, her voice firm but warm.

Johnny smiled. 'Go on, baby . . . And Molly, Daddy loves you, remember that. Tomorrow you and me will go into town and I'll buy you something special.'

Molly's face lit up as she squeezed the teddy bear she held under her arm. 'A unicorn. I'd like a unicorn.'

Johnny winked at his daughter. 'Then if that's what you want, that's what I'll get you. Now go on, close the door.'

Johnny turned back to Bree. He pulled a small brown bottle out of his pocket, then crouching down, he said, 'Drink this.'

Bree shook her head. She spoke in a tiny voice. 'No, Johnny. I don't want it.'

'I know you don't, but it seems to me you don't learn . . . I said, drink it! Fucking drink it!' He pulled back her head, clamping it in the crook of his arm. 'Hold her nose, Ma.'

Ma Dwyer bent down, roughly pinching and holding Bree's nose hard between her fingers, causing her to open her mouth.

As he poured the clear liquid down her throat, Johnny whispered, 'Next time Bree, perhaps you'll learn not to be such a bad girl.'

39

With Lola and Janine out shopping on Chigwell High Road, Alfie, Vaughn and Frankie sat in the games room, cigars alight, brandy on the side and discussions about the events of the week progressing in relative peace and calm.

Standing up and chalking his cue, Vaughn bent over the table, concentrating hard.

Aimed.

Shot.

'Shit!'

The blue ball bounced off the side to hit and send the black ball careering into the top, left pocket.

Pulling deeply on his cigar, Frankie chuckled. 'You're losing your touch, Vaughnie.'

'That's what I've been telling him, but he won't have it.'

Vaughn stared at Alfie. 'What's that supposed to mean? Are you having a pop?'

'I see it. I call it.'

Taking a gulp from the red Waterford brandy glass, Vaughn said, 'Well, don't.'

'Then if you don't want me to, let's sort this out once and for all. We need to sell the diamonds, and quick, before every bad boy comes down on us.'

'And that's why we shouldn't do it. We ain't got the manpower needed. We need to leave them hidden where they are and just forget about them.'

Alfie stared at him in bemusement. 'You want to leave millions of pounds' worth of diamonds shoved down the drains?'

'If that's what it takes to keep us above ground, yes. I'm not ready to be six feet under. I'm leaving well alone.'

Alfie snarled. 'It's too late for that, ain't it? Franny's ripped us all off so we ain't got much choice.'

Vaughn wondered, not for the first time, how things had gone so wrong so damn quickly.

'Alfie, that's my final word. I've told ya.'

'No, mate. We're all in this together, so like I say, there is no backing out.'

Leaning against the window seat, Vaughn's green eyes pierced into Alfie. He shook his head and chuckled scornfully. 'I ain't picking up the pieces.'

Coldly, Alfie answered, 'And I ain't letting this deal with Reenie piss by. Besides you owe me.'

'I don't think so. It wasn't me that trusted Franny was it?'

'You're missing the point, Vaughnie. I ain't talking about the money, I'm talking about how you jeopardised my life. And for that, you *owe* me.'

Frankie Taylor, undoing the button on his trousers to get a bit of comfort, looked at Vaughn. 'What's he on about?'

Vaughn shrugged. 'Who fucking knows? But that's Alfie, a law unto himself.'

Trying not to let his temper and his fists get the better of him, Alfie sniffed contemptuously, rubbing his hands. 'What I'm on about Frank, is this muppet thought it was clever to say me name when we jacked the lorry.'

'What?' Frankie asked incredulously.

'Exactly. Number one rule: no names.'

Still unable to get his head round what he'd just heard, Frankie directed his conversation to Vaughn. 'What were you thinking, Vaughnie? What were you playing at?'

'Don't you start, Frankie, I've had enough from him. Okay, so I made a mistake. But no harm done.'

Alfie threw down the cue he'd just picked up. 'No harm? Think about it. How else are they onto us? And why else is some geezer all of a sudden looking to turn me over?'

'Because you've always had enemies, Alf, that's why.'

Alfie exploded. 'No, Vaughn! Because you fucked up and now every face and would-be gangster knows we have the diamonds. Look, this is how it's going to work. From tomorrow we're going to start shopping them out. We'll start with Timmy Green, see what he has to say and if he's in the business for buying, and then we'll take it from there. Because fuck knows, we might as well sell them because at least that way we'll be able to afford to pay for our bleedin' coffins!'

Jason Robinson stared at Eddie Styler. How the man ever thought he was going to be a face to be reckoned with, he didn't know. He couldn't think of one person who had any kind of respect for Eddie. Not even his own missus did.

The man had been chasing his tail for as long as he could remember, giving it large. Ducking and diving, running up bills and favours left, right and bleedin' centre. The geezer was a liability, a low-level conman who had finally been brought down a peg or two.

But then, if Eddie did manage to pull off getting the diamonds back, and it was one great big *if*. Maybe, just maybe, he'd have to rethink and give the man a smidge of respect. Though until that happened, Eddie Styler was on dangerous ground. One wrong move, and it'd be curtains.

Jason broke off from his thoughts, knocking back the glass of cheap complimentary champagne they'd given him on the way into the bar. Why Eddie had suggested meeting in a dive in Clacton, he'd never know. 'So?'

Eddie looked at Jason blankly.

'Oh for God's sake Ed, this ain't a social, you ain't called me down here to show me the nightlife. What's happening about the rocks, cos I ain't going to wait around forever for me dough.'

'Oh yeah, sorry.' Slightly distracted, Eddie's eyes darted round. He was feeling edgy, although this place they'd come to, he'd bet hands down that Johnny or any of his goons wouldn't be here. And that was the way it needed to stay, because he couldn't afford for Johnny or for Jason to know about each other. If for one minute either of them sniffed out he was doing a deal with the other, he wouldn't even live to see daylight. But what he was banking on, the only thing he had, was the fact that the mutual loathing between Jason and Johnny would keep them apart for the time he needed. And after that, well, they could do what they liked.

It was a risk. No doubt about it. But what else could he do? It was the only way he could see around the mess that Alfie Jennings had put him in. And when he eventually pulled off this little number, what a sweet day that would be, and he'd make certain that one way or another, next time the bullet with Alfie's name on didn't miss.

The other reason he'd chosen this place with the smell of piss and the faded plastic red chairs and the barmaids looking like they were all on crystal meth, was because of Sandra. He hadn't wanted to have the meeting at home. She'd been acting oddly recently, secretive even. Maybe it was because she still hadn't found Barrie or maybe after Jason had threatened her it'd got her thinking. But whatever it was, it seemed prudent not to let her in on anything else. After all, her number was going to be up very soon.

'Am I talking to my fucking self, here, Ed?'

Eddie was preoccupied for a moment by Jason's veneers giving off a strange white glow under the lights. 'What? No, sorry. Long day and me eye's giving me a bit of gyp. Had a bit of an accident the other day.'

'I must say Ed, I've seen you look better . . . Anyway, fuck the beauty talk, let's chat about why I'm here. See the thing is, I'm getting a bit worried again. You ain't been in touch and whenever there's radio silence from you, it makes me anxious. Makes me think I've been a mug to trust you. Perhaps there ain't no diamonds at all and you're just looking to buy time. You see where I'm coming from.'

Eddie Styler could certainly see where Jason Robinson was coming from and if he could have it his way he'd like to tell him where to go, but instead he smiled, feigning warmth and brewing revenge. 'Jason, I can only apologise. I'm on the case. My men—'

Jason interrupted. 'Your men? Rumour has it, you ain't got anyone working for you anymore.'

'You know what they say about rumours: take them with a pinch of salt. I'm hoping to lay me fingers on the ice very soon.'

Deciding he may as well drink Eddie's complimentary champagne as well, Jason gulped it down, not noticing the smears of grease on the plastic gold flute glass. 'Hold up. So, let me get this right, you're telling me you don't actually know where the gems are?'

Comfortable with lying, Eddie said, 'No, no! Jesus Jase, where ever did you get that idea? No not at all. I'm just setting the deal. It's all under way.

'You don't sound so sure.'

Feeling under pressure, Eddie forced a smile. 'Of course I'm sure. I'm not saying there wasn't a bit of bother at the beginning, it was a bit tricky, but it's all sorted now.'

'So why aren't they here? Are you sure you ain't mugging me off?

'Jason, please! This is me you're talking about.'

'Exactly, and that's why I'm asking.'

With his mouth becoming dry, Eddie licked his lips nervously. 'I didn't want to bore you with details, but my source now has the diamonds in his hands. Now it's just a question of him getting them to me.'

'What do you mean?'

'He's abroad . . . Just for a couple of weeks. Like I said, it's all sorted, it's going to run like clockwork.'

'And you're sure you're being straight with me, because you know what happens when people take the piss. And you, my son, have already burnt all yer chances.' Jason paused, cracking his knuckles as he stared at Eddie before adding, 'You hear what I'm saying, Ed?'

Although Eddie Styler knew that Jason Robinson had never been one of the smartest of men, he knew that what he was, was one of the toughest of men, so feigning a smile, Eddie nodded, slapping Jason gregariously on the back. A nervous laugh mixed with his words.

'Jason! Come on! Turn it in, of course I'm being straight, but these things take time, you know how it goes. Once everything is set up on the table, well, that's when I'll be calling you. We got a deal, ain't we? And I'm grateful to you. Listen, I want this as bad as you do, Jase.'

Jason stared at Eddie, watching him squirm.

'Am I making you uncomfortable, Ed? If there's anything you need to tell me, it's best you spit it out now. I'm not keen on surprises, makes me want to do somebody some serious damage.'

'Ain't no surprises, Jase. All you have to do is just sit back and watch.'

Outside in the car, Eddie picked up the phone, his hand shaking. 'Johnny, it's Ed. I got a bit of pressure on my end, I need to know how long it'll be until your missus makes a bit of headway.'

Johnny spoke flatly. 'I told you, don't call me.'

'I know but, you got to . . .'

'I don't have to do nothin', Ed. You're lucky I'm still cutting you in.'

Eddie paled. 'What . . . what are you talking about?'

'Well let's have it right, Ed. The ball's in my court when it comes to this job. So, if I decide not to bring you in, then ain't nothing much you can do about it. After all, Bree won't be telling you what she finds out, will she? It'll be me.'

Eddie gripped the phone. Tightly. It took everything in him not to smash it down on the dashboard. Breathless, he said, 'Come off it. It was me who told you about them in the first place. That ain't fair.'

'Don't whine at me, Ed. If there's one thing that gets on me wick, is a geezer thinking they're a bird.'

Watching a seagull rip into a piece of battered fish lying on the side of the pavement, Eddie tried to keep his voice calm. 'I ain't looking to piss you off, Johnny. I'm just a bit put out by what you've just said. You wouldn't really do that to me, would you?'

'You mean after you skanked me. Put one over on me by making me think it was the old marching powder we was carrying on that lorry?'

'Johnny, look, I get it, okay, but I'm begging you . . .'

'Ed, Ed, listen to me. Calm down. I never said I *would* cut you out. I'm just thinking about it. So, you just need to remember who holds all the cards and start being nice to me. I'll be in touch.'

The phone went dead and it took Eddie Styler a good couple of minutes before he was able to prise his own hand off the steering wheel without fear he'd smash his fist through the windscreen.

Johnny Dwyer had just crossed the red line and he was going to make sure he paid. Essex wouldn't only be hearing Alfie Jennings scream, they'd be hearing Johnny. Very loud and very, very clear.

40

Seven miles north of Braintree, Alfie found himself looking out of the car window, as they drove past the tree flanked River Colne in Halstead. The picturesque small market town full of cafés and boutiques seemed deserted as they passed St Andrews Church and the former silk-weaving mill at the bottom of the high street.

He sighed. He'd been thinking about Bree all morning. All night actually, and if he were to be honest, most of the day. He'd wanted to call her but he'd also wanted to play it cool. He hadn't wanted to look too eager but mainly he didn't want to look too much of a fool.

It wasn't just because she was beautiful but of course she was. And it wasn't just because she had a banging body but of course she did. It was because Bree was special. She always had been. And he was looking forward to seeing her again. The problem was there was something he couldn't put his finger on, something that was troubling him but he didn't know what.

Perhaps he was just being cautious because he was hurt about Franny. Angry with Franny. But he had to put her in the past now. They were *over*. Of course, that didn't mean he was going to let her off with the money. Like Frankie had said, when everything was sorted, he'd look for her. Or rather he'd look for his money. But he didn't want Franny in his life anymore, because she'd left him with something he thought he'd never have when it came to a woman. And that was a broken heart. The feeling was alien, but Christ it hurt. He was larging it up in front of Vaughn. Pretending it was just what it was. But what it was, was the worst he'd ever felt for as long as he could remember.

So maybe that was all it was, maybe the problem, the sense of something not being quite right with Bree showing up, was that it simply boiled down to him liking her . . . and him being scared of what that entailed.

'Alf, you ready? We're here. We don't want to be late for Timmy, he can be a bit of a prick about time.' Frankie turned around from the front of the Range Rover, a big grin on his face, feeling surprisingly well.

'Yeah, just having a bit of a think.'

Frankie laughed, winking at him. 'Let me guess. About that bird? She was a bit of a sort. I'd proper bone her. Give her the night of her life.'

Alfie narrowed his eyes at Frankie. He wasn't going to get into it. 'Well ain't she the lucky one. What woman could resist?'

Frankie nudged Vaughn who'd just parked by a tall Georgian town house.

'Maybe I'll have a go, then.'

Alfie sighed. 'Be my guest, Frank, crack on.'

'You wouldn't mind?'

Alfie chewed the inside of his cheek. He answered coldly. 'Why would I? But I think Gypsy would, don't you? Think she'd have something to say about her old man chasing a bit of skirt when he's supposed to be sorting out this mess.'

Frankie filled the car with his laughter. 'So you do like her! I knew it! I knew it! I said to you, didn't I Vaughnie, that Alf was proper soft on her.'

'Fuck off, Frank.' And with that, Alfie Jennings stepped out of the car.

* * *

Timmy Green liked his food. He liked it so much that he even had a chef on twenty-four-hour call. It'd always been the case since he was a kid, and his mother had been happy to indulge her only child with whatever food took his fancy. When she'd suffered a heart attack, he'd mourned her passing, admitting to himself it was more about the loss of her secret recipe for jambon persillé, which she'd taken to her grave, than it was for her untimely demise.

He'd been married three times, all short-lived. The first two he divorced for their lack of cooking skills. The third one, a South East Asian mail-order bride, he divorced after Timmy had developed a sudden allergy to most Vietnamese foods.

The only thing Timmy Green liked better than food was gems, in particular diamonds, and he wasn't bothered by where he got them, who had robbed them or who had died for them, all Timmy wanted to know was . . .

'What's the price?'

'You tell us, Timmy.'

Timmy looked at Alfie as he sat in the large wooden drawing room of his four-storey Georgian house full of antique dishes and vases in glass cabinets. He picked up the diamond, twirling it round between his fingers before lifting it up to the light. 'You say they're all like this?'

'All of them.'

Timmy whistled. 'Not bad, Alfie. Not bad at all. By the way, it's nice to see you musketeers back together again. Essex ain't been the same without you.'

Vaughn shrugged. 'Well, we don't know if we'll be here forever.'

'Who is, Vaughnie? Who is?'

Leaning across to take a bite from the steak béarnaise next to him, Timmy pulled a face.

'Where's the bleedin' salt? For fuck's sake, do I look like I'm on a low-sodium diet? What's wrong with you muppets?'

A small, sinewy man in his late fifties, who'd been sitting quietly in the corner of the room, scuttled across to Timmy holding a large stainless-steel mill.

'Sorry, boss.'

Snarling, Timmy wiped his mouth with the edge of his serviette. 'Less talk, more action.'

The man nodded and proceeded to grind a vast amount of salt on the steak béarnaise as Timmy picked up the conversation with Alfie.

'So, if what you're telling me is true – though I'll obviously have to check each stone – and you have the amount you say, well, I'd be willing to offer you a good deal. Especially as we all go back a long way. Ain't never forgot you giving me that first job, Vaughnie. Put me on the ladder that did. It means a lot, as you all do to me, and as such, I'll offer you one million big ones. Ain't going say fairer than that.'

The three men looked at each other, then at Timmy, who was now enjoying taking a mouthful of the salmon fillet from one of the numerous plates he was surrounded by.

Alfie rubbed his face. One million was not even an option. It was only half of what they needed. Timmy was taking the piss, but now was not the time to let his temper show.

'Timmy, like you say, we go back a long way and in all that time, I've never disrespected you, none of us has, but I don't think the same can be said about you. Those beauties are worth way more. You know it sunshine, and I know it.'

Timmy, with his brown eyes magnified by his bifocal glasses, looked evenly at Alfie. 'I agree with you, they're worth fuckloads more. But that ain't the point. I ain't going to offer you more than a mill. And I ain't forcing you to take it either. I'm happy either way.'

Alfie stared at Timmy tucking into a perfectly folded crêpe. He wasn't so much fat than big. Big feet, big hands, big shoulders, big everything, even the size of Timmy Green's head was big. 'We can't afford to let them go for that little.'

Timmy waved a fork at Alfie as he spoke. 'But can you afford not to let them go? Can you afford to turn this offer down? I understand that you're buying Reginald's business. That's what you want this money for, ain't it?'

Alfie answered coldly. 'It ain't actually. We already got that covered.'

Timmy raised his eyebrows. 'Glad to hear it, Alf. You don't want an opportunity like that to slip through your fingers. Anyway, it's down to you. To sell or not to sell, that is the question.'

Timmy grinned as Frankie stepped forward. He scowled at Timmy who was clearly enjoying playing with them. 'Do me a favour, turn it in. How about I ask a question now? Ready? . . . For most of his life, this person has been a muggy cunt.'

Alfie Jennings banged down his hand on the table. 'Boom! I know this one.'

Frankie nodded. 'Go on Alf, you buzzed in first.'

'Who or what is Timmy Green.'

Timmy's face darkened, he spoke through gritted teeth. 'Don't come in here and take the piss, thinking you can give it large. I don't owe you fuck all. I saw you as a favour and if you don't like what I offered, don't take it. Turn around and walk away. Go find another buyer. But let me guess, that's easier said than done, ain't it? I see what you want. We've all been in this game long enough to know that you need to get rid of the stones before every gangster hears about it and thinks they can come help themselves.'

Vaughn, who'd kept quiet until now, chimed in. 'Then if you know that, why don't you want to give us a squeeze?'

'When did this business ever do anybody any favours? We ain't in it for Grandma's day out. I like you. Always have, but that don't mean I'm going to pluck out me intestines and give them to you . . . Look, I get it that you need to move sharpish, and you feel like I ain't giving you a touch, but actually I am, gentlemen.'

Alfie snarled. 'How do you make that out?'

'Think about it, Alf. I'm willing to give you *one* million quid for the rocks, which means within twenty-four hours you can walk away with a big bag of money, and without any hassle. More to the point, no one will know so you won't have every prick crawling out of the woodwork ready to turn you over for the ice. I ain't going to tell anybody that you've been here, and I trust me men to a point, but there's eyes everywhere and it only takes one tiny word in the wrong lughole and the lion's out of the bag.'

'And what are we supposed to do with a poxy million quid?'

Timmy, deliberately missing the point, grinned. 'Whatever you want, Alfred. Your choice. Go back to Spain. Stay here. Put your feet up. Anything.'

Alfie reached over, scooping up the rest of the crêpe suzette off Timmy's plate. He took a large bite out of it before throwing it back down. 'When I want a life coach, Timmy, I'll let you know, until then, fuck you and fuck your money.'

Outside, Alfie stormed to the car. He shouted over his shoulder. 'Before you or Vaughnie say something, don't.'

'Maybe we should've thought about his offer a bit more.'

Alfie looked at Vaughn incredulously. 'I never heard you say that in there? And if it hasn't escaped your notice we can't afford to let them go for that.'

'I know but he's right, ain't he. One million is one million more than we got.'

Alfie turned around, stomping up to Vaughn. 'And it's two million less than it should be and one million less than we need.'

'Maybe it's worth it to stop the hassle.'

'Lose our chance just so we don't get a bit of agg? Turn it in.'

Vaughn pulled the car key out of his pocket. 'Getting shot, getting jumped on, getting put down, ain't a bit of agg, Alf. I've told you before this ain't sensible.'

'Just wind your neck in! How sensible do you think it'll be with only a million between us and nothing else? It's not going to buy us what we want, is it? The opportunity we've got ain't going to come around again.'

Frankie nodded. 'He's talking sense, Vaughn. We can't afford to lose so much money.'

Starting up the engine, Vaughn shook his head. 'So you want us to put our heads above water and basically become sitting targets for the whole of the criminal fraternity?'

Alfie stared out of the blacked-out window. 'If that's what it takes, Vaughn, that's exactly what we'll do.'

Turning a tight right, Vaughn put his foot down. 'It's madness, Alf. We're going to open the floodgates and it's not just us we have to think about. There's Janine and Lola, they'll be sitting ducks, and Christ how this business likes to go in for the nearest and dearest. Let's go back in there, and take the money.'

'No can do, Vaughn.'

'So, you're calling the shots now are you? I don't think so.'

Alfie slammed his fist down on the cream leather seat. Frustrated, he yelled at Vaughn. 'It's not about calling any shots, it's about our future, it's about—'

Alfie's phone rang, stopping him in mid flow. Angrily he answered. 'Yes!'

'Sorry, have I caught you at a bad time? It's Bree.'

41

Johnny Dwyer stood with Big Billy Baldwin looking at the most recent banger car rebuild.

'Not bad, boss, it's come out nicely and it'll certainly give the other team something to think about.'

Wiping his petrol-covered hands on his blue overalls, Johnny nodded, pleased with the finished result. 'You're telling me, we got the extra reinforcement in there so when they hit it, they'll be lucky to walk away . . .' About to say something else, Johnny stopped as he saw Bree coming out of the mobile home. He cricked his neck, trying to take the tension out of it. His tone was hard and cold as he called her. He hadn't forgiven her for what had happened to Molly, but then, he hadn't forgiven her for so many things she had done. She was a tease. A head-fuck. But she was his and she'd do well to keep remembering that.

'Bree! Come here! Billy, can you give us a moment . . .'

Big Billy Baldwin nodded, making his way over to Ma, who stood, arms folded, by Kieran's quad bike.

Johnny watched him go then turned his attention to Bree, who sauntered across, her dress showing and accentuating her curves. He ground his teeth, the noise in his head suddenly becoming louder. He pressed his palms against his temple as he spoke. 'Why do you have to do that?'

'Do what?'

'Flaunt yourself like you're looking for sex. Is that what you want, Bree? You want Billy? You want him to notice you?'

Bree's gaze went from Johnny to Billy, who was deep in conversation with Ma. She spoke breathlessly, her nerves showing in her voice. 'No! Of course not. I didn't even realise he was here.'

'But if you had done, did you want him to look at you? Were you imagining what it'd be like to be with him?'

Bree shook her head. 'Please, Johnny, don't do this again. I came over to see *you*. I just wanted to let you know that I've spoken to Alfie.'

Johnny took a deep breath, trying to get his thoughts in order. 'And?'

'And, like you wanted me to, I've arranged to meet him again. I'm seeing him this evening . . . If that's okay with you.'

Johnny held Bree's stare, then he smiled, although it didn't quite reach his eyes. 'You know what happens if you turn us over, don't you, Bree? Ryan will have to pay. He'll be the one to get it. He'll be in more trouble than he's ever been in . . . Ain't that right, Ryan?' Johnny stopped and turned to look at Ryan, who sat on the bench looking handsome in his grey marl tracksuit as he played with one of his kittens.

'Ryan, tell Bree what happens . . . Tell Bree that Ryan gets it.'

'Ryan gets it. Ryan gets it. Ryan gets it . . .'

Johnny turned back to look at Bree as Ryan continued to chant. 'See, even he knows it.'

Unable to hold back the tears, Bree shook her head. 'How can you even think like that?'

Taking the screwdriver he was holding, Johnny began with menacing slowness to trace Bree's face with the sharp, metal end. He then traced her neck, dragging the point across her skin, eventually stopping at her chest. He poked the tool hard against her body. 'I love my brother, so the last thing I want is to have to hurt him, and I know you don't want to see that either. So that puts us on the same page. We both want what's best for him. And it's real easy for us to keep him safe. I tell you what I want, and you do as you're told. That ain't hard, is it? . . . I said, is it?'

'No, Johnny, it's not.'

'So, all this talk of how you don't want to hurt *Alfie* is a thing of the past? You need to worry about *Ryan*. Right?'

Bree nodded quickly. 'Absolutely.'

Satisfied, Johnny threw down the screwdriver, picking up and taking a sip of tea Ma had brought him earlier. 'So how long are we talking? How long until you get some info out of Alfie?'

'I don't know if he'll even tell me, Johnny. I haven't seen him for years so he's hardly going to just open up about what's going on, and if he does, then it's going to take time.'

Slamming his tea on top of the car's bonnet, Johnny raised his voice. 'But you ain't got time because I ain't got time. So *you* need to find a way around this. Find out what's going on. I don't care what you have to do.' Johnny stopped and grabbed her face hard. 'I don't care, as long as you don't enjoy it. You hear me, Bree? Don't you enjoy it. You're mine, every single bit of you.'

Bree trembled, terrified to think of what would happen if she didn't manage to pull this off. 'Yes, Johnny.'

'Good. See, that ain't hard, is it? Go on, baby, get yourself dolled up.'

As Bree walked away, Johnny, his voice warm and cheerful, said, 'Ain't you forgetting something, Bree?'

She turned around, forcing a smile, walked back towards Johnny and planted a kiss on his cheek.

'And Bree, don't forget, I love ya . . . Tell her, Ryan. Tell her I love her.'

'I love her. I love her. I love her. I love her . . .'

With her back turned to them, tears ran down Bree's cheeks,

her lips barely moved as her whisper caught in the wind. 'And I love you too, Ryan. *Always.*'

At the wetlands of Abberton Reservoir, which spanned twelve hundred acres, close to the coast of Essex, Bree could see him standing by the long marsh grasses. She stopped before calling out, watching him as he stared out across the lake, tall and handsome as the wind swept through his soft black hair. Waiting for a moment to calm herself, she took a deep breath.

The low greyness of the evening sky added to the remoteness of the area. A long time ago she'd visited when the sun shone high and the wetland was an explosion of life – in happier times – but in the rain, the desolate silence, the trees and bracken gave the whole area an oppressive undertone.

As Bree opened her mouth to shout his name, he turned, smiling, sensing her presence and putting her slightly more at ease. She watched as he walked towards her. Perhaps it would be easier than she thought. Perhaps he'd just tell her what she needed to know.

Alfie smiled. 'Hello, you.' His voice was a combination of velvet softness and the coarseness of his life. He lent forward to kiss her gently on her cheek, producing a smile on the face of the carp fisherman who was watching them, unnoticed on the opposite side of the lake.

'I've always loved this spot. I used to come here as a kid. When me old man came down to visit one of his mates, instead of staying around to watch him get pissed, I use to nick the boy next door's bike and cycle off for hours. I tell you, round this place, I felt free. Like I was flying. Anyway, I thought it'd be nice to meet here. Bit of peace and quiet and away from nosey ex-wives.' He stopped and grinned, wondering if his chatting was down to nerves. Then he added, 'Maybe you'd have preferred a restaurant?'

Bree shook her head. 'Not at all. You'd be surprised how little time I have just to get out and about.'

'Would I?'

Bree shifted her feet uncomfortably. 'I mean, you know, with the kids. Life. It gets busy, don't it?'

Alfie looked at her. 'Does it? So, tell me about your old man. You never told me anything before. I take it you're with someone.'

Bree spoke quickly. 'No. I was. But it didn't work out. These things happen.'

With his words filled with careful compassion, Alfie said, 'So, who did that to your face then?'

Bree's hands rushed up to touch her bruised cheek. Taken aback, she reddened, more uncomfortable than ever. 'What? Oh this, it's nothing. I . . . I do martial arts. Wanted to learn self-defence a while back and it took off from there. Even the kids do it.'

'Really?'

'Yeah. I love it.'

'What kind? What kind of martial arts.'

Bree's head was whirling. This wasn't how it was supposed to be. 'Sorry, do you mind if we go back to the car? I'm really cold.'

Alfie's gaze was steady. 'Whatever you want.'

And with that, Bree turned to walk back to the car, followed by Alfie, the troubling doubt coming back into his head.

With the car windows of his Range Rover steamed up, Alfie sat in the back next to Bree, both of them having decided to leave the packed supper Lola had lovingly made.

'I'll have to dump it before I get home. She'll be well gutted if she found out we didn't eat it.'

'She sounds nice. Everyone does. You're lucky to have good people in your life.'

Alfie thought for a moment, then nodded. 'Yeah, I tend to take a lot for granted. It's been good. Not all of it, but it's certainly been an adventure.'

She smiled, her face lighting up as she looked at him. 'It really is good to see you, Alf.' She paused, trying to edge into the next part of the conversation naturally. 'So, what is it that you do now?'

'Me? Nothing much. You know how it is?'

'No, not really. Tell me. I'm interested.'

Bree slipped her shoes off and cosied her legs underneath her on the heated leather seat of the car.

'Are you, Bree?'

'Of course I am. Why wouldn't I be?'

A frown appeared on Alfie's forehead. His handsome face looking troubled. 'I don't know. You just seem odd.'

Bree gave a half laugh. 'I'm sorry. I'm just nervous. I'm not very good at this. It's been a long time. Look, if you'd rather do this another time, we can.'

Alfie was quick to reply. 'No. It's probably just me. Been in the game too long. I get paranoid and edgy and I think I'm a bit nervous too.'

'Well how about I start off then. I'll tell you about me, and then you tell me about you. How's that?'

Alfie grinned, relaxing slightly and feeling a rush of happiness. 'Sounds like a pukka plan.'

'Well don't get excited, there isn't much to tell. I left care, got a job and trained as a hairdresser, then I worked on the cruise ships a bit, which was fun. Met this guy, came back to Essex and married him, had a family but we separated last year.'

'What's his name?'

'Who?'

'Your ex.'

The pause, although fractional, was noticed by Alfie.

'Andrew.'

Alfie nodded. 'Bree, why are you lying to me?'

Red-faced, unable to look straight at Alfie, Bree's eyes darted around. 'What? I'm not!'

'You are! Listen babe, I'm not proud of it but I've made me living out of lying, and I've spent more hours than you can imagine getting the truth out of liars. Not only that but most of my working days I've been surrounded by liars and they've been good ones. So, I think I'm qualified to know when someone's lying to me, especially when they ain't good at it.'

'Alf, I swear . . .'

A tinge of sadness came into Alfie's voice. 'Why you doing this?'

'I'm not doing anything.'

Gently grabbing her hands, Alfie pulled Bree towards him, looking into her eyes. His face inches away from hers. 'Sweetheart, I've known you for so long and when I saw you the other day, I couldn't believe me luck. I ain't stopped thinking of you. You've always held a special place in me heart, but now you're breaking it, cos the Bree I know wouldn't have lied to me . . . What's going on, darlin? Why you mugging me off?'

Bree pulled her hands away. 'The Bree you knew was a long time ago, and a lot of things have happened since then, but I ain't lying to you. I don't know why you think I am.'

'Oh, Bree.' He leant over and gave a kiss on her cheek, closing his eyes as he did. Then he opened the door and simply said, 'I think you'd better go.'

42

Bree sat on the sofa looking down at her pregnant stomach. She was exhausted. She still had a couple of months to go but at times she felt so big and fat she wished she could get the pregnancy over with. She also wished she didn't have to get up. The effort seemed so much but Ma had insisted, and even though Ryan had kept on at her to get up, she just couldn't find the motivation.

'Baby kicking?' Johnny spoke as he looked up from the paper he was reading whilst checking the time on the clock on the wall.

'A little bit. Not too bad. Last night was worse. I couldn't sleep, Ryan had to rub my back for me.'

Johnny nodded, saying nothing, and continued to read his paper. The room fell silent save the ticking of Ma's grandfather clock which took pride of place. And in the warmth, Bree began to drift off to sleep.

It felt like only moments later when Bree was crudely awoken by Ma barging through the door. She stared at Johnny, then looked at Bree.

'There's been an accident.'

Bree, trying to get her bearings after having been asleep, sounded puzzled. 'What?'

'It's Ryan. Ryan's had an accident on the racetrack.'

43

Exhausted, having not been able to sleep, her mind had been whirring all night thinking over what happened with Alfie, and the bag she'd found in Kieran's duffle, which now sat hidden in one of the boxes in the barn. Bree looked at Kieran who sat at the breakfast table sharing his fruit pop with Molly.

She was worried about him. About both of them. Kieran had been very secretive lately and neither she nor Johnny had been able to get to the bottom of how and why Molly had fallen into the stream. And Molly, usually one to talk, had been particularly quiet; each time Bree had spoken to her, she'd clammed up. A nervousness about her that wasn't usually there.

Without saying a word, Kieran picked up his bowl of cereal and threw it in the sink before stomping out of the kitchen, a big scowl on his face.

Hearing the front door open before being slammed closed, Bree sighed, moving to sit next to Molly. Taking her daughter's hand, she smiled.

'Molly, sweetheart. Is there something you need to tell me?'

'No.'

'Are you sure? I mean I still don't know what happened with Kieran and why you fell in the stream.'

Molly pouted, shrugging her mum's concern away. 'Just did.'

'But you don't just fall in the stream unless you went too near it. Is that what happened, where you playing too near the water?'

'No.'

Bree looked up, watching out of the window as Kieran skipped across the yard. She frowned, turning back to her daughter. 'Is this about your brother? I promise I won't tell anybody . . . Molly, please talk to me. Is this about Kieran?'

Molly nodded, a tear running down her cheek. 'I can't tell you.'

'What can't you tell me? Molly, I'm worried. I promise and I cross my heart I won't say anything to anybody.'

Looking up at her mum, her big wide eyes full of fear, Molly spoke in a whisper.

'Kieran's got a secret but he said if I told anybody about it he'd hurt me again.'

Alfie Jennings sat at the table with his sister looking at the unopened texts on his phone. He could see they were all from Bree but so far, he'd resisted reading them. Not that he hadn't wanted to, he had, it was just when it came down to women perhaps it was best for him to leave well alone.

'So, what do you think?'

'You're asking me for advice? I married Eddie, so I don't reckon I'm the best person to give you relationship advice, do you?'

Alfie got up, switching the kettle on. 'What's wrong with you? I ain't looking to marry her. I just don't know what to think. You were best mates with her.'

'About a hundred years ago. I don't know anything about her now. A long time ago I heard she was in the area, but I wouldn't know any more than that.'

'Well, thanks for nothing.'

Sandra looked at her brother. 'What do you want me to say, Alf? So, you think she lied to you, but you don't know for sure.'

'I do. I could see it in her eyes.'

'Have you heard yourself? Maybe she just don't want to tell you about her life. Maybe there's stuff she's embarrassed to talk about and the last thing she needs is some tactless oaf grilling her like she's under arrest. Anyway, it's not like you ain't a liar.'

'Thanks for that, Sandra.'

'Well it's true. When was the last time you were fully honest about your life? Just enjoy it for what it is.'

'I wish I could but . . .'

'But what?'

Pouring too much milk in his tea, Alfie said, 'It's not just that, though. There's something else I can't quite put me finger on. I just got a bad feeling about her.'

'You're just too paranoid.'

'Maybe. Anyway, let's forget it . . . Have you found Barrie by the way? That cat has more lives than a rechargeable battery.'

Before Sandra was able to launch into a monologue, Alfie put his hand up. 'Shhh, did you hear that?'

'What?'

'Shut up . . . There, you must've heard that?'

Sandra nodded as Alfie went over to the kitchen drawer quietly, opening it up and carefully pulling out a gun. 'You stay here.'

'What are you doing?'

'Shhh, Sandra, don't make a noise, and *don't* leave this room.'

She nodded, her face tense. Then making his way across the kitchen, Alfie pulled the gun up to his chest, holding it close. He edged the door open, pulling it with his foot.

'Alfie! Maybe I should come with you.' Sandra, suddenly becoming scared, ran across to her brother. He spoke in a whisper back to her.

'It's fine, just stay here. It's probably nothing.'

He gave a tight smile, his gut not quite allowing him to believe his own words.

Tiptoeing slowly along the hallway with the gun still held tight,

Alfie followed the noise. He could hear his own breathing in the silence of the house.

Getting to the back door, he slowly and carefully opened it, looking around before stepping out into the courtyard.

Sidling along as quietly as he could, Alfie craned his neck around the corner. He pulled back quickly at the sight of three blacked-out Range Rovers parked and spread across the entire width of Janine's driveway. The driver's door of the end car opened and a man Alfie didn't recognise got out, but what he did recognise was the large sawn-off shotgun he held in his hand, and there was no mistake about that.

'Shit!'

Alfie charged back to the house, along the corridor and back into the kitchen to Sandra. He burst in, dragging her off the chair.

'Hurry up! Come on! Run! We have to go!'

Without asking questions, Sandra, terrified, ran as fast as she could, holding on to Alfie's hand as they made their through the newly built extension to the sound of the front door being kicked in.

Alfie, with his gun drawn, signalled to Sandra as they made their way into the garden.

'Listen, we need to get out of here, we can't be seen.'

'What's happening? Who are they?'

'Ain't got time to explain now, but whatever you do Sand, stick with me and don't look back.'

Bending down by the roses Alfie gestured to Sandra, but he froze as he heard voices, knowing whoever it was they were only metres away on the other side of the courtyard.

Running to the end of the wall, he craned his neck. He could see at least four men, all armed, walking by the trees. The whole place seemed like it was surrounded and if he didn't think of something quickly they were in deep trouble.

Scanning the grounds, looking for an obvious way out, Alfie's eyes rested on the garage.

He whispered urgently to Sandra. 'If we can get over there, that will be our best bet . . . You okay?'

Shaking, Sandra nodded. 'Ask me after we get out of here.'

'It'll be fine. Come on, let's go.'

He ducked down, checking around as he ran with Sandra following closely behind. She slid up next to him by the corner of the stables, petrified, and spoke in the smallest of voices. 'How many do you think there are?'

'I reckon, worst-case scenario, a dozen.'

Sandra's eyes were wild and panicked. 'And the best?'

'Half, but every single one of them is probably armed. Come on, Sand, the place is crawling and if we don't get a move on, any minute now we're going to be spotted and that won't be good . . . It ain't far. Just there.'

He pointed to the garage and Sandra, her face pale, shook her head.

'We'll never make it, Alf. I can't. I can't.'

Seeing the men walking around the grounds and coming ever nearer, Alfie looked at his sister. 'We'll never make it if we just stay here. They'll kill us if they find us. I'll look after you. I promise. Take my hand. It'll be alright.'

With only a slight hesitation, Alfie ran ahead, holding Sandra's hand and stopping at the large tree. He turned to her.

'You still okay?'

She nodded.

'Good. Then we'll go on the count of five.'

Sandra, her legs shaking so much she could hardly stand, watched Alfie count with his fingers from five to one before mouthing, 'Go!'

With a warm wind picking up, they sprinted across the lawn, neither of them looking back as they panted and ran for their lives.

Getting to the side of the garage, Alfie slammed his body hard against the wall with Sandra split seconds behind. Then, breathing heavily, Alfie passed his gun to his sister.

'Listen, Sand, I need you to cover me.'

'What? I can't.'

Trying to reassure her, Alfie said, 'You can. If anybody comes, just shoot. Just pull the trigger.'

'What are you going to do?'

'I'm going to try to climb in and get the car out.' Alfie nodded to the small window of the garage.

'You'll never make it through . . . Let me.'

'No way. Sand, just go and hide in the bushes until I get the car.'

'Alf, this ain't the time to play the big brother. Let me do this.'

Alfie looked at Sandra and then at the men stalking the grounds near the house.

'No, I can't! No way. I ain't going to let anything happen to you.'

'Alf, we ain't got another choice. Just let me do this.'

'I dunno.'

Sandra's voice was urgent. '*Please.*'

'Fine, fine, but take the gun. You'll find the spare keys to the car by the tool box. There's also the spare garage door keys next to them. You can't miss it. You ready? You okay?'

Sandra gave a nervous smile.

'Here, I'll help you. I'll give you a leg up,' Alfie said.

With her heart racing, Sandra managed to pull herself up on the ledge, tucking her legs in and through the small window before vaulting down onto the workbench and jumping down onto the garage floor.

Sandra quickly looked around the garage. Seeing the keys by the tool box as Alfie had said, she grabbed them and jumped into the car as fast as she could.

Taking a deep breath to settle her nerves, she pressed on the brake and pushing the start button to switch on the car, she pointed the remote at the sensors. Slowly and smoothly it began to open . . . then stopped.

She spoke out loud to herself, her hands trembling. 'No, don't bleedin' do this to me. Come on!'

She pointed the remote, first shutting the garage door again before once more pressing open. This time the garage door didn't move at all.

'No, no way.' She held her finger on the button, pressing it over and over again.

'Sandra! Sandra! What's going on?'

Sounding desperate, she yelled, 'The door won't open!'

'What?'

'The door, it won't open.'

'Look, I can't hear you . . . But you got to hurry, they're coming! Sand! Sand!'

Revving the Range Rover, Sandra, her mind racing, stared at the door, then taking a deep breath she closed her eyes, pushing her foot right down on the accelerator, causing the car to speed off, crashing it through the garage door, ripping it off.

She crunched the Range Rover into reverse, spinning it round and sending a spray of lawn and mud as Alfie ran, jumping in and scrabbling into the back passenger seat. He yanked up the carpet from the floor, pulling out two small machine guns.

The Range Rover weaved and snaked through the garden, throwing Alfie around and across the seat as Sandra sped over the lawn.

'Fucking hell, Sand!

Alfie looked behind him and saw some of the men running to their cars.

'Head for the gates! The gates!'

Sandra spun hard on the wheel. 'Hold on!' But directly in front of them there was a line of trees and for a moment Alfie thought Sandra was going to hit them straight on, but she slammed on the brakes, throwing him into the back of the driver's seat. She put the Range Rover into reverse once more, speeding backwards, sending mud and flowers and plant pots flying everywhere.

'Sand, be careful, they're shooting!'

Flicking the safety catch off the guns, Alfie bobbed down as the back window was shot out, sending tiny fragments of glass ricocheting around the inside of the car as the bullets continued to fire.

The three Range Rovers trailed Sandra, making it impossible for her to get to the entrance of the house. Round and round the water fountain she went, tearing up the lawn as the other cars followed.

She screamed out, tears in her eyes. 'Alfie!'

'Keep going, Sand, you're doing good!'

Leaning out of the window, Alfie started to shoot whilst a hail of bullets pumped out from the other cars. Covered from the spray of mud from the spinning tyres, Alfie fired a round of bullets at one of the oncoming Range Rovers. The bullets hit and blew out the front tyres, causing the driver to lose control, sending the 4x4 into the trees where it flipped in the air, twisting round and landing in the path of the other two cars.

Seizing her opportunity, Sandra accelerated, driving through the bushes and through the gates and onto the road, heading into the darkness of the countryside.

After a minute, checking they weren't being followed, Alfie punched the air. He bellowed, charged and full of adrenaline. 'Fucking hell, Sandra, I didn't know you had it in you, I reckon we've lost them! You go, girl! You go . . . Sandra? You okay?'

Sandra, looking in shock, spoke timidly. 'I think I got some glass in me arm.'

'Pull over!'

'No, it's fine.'

'I said, pull over! Now!' From where he was, Alfie could see a large piece of glass sticking out of Sandra's arm. Blood pouring down. He quickly tore at her top to get to the wound, looking at her with concern. 'We need to get you to hospital.'

'I said, I'm fine.'

'Look, don't argue. I'll drive you.'

Sandra gave Alfie a steely stare. 'I'm not going anywhere until you tell me what the hell that was about.'

Alfie's temper began to rise. 'Just move over so I can get you to the hospital.'

'No.'

'You always were a stubborn mare, but now ain't the time.'

'Then tell me.'

He thumped his fist against the door. 'Looks like you ain't given me much choice.'

And as Alfie sat in the country lane telling his sister the story of the diamonds, he had a creeping suspicion Vaughn had been right. Maybe trying to sell the diamonds was opening a can of worms, far bigger and far stronger than they were.

44

'What happened?' Eddie Styler glared at his wife who sat with her arm wrapped up in bandages. He was irritated by her as she lounged in front of the heatless flames of the white wall-mounted faux fireplace.

Sipping on a mojito Sandra glared back at Eddie. She'd had strict instructions from Alfie not to mention anything about the diamonds, which she had to admit was proving harder than she thought because quite frankly she wanted to wring his neck.

And it wasn't only Eddie she was furious with, she was angry with Alfie as well. He'd explained about the lorry, the diamonds and about how he'd had them all along, but hadn't told her simply because it came down to trust. He'd been worried her allegiances were with Eddie, which had been the biggest joke of all.

She'd been hurt, and had given him an earful vowing never to speak to him again, but they both knew that wouldn't happen. He was her brother and she loved him in the same all-consuming way she'd loved her other brother, Connor. So eventually she'd forgive him; after all, family was family and it had to be treasured.

Eddie, however, was a different prick altogether, and one way or another he was going to have a mighty nasty fall. The more Alfie had told her, the more her hatred for her husband had grown.

The diamonds, and the running up of debts in Reggie Reynolds' name, along with remortgaging her house had been bad enough. But now that she'd discovered the spineless fool had used Barrie to get out and about, no doubt playing a part in his disappearance, Eddie was going to come a cropper.

Alfie had asked her to find out if Eddie knew or suspected that he and Vaughn had the diamonds, and report back anything else of interest. Not that she'd agreed to it, she was too angry. But that was then. This was now and now was as good a time as any to start, but she knew she'd have to be discreet.

'So, Eddie, about those diamonds.'

'What? What are you talking about?'

'Don't try to kid me. I heard you. I heard you with Jason.'

Eddie's face contorted in rage. 'You better not tell anybody!'

'Oh, believe me, I won't. I'm not having anybody trying to come and make a claim on those. I ain't that stupid! But what I want to know is how you came to have your finger in such an expensive pie.'

Gulping down the tumbler of whiskey he'd poured himself, Eddie frowned. 'Since when have you started asking me about me business?'

Taking off her shoe, Sandra threw it at Eddie's head. It skimmed the side of his temple before crashing into the glass decanters. 'Since we had a bleedin' gorilla knocking the door down. That Jason didn't seem like he was having a laugh and the last thing I want is some comedian kicking in me Everest double glazing back door. So you Eddie, need to tell me exactly what's happening, otherwise you and me are going to fall right out.'

'Look, don't worry about it, I've got it all in hand.'

'The only thing you've ever had in your hand, Eddie Styler, is your cock, so don't play the big businessman with me. You won't be stepping into Richard Branson's shoes anytime soon.'

Snorting in anger, Eddie snapped. 'Look, those diamonds are nothing to do with you.'

Playing him like a fiddle, and wishing she could rub it in Eddie's face that in actual fact it was Alfie and Vaughn who had the diamonds, Sandra said, 'Are you joking? Three million quid will always be my business. Ain't it you that tells me we're married and as such what's mine's yours? It works both ways, Ed. So, come on, spill the beans, where are these diamonds?'

Eddie stared at Sandra. The sooner he was able to do a moonlight flit the better, but at the moment everything rested on Johnny's missus, so the pressure was on, and the last thing he needed or could cope with was Sandra sticking her nose in, because if she wasn't careful he'd just have to chop it right off.

His wife had always been a nosey cow, but her sudden interest in his affairs wasn't about curiosity, it was about greed. The minute she smelled money she was like a pig in a trough, but if she thought for one minute that she was going to get her grubby hands on his bling, then he'd have to take her head out of her arse and make her think again.

45

It was dark apart from the moonlight as Bree crept into the barn. She stood in the doorway for a moment, making sure no one had heard her. The night seemed warm and the stillness of it felt comforting.

Johnny was out and Ma was asleep, snoring heavily in front of the TV, so it was the perfect time to do what she needed to do and try to put her mind at peace.

The contents of the bag she'd found in Kieran's bag had played on her mind. The bones had been so tiny. The remains of what? She didn't know for sure, but she'd had a bad feeling. She'd been worried, but instead of doing anything about them, because in truth she didn't know what to do, she'd hidden them away in a box in the barn, thinking she could just forget she'd ever seen them. But she hadn't. If anything, knowing that they were just lying there had made it worse.

Each day she'd woken up and looked across at the barn. Each afternoon she'd fed the dogs and stared at the barn. Every night when she'd closed her bedroom curtains, all she could see was the barn, and the box, and the bag, and the bones.

So, she'd decided to do something about it. She'd take them and post them to the hospital perhaps, to the police, to a church maybe, to somebody who'd know. But wherever she sent them tomorrow, at least they'd be away from here.

Switching on her torch and being careful to shine it on the ground, Bree tiptoed into the barn. She could smell the hay and straw, the feed and the stable bedding piled up high. At the far corner of the barn, she paused, looking back at the doorway, making sure no one had followed. Confident, she was on her own, Bree climbed up on the haystack and carefully hauled the box out, pulling it down.

Quietly she opened it. Then froze. The box was empty. There was nothing there. The bag she'd so carefully hidden had gone, somebody had taken it.

Hearing a noise, Bree quickly slid the box to the side, hurrying out of the barn, not seeing the person in the shadows watching her.

46

'You're having a bubble. You are off your head. You've lost the bleedin' plot if you think I'm staying here! That mattress looks like it's from a crime scene off *CSI*, the shower looks like it ain't been cleaned since they invented running water and there's more hair in that sink than a Saturday afternoon in Toni and Guy's.'

Alfie sighed as he looked at Janine who was standing, hands on hips, in the middle of the family room of the bed and breakfast in Southend. 'Look, Janine—'

Squawking, she interrupted. 'No, you don't. Don't try and give me *look Janine* when you've brought me to this poxy place. I could be lying in a bath at home with me Jo Malones.'

Alfie shivered at the image. 'You could be, but you ain't, and you won't be able to until this mess is sorted. It's not safe to go back home.'

'Ain't safe! And you're saying this place is. It's a bleedin' health hazard. Look at all those bugs in the bathroom, it looks like an episode of *Life on Earth*. I'm half expecting to be sitting on the carzey and David Attenborough to come crawling up into the bowl.'

'For God's sake, Janine! Can't you put a sock in it? So it ain't the most salubrious of places but what it has got going for it, is the fact that nobody will know we're here. Janine, all I care about is keeping you alive.'

Lola gave Janine a sympathetic smile. 'Alf, she's got a point, this place is a dump.'

Janine threw up her arms in the air. 'Finally, someone's talking sense.'

Alfie glared at Lola, though he kept his voice quiet. 'Look, I ain't denying it's a dump, but it ain't really clever for us to check in at some big hotel just so she can get a perfumed pillowcase. It won't be for long, but for now, it's the safest bet. And at least it's a big enough room so we can all shifty up together.'

Vaughn was sat on the edge of the bed, now regretting it due to one of the mattress springs catching and scratching his leg. 'This wouldn't be happening if you'd just listened to me.'

Alfie shot Vaughn a stare. 'And that's helpful how?'

'It ain't supposed to be helpful, but what I was going to say to Janine is, Alf's right. I know it ain't a great situation we've got ourselves in, and more to the point, got you and Lola in, but I'm sorry, we can't afford to let anything happen to you. Those geezers coming to the house is probably just the start of it. It ain't safe for you to be there, these guys won't be messing. For three million pounds' worth of gems they'll be willing to put a bullet in yer head before you've got time to put yer hands up. Until word gets out that we've got rid of the diamonds, they're going to keep on coming. Whether it's busting into your house, or trying to take you off the road late one night, even kidnapping you, they won't be satisfied until they have them in their hands or they know the bling has been sold. With it being only me, Alf and Frank, we're no match at the moment for every foot soldier out there. So we hide, keep our heads down, make the most of it until we manage to sort this out. And we will.'

Lola looked at Vaughn, appreciating his care. 'Wouldn't it be better for us to get out of the country? Maybe go to Marbs?'

Vaughn shook his head. 'I wish, but it's not so easy to slip you out of the country without anyone knowing, and staying in some big place ain't sensible. The Costa will be just as bad as here. Word travels. I'm sorry.'

Janine pulled down her pink cashmere jumper and gave a small smile. 'At least someone's sorry.'

Frankie nodded as he looked around for a smoke alarm, and seeing there wasn't one, he lit up a large cigar. 'Janine, we'll sort this as soon as. I've got a couple of contacts we can try to sell the diamonds to, hopefully they'll bite, even if it means coming down in price a bit. We've got a two-million-pound target we need to hit, so it might take a bit of time. But one way or another we'll get rid and then it'll be safe to go back. Just give a week or so.'

Vaughn turned to Alfie as he headed for the door. 'Where are you going?'

'I have to go out.'

'Go out where? I thought we were all going to go out later for some food.'

'Not everything's about bleedin' food.'

'What's that supposed to mean?'

Irritated, Alfie snapped. 'I don't have to explain meself to you.'

Vaughn leapt up, blocking Alfie's path. He gritted his teeth angrily as he spoke. 'That's where you're wrong, mate.'

'I'd move if I was you, Vaughn.'

'I don't think so. After what Franny did, let me tell you, I don't trust you completely anymore, and I hold you responsible for this shit. We are always cleaning up your mess and I'm sick of it. I'm sick of you doing things behind me back. Bringing Frank into the business without telling me when we were supposed to be partners. I don't know why I thought you'd changed, Alf. Maybe the offer of Reginald's business blinded me from the truth of who you are. And the worst thing is, I can't even pull out now because I need to make this work, and that means knowing what's happening. So you need to tell me *exactly* what you're doing and where you're going. None of us want any more surprises.'

Alfie pushed Vaughn hard. 'Fuck you. I ain't Franny's keeper, she did this to me as well. How do you think that feels?'

'Right now, Alfie, I don't care how it feels.'

'No, of course you don't, just like you don't want to remember it was actually *you* who got us into this mess, because if you hadn't sounded off, saying me name, *nobody* would know to come looking. So, the blame sits right at your doorstep. Now get out of me way.'

Vaughn shook his head. 'I told you, not until you tell me where you're going . . . I don't trust you, it's as simple as that.'

'What? What do you think I'm going to do, hey? You think Franny is waiting for me with a swag bag of money? Or maybe you think that I'm going to call Eddie? Cut a deal with him?'

'No, actually, but what I do think though, is you'll do something stupid. Have some Alfie Jennings game plan going on, some big idea that ends up fucking us all over.'

With as much hostility as he could muster, Alfie snarled back. 'If you must know I'm going to call Sandra. I ain't heard from her, and I'm going to check she's alright.'

'No, you ain't. You can do that here.'

Alfie burst into laughter. 'I thought for a minute you said "No I ain't".'

'That's exactly what I said.'

'Listen Vaughn, I never listened to me old man, I never listened to me teachers, I never listened to the old bill or the judge, so I reckon it's unlikely that I'm going to start listening to you. So save your breath.'

'Give me your phone, Alf.'

Alfie laughed scornfully. 'You've lost it mate, but I'm going to tell you what's going to happen. In a moment, I'm going to walk out of this door, cop some sea air and then phone me sister to make sure she's alright. And you, my son, ain't going to do fuck all about it.'

Alfie turned to walk away but was held back by Vaughn grabbing his jacket.

'Get off me!'

'I told you, you ain't going nowhere. For starters we're waiting on a call from one of Frankie's contacts and I'm telling you, you ain't going to fuck that up.'

'And I told you, you ain't me dad.'

Then, without hesitation and with expert speed, Alfie channelled his anger and threw a right hook, catching Vaughn square on his mouth, splitting his lip. He followed it through with a hard body shot to the side of Vaughn's ribs.

Seeing Vaughn coming back at him, Alfie quickly ducked, curving his strong body out of the way to avoid the counterattack. He moved to the side, powering a left punch to Vaughn's jaw, causing Vaughn to stumble backwards. And with that, Alfie Jennings walked out of the room, slamming the door behind him.

Outside the air was brisk. Cold and bracing. The sea rolled and smashed and crashed against the wall, and the dark sky merged with the darkness of the ocean. Pulling out his phone, Alfie looked around. The promenade was empty save the seagulls eating the remains of the day's rubbish.

He blew out, watching his breath form into small clouds, not knowing if he was doing the right thing, but not wanting to stop himself either.

He pressed call.

'Hello?'

'Bree, it's me. I got your messages, I thought we should meet.'

47

Bree stood with Johnny, looking down at Ryan in the hospital bed. He was asleep and to Bree he looked so helpless, so pale, so white; as white as the starched pillowcase he lay on.

A computer monitor sat on the wall behind him, connected to a multitude of coloured wires that ran over the bed, attaching to Ryan's bruised and battered chest and hands. A red wire ran under the bandage wrapped round his head, whilst a central line remained fixed into place on the side of his neck.

She was tired, scared, and for the last seventy-two hours, Ryan's life had hung in the balance. Gently squeezing his hand, Bree smiled sadly. 'Hey, sleepy, it's me.'

Ryan's eyes began to flicker open. He gave a small smile back as he glanced from Bree to his brother. His lips were dry and cracked as he took off his oxygen mask. He spoke in a husky whisper as he reached out his hand, placing it gently on Bree's large, pregnant stomach. 'I know it's you, Bree. I crashed my banger car, I didn't lose my memory. It's good to see you though, thanks for bringing her, Johnny. How's my baby doing?'

She smiled. 'Kicking a lot. What happened, Ryan? Can you remember the accident at all?'

Ryan glanced at Johnny, who stood next to Bree, his eyes dark and cold. Ryan shook his head, his eyes closing from the effort of talking. 'No, it's just a blank . . . Johnny, can you give us a minute.'

Without saying a word, Johnny nodded and walked out of the room. Ryan watched his brother going to stand on the other side of the door with Ma, who was staring coldly through the glass.

He turned to Bree, staring at her for a moment. 'Bree, I love you.'

'I love you too.'

'Listen to me, we got to leave as soon as I'm out of here. We got to make sure we do what we said we'd do. It's not safe for you to be back at home. You can't trust Ma. There are some things you don't know about. Things I should've told you before.'

'Ryan, stop! You're frightening me! . . . And anyway, it's fine now, you know that. It's not like how it used to be. Ma's been brilliant.'

There was a relentless hissing from the oxygen mask strapped loosely to Ryan's face, now pushed to the side of his cheek.

'No, Bree, you don't understand. This is what she does. I've seen it before. Don't trust, Ma. You don't know her like I do . . . I need you to promise me something.'

'Anything.'

'I want you to go to a doctor.'

Bree shook her head fiercely. 'I don't need to, Ma's been great. She knows everything any doctor would know. Probably more.'

'Bree, sweetheart, she doesn't. I keep telling ya, it's been a long time since she was any kind of nurse, not everything she says is right. We'll never be free if we stay with her. Why won't you just listen, babe?'

Sighing, Bree looked around at the large syringes filled with various medications, each clipped to its own mechanical pump. The drugs streamed down plastic lines into Ryan's veins with screens displaying such names as Noradrenaline, Fentanyl, Keppra, all of which meant nothing to Bree.

'I don't want to argue with you Ryan, but you know how I feel

about going to the doctors. You know I'm worried about what they'll think of me. Even Ma agrees I should stay away.'

The sound of the glass door opening made them both stop talking. Bree smiled as Ma walked in, her heavy thighs rubbing together. Her breathing hard as her chest fought against the heavy rolls of fat.

'Bree, you look tired. I think you better go and get a cup of tea. Johnny will take you down to the canteen.'

As Bree left, Ma turned the silver dial to close the door and window blinds. 'There you go, a bit of privacy.'

Ryan's gaze darted to the door.

'Hey son, don't look so worried. You and me are just going to have a little chat.'

'I'm tired, I need to rest.'

Ma smiled nastily. 'You're in bed, ain't you?'

'What's this about?'

'It's about Bree. I want you to stop putting things in her head. Before the accident I heard you talking, planning on leaving. Where would you go, son? Where would you go without me?'

'You ain't doing this to me anymore. No more mind games.'

'It ain't a mind game, I just want to know that you ain't thinking of leaving when you get out of here. Can't a mother care? You and Bree, well you got a home with me.'

Ryan's face screwed up. 'I should've left you a long time ago, got on with me life, and that's exactly what I'm going to do now. No more, Ma, no more. You broke me a long time ago and it took meeting Bree to help put me back together again.'

'Son, don't do this. You're making a mistake.'

'Goodbye, Ma. I want you to go now. There's nothing you can do or say to me anymore. It's over.' Ryan reached for the nurse's bell.

Ma nodded sadly. 'You're right, it is.'

Quickly she grabbed for the bell, knocking it out of Ryan's hand. She squeezed his face brutally hard. 'You never learn, do you?'

He scraped at her hands, trying to prise her fingers off him. Terror in his eyes. 'You're hurting me, get off! Ma! Get off!'

Stretching over, Ma reached for the Noradrenaline syringe, easily detaching it from its pump.

'What are you doing, Ma!'

Ma slammed her hand over Ryan's mouth as she bent down and kissed his head. 'I love you son, but I told you before, nobody ever leaves Ma . . .'

Then Ma expertly pushed the plunger hard, quickly forcing an unnoticeable volume yet potent dose of the powerful, fast-acting drug straight into Ryan's veins.

A fierce wave of heat rushed through Ryan's body and as he tried to call out his eyes rolled back into his head before he quickly lost consciousness.

Hurriedly, Ma put the syringe back in its place, pressing the green resume button on the pump. Reaching up to the monitor, she glanced at the door before clicking the two-minute suspend alarm tab on the screen. She stood back and watched the numbers on the monitors start to change. His blood pressure climbing higher and higher. 240 . . . 280 . . . 340. And then calmly watched as Ryan's oxygen levels began to fall, his body beginning to convulse and tremor.

As the two-minute counter reached zero, the alarms burst back into life and taking a breath, Ma walked to the door, stepping out into the corridor. 'Help! Nurse! Help! Somebody, please help!'

Within moments, medical staff began running into the room. A tall, thin doctor, seeing immediately what was happening, shouted his instructions as Ma stood and watched.

'He's fitting! Give him five of diazepam. Stop the Noradrenaline quickly, we need to get his pressure down otherwise he'll have a cerebral bleed.'

As the ICU team continued to work on Ryan, Bree came around the corner with Johnny. She froze. Her eyes wide and terrified, darting from Ryan to Ma. Her voice barely audible as fear set in.

'Oh my God, what happened? What happened, Ma?'

Glancing at Johnny, Ma took Bree into her arms. 'Shhh, Bree, don't get yourself upset, we need to get you home. This ain't a place for you in your condition.'

'Is he going to die? Is he?'

'No, Bree, he ain't going to die, but the damage has already been done.'

48

Bree stepped into her grey Mercedes 4x4, turning the engine on. She sat staring ahead, mesmerised by the motion of the rain sensor windscreen wipers, which gave out a dull screech as the blades dragged back and forth against the glass.

It was cold and she was tired, and the thought of Alfie played on her mind, weighing heavy on her heart, causing her chest to feel tight and her breath to become short. She thought about his kindness. His care. His love. How he'd protected her from the harshness of her life as much as he could. And all done from the goodness of his heart. He had saved her. Picked her up when she was young and broken, and now she was going to repay him by taking his hand once more, leading him straight into a trap.

'Bree, you better get a move on! Don't fuck this up.' Johnny banged on the side of the car, making her jump.

She watched as he walked across to the far side of the mobile site, disappearing for a moment before reappearing a few seconds later with Ryan who was smiling and completely unaware.

Through the rain-dotted windscreen she saw him grin, then watched as Johnny put his index finger to Ryan's throat, slashing it across his neck.

Johnny shouted to her. 'Make it count, Bree. Make it count. Time's running out, babe. Don't make me have to do it to him.'

Reversing out of the caravan site, Bree kept her eyes on Ryan, blowing him a hidden kiss, smiling and waving until she couldn't see him anymore.

As soon as she'd turned the corner, Bree pulled up by the side of the lane and cried. She banged her palms against the steering wheel over and over again as the tears ran down her face and the car filled up with her desperate screams.

49

Sandra Styler bent over, pushing her ear against the white wooden bedroom door, attempting to listen to Eddie speak on the phone. She screwed up her face as she concentrated on his words.

'. . . I ain't having a go. I'm just saying it's taking some time . . . I get that Johnny of course I do, and all I mean is that if we don't move quickly . . . Yeah, okay . . . Then how long does Bree think it'll take?'

Hearing the name Bree, Sandra jolted up, banging into the glass vase on the landing table behind her. She cursed as it crashed into pieces on the wooden floor.

'. . . Hold up Johnny, I'll call you back.'

The door of the bedroom flung open and Eddie stood staring down suspiciously at Sandra.

Carefully picking up the pieces of broken glass, she frowned. 'Oh, there you are, I was wondering where you'd gone.'

Eddie's eyes darkened. 'How long have you been there?'

'What? On me hands and knees picking up this poxy vase? I don't know Eddie, should I have been timing meself?'

He paused, trying to read her face. 'No. Outside the door, listening.'

Snapping, Sandra pointed a piece of glass at Eddie. 'If I'd been listening, then I would've known where you were, wouldn't I?'

'You're up to something. I know it.'

'Then you know more than I do, and the only reason you think I'm up to something is because you must be. What are you hiding, Eddie?'

Eddie shuffled. 'Nothing.'

'Well you look suspicious for doing nothing, but maybe instead of standing there gawping, you can start helping me pick this up, cos when Barrie does turn up, he won't want glass in his paws, will he? . . . Where you going? Ed! Ed! I'm talking to you!'

As she watched Eddie stalk off, leaving the smell of alcohol in the air behind him, Sandra let out a sigh of relief and slumped down. She threw the pieces of vase to one side. She needed to speak to Alfie and quickly.

Waiting for the front door to shut, Sandra pulled out her phone. She wasn't quite sure what was going on, but there was no way it could be a different Bree. No way. She hadn't come across that name for years. There was coincidence and there was blatantly obvious. And whatever it was, it was obvious Eddie was up to no good. And Bree, the little bitch, was in on it too. How, she didn't know. What it was, she couldn't guess, but Alfie had been right that Bree wasn't all that she seemed.

Alfie's phone went straight to voicemail. 'Alf, it's me, Sandra. I need to talk to you. It's about Bree. Call me back as soon as.'

A sound to the side of her made her look up.

'I knew you were up to something.'

Eddie Styler stood looking down at Sandra, a claw hammer in his hand.

On a large grassy verge by the sand and shingle beach of Shoeburyness, three miles east of Southend-on-Sea, Alfie Jennings sat listening to Sandra's voicemail. He shook his head and smiled. *Now* she had something to say about Bree, no doubt bored and looking for a bit of gossip. A bit of a nosey. Well she'd have to wait. He'd call her later, or maybe tomorrow, and see if she'd found out anything more about Eddie and what he knew, but for now, his sister would have to find her natter elsewhere.

Seeing some headlights approaching, Alfie stuffed his phone into his pocket and got out of the car, waiting for the SUV to stop. Smiling, he looked at her as she turned off the lights.

Smiling, she looked at him as he waited in the warmth of the evening. His handsome face lighting up. Taking a deep breath, her eyes sore from crying, Bree got out of the car, doing what she knew needed to be done. Pushing every other thought away. This time, as Johnny had said, *she had to make it count.*

'Hey, Alf!' As her heart raced, Bree hoped her tone sounded casual.

'Hey, sorry to meet you out in the open . . . again! It's becoming a bit of a habit.'

She shrugged, ignoring the way he smiled at her. Ignoring his warmth. She had to think of him as the enemy, it was the only way she could do this. To see him as the person who stood between Ryan and his safety.

'No matter. It's just nice to see you. Thanks for meeting me Alf, especially after the last time. I didn't think you would.'

'It's hard to ignore ten messages, unless of course they were from Janine that is.'

She grinned. 'It wasn't good how we left it last time. I just wanted to explain.'

Alfie gestured to both cars. 'Okay, but your place or mine?'

She laughed. 'How about my place?'

'Thought you'd never ask.'

They got into Bree's car, looking at each other, not saying anything. Unable to hold Alfie's gaze, Bree turned away, playing with an unseen thread on her top. 'Like I said, I needed to explain . . . I did lie to you, Alf.'

'I knew it . . .'

She looked at him oddly.

He shrugged. 'Sorry. Go on.'

'There is no Andrew. I mean, that's not my ex's name. I made it up because it felt easier. His real name is Mick and . . .' She trailed off, struggling, hating herself more and more with every passing word.

'And?'

'I've had a lot of trouble with him. He ain't a nice man. I was embarrassed and you seemed like you had it all sorted out. Your life seemed great.'

Alfie gave a wry smile. 'If only you knew because, sweetheart, if you did, you wouldn't be saying that.'

'The point is, my life's a bit of a mess at the moment, and like I said, I was embarrassed.'

Alfie nodded thoughtfully. 'I have to give it to Sandra, she said as much. She said you probably had stuff you didn't want to talk about. She was right, and there's me steaming in like a bleedin' gorilla. I'm sorry.'

'It's not your fault. I just didn't want you to think . . . well, I didn't want you to think badly of me. My ex is trouble and I thought if I told you . . .' Bree trailed off, biting her lip.

Alfie gently put his finger underneath her chin, lifting her face up to his. 'That I would be put off?'

She nodded, feeling sick at his kindness. 'Yeah.'

'Bree, baby, you don't have to impress me. You should see some of the birds I've been with . . . No, that sounds bad. What I mean is, I ain't nothing special. I'm Alfie. Alfie that used to hold yer hand, Alfie that used to distract the ice-cream cart man whilst you and Sandra nicked the 99s. And Alfie that missed you when you went away, girl.'

Bree burst into tears, sobbing loudly, her body heaving. Alfie passed her a tissue which she gratefully took.

'That's the second time you've done that to me. You alright, Bree?'

Bree managed only to nod her head then quickly opened the car door and promptly vomited, her nerves playing havoc with her. 'It must've been something I ate.'

Alfie grinned. 'Now that's more like it. I'm home from home now. I'm used to birds and old Toms throwing up on me. Makes me think I'm back in Soho.'

Wiping her mouth, Bree shivered, but smiled. 'I'm so sorry.'

'No need to apologise. A bit of sick always breaks the ice. Did he do that to you? This Mick? Did he hurt you?' Alfie gently touched her face, moving his finger down her bruises.

Picturing Johnny in her head, Bree spoke sincerely. 'Yes, he did. He's hurt me a lot.'

'I want to kill him. I want to wring his neck. Let's see if he's so handy with his fists when I go round. Tell me where he lives.'

Bree put her hand on Alfie's clenched fist. 'It's fine, well, it is for now. Let's not talk about him . . . What did you mean when you said "if only I knew"?'

Alfie said nothing, trying to push doubt away, but he was tired of not having anyone to share how he felt with. He was hurting from Franny, stressed from everything that was going down with the diamonds, pissed off with Vaughn and fed up of Janine. So maybe having someone to talk to, someone gentle, someone beautiful, someone he'd known when life seemed so much simpler, was just what he needed. Maybe he needed Bree.

Bree shrugged. 'No, it's okay if you don't want to answer. Forget I said anything. I don't want to pry.'

Firmly, Alfie said, 'No. It's fine. Fuck it. Why shouldn't you ask. I spent me whole life being paranoid, looking over me shoulder, checking what I say and who I say it to. The business I'm in makes you like that, it plays with your mind, but I'm sick of it, and why should I be paranoid about you? It's just you and me, ain't it? Just Alfie and Bree.'

He paused, watching as Bree's eyes slowly fixed on his, a smile beginning to pull at her lips. And with that, Alfie Jennings closed his eyes, feeling a sense of real happiness as he leant in for a warm, long, sensual kiss.

50

'I will kill him. I will bleedin' well kill him.'

'I'll second that.' Janine stood looking at Vaughn as he paced along the worn-out carpet of the B&B.

Ignoring Janine, Vaughn looked at Frankie who sat smoking yet another cigar. 'He *knew* that we were waiting on a call. You *told* him that you had contacts who were interested in buying the stones but they wouldn't wait around. And now, Perry wants us to meet him and Alfie's nowhere to be seen. He ain't answering his calls and his car's gone.'

Frankie, usually the one to let his temper have the better of him, inhaled deeply and calmly. He blew the smoke out with his words. 'You think he's gone to see Sandra? She was hurt after all, and he did say he was going to call her. Maybe she needed to see him.'

Vaughn scowled. 'What? A little bit of glass in her arm, it's hardly Vietnam. And anyway, he could've phoned on the way. Plus, he knows to stay away from that part of Essex. He's going to fuck everything up if he don't start toeing the line. His head's all over the place.'

'Then if he ain't with Sandra, where the hell is he?'

Irritated, Vaughn looked bemused. 'Well that's what I'm trying to work out, ain't it, Frank?'

Lola pulled a face. 'Maybe he's had an accident, Vaughnie.'

'He'll wish he had one when I finish with him. The meeting with Perry starts in an hour and we ain't got anything to show him. Alfie's the only one with the tester stone. I should've thought to get it from him.'

Janine slumped on the bed, eating her way through a family-size packet of Maltesers. 'Then you'll have to postpone.'

'We can't. If we don't go or we call to cancel they're going to think we're just taking the piss. We ain't got many options at the moment, and if we want to offload them as soon as we can so we don't mess up the Reynolds deal, we can't get mess this up.'

Janine, incensed by Alfie, grabbed her phone, dialling Alfie's number. 'I'll call him again.'

Vaughn sighed. 'It'll just go to answer machine.'

'Then I'll leave him a message, won't I? . . . Alfie, it's your wife. Ex. Where the fuck are you? You need to call us and sharpish, and you better have a good explanation as to . . .'

'Where you been?' Vaughn spoke as Alfie walked in.

The grin on Alfie's face quickly disappeared as Janine, Lola, Vaughn and Frankie stood facing him off. Throwing his keys on the side, he said, 'What's going on?'

Vaughn stepped forward but was held back by Frankie. 'Oh, nothing Alf, everything's just cushty with us. Everything's sweet as.'

Alfie held Vaughn's stare. 'Then there's no problem, is there?'

Janine, unable to contain herself, exploded. 'No problem! You are about to lose your second chance, so you need to pull your head out of your arse and get it together.'

Alfie looked dumbfounded. 'What the fuck is she on about?'

Vaughn, deciding it was best to take the lead on this one, put on his jacket. 'We ain't got time to go through the ins and outs, we got to go if we're going to get to this meet. Perry Wickes is wanting to see us, but you know he don't like people being late.

So, if we want to turn this round, and get out of this shit hole and be able to put our heads above water again, then we need to make this work, because if we don't, we are all well and truly fucked.'

Sandra Styler could hear a voice but she couldn't tell quite where it was coming from; she didn't bother opening her eyes to find out. Every single part of her hurt. She'd tried to move but the attempt had caused crippling, throbbing pain. Her tongue felt swollen and her lips were parched and she could feel the dry blood stuck on her face.

'Here.'

A tray of food and a bottle of water was thrown down, slamming on the floor next to her as Eddie Styler stood by the door. Seeing no movement, Eddie walked over and prodded Sandra in her side with the toe of his shoe.

'Fine, have it your own way. Don't talk. Don't eat. You've always made the rules, only this time Sandra, you're not going to tell me what to do. In fact, you ain't going to tell me what to do ever again. And by the time they find you, I'll be long gone, and you, darlin', can rot in hell, the place I've been living for the whole of this marriage.'

And with that, Eddie Styler, feeling exceptionally pleased with himself, slammed and locked the door of the basement, leaving Sandra in the cold darkness.

51

'Is he going to bite?' Johnny stared at Bree as she finished locking the chickens up in their coop.

She nodded, not wanting to look at Johnny as she thought about Alfie. 'Yeah, I think he is.'

'You only think?'

Trying not to aggravate Johnny, Bree attempted to be more specific. 'Sorry, I meant I'm sure he will. I'm certain of it. He started to open up to me. Answered my questions, but I didn't want to push it. I need him to trust me. I don't know how long that will take.'

'Bree, how many times have I told you, you ain't got time. I need to be able to tell the men that the job's on, everyone's looking at me to get this sorted. There's a lot of money involved, let alone what might happen to Ryan, but you don't seem to get that.'

Bree flinched. 'I do. Of course I do. How can I not, Johnny?'

Johnny's eyes went cold. He pressed his temples, the white noise in his head getting louder.

'Don't give me lip, Bree. *Never* give me lip . . . I tell you what I'm going to do. I'm going to shake it up, because no matter what you tell me, I don't think you're taking this seriously. I don't think you're trying.'

'That's not true!'

Slamming Bree hard against the chicken coop, Johnny spoke in a whisper. 'You calling me a liar, Bree?'

'No, no. I'm just saying what you think isn't right. I'm doing everything I can. I'm trying, Johnny.'

He breathed hard and Bree could see the cocaine residue sitting at the bottom of his nostrils. 'Then try harder! And the next time you go and see Alfie, I want you to find out exactly what he's doing with those diamonds. And if you don't, then Ryan gets hurt.'

'No! No! No! That's not what you said, you said if I broke your trust you'd do something to him.'

Screaming in Bree's face, Johnny spat out his words. 'And now I've changed the rules!'

Covering her face with her hands, Bree broke down. Her tears seeping through the gaps between her fingers. 'Please, please, I'm begging you. Don't do this. Don't do this, Johnny.'

Taking her in his arms, Johnny stroked Bree's hair. He smiled and kissed the top of her head. 'There's no need to cry, Johnny's here . . . Hey Bree, stop crying . . . *I said stop crying* . . . That's it . . . Look, nobody loves Ryan or you more than I do, so it's going to be alright. You do trust me, don't you?'

In a whisper, Bree said, 'Yes, Johnny.'

Johnny pulled Bree's hands away from her face and stared into her eyes. 'Because you'll do whatever it takes to save Ryan and then I won't have to hurt him. Promise me, Bree, that you won't make me hurt him. *Promise* me.'

'I promise, Johnny. Whatever it takes.'

He nodded and this time, it was Johnny who began to cry. He buried his head in her shoulder. 'I love you, Bree. I love you. Now say it.'

'I love you too.'

'No, not that, say it!'

Bree closed her eyes, her body rigid. 'I'm never going to leave, Johnny.'

52

In the large study of his ten-bedroom house on the edge of the village of Layer de la Haye, a few miles from Colchester, Perry Wickes sat in his claret and blue wheelchair. He wore a custom-made blue velvet flat cap along with a claret Ralph Lauren tracksuit he'd had imported from the States. A lifelong supporter of West Ham, everything Perry was able to pimp out in the Hammers colours, he did.

Perry grinned, taking a sip of coffee from a Millwall FC mug. He gestured to the cup. 'Me brother thought it'd be a laugh. He's got a hundred-pound bet that I won't last more than a month drinking from it. It's been a week, and I have to tell you fellas, I feel sick every time I put it to me lips. I feel like fucking Judas at the last supper drinking the old Calvin Klein.'

Frankie and Vaughn laughed, but Alfie kept quiet. His mind was on Bree. And it pissed him off. Not that *she'd* done anything. He was pissed off with himself. It was stupid, but he could feel himself falling for her already. Or perhaps it wasn't so much him falling for her as just a classic rebound caused by the pain from Franny. Maybe he needed to find something, or rather *someone*, to fill the void inside him which seemed to grow bigger every day.

But whatever it was, she made him feel good. He didn't know if it was just about the memories they shared, or it was something more, but he felt so relaxed in her company. He'd been able to talk to her. Open up. He was able to be himself without worrying she was going to judge or try to pull one over on him. And he certainly respected her for admitting the truth of why she'd lied about her ex. That can't have been easy for her, but it went a long way with him. Which was ironic really, because the truth and him rarely walked hand in hand.

But everything about Bree was so refreshing and although it was the earliest of days, and Franny was still very fresh in his mind, perhaps he and Bree might have some mileage. Maybe they could make a go of whatever it was they had.

He already wanted to talk to her again, and he knew that was stupid, but what could he do? He'd felt like that since the moment she'd driven off. He'd wanted to call her but thankfully he'd resisted and he'd called Sandra instead, wanting to share what had happened, knowing his sister would love hearing every gossipy word.

Annoyingly he hadn't been able to get through, so now he was fit to burst wanting to tell somebody how he felt about Bree, that maybe she could help heal his battered heart, so the very last thing he wanted to do was stand and hear Perry reminiscing about West Ham's 1978 victory against Millwall.

'Alf? Alfie? Did you hear what I just said? Bryan Robson's shots, well, you had to be there to believe it. It was like the whole of Upton Park held their breath. All three goals Robson got. All three. Can you believe it?'

'Not really mate, cos I weren't there.'

Perry Wickes stared coldly at Alf. 'Are you being funny?'

Alfie sniffed. 'No.'

'You know I don't trust a man that doesn't like football. It's like he doesn't like life. Something must be missing, something's not right. I mean, what are you supposed to talk about with a geezer that don't know about football? Seriously, what else is there. Fucking cooking? Embroidery? Emotions? Fuck that. Nah, it don't sit well with me. Never do business with a man that don't know his Bobby Moores from his Bobby Zamoras.'

Alfie glanced across at Vaughn and Frankie who were giving him harder stares than Perry. He shrugged. 'Pel, it ain't that I don't like football, I do. I could sit here and tell you how many times I've wept at the final whistles but it's pointless, because what can you do if you have a shit manager and the people in the board room don't want to listen to the fans.'

Perry's face lit up. He banged down his hand on the table before pointing at Alfie.

'Exactly! Exactly!' Perry paused, looking vindicated as he pushed back the thick brown hair from his forehead. 'Anyway, we ain't here to put the FA to rights, so let's get down to business.'

Turning his back to Perry, Alfie winked at Vaughn, who scowled as Frankie began to talk.

'So, first off, I appreciate you seeing us Pel, especially as you know you weren't the first person we came to. Though that ain't nothing to do with respect, it just comes down to who was available in that moment, because as you know, and I ain't going to make a secret of it, we need to get shut and quickly. But obviously we're looking to get a decent price and to do that we're calling in the favours.'

Alfie placed the diamond on the table in front of Perry.

'They're all like this. All perfect. None of them have any visible hues, the clarity's beautiful Pel, no natural flaws that you can see. They've got a brilliant cut and they hold some proper weight. You won't find better.'

Perry passed the stone to a small, wiry grey-haired man who began studying the diamond in earnest, looking at the colour, clarity, cut, and carat weight. 'So, Frankie, if they are all pukka, and they all check out, you say you want to sell them along with pulling in the favours, which I suspect makes the price go up.'

Frankie watched as the grey-haired appraiser nodded at Perry, passing the stone back to him.

'Absolutely, Pel. Stones plus favours. So, what do you say?'

Perry glanced at the three men. 'I have to say, they're a tidy bit of stone. I ain't seen such good ones for a while. I don't suppose you fancy telling me your source?'

Frankie grinned. 'What do you think, Pel?'

Perry chuckled. 'Well, I'll easily be able to knock these out.'

'So, we have a deal?' Frankie asked.

'I think we do . . . and what do you say to two million? Two million big ones.'

At this point Perry Wickes raised his Millwall FC mug, looked at it and said, 'Cheers!' before throwing it against the wall.

53

Bree got up. She could feel herself shaking. She was cold but her sweat-drenched nightie clung to her. Her pregnant stomach felt hard and her back ached as she attempted to wander through to the kitchen to get a drink.

She felt dizzy and the continual flu-like symptoms racked her whole body. She couldn't remember the last time she'd been well. Each day she either slept or was violently ill, and usually Ma had to help her get up and walk anywhere further than a few steps.

But tonight she'd needed a drink of water and there was no way she could get back to sleep feeling so thirsty.

Halfway down the passageway of the large mobile caravan, at Ryan's room, Bree paused to catch her breath. She leant on the wall, pains rushing through her sides as her whole body shook.

She looked in, seeing him asleep, looking like he always had; so gentle, so handsome, but that was all she recognised. The person who'd come home from the hospital last week had been a stranger. The light in his eyes had disappeared. The understanding was gone.

The sudden but not uncommon cerebral bleed had caused irreversible, irreparable damage. But she wouldn't give up hope. She'd never give up. There was a chance over time things might improve, the doctors had said sometimes they did. And she was holding out for that. For the day when he would look at her and know who she was, because somewhere inside him, Ryan was still there. But nothing could stop her loving him. After all, she was still her and he was still him.

Walking into the room, Bree sat down on Ryan's bed. She smiled, watching him sleep. Then she heard voices; Ma and Johnny were coming down the passageway. About to call out a greeting, Bree stopped herself, suddenly curious to hear what they were saying.

'. . . It ain't my fault you know. So, stop saying that.'

'If you'd done it properly, then I wouldn't have to, would I? You got somebody else to do your dirty work because you were too much of a coward. And yet again, I've had to pick up your pieces.'

'I did what you asked.'

'Don't kid yourself. Ryan was perfectly fine after the crash. In fact, he felt better than ever, couldn't wait to tell me how he and Bree were going to leave.'

Bree froze, her eyes wide, her body rigid as the enormity of what Ma and Johnny were saying began to sink in. Afraid she was going to cry, she put her hand over her mouth as she continued to listen.

'You don't get it, do you?'

'What don't I get, Johnny? Because I know Ryan was going to leave us. He was going to break your heart. Your own brother was going to leave you.'

'Ma, look . . .'

Angrily, Ma raised her voice. 'No, Johnny! I told you what I wanted. I told you after the crash I didn't want him to be able to walk away, but that's not what happened, is it? The doctors said he was fine, that he was going to make a full recovery. So, whether you like it or not Johnny, you're to blame . . . You.'

Bree flinched as she heard a loud slap before craning to hear the rest of the conversation.

'Don't hit me, Ma, you got to stop, you hear me? I ain't Ryan that you can just knock about when you feel like it.'

'Get off me!'

'Then you need to calm down and listen. Big Billy tried his best,

but there's a fine line between injuring and killing a person when you're speeding round a track. It's not like ordering a pizza, Ma. We told you we couldn't guarantee what would happen, but you still wanted us to go ahead. The only thing we promised was we'd keep Ryan alive, which we did, Ma. We did.'

'And I had to make sure he couldn't leave you. So you need to be thanking me for clearing up your mess . . . He ain't going to leave you now, Johnny, not no more. I've given you your brother back.'

The bile flooded into Bree's mouth. She felt sick. She could hardly breathe. It all made sense now. Ryan had warned her, and she'd just ignored it. But if she'd listened, Ryan wouldn't be lying here now, lost forever.

She heard Johnny going into his room and Ma leaving to go back to her mobile caravan. Bree tried to push aside the pain that was coursing from her stomach right across her back. She struggled as she attempted to hurry across to Ryan's drawers. She pulled some clothes out quickly before quietly and gently shaking him awake.

'Ryan, it's me, Bree. Wake up, honey.'

He opened his eyes and grinned, but the recognition wasn't there.

'Ryan, I need you to get dressed. We got to be quick or Ma will catch us.'

He looked at her, then slowly said, 'Big trouble.'

Bree's face lit up, she hugged him, then stroked his face, placing a gentle kiss on his lips.

'You are there Ryan, aren't you? I knew it. But that's right, there'll be big trouble, so come on . . . And Ryan, I love you; whatever happens, I'll never leave you.'

With shaking hands and tears running down her face, Bree helped Ryan to get dressed as silently as she could, not being able to contemplate what would happen if she got caught.

Part way down the corridor, Bree, holding Ryan's hand, stopped as the flu-like symptoms came on hard and fast and her pains began to get worse. A sudden thought struck her. The medicine. Ryan's medicine. She couldn't leave without it.

Smiling at Ryan, she pulled him back towards the kitchen, putting her finger to her lips.

'Shhh, we have to be quiet, Ryan. Really quiet.'

The kitchen was dark apart from the light from Ma's caravan opposite. Bree began to look around the kitchen. She knew Ma kept it in here, but where?

Going to open the cupboard next to the stainless-steel oven, Bree realised it was locked by a small gold padlock. Yanking open the cutlery drawer, desperate not to make a sound, Bree grabbed the penknife as pain gripped her and the cold sweat continued to pour down her face and down her back.

Pushing the tip of the blade into the padlock, Bree pressed down with the end of the knife, feeling the springs and the tension of the lock. She wiggled the knife and a moment later the lock came open.

Inside the cupboard there were various everyday medicines, but right at the back, marked clearly, were Ryan's medications.

Grabbing the packets of pills, Bree's hand banged into a bottle, but before she managed to catch it, it dropped out, rolling onto the floor. Thankful it hadn't made too much of a noise, she picked it up, placing it back in the cupboard, but as she did, she noticed her fingers were wet. The contents of the bottle were leaking out. About to push it into the cupboard anyway, Bree suddenly stopped. She smelt the air, then put her fingers to her nose, smelling the medicine, which had covered her hand.

It was the same pungent, fruity smell as the drink Ma gave her. The same nauseating aroma that always made her feel so sick. She put her tongue to her fingers, tasting it. And yes, although it was usually mixed with water in the drink Ma brought her twice daily, there was no denying the taste of the bitter medicine.

Curiously, Bree turned the bottle round to see the label. She stared, blinking, not quite believing what she read.

Morphine Sulphate, oral solution.

* * *

Morphine! Ma had been giving her morphine! The whole of her pregnancy she'd been given this. Her tiredness. Her lethargy. Her confusion. Was it all down to this? When Ma had been late bringing her drink, she remembered the restlessness, the cold sweats, the cramps and the pains. Like now . . . She hurt so bad.

A thought crossed her mind and quickly unscrewing the bottle, Bree took a swig, careful not to take too much. If she was right, it would help and take away some of the pains, making it easier to get away.

Throwing the leaking bottle into a bag, along with Ryan's medicines, Bree hoped the morphine would kick in soon. Then opening the back door and taking Ryan's hand, Bree ran out into the night.

54

'Result! Result!' Frankie, raising a plastic cup full of brandy, grinned at the others as they stood in the B&B, which suddenly didn't look so bad. 'I knew old Perry would come through. But fuck me, it was proper squeaky-bum time, Alfie, when I thought you were going to blow it. Everybody knows Perry loves his football, the geezer's obsessed with it, and he don't do business with anyone who doesn't love the beautiful game or who supports Millwall.'

Alfie sat down, slightly distracted. 'Yeah well, I was tempted to give him a bit of grief, but the idea of having to put up with you bunch of muppets giving me the chip-chop and chewing me ear off, well, it was worth pretending I was a football fan rather than a rugby man. And at least now we can sort out what's needed to be done.'

Frankie nodded. 'I'll second that because we are back, son. We are back. I think we should raise a toast to Reggie Reynolds! Our empire awaits.'

Lola raised a can of Fanta orange. 'This is one of the best days I've had for a long time. Me boys are back where they belong and on top of that me bunions ain't giving me any grief.'

Alfie placed a kiss on her cheek. 'Well that's a cause for

celebration if ever there was one. Of course, we still have to do the handover of the diamonds, which is planned for next week. We'll obviously lie low till then, because the vultures will be out in force, especially as Perry can't keep his trap shut. But then, boom baby, we're on it. Actually, I better call Sandra, stupid mare ain't picking up her phone. But I just wanted to bring her in on it.'

Janine scowled. 'Why?'

Alfie, his good mood beginning to subside, put his plastic cup down as he walked over to Janine. 'Why what?'

'Why you bringing her in on it? I don't see her putting any hard graft in. I told you before, I ain't sharing my readies with her.'

Alfie burst out into scornful laughter. 'Your readies? Janine, darlin', you've lost your fuckin' mind. Let me just remind you that those stones actually belong to her husband, so by rights they are actually *hers*. In fact it's *us* jumping on *her* bandwagon, not the other way around.'

Janine poked Alfie hard in the chest. 'Finders keepers, losers, and it ain't my problem you weepers.'

'Shut up, Janine. Most, if not all, of that money will be given to Reenie Reynolds, but Sandra will certainly be having a cut of the business once it takes off, whether you like it or not.'

'I don't like it, and I'll tell you something, it'll be over my dead body.'

'Don't fucking tempt me, girl.'

Janine bit into her cold cheese-and-ham panini and narrowed her eyes. 'You're mugging yourself off anyway. She's obviously blanking your calls. If she wanted to talk to you, she would, but you still want to play the generous brother act.'

'If it wasn't for her, I might not be here. I might've had a bullet in me head.'

Janine pulled a face. 'How convenient.'

'Convenient? What are you talking about?'

Janine looked at the others. 'It ain't just me that thinks it, it's a bit odd that Sandra just so happened to be around when those geezers came to blow you away, and then she came away without a scratch.'

'Apart from a piece of glass in her arm.'

Janine shrugged. 'That's just collateral damage, ain't it? Come off it Alfie, she's married to Eddie, ain't she? Her loyalties lie with him, not you. She's proper shady.'

Alfie stared at Janine then gave a piercing look to the others, none of whom could look him in the eye. 'I understand why Janine would think that, cos apart from the fact she's never got a nice word to say about anybody, she's never liked Sandra from the day she's known her. But you lot? You've all been slagging me off behind me back? If anybody's being shady, it's you guys. You all know her and she'd never backstab any of us and it fucking hurts to know that's what you think.'

Vaughn spoke evenly. 'We thought Franny wouldn't do the dirty, but look what's happened there.'

Joining in the conversation, Frankie said, 'Alf, listen. You know I like the girl, and we ain't been bad-mouthing you, but we just reckon you should be careful. Especially when we're so near to pulling this off with Perry. See it from our point of view, you could end up trusting her when all the time she's in Eddie's corner.'

Alfie's face was red. He pointed at Frankie. 'You bastard. That's my family you're talking about. So do yourself a favour and keep out of it mate, unless you want me to put you against that wall.'

Lola walked up to Alfie. 'Sweetheart, we're only worried about you.'

'You're not worried about me, you lot are only worried about the money.'

Vaughn snarled. 'Do you blame us?'

'I tell you what, I'll prove it to you that she ain't a grass . . . Where's my phone? I'll call her, shall I? See what she has to say.'

Alfie punched out the numbers, staring hard at Vaughn. The phone rang then switched onto answer machine. He tried again, and again it went to voicemail. He looked around the room.

'So, she don't answer her phone, that don't prove anything.'

Vaughn said, 'Are you sure about that?'

Alfie took a deep breath, refusing to let the doubts seep in. 'Have you thought something might've happened to her, rather than she's plotting something? Cos it just don't make sense, if she *was* plotting something, don't you think she'd answer?'

Vaughn stepped in close to Alfie. 'Fuck this deal up and I'll kill you.'

Fuming, Alfie grabbed his bag, storming towards the door. 'Well I'm worried about her even if you lot aren't. But in the meantime, I ain't staying here. You guys make me sick, so I'm going to find meself a room, don't matter what, because sharing a bed with fleas and cockroaches would be better than seeing your boat races right now. And before you say it, don't worry, I'll be there next Tuesday with the rocks, but till then, it's good to know that I have mates like you. Thanks for nothing.'

55

Alfie Jennings lay on his bed watching the sun rise in the small, but surprisingly clean room of the quaint bed and breakfast on the outskirts of Southend-on-Sea. Sighing, he looked at his phone, then angrily threw it against the wall. There were several missed calls from Vaughn and Frankie, a couple from Lola and a stonking message from Janine, but nothing at all from Sandra.

He'd tried several times to get through to her, but he'd had no luck. He'd even tried the home phone, withholding his number in case Eddie had picked it up, but again, there'd been nothing.

He'd flitted in and out of sleep and in the end, he'd got up, taking a stroll along the front to try to clear his head. Walking down to the pier with its locked-up fairgrounds and sweet stalls, watching the sea, watching the boats and the early morning walkers. But it hadn't helped, not one bit, in fact it'd made it worse. He'd even tried to call Franny, and he'd left an angry, vicious message which he regretted the moment he had done it. And now all he could think of was what the others had said about Sandra. And, like so many things, doubt had started to creep in, which pissed him off no end.

All he needed to happen was for Sandra to pick up the phone and just speak to him, so he could put his growing suspicion aside.

But the longer the silence went on, the longer he thought that perhaps, just perhaps, the others might have a point. After all, it was true they hadn't been close for a while.

Would he blame her for betraying him when that's essentially what he'd done by not being there for her? Marrying Eddie because she'd just needed somebody, anybody, to be there. When he'd been living the life in Soho, he'd seen her, but he'd been so wrapped up in himself, living it large and becoming a face, that Sandra's feelings weren't ever a concern. Yes, his betrayal of her was bigger than anything she might've done, but that didn't mean it didn't hurt.

A knock on the door saved Alfie from his thoughts.

Carefully, he slipped the gun off the bedside table and eased himself up from the bed. He tiptoed across, pressing his eye against the door viewer to see who it was.

Throwing the gun on the bed behind him, he opened the door and smiled. 'Thanks for coming, I didn't think you would.'

Bree Dwyer smiled at Alfie. 'Well thanks for inviting me, it was a lovely surprise.' She craned her head, looking around. 'I'm impressed though, a room instead of a car, you're spoiling me, Alf.'

He laughed. 'Come on in, let me show you my palace, and no, that ain't an innuendo.'

It was Bree's turn to laugh as she stepped into the room. Then taking a deep breath to steady her nerves, she sat on the bed. 'So, what's with the bed and breakfast by the sea?'

'Just like to get away sometimes.'

Bree raised her eyebrows. 'To here?'

'Well you know what they say, it ain't the place, it's the people . . .' Alfie slumped down on the chair. He looked at her intently. 'You don't believe that any more than I do.'

'You don't have to say. We can just sit here or go for a walk, watch TV. Whatever makes you comfortable.'

'That's what I like about you, Bree. Ain't no pressure. If you were Janine, Christ almighty, I'd be having me ear chewed off now whilst you try to find out every last detail about me business.'

Thinking about Johnny and Ryan, Bree knew how carefully she had to play it. 'Well, I know what it's like when you don't want to say, but I'm here if you want to talk.' She looked at him, her big, beautiful eyes drawing him in.

Pushing back his hair, which flopped across his face, Alfie shrugged, pulling out a cigarette from the box on the table. Lost in thought, he lit it, inhaling deeply as he gazed at Bree.

'Can I ask you something?'

She smiled. 'Anything.'

'Would you say Sandra was trustworthy?'

'Sandra? I mean, I don't know her now, but she was one of the most trustworthy people I knew. I loved her, I would've done anything for her. She was a fantastic best friend.'

Alfie beamed. 'Thank you. That's just what I needed to hear.'

Curiously, Bree said, 'If you don't mind me asking, what's this about?'

'It's difficult, cos there are some things that I can't say but let's put it like this. The people I thought were me friends have proper mugged me off.'

'Has this got something to do with why you're staying here?'

'Kind of. But like I said on the phone Bree, I'd appreciate it if you wouldn't tell anybody I was here.'

'Like who?'

He winked at her, saying nothing but knowing it felt good to talk.'

'Can I ask you another question then?'

'Anything. Well, you can, but I might not answer.'

Bree, feeling her heart race, thought again about Ryan. Thought again how she needed to feel nothing for Alfie and yet she did. It felt so good to talk to him, to be in his presence. But she needed to think not about that, but how much Alfie was her enemy. *Ryan's* enemy. 'Do you trust her, Alf? Do you trust, Sandra, because if you need to ask me, it's like you're having doubts about your own sister.'

'It sounds terrible Bree, but I don't know anymore. I don't know who to trust. And I know that sounds fucked up, but it's true.'

'You can trust me.'

Quietly, Alfie said, 'Can I?'

'Of course. You can tell me anything you want. We go back such a long way Alfie, and we went through such a lot, it's like you . . .' She stopped to take a breath. He was her enemy, that's all he was. That's what she had to keep saying to herself. '. . . It's like you were the family I never had back then. You saved me, and I loved you.'

Not for the first time in the last twenty-four hours Alfie Jennings choked up. He smiled so warmly, Bree had to look away. 'You soppy cow, you'll have me welling up, but whilst we're putting it out there, well, it broke my heart when they took you away. But look at you now, you're beautiful both inside and out.'

She shook her head. 'No, I'm not.'

'You are and don't let anyone tell you different.' He got up and walked over to her, then kneeled down in front of her as she sat on the bed. 'You really are special Bree, you always were.'

She smiled, thinking about her mantra: the enemy. The enemy. That's all he is. 'You're special too, Alf.'

As she sat there, he looked up at her with his warm blue eyes and kissed her so gently on her lips it seemed electric. He felt her body through her dress as he caressed her back then he reached up and started kissing the nape of her neck. Undoing her top, Alfie bent over, slipping off the rest of her clothes.

He smiled, lifting her naked body up the bed, watching her as she smiled back at him. Laying her against the pillows he kissed her, letting himself savour the moment. He closed his eyes, his mind thinking about nothing but Bree.

'Alfie . . .'

Her voice broke into his thoughts. He looked down at her tenderly.

'You alright?'

'I just . . . I want to take it slowly, I . . .'

Resting on his elbow, he reached across, playing and stroking her hair. His naked body still hard against hers. 'Bree, you know we don't have to do this if you ain't ready.'

'I want to, it's just . . .' She trailed off, picturing Ryan, feeling so much love in her heart for him, but a long time ago she'd given up thinking that they'd ever be physically intimate again, so why did she feel like she was cheating on him when she never did when Johnny forced her – as he did every night – to sleep with him? Perhaps, just perhaps, it was because being with Alfie, being next to his body, felt so good.

'I'm sorry, Bree.'

She touched his face. 'Don't apologise, you ain't done nothing wrong. The gentleman as always.'

Alfie pulled a face. 'I don't know about that, and I don't know if many people would agree with you either.'

'Then they don't know you.'

'Maybe it's *you* that don't know me. You only see this side of me, there's a lot more and it ain't good. I've done things I ain't proud of and I still do.'

'Like what?'

'Things.'

Bree sat up, turning on her side to look at Alfie. 'No, go on, I'm interested. You keep saying all this stuff and you say you trust me, so I hope you know I won't judge, but I've no idea what it is you do exactly.'

Alfie gave a crooked smile. He traced his finger along her face, pushing her long hair behind her ears. It was so good to talk to her. In fact, it was so good to talk to anybody that wasn't somehow connected to the business. So good not to worry. Refreshing didn't even come close. He grinned at her, his tone turning playful. 'If I tell you, and you repeat anything I say, you know I'll have to kill you.'

Bree grinned back. She leant over to give Alfie a quick kiss on the lips.

'Then I'll just have to make sure I keep me mouth shut, won't I?'

He kissed her back. 'I guess you will . . . So let's see if you think I'm still a gentleman after I tell you *exactly* what I do. I'll bet you'll be running for that door.'

'Try me.'

'There's this job, right, and it involves a whole heap of diamonds . . .'

And as Alfie Jennings told Bree all about Eddie, the lorry, the diamonds, his fears and his suspicions, Bree asked questions, nodded at the right places and made a mental note of everything. And when he'd finished Alfie looked at her and said, 'So, that's it really. We're meeting Perry next Tuesday. Can you believe the geezer wants us to do the drop off on the beach on Mersea Island at the dead of night? I reckon he thinks he's in *Pirates of the Caribbean*. Mug. Anyway, there you have it. My life in a nutshell. What do you think. Still think I'm the gentleman?'

She smiled, her heart breaking. 'I think you'll never really know what it means that you trusted me enough to tell me everything. Thank you . . . And Alfie?'

He looked at her softly. 'Yeah?'

'Kiss me.'

'What?'

'Kiss me. I know I said I wanted to take it slowly, but . . .'

'Are you sure?'

'Yeah.'

And as Alfie began to kiss Bree, his strong, muscular body hard on top of hers, she closed her eyes, knowing this may well be the last time she saw him alive.

56

Bree didn't know how long she and Ryan had been running through the woods, but she was tired and it was clear Ryan didn't understand why they needed to keep on going. The morphine didn't seem to be working and the pain in her abdomen was getting worse.

They were soaking wet and she could see Ryan was cold and anxious, but there was no other way. They had to get away.

'Ryan, it'll be alright. Let's just go a little further. We might be able to find somewhere to hide.'

He gazed at her blankly, his face so worried and so unsure. Bree was about to say something else when she felt a pain she'd never experienced before shoot through her. The agony of it sent her stumbling forward and she fell, slipping and sliding down the muddy track. As she tried to stop her fall, her foot got caught, spinning and twisting her round, sending her crashing down on her back. She screamed out, turning her head to bury it into the wet ground, wanting to mute her cries. She felt a sudden warmth between her legs and in the moonlight she could just make out the blood on her dress. She was bleeding.

'Bree! Bree! Come out, come out, wherever you are! Ryan! Ryan! Answer me, Ryan!'

Getting up, she slammed her hand across Ryan's mouth who

looked terrified and confused. She shook her head, speaking softly to him. 'Don't say a word. Don't say a word.'

Carefully she took her hand off Ryan's mouth. Bree, hardly able to walk from the pain, led Ryan towards the hill, each step she took hurting.

'Ryan, don't cry. We'll walk a little bit further and then we'll rest. I promise we'll rest.'

As they stumbled through the woods, Bree could hear the sound of Johnny's voice coming nearer.

'Where you going Bree? There ain't nowhere to run. Why are you making it harder on yourself, Bree? Come back, we're going to find you anyway. Bree! And Ryan, you can't take Ryan, you know that, Bree! He ain't yours anymore. He's ours. Ryan belongs to us.'

They needed to move faster, she could hear the dogs. They didn't have long.

'Come on Ryan, come on!'

The panic began to rise as the pains became worse. It was almost as if she couldn't breathe. The agony holding her, slowing her down, making her not want to move and she didn't know how long she could bear it.

The velvet darkness surrounded them as the storm picked up and Bree tried to smile. 'Ryan, hold my hand. Keep holding my hand.'

'I want to go. I want to go. I want to go.'

'Shhh, Ryan, quiet.'

Seeing some bushes up ahead, Bree decided it might be a good hiding place and gently pushed Ryan, guiding him underneath the large rhododendron bush.

She cradled him close, squeezing his arm, feeling the guilt of what she'd caused as she listened to the dogs. Then an awful thought crossed her mind. The blood. The dogs would smell the blood if she didn't cover it up.

'Stay here, Ryan. I'll be back soon.'

Crawling out into the moonlight Bree saw the trail of blood and as the rain poured and the wind crept up she saw them. They were coming. Johnny was less than ten metres away.

Trying to manoeuvre slowly backwards, the wave of pain hit Bree again. She bit into her sleeve, trying to stop herself crying out. But the pain was too much and she heard herself scream.

And as Johnny heard her cries, he turned and smiled, dark eyes staring coldly at her.

'Bunny ears, bunny ears, playing by the tree, bunny ears, bunny ears, trying to catch Bree . . . Hello Bree, I told you I'd find you. We've got a lot to talk about, don't you think?'

With the pain ripping through her, her hands and knees sunk into the wet earth as Bree crawled forward towards Johnny's feet, her blood mixing in the mud.

'Help me. The baby. I'm bleeding. The baby's coming.'

'If you want me to help you, then you need to say please, and promise me that you and Ryan will never leave Johnny again.'

'Please Johnny . . . please, just help me.'

'Say it!'

Barely able to utter the words, Bree whispered. '. . . I promise . . . I promise I'll never leave Johnny again.'

And with that, Bree blacked out.

57

'Well? What's it going to be? Good news or bad?' Johnny Dwyer stared at Bree as she sipped her tea in the kitchen of the mobile home. It was spotless as always, and the smell of bleach sat heavily in the air. The Swarovski crystal handles on the cupboards glistened in the late afternoon sun.

'Alfie told me everything,' Bree said flatly. 'I've got all the details. He's staying in a bed and breakfast near Southend. Seems like he's had a falling-out with the others. Anyway, I was going to call you on the way back, but I thought it was best to wait to tell you in person.'

'Ma! Ma!' Johnny shouted through the window. A moment later the door of Ma's caravan opened. She stood, frowning, her cream and coral polyester nightie clinging to every bulbous curve.

'What are you shouting about? Fucking hell, what's happened now? I tell you, if it's Ryan and those bleedin' kittens of his, if he's still letting them piss everywhere, then I'm sick of it. Just give him a good hiding and be done with it.'

'Shut up Ma, and come here, I got some news.'

Waddling over in her slippers as the sun seeped through the clouds, Ma walked into Johnny's and Bree's home, muttering to herself as she ambled down the hallway.

Standing in the doorway, wheezing, she shrugged. 'Well what is it son? Where's the fire? And this better be worth it.'

'Oh, it is! Guess what, Bree's done good. She's got it out of Alfie. We're on.'

Ma turned to look at Bree. Her stare cold and nasty. 'Is that right?'

Bree glanced down at the floor, Ma's gaze making her feel uncomfortable. 'It is.'

Ma sniffed, running her finger along the worktops checking for dust. 'And what did you have to do Bree? What did Little Miss Muffet have to do for three million pounds' worth of shiny diamonds?'

'Sorry?'

'Don't give me the innocent virgin act, it don't suit you. Especially as I know how you seduced my boys. I watched you, remember?'

Bree's head shot up and she frowned, shaking her head. 'That's not true, you know it's not.'

'I see sleeping with Alfie has given you some lip.'

'I didn't sleep with him, Ma,' Bree said, lying.

'Oh, come on. I can smell him on you . . . You like him, don't you? I can see it.'

Vehemently, Bree shook her head. 'That didn't even come into it.'

Ma stepped towards Bree, her underarm hair long and wet from sweat. 'You can't fool me, I'm a woman. I know these things.'

'Well you're wrong, Ma. I just did what Johnny asked me to do.'

Ma's hand shot out quickly, slapping Bree hard across the face. 'Don't speak to me like that.'

'Leave her alone, Ma.'

Whirling around to stare at Johnny, Ma spoke, a cruel tone layered in her words. 'Son, I'm just looking out for you. You'd be a fool to trust her. But then, you've always been a fool when it comes to her, ain't you? Even when Ryan had her, you wanted her. Sent you crazy. You couldn't stand to see him with her, nearly drove you insane. Problem is you've never known how to keep her.'

Ma laughed nastily as Johnny raged, his head beginning to hurt.

'Just shut it Ma, shut it! You should be happy, celebrating. Alfie Jennings is on his last supper but instead you do this! You can't help yourself can you? Bree got what we wanted, so drop it.'

'Yeah but Johnny, what did she have to do? What did she do? Go on, ask her if you dare. Ask her what she did with Alfie.'

Like a child, Johnny put his hands over his ears. 'Why you doing this? Why you doing this to me? I don't wanna hear it! Just shut up or get out!'

Ma stared at Johnny, then at Bree. She snarled at her son. 'Is that how it is? You're siding with this slut over me. Your own ma. Don't you love me no more, Johnny?'

'Stop!'

'Then tell me you love me.'

Johnny rubbed his eyes, the noise getting louder in his head. 'I said *stop*!'

Ma's eyes were wide and intense. Loose fatty skin hung down from her pale white open arms. 'Just show me then. Show me you love me. Come on son, give your Ma a hug.'

He shook his head.

'I said, come on!'

Kicking the table over, Johnny clattered out the room, shouting as he slammed open the front door. 'No more, Ma, no more!'

Eddie Styler grinned as he pressed the phone to his ear. The news couldn't be better. Things were certainly looking up.

'Johnny that's sweet. Your missus did well. Alfie and Vaughn, or rather Tweedle Dum and Tweedle Dee, won't know what's hit them. But it's best if I come around to yours and discuss details, I'm a little bit, how shall I put it . . .' He stopped and turned around to throw a roll of toilet paper at Sandra who sat, knickers around her ankles, on the lavatory, glaring at him.

'. . . occupied. I've got me hands full a bit here. It's a little bit awkward . . . Okay . . . yeah great. I'll see you then.'

As Eddie put down the phone he immediately dialled a number. It rang for a moment before a deep voice answered. 'Yes?'

'Jason, it's Eddie.'

'I know who it is.'

'Well I was just phoning to tell you that we're finally on with the stones, so it looks like it's only a matter of days until you get your money. I'll let you know all the details soon.'

As Eddie put the phone down on Jason Robinson, he stared at Sandra, gesturing her out of the bathroom with his gun. He smiled. His plan was working out better than even he could've imagined and soon – very, very soon – he'd be lying on a beach in the sun.

Sandra Styler paced around in the darkness of the basement. She'd got used to it. In fact, if she were to be honest with herself, under different circumstances she wouldn't mind it at all. The one thing she hadn't been keen on was the bucket in the corner Eddie had tried insisting that she used, but eventually, after loud protestations, he'd succumbed and allowed her to go to the downstairs bathroom under his strict supervision; watching her and making sure she didn't make any moves.

The chronic pains she'd suffered from the blow to her head had ceased and now the only things left were a few bruises and of course, the burning, simmering hatred for Eddie, which rose above everything else – above the darkness, above her own anxiety, above the pain, blocking any other thought than revenge.

And as she paced around the room in the darkness, sitting bitterly in her heart, Sandra could taste it, the retribution that would eventually come to him. But first, she needed to think of a way to contact Alfie. She needed to warn him against Bree, and once she had done that, once she was free, then Edward Robert Albert Styler would have it coming, boy would he just, and she would enjoy every last moment of it.

58

Bree opened her eyes and for a moment she wasn't quite sure where she was. Her mind was hazy; she didn't recognise the room she lay in. And then it hit her. In one suffocating wave it came flooding back to her. The woods, Ryan, the pain. Her baby . . .

Quickly she sat up, looking down at her stomach.

'Hello Bree, finally, Little Miss Muffet's decided to wake up.'

Bree jumped, panic suddenly setting in as she realised Ma was in the room. 'Oh my God, what's happened? What's happened? The baby, Ma! The baby!'

'I'd calm down if I was you, Bree.'

Bree screamed. 'Not until you tell me what's happened!'

Ma leapt up, moving surprisingly quickly for her overweight frame. She flew at Bree, grabbing her shoulders, shaking her hard. 'I said calm down! Calm down!'

Bree continued to cry and savagely, Ma raised her hand, striking her across her face leaving a raised red welt. 'Shut up! Shut up! I told you to shut up!'

As Ma shook her, Bree's head whipped back and forth, her desperation palpable. 'I'm sorry, I'm sorry, just tell me what happened, please.'

Releasing her grip slightly, Ma stared at Bree. 'You gave birth Bree, but it's all fine.'

'What? What are you talking about?'

'You gave birth shortly after Johnny carried you back from the woods. But me and Johnny think it'd probably be best if someone else, someone more stable, took over your role for the time being.'

'I don't understand. What do you mean, take over my role?'

'As a mother, Bree. You're in no fit state to be a mother. Look at you. You're a mess. You can't even look after yourself. We've got family in Ireland, good people who'll be better at caring than you.'

Bree, almost hysterical, screamed at Ma. 'No! No! You can't do that. It's not your child!'

'Like I say it's for the best. I've got me hands full looking after Ryan, let alone becoming some kind of nursemaid.'

Defiantly, Bree said, 'I want my baby. I'll go to the police . . .'

Ma's laugh was cruel and filled the room. 'Oh Bree, who are you kidding? But if that's what you want to do darlin', go ahead, be my guest. But let me warn you, you'll never have any chance of becoming a mother, not with that lot anyway. Police and social services will take one look at you and see you for what you are. You're unfit to be a mother, Bree. You ain't got no home, no money and no job. And to top it off Bree, you didn't even go to get a check-up when you were pregnant, what mother does that? Not one that cares. You're also an addict.'

And suddenly it all came flooding back to Bree. The bottle she'd found. The morphine. She stared in horror at Ma. 'You . . . you fed me morphine. This is all because of you.'

Bree broke down crying. She screamed. 'Why would you do this to me? What did I ever do to you, Ma? What?'

Ma, sitting heavily on the pink cotton sheet covering the bed, looked at Bree nastily, her tone full of malice. 'If only you'd listened to me when I told you to, none of this would've happened. You were the one who got yourself into this situation.'

'I want my baby!'

'All in good time Bree, when you're well. When you know what's good for you. When you learn to listen.'

Bree scrunched up the sheets in her hand, clinging on to them as she rocked back and forth. 'You can't do this! You can't do this!'

'Take this. Drink this, it will make you feel better. Calm you down a bit.'

Bree hit out, knocking the drink out of Ma's hand. 'I don't want it! I don't want it!'

Coldly, Ma said, 'You might not want it, but that don't mean you don't need it. Give it an hour and you'll be begging me for it. Climbing those walls.'

Bree covered her face, huge tears running down her cheeks.

'Why, Ma? Why? Why did you do it to me?'

'I've already told you. Nobody leaves Ma.'

Ma turned her head slightly, shouting over her shoulder. 'Johnny! Johnny! Come in here! Our sleeping beauty's finally woken up and talking.'

A few seconds later, Johnny Dwyer appeared at the door looking tall and handsome, his Romany features darkening as he stared at Bree. 'Hello Bree, thought you'd never wake up properly. It was a job to feed and bathe you, you were so far gone. Ain't that right, Ma?'

Ma grinned. 'It was and now she's all yours, Johnny. Your reward.'

Bree glanced at Ma, then at Johnny. Her eyes filled with tears. 'Please, what are you talking about?'

Emotionless, Ma stared back. 'Shut up and listen. This is how it's going to go. You're going to stay here and be with Johnny . . .'

'. . . What! No!'

Ma leant across to Bree, putting her fat, nail-bitten finger on her lips. 'If you know what's good for you, I'd listen. You'll be with Johnny now.'

'I won't! I won't do it!

Ma spoke coldly. 'It's up to you, Bree. Leave here if that's what you want, but I can't promise you'll ever get your family back from Ireland if you do. And it's no good reporting it either, the birth was never registered, and you never went to the doctor, so there's nobody apart from us who knew you were pregnant. And if you do leave here and decide not to be with Johnny, then the thing is, I can't promise I'll be able to keep Ryan safe. I can't promise we ain't going to hurt him.'

Bree shook her head, horrified. 'Please, no!'

Ma shrugged. 'It's your choice. And don't worry, once you learn to stay here without complaint and do exactly as you're told, we'll even help to wean you off that stuff. We're here for you Bree . . . Ma's always here for you. But in the meantime . . .' She stopped to chuckle at her own joke. '. . . Here's Johnny!'

At that point, Ma Dwyer got up and left the room and Johnny slowly began to undo his belt.

59

It was three in the morning and Alfie couldn't sleep. He hadn't been able to sleep properly since the day he saw Bree. He was restless and his mind wasn't on the upcoming deal, which he knew could be dangerous because although he trusted Perry, well as far as anyone trusted anyone in the game they were in, he realised he had to be on the ball, especially as the whole of Essex seemed to be wanting to put their hands on the rocks. The whole of the South East even, and the Med too. And right now, he was so far from being on the ball, it was untrue. He needed to concentrate.

The problem was how, though? How could he focus and push Bree aside in his mind, because it wasn't happening, no matter how much he tried, how much he thought of the diamonds. Although he'd rather not, he needed to make plans, he needed to speak to Vaughn and Frankie about the handover with Perry before it went down, and – much as it was on his mind that he was still no closer to contacting Sandra – the fact was he just didn't care about any of it *enough*.

All he could think of was Bree and the hours they'd spent together. He could still smell her perfume on the pillows and he could still remember how she'd felt, and damn it, he wanted her again so badly it actually hurt.

In the darkness his phone beeped loudly, vibrating furiously and causing the packet of gum on the bedside table to jump and dance around in circles. Pulling himself slowly away from his thoughts, Alfie rolled onto his side. He reached across, picking up his phone to look at the text. It was from Bree.

You there Alfie? It's Bree by the way.

Alfie smiled, feeling a rush in his stomach and it didn't escape his notice that the last time he'd felt so connected, so consumed by a woman was when he was with Franny. It also didn't escape his notice that when he thought of Franny now, it wasn't like someone had punched him in the stomach, in fact he didn't really picture her at all. She'd made it clear from what she'd done that she didn't want to know, so the only thing he wanted from Franny now was his money.

Flicking on the light, Alfie lay back on his pillow, reread the text, thought for a moment and then replied.

I know who it is, silly! You ok? It's good to hear from you, but what are you doing awake at this time of night? It's late!!!!

I could ask you the same question!

I asked first!

Stuff on my mind.

Want to share?

Oh, it's nothing. Just sometimes my mind races overtime.

I hate it when that happens, my mind does that all the time, sometimes I wake up and I still think I'm married to Janine. Thank yourself lucky you don't have that, you'd never sleep again . . . But seriously, are you sure you're ok though?

Yeah, I'm fine. You? You still got that job lined up for next week?

Yeah and yeah.

That's great. I'm pleased for you. So how about you take me out to dinner afterwards? We can celebrate your success. We'll go Dutch though!

I'd love to take you out to dinner but no chance on going Dutch, I've never let a lady pay. Not now. Not ever. Call me old fashioned!

Who says I'm a lady ;)

Alfie read and reread the last text and closed his eyes, resting the phone by his side; trying not to let his mind drift to what she might mean; trying not to let his mind get lost in his desires; and trying desperately not to picture her perfect, naked body. He exhaled once, twice, wanting to be a gentleman. Finally, he wrote back.

Been thinking of you by the way . . .

All good I hope!!!

Ha maybe! So, you fancy going out after I've sorted this job?

That would be nice . . . I'd like that.

Ok, it's a date????

Yes. I'm looking forward to it.

Me too Bree. I'll call you soon.

Ok . . . Night night xxx

Night night xxx

Bree put the phone on the table. She looked up at Eddie, Ma and Johnny who sat opposite her in the kitchen of their mobile home. It was Johnny who spoke first.

'Well, Bree?'

She looked down at her phone, feeling the warmth in the messages Alfie had sent her and hating herself she whispered, 'It looks like the job's still on. The deal's still going ahead.'

60

Vaughn looked at Alfie. There was something different about him today. Something he couldn't quite put his finger on. He seemed distracted, subdued, like his mind was on something else. But perhaps that was just because Alfie hadn't wanted to come to meet him and Frankie. Perhaps he was just annoyed that they hadn't given him any choice. Or perhaps Alfie was having second thoughts about going into business with him, looking for a way out.

Who knew, maybe even after everything Franny had done, Alfie missed her, like he missed Casey. The problem was neither of them spoke about their feelings. Even thinking about feelings made him feel stupid. All of them had been brought up to be hard men, tough men, men that don't cry. And although he had no desire to start bringing out the Kleenex, and he was still angry with Alfie, it would have been nice on occasion over the years to have known that they could talk and make sure one another was alright.

Throwing down a large submachine gun on the bed in the B&B, Vaughn nodded to Frankie. 'You think we got enough here? It ain't as easy as it once was to get cheap, untraceable guns. I had to pull out all the stops with old acquaintances who weren't so keen to give them up. I hope there ain't any nasty surprises with Perry.'

Frankie picked up one of the Uzis that lay on the bed with the pile of other semi-automatic weapons. 'Yeah, I think this will sort us. I'm not seeing any problem with Perry. It's the rest of them that I worry about. But the drop-off is at the perfect place, and Perry says he's kept it under the radar, so he ain't been blabbing. It's still hush-hush. So, we don't have to go overboard, these will do just as a precaution.'

Janine, spitting on one of the guns and then wiping a smudge off, spoke over her shoulder to Frankie. 'Precaution is putting a condom on your dick when you sleep with some Tom. Sorry Lola, no offence . . .'

Lola was eating a bowl of cereal and shrugged. 'None taken.'

'. . . Not a bed full of guns.'

Frankie frowned, taking the gun back from Janine. 'You're a bit handy with that, girl. It's loaded you know, and what you doing spitting all over it, you dozy mare? You got your DNA on it now! Bleedin' hell. Rein her in, Alfie.'

Janine picked a honey puff out of Lola's bowl and scowled. 'Listen Frank, I don't know who you think you are but let me tell you, I can whip out ammunition and clean a weapon quicker than I can get me knickers off.'

'And believe me Frank, that ain't a sight you want to see,' Alfie said with a raised eyebrow. 'It's like seeing Medusa's fucking head. The sight of Janine with her Alan Whickers round her ankles will turn you to stone.'

Not impressed, Janine glared at Alfie as she bit into a strawberry jam waffle. 'You're the fucking comedian today, ain't you? What's wrong with you anyway? You licking your wounds now you've had to do a U-turn after your dramatic exit?'

'Only a mug would go and meet Perry without sorting out the last bits and pieces, and I ain't a mug.'

Cuttingly, Janine said, 'So how is Sandra?'

Not wanting to divulge to any of those assembled that he still hadn't been able to contact her, Alfie gave Janine a tight smile.

'She's great. Sends her love to everyone. She's been away. Decided to take a trip down to Devon to see one of her pals. Satisfied?'

Janine turned her head to one side, staring at Alfie as he stared back, playing his best poker face. 'I think you're hiding something Alf?'

Alfie sighed. 'Think what you like Jan, you always do. But in the meantime, let's finish up here. I need to get off in a minute . . . So, Frank, Vaughn, we're all agreed we'll meet at the Peldon Rose pub on Mersea Road? We'll just take one car across to the island, and we'll leave mine around the corner from the pub. There's a cul-de-sac which ain't got no CCTV. It's perfect. We should be able to do the drop-off and get back within three hours. It should run like clockwork.'

Vaughn gave a wry smile. 'The last time you said that Alfie, we all ended getting banged up.'

As Alfie headed for the door, he shrugged. 'What can I say? This time I feel lucky. I'll see you Tuesday.'

As Alfie walked down the landing of the B&B, Vaughn rushed after him.

'Alf, wait. Listen up! Are you alright mate? Look, I know we ain't been seeing eye to eye and we've got a lot to sort out, and I ain't saying I'm not still pissed off with you, but you seem a bit distracted. And now of all times, we've got to be on the ball.'

'I'm sweet as.'

'Are you sure? I know we haven't been close and the stress of everything has driven a bit of a wedge between us. But you know you can talk to me, right?'

Alfie, still annoyed with Vaughn, stared at him as if he'd just grown two heads. 'Hold on, did I just hear right?'

Straight-faced, Vaughn said, 'Look, men need to talk too.'

Alfie placed his hand on Vaughn's shoulder, a small smile at the corner of his mouth.

'I don't know if you've been reading them magazines Janine

and Lola left lying around or what, but you need to put them down and step away if you have. You're going stir crazy in there with them two. If anybody needs to talk, it's you. To yourself. Look in the mirror mate and have a word.'

Alfie turned to walk away but then said, 'But it's all going to be fine. Stop worrying.'

Irritated by Alfie's knock-back, Vaughn said, 'I've known you a long time Alf, and I know there's something you ain't telling us. Can't help worrying because we can't afford for this to go wrong. None of us can. I don't want to pick up any more pieces.'

Alfie tried to hide his smile as he thought about Bree. 'Vaughnie, listen to me. Stop. I'm fine. It's fine. In fact, things haven't been this fine for a long time.'

Bree sat by the toilet, throwing several pieces of tissue paper into the bowl before covering her mouth with a towel in the small but pretty bathroom, trying desperately to mute the sound of her vomiting travelling through the whole of the mobile home.

Nerves always made her ill, and every time she thought of Alfie it made her feel sick. She took a sharp intake of breath, trembling as she drew herself up to the basin. What was she doing? How had it even come to this? When was the moment she'd become like this? Was it Monday? Was it Tuesday? Was it last week? Last year? When had the door been closed and locked on her escape? How was she supposed to look at herself when she hated what she saw? And how could she live with herself when she was going to do this to Alfie?

She stared at herself in the mirror before suddenly picking up the hairbrush on the side, smashing it into the glass, over and over again.

'What's going on in there? What's that noise?'

Bree jumped, forgetting Ma was in the lounge. She shouted through the bathroom door, leaning the weight of her head against the cabinet as tears rolled down her face.

'Sorry, I closed the bathroom cabinet too quickly, the mirror's broken!'

'Well make sure you clean it up. I swear to you Bree, if I get a piece of glass stuck in me foot, you won't know what's coming, lady!'

Bending down to pick the pieces of mirror out of the basin, Bree saw the small drops of blood. She touched her forehead feeling the tiny grains of glass that had got stuck in her skin. She hadn't even noticed the pain.

Washing her face carefully, the water mixing with her tears, Bree heard Kieran outside the window, shouting to Ma.

'I'm going up to the woods.'

'Well make sure you're back before tea, Kieran. And put a jacket on, this ain't the Costa del Sol.'

'It's fine, I won't be long.'

'Suit yourself, but don't come complaining to me if you get cold. Off you go then, have some fun.'

Quickly, Bree ran out of the bathroom, not bothering to dry her face. She wanted to see where Kieran was going. He'd been so secretive and withdrawn and it'd only got worse since the day Molly had fallen in the river.

She'd tried to talk to him about Molly, about what she'd said about him hurting her. But each time she'd tried, he'd lashed out or clammed up, or Ma or Johnny had been about. But whatever it was, whatever was troubling Kieran, she was determined to get to the bottom of it.

Running through the fields, Bree found herself having to duck down by the hedges and fences, by the bushes and streams, as Kieran constantly stopped to look around, checking nobody was following.

She watched him as he got to the woods on the hill, and for a moment she thought he'd spotted her as he stared intently in her direction, but an instant later he turned, continuing to run through the copse.

Coming out of her hiding place, Bree cautiously began to follow.

'Bree!'

Startled, she stepped back. 'Ryan! You gave me a fright! What are you doing?'

'Kittens. My kittens. Can't find them.'

She smiled at Ryan, but she was distracted and her eyes flitted and darted towards where Kieran was going. 'Ryan, why don't you go home. I've got to do something. Go on.'

'No. I want my kittens.'

'You've lost them again? Oh Ryan, what am I going to do with you?'

'Hit me.'

Bree flinched, knowing exactly who those words had come from. 'No Ryan, that's not me. I'll never hit you ever. You know that, don't you?'

She sighed as she saw Kieran disappear out of view. She wanted to follow, to find out why it was Molly had become so frightened of him, but she wasn't going to leave Ryan. So, giving one last glance towards the woods, Bree took hold of Ryan's hand and kissed him gently on his face.

'It seems like I ain't been on me own with you for ages. I've missed you.'

His face lit up. 'Missed you.'

'You're funny, Ryan and I love you.' She giggled, but the moment was bitter sweet.

'I love you.'

She took a deep breath, looking deep into Ryan's eyes. 'Are you okay? Sometimes I just don't know.'

Ryan stared at her without saying a word then watched a bird pick up a twig before flying away.

Bree squeezed his hand. 'That will be us one day, Ryan. We'll get away and we'll be as free as that bird. You and me.'

He nodded, 'You and me, Bree.'

Her smile light up her eyes. 'That's right, Ryan, you and me, like we once planned. Remember? But I promise you, I promise I'll figure out a way of getting us out of here.'

He stared at her again and Bree could see he hadn't understood everything she'd said. But that didn't matter, because today was a good day for him. For her. When he spoke, when he interacted independently, it was more than she'd ever thought she'd get, because there'd been many dark days, dark weeks, when the only thing she'd got from Ryan were grunts and sounds with no light in his eyes at all.

She led him to the large pine tree where years ago they'd carved their names, and sitting down she smiled. 'What am I going to do, Ryan? It's all a mess. It's all falling apart. I wish you could help me. Tell me what to do.'

'What to do.'

'Exactly, what to do. What am I supposed to do, Ryan? I can't do it, I can't hurt Alfie.'

'Can't hurt Alfie.'

'I know but then I can't let them do anything to you, baby. But this isn't me. It's not who I am. It's not.'

Ryan gazed blankly, repeating her words. 'It's not.'

She squeezed his hand again, feeling so much love towards him. 'Do you think I should tell Alfie?'

'Tell Alfie.'

'Really?'

'Really.'

She shook her head, looking down at the moss as she played with some stones. 'But what happens if Johnny finds out. I don't care what he does to me, but you, I don't want him to do anything to you.'

'I don't want him to do anything to you.'

Bree leaned her head on Ryan's shoulder and closed her eyes. 'You're so sweet, thank you for caring. So, you think I should tell Alfie, yes?'

'Yes.'

'I'll do it, I'll do it somehow.'

'Do it, somehow.'

She reached out and gave him a hug. 'Thank you, Ryan, thank you for helping me. I knew I could rely on you . . . Now, come on, let's go and find those kittens of yours before it gets dark.'

61

Eddie Styler could hardly contain himself. Everything was set up and was going just how he imagined it to be. And if all went well, then this time tomorrow he would be on a train and it'd be goodbye Essex, hello new and successful life.

'What are you looking so pleased about?'

Eddie scowled at Sandra who, after five minutes, was still sitting on the toilet.

'If you must know Sand, I'm thinking about me life.'

'You're life's a joke. Ain't worth putting in the bin let alone thinking about.'

The scornful laughter that came from Sandra almost dampened his good mood. Almost. But instead he stared at her evenly.

'I don't know what you're laughing about Sandra, because if anybody's life's a joke, it's yours. It may not have occurred to you, but you've been locked up here for some time now, and I don't see anyone coming to your rescue, do you? I mean I don't see mates or relatives coming to see what's happened. Worrying about your whereabouts. Even Barrie the bleedin' cat has pissed off.'

Sandra's face dropped. Far from it not occurring to her, it'd played on her mind constantly when she'd been working out who would actually miss her and who it was who'd actually come looking.

She didn't have a job, so she had no boss or work colleagues to wonder where she was, and most of her friends were actually only afternoon coffee and manicure-on-the-high-street acquaintances. Truth be told, she had a closer relationship with her hairdresser than her so-called friends, and it'd been a while since she'd bothered to get her roots done. The gardener had been dismissed due to money problems, as had their cleaner. So, who was left? Who would notice she was gone? The only person she could come up with was the nurse who'd insisted on making an appointment for her smear test, and she doubted that the gynae department at Basildon Hospital stretched to search and rescue. So that only left the one person who she couldn't bear to think had abandoned her, didn't care whether he heard from her or not. And that person was . . .

'Alfie. Alfie will have called, he'll be wondering where I am.'

Eddie pulled out Sandra's phone from his pocket. There were dozens of missed calls from Alfie. He shook his head. 'No, don't look like it.'

Trying to disguise her hurt, Sandra swallowed down her tears. 'You're lying, Eddie.'

He grinned, seeing the pain in her eyes. 'Perhaps he's calling a different number, cos he's certainly not calling this one.'

'I don't believe you.'

Eddie shrugged. 'If it makes you feel better to think that I ain't telling the truth, well fine. I'm lying. But face it Sandra, he don't give a shit about you. The only thing he cares about is them diamonds and, by all accounts, Johnny Dwyer's missus, Bree.'

'What?'

Sandra felt shocked. Everyone in the criminal world had heard of Johnny Dwyer, he was a thug, cold and dangerous. Certainly not right in the head, but she had no idea he had a wife, and certainly no idea that Bree was even connected to him. How? How did someone like Bree end up with someone like Johnny? She'd clearly changed because the Bree she'd known had been warm and kind, vulnerable, funny, beautiful and special. Not someone who would've gone within an inch of a person like Johnny Dwyer.

But then she guessed people changed and apart from realising Bree must have turned into one of the biggest bitches, she felt sick because she had a growing suspicion that Alfie, her brother whom she loved so much, could be in grave, grave danger, and she couldn't, she just couldn't lose another brother.

Seeing Sandra's concern, Eddie gloated. 'Oh, I might as well tell you, cos you'll find out soon enough. Your brother got well and truly mugged over by this bird Bree. She's a proper sort. Apparently, she knew Alfie back in the day, nobody knows how. I don't think Johnny asked her. You never knew her, did you?'

Sandra could hardly speak, and she just about managed to say, 'No.'

'Well anyway, your brother's been thinking with his dick and not his brains, turns out he gave her a whole heap of pillow talk. She found out all about the deal he's making with the diamonds. I'm not surprised he told her everything. Fucking hell, I don't blame him, I'd spill the beans too if I had Bree's lips around me cock. Anyway, Johnny got Bree to find out everything and now, what do you know, we're in the money.'

Eddie grinned as he watched Sandra blanch. He wished he'd be able to see Johnny do the same when he realised that he wasn't going to get any part of the diamonds. What he planned was going to be sweeter than he could've ever imagined.

62

It was early morning and Bree picked up her phone. She'd been trying to call Alfie for the best part of the night, but each time it'd gone straight to voicemail. She'd been afraid to leave a message for fear he'd call back, just in case Johnny picked up her phone, which he so often did. Answering it, checking it, getting itemised bills, making sure she didn't call anybody she shouldn't.

If Johnny knew or even suspected that she'd been trying to contact Alfie now that they'd got all the information they needed, he'd know immediately something was up. She had to be careful, really careful. She knew she only had one chance and both Ryan and Alfie's lives depended on her getting it right.

Sighing and trying to ignore the nausea that was bringing a sickly sweetness to her throat, Bree tried Alfie's phone again, but still there was no answer. Her nerves were playing havoc with her and she could feel herself trembling. Her legs were shaking so much it was causing her back to hurt.

Everything was such a mess. Though the one thing she was grateful for was that Kieran and Molly had gone to one of Ma's friends over in Wickford because there was no way she'd be able to pretend that everything was alright.

She had no idea what she was going to do. No idea at all. But she knew that time was running out. She had less than twelve hours – if that – to somehow get in contact and stop Alfie going through with the drop-off. That is, of course, if he'd listen. Because not only would she be admitting she'd lied to him, but she'd be asking him to throw away the two-million-pound deal he'd set up and he so badly needed.

Hearing Johnny come out of the bathroom, Bree quickly deleted her call log to Alfie before putting her phone away, stuffing it in the back pocket of her jeans.

She smiled as he came into the kitchen and looked at her suspiciously, frowning, her beauty riling him, taunting him, causing his jealousy to ignite as it so often did.

'Why you here? Where's Ma? What you doing in the kitchen anyway?'

Bree spoke softly, desperate not to inflame Johnny any more than he was. 'I don't feel so great. I was just getting some water.'

He walked up to her, stroking her face. His handsome features brooding as his hand slid down to clutch her throat. 'I love you Bree, you know that. I always have. Ryan never deserved you. I'm the one who looks after you.'

Her body went rigid as she pushed herself away from him, the curve of her spine pressing against the worktop. 'I know, I know you do, and . . . and I love you too.'

Johnny leaned in and almost nose to nose, he said, 'Do you?'

'I do.'

'Say it, let me hear you say it. Tell me you love Johnny?'

She looked at him, trying to hold his gaze, watching the vein on his temple pulsate. 'I do. I love Johnny. I always have.'

Letting go of her throat he continued to stare at her. Thoughts rushing through his mind, then a moment later, satisfied, he nodded, speaking quietly to her as he rubbed his temples from the noise in his head. 'Have you seen Ma? I need to go.'

'I think she's down by the chicken coop, well she was the last time I saw her.'

Getting a drink of water for himself, Johnny shouted at the top of his voice, 'Ma! Ma! I need to go. Ma!'

A few minutes later, Ma appeared, red-faced, waddling in with a blue plastic tub full of chicken eggs tucked under her arm. 'What's with all the hollering, son? I can hear you calling from the other side of the yard.'

'I'm going. I'll be back tomorrow. I want you to keep an eye on her. You hear me? Make sure she don't go anywhere. She's *my* wife, nobody else's.'

Lacking any force behind it, Ma slapped Johnny across his chest. 'What's wrong with you? You know you don't have to tell me that. You're the one who's too soft with her, not me. You're forgetting if it wasn't for me, Little Miss Muffet here might never have been yours. Remember that. Now get gone. Be safe, son.'

Without looking back, Johnny stalked out of the room leaving Bree with Ma, who sniffed, staring at Bree in disgust. 'Right, don't think because Johnny's gone that you can slack off round here. Johnny may be a soft touch, but I ain't. There's cleaning to be done and lunch and dinner to cook. There's beds to be made and there's a pile of ironing in my house that needs sorting.'

Ma turned on her heel without saying another word. She slammed the door closed and Bree stood listening to Ma's heavy footsteps crunch across the gravel yard to her own mobile home. And then there was silence apart from the dogs barking in the yard.

Pulling the net curtain back and checking Ma had really gone inside, Bree whipped out the phone again, punching in Alfie's number. 'Come on. Come on, answer. Please answer.' But it was as she feared; straight to voicemail.

Looking up at the clock, Bree knew she needed to think of something quick.

Ten minutes after Johnny had gone, Bree was still trying to contact Alfie. She'd even texted him to call her but she was no further forward in either speaking to him or coming up with an idea of what she was supposed to do now.

'Bree! Bree! Make me a cup of tea. Not too much milk and make sure you put sugar in!'

Answering Ma's boorish request, Bree called back, shouting out of the window to the other mobile home. 'Okay Ma, I won't be long.'

Quickly Bree filled up the kettle, getting a tea bag out of the jar before rushing over to the crockery cupboard, making sure she chose exactly the right cup for Ma.

Bringing the red and pink flower cup back across to the kettle, Bree suddenly froze, a thought hitting her. Standing motionless in the middle of the room her mind began to race and slowly, slowly, she turned around, tiptoeing softly back as if she was walking on glass, as if Ma could hear her every move.

She stopped, trying to push down the tension rising in her chest, taking a deep, long breath before she flung open the cupboard door to stare at what she'd just seen. And there it was on the top shelf. There at the back was perhaps her answer. A bottle of morphine Ma always liked to keep, just in case.

Ma had weaned her off the drug a long time ago – painfully and slowly – after she showed that she could be trusted not to run away, not to alert any of the authorities, not to do anything that might make them think she was planning to leave.

On the odd occasion over the years Ma and Johnny *had* given it to her again, forcing her to take it when they'd seen her as being defiant, being troublesome. The last time they'd made her take it was when Molly had fallen into the river. It'd knocked her out and when she'd woken up, in between her thighs had been covered in bruises, and as usual after waking up from the morphine, she had no memory of what had happened whilst she'd been unconscious.

And in truth the *defiance*, the *trouble*, had only been when she'd broken down hysterically, begging for compassion, unable to cope anymore with the overbearing, violently oppressive situation in which she found herself imprisoned.

'Bree! Bree! Where's my bleedin' tea!'

'I'm coming, Ma! Kettle's just boiled.'

Grabbing the almost empty bottle, Bree took it over to the side, making sure she made the tea first in the way that Ma liked it. Then carefully she poured in the morphine sulphate.

There wasn't a lot left, but Bree knew what there was might do the trick, knocking Ma out for the vital hours she needed. She could put Ma to sleep without her knowing she was gone. Of course, it was a risk. She was terrified, and she would never think about doing anything like this if she wasn't desperate, mainly because there would never be anywhere far enough from Johnny for her to run.

But what else could she do? She knew Alfie would get there early and hopefully she'd be able to contact him sooner rather than later, and certainly before he went onto the island. But in the worst-case scenario, the very worst, Mersea Island wasn't so big, taking only half an hour to drive the whole way around.

But that was the last thing she wanted to do, to go on the island itself. She couldn't bump into Johnny, because if she did, it would be over for all of them.

Adding three heaped teaspoons of sugar – which disguised the taste of the morphine – and stirring the tea thoroughly, Bree walked it across to Ma, hoping what she was planning wasn't written all over her face.

Going into the lounge of Ma's mobile home, Bree smiled, trying to concentrate on stopping her hand from shaking too much. 'Here you are Ma, just as you like it.'

Ma glanced up at Bree as she sat slumped on the clear plastic cover of the blue leather sofa. Not bothering to say thank you, Ma grabbed the cup.

'Well go on then, what are you standing there for? Ain't you got jobs to do?'

'Sorry, I was just making sure your tea was okay and it had enough sugar in it.'

Keeping her eyes locked on Bree, Ma took a sip of her drink. She tasted it noisily before nodding, turning her attention back to the TV.

'I'll start on your ironing, Ma. I'll be in the kitchen if you need me.'

Standing in Ma's lilac and silver kitchen, Bree watched the clock. She could feel her breathing was shallow and tight; nerves were kicking in, making prickles of sweat drip down her back.

As long as Ma drank all her tea, it'd take fifteen to twenty minutes for the morphine to kick in, and once it did, she'd make her way down to Peldon, Colchester. It was early morning, so the traffic through Saffron Walden and beyond shouldn't be too bad, and if she got lucky the drive would take her no more than an hour tops.

One of the main problems was that she couldn't take her own car because Johnny always wrote down and had a record of her mileage, checking each time she used it that she hadn't gone further or where she wasn't supposed to. Which meant she'd have to take one of Johnny's or even Ma's cars.

It was chancy, and she'd have to make sure she drove carefully, no speeding tickets, no parking tickets, nothing that would come back and haunt her.

As she stood watching the minutes tick by, wanting to but resisting the temptation of checking on Ma, Bree suddenly thought of Ryan. She couldn't leave him on his own and she certainly couldn't take him.

Hurrying out of the kitchen, Bree made her way along the hallway of Ma's mobile home. Seeing that Ma was still awake, she called to her, wanting to reassure her that everything was as it should be.

'Ma, I'm just popping over to get something and I'll see if there's any more of your clothes over there which need ironing. I'll be back in a couple of minutes.'

Not waiting for a reply, Bree ran across the small gravel path to her own home, making her way to the kitchen. Quickly she grabbed the bottle of morphine again, pouring it into a glass, mixing it with Ryan's favourite strawberry squash.

Giving Ryan some morphine was the very last thing she wanted to do, but at least this way she'd know he'd be safe. Safely tucked up in bed without any chance of him getting up, needing food, needing some loving care.

Carefully putting the bottle back in the exact place Ma had left it, Bree hurried back across to Ma's.

Passing the lounge Ma shouted, her tone irritated. 'What have you got there?'

Bree froze, her heart beating quickly as she spoke from in the hallway. 'Nothing.'

'Ain't nothing, if you've got something in your hand. Come here!'

Bree attempted to dispel her rising panic. Hesitantly, she walked to the lounge, standing in the doorway. 'It's just juice, Ma. I was a bit thirsty.'

Ma gestured to her. 'Give it me. I could do with a cold drink.'

'What about your tea?'

'I don't want it.'

Bree stared at Ma, knowing that the amount she'd put in the drink for Ryan had been so much less than she'd put in the tea, and with Ma's obese weight it meant the sedative effects of the morphine would probably only knock her out for about three to four hours, nowhere near long enough for what she needed to do.

Trying not to panic, Bree began to stutter her words.

'But . . . but . . . but your tea, I made it nicely. Why don't you have that instead? It's a cold morning, a hot drink is always nice.'

'Shut up, Bree! What's wrong with you? Do I look like I don't know what I fucking want? Now just give me that bleedin' squash before I die of thirst.'

Bree's hand shook, there was a possibility that Ma would be

able to taste a slight residue in the squash or even smell it, although she hoped the strong scent of strawberry would hide the smell.

'I said, give it me!'

Deciding too late it was probably best to drop the glass on the floor, Ma grabbed it out of Bree's hand. She put it to her lips and began to drink it. Then stopped and screwed up her face. 'That's horrible. Taste it.'

Bree shook her head. 'No, it's okay. If it's not nice I won't bother.'

Ma wiggled forward, her sweaty thighs rubbing on the plastic sofa cover making a loud, noisy squeak.

'I've already told you, just because Johnny ain't here, don't meant that you can have an attitude. You understand, Little Miss Muffet?'

Bree gave a tiny nod.

'So, when I tell you to do something, you do it. Now go on, taste it.'

Pausing, panicking, Bree looked at Ma before putting the glass to her lips, letting only the smallest of drops into her mouth. 'I can see what you're saying, Ma. It ain't nice, I'll make you another one.'

Ma's eyes stared at her coldly. 'You never tasted it properly.'

'I did! It's not nice.'

'Drink some more.'

'What? No, I mean, I can see what you're saying Ma, I agree with you. I must've put too much squash in. The strawberry taste can be too much if you do that.'

'And you think it's alright just to waste stuff, do you? I don't see you paying your way around here, but you think it's still alright to waste other people's money just because something's not nice.'

Wanting to run, wanting to flee, Bree's legs trembled, threatening to give way. 'No of course not, I just don't like it that's all. I don't want it. I'm sorry, I haven't been feeling so great.'

'You made it, so you drink it. Then next time you'll know to make it properly, won't you?'

'No . . . I . . .'

Ma raised her voice. 'Drink it! Do as your told. Don't think you can waste my money.'

It was no good now to spill the contents of the glass on the floor, Ma would know she'd done it on purpose and it would only result in her being locked in her room and probably worse and that wouldn't help anyone, certainly not Alfie. So tightly, her voice filled with fear, Bree nodded. 'Okay . . . okay.'

She drank a mouthful. Then another. Then stopped.

'All of it!'

Without saying another word Bree finished off the glass, her thoughts racing as she did so.

Ma watched her, chuckling, then reached for the mug of tea, slurping it down in loud, large gulps. She burped, waving the empty mug at Bree. 'Take this, and next time don't put so much sugar in. Go on then, piss off.'

Bree turned, walking out quickly, heading for Ma's front door. She closed it quietly then began to run.

63

Bree leant over the toilet bowl, sticking her fingers down her throat, trying to vomit out the squash, but her stomach was empty so there was no food to bring up, making it difficult for her to retch the liquid. And with no breakfast inside her, Bree knew the morphine would start absorbing into her bloodstream straight away.

She was desperate, and the back of her throat was sore as her nails scraped at it, her body refusing to expel the drink. She wanted to scream, she wanted to cry, but it wasn't going to help and she needed to act fast before the drug began to kick in.

The small amount of the juice she'd been able to bring up wouldn't make a difference. The only chance, the only hope she had was her body over the years had become more tolerant of the morphine, making the dose she'd just drunk less effective.

Quickly she ran to the kitchen making another drink for Ryan, but this time she was going to hide it from Ma.

Emptying the bottle of distilled water she used for ironing, Bree did a quick swap for the medication before running back across to Ma's mobile home.

'Only me, Ma! Just going to get on with the ironing.'

Bree moved quietly down the hallway, going past the kitchen

and straight into Ryan's room. He was asleep, and the room was warm and silent, save the ticking of the cuckoo clock he loved.

She paused momentarily, smiling at how peaceful he looked, then moving quickly, she ran across to his bed. 'Ryan, Ryan, wake up, it's me. Bree.'

Ryan's eyes began to flutter before they opened wide. He stared at her and then she smiled.

'I need you to drink this, Ryan. Sit up.'

She helped him up as he looked at the bottle before he opened his mouth wide with Bree quickly putting it to his lips. As he drank it down she kissed him gently on his head.

'Now go back to sleep.'

Having made sure Ryan was settled, Bree quietly left the room. She passed the lounge, then paused, walking back a few paces.

'Ma?'

Ma Dwyer lay on the settee, her mouth gaped open as she snored loudly. Creeping in, Bree spoke again. 'Ma?'

There was no response and cautiously she reached out to shake her. 'Ma?'

Nothing. The morphine had worked.

Immediately, Bree turned and ran back across to her mobile home, charging into the kitchen where Johnny kept his car keys. Grabbing them, she spun round, dashing out, but suddenly her legs buckled as a wave of dizziness struck her. No, no, no. It couldn't be happening. She thought she might have longer. She had to get to the car, she had to get to Alfie. Whatever she did, somehow she had to be able to contact him. She had to tell herself she'd be fine. She'd be fine if she just got to the car, fine once the cold air hit her.

Using the walls to steady herself as the morphine overwhelmed her, Bree tried to fight the feeling, staggering to the car, fumbling with the key before getting in. She looked up at the morning moon, opened the window and began to drive.

* * *

The oncoming car headlights on the A120 strobed across Bree's face as she struggled and fought to keep her eyes open. Although it was early morning it was still dark, and the moon was still out. Bree tried to focus on keeping the car straight but the white central lines slipping by hypnotically only made her drowsiness worse.

Alfie had told her he was planning to get there early and she hoped that she hadn't missed him. She needed to warn him, no matter what, but her hands shook, and her palms sweated. The morphine was making her limbs feel heavy, striking hard into her muscles making it difficult for her to move her legs.

She felt tired. So tired. No. No, she couldn't focus on that but keeping awake was painful, the burn behind her eyes, the cramp in her back as her body fought against her mind. She couldn't, she wouldn't think about sleep. On closing her eyes, on—

A screeching horn forced Bree's eyes wide open as she swerved across the road, narrowly missing an oncoming car. Concentrate. She had to concentrate. Slow down, slow down.

Leaning out of the driver's window she drove along, letting the rushing wind hit her face. The sound of the passing cars filled her ears with whining noise, distorted in the fog of her mind.

Her body began to tremble. So cold. She felt so cold.

'Come on, come on!' She shouted out loud, moving her hand to switch the radio on, biting down on her lips harder and harder, trying to do anything to keep herself awake.

Gripping the steering wheel, Bree's head jolted as it nodded forward. She blinked quickly, trying to shake away the drowsiness, trying to make out whether in front of her there were two lorries or one as double vision obscured her senses.

The road stretched out ahead, miles upon miles, and the Sat Nav said she still had twenty more to go.

Feeling sick, Bree indicated to pull over in the lay-by.

Stopping the car, she breathed out a huge sigh of relief, grateful for the break. She stared at her phone, trying to make out the right number. Then pressing redial she waited for it to ring. She was so tired. Maybe if she just rested her head, just for a moment. No, no, she couldn't. Alfie. She had to think of Alfie. But if she just closed her eyes, while the phone rang, just rested them, maybe that would be alright. Just for a moment . . .

'Hello? Hello? Bree, is that you? Hello . . . Hello? Anybody there?'

64

'Hello? Bree? Bree? Hello, I can't hear you . . .' Alfie pressed the phone against his ear, puzzled, before clicking it off as he sat, heater on, lighting a cigarette in his blacked-out Range Rover by the Peldon Rose pub.

When he'd turned on his phone in the early hours of the morning, hoping to contact Sandra, there'd been several missed calls from Bree. At first he'd been worried, wondering if something was wrong, though the more he thought about it the less convinced of that he was. He couldn't imagine that Bree would've phoned over twenty times without leaving a voicemail if anything had happened. No. Without a doubt her phone had been playing up, just as it was now; she clearly couldn't hear him, though he couldn't help smiling that she'd bothered to call at all.

He'd catch up with her later but for now he had to push thoughts of her to one side and concentrate. Keep his mind on the next few hours, make sure he stayed alert. There was simply too much to lose. He'd come down early – hours early – making sure there were no hitches along the way. Nothing that would stop their big chance from happening. *The* chance to get themselves out of the shit Franny had put them in. Two million quid's worth of chance.

The sudden banging on the window made Alfie jump. It was Frankie and Vaughn.

Pushing the electric window button, Alfie grinned, looking at Frankie's red nose.

'Alright, guys? Didn't expect to see you here yet.'

Frankie stuffed his hands in his pockets. 'Stop gassing and let me in. It's fuckin' freezing. I forgot how bleedin' cold it is down here.'

Alfie shook his head looking at Frankie's fading tan. 'Mate, problem with you is that you've got too accustomed to the Costa, all that sunshine has made you a pussy, son.'

Not bothering to reply, Frankie winked, jumping into the back of the car with Vaughn, who leaned forward, helping himself to Alfie's cigarettes.

Inhaling deeply, he said, 'Alf, I'm taking it that you've got the rocks on you?'

'What do you take me for? Pull the carpet up on the floor next to your feet.'

Vaughn did so, revealing the hidden footwell that contained a small blue bag. Grabbing it, he passed his cigarette to Frankie before carefully opening the bag on his knees. A large grin hit his face and he whistled. 'They look better than I remember.'

Alfie glanced at him. 'Maybe that's because they're not covered in horseshit this time. But I reckon it'll be smiles all round, don't you? I think when Perry sees them in their final glory, he'll be blowing the final whistle. It'll be sweet as. Cushty.'

Vaughn smiled, feeling more relaxed than the last time he'd seen Alfie. 'You're not wrong there, thought this day might never come. Though we've still got a few hours to burn before the swap, what do you want to do? Hang out here or go across to the island?'

'Well as long as I don't freeze me bollocks off I don't mind,' Frankie said. 'The problem with going across to Mersea now though, is that it's so small, someone might think it's suss seeing three geezers sitting about in a big car.'

Alfie cranked up the heat. 'Maybe you should've brought your binoculars then, you could pass as a birdwatcher.'

Vaughn grinned. 'That's exactly what his missus has been worried about all these years. Ain't that right, Frank?'

Just as Alfie was going to add to the banter, his phone began to vibrate before ringing out loudly. He glanced at his mobile and then at the others, knowing full well who it was, not wanting to talk in front of them.

Sending the call through to voicemail, Alfie shrugged, only for the phone to begin to ring again. And again, he locked it off.

Vaughn, seeing Alfie looking slightly awkward, tilted his head, giving a mystified smile.

'Who's that then? Seems like they're desperate to speak to you.'

Alfie, not appreciating the questioning, changed his whole demeanour. 'What? Suddenly you're my keeper now?'

'No, far from it, but where I was *slightly* interested before to know who it was, now I'm *really* interested because only a man who has something to hide reacts like that.'

Frankie, wanting to diffuse the tension between the men, tried appealing to them. 'Hey guys, this ain't the time. We're this far away from being quids in, so let's not be stupid and do anything to fuck it up, okay?'

Alfie growled. 'Shut up, Frankie. The geezer gets on my wick. Always trying to wind me up and get a reaction.'

Vaughn shook his head. His tone condescending. 'I think the only person winding themselves up is you, wouldn't you say. I only asked a simple question, you're the one who's got their finger stuck up their arse all of a sudden.'

Alfie's phone rang again, and all the men stared at it. Vaughn pointed at the mobile. 'Go on then Alf, pick it up.'

'It's fine, thanks.'

'You want me to then?'

Before Alfie had a chance to stop him, Vaughn quickly picked up the phone. 'Hello?'

The voice on the other end was slurred. 'Alf, Alf, you got to listen to me . . . Listen to me . . . I'm nearly there. I'm nearly at Mersea. Wait for me . . . I . . . Johnny, Johnny . . . he knows about the diamonds.'

Then the phone went dead.

Vaughn stared at the phone, then he dropped it as if it were on fire, staring at Alfie as he tried to comprehend what he'd just heard. He roared, yelling at him, the sound of his voice loud and aggressive in the confined space of the car.

'What the fuck are you playing at? Are you trying to turn us over? Who are you working with? Who?'

Vaughn reached into his pocket, pulling out a gun and pointing it at Alfie as Frankie looked on in disbelief.

'I'm speaking to you, Alf! You better start talking cos I won't be responsible for my actions. Let me tell you something son, I'll be happy to pull this trigger and you know I will.'

Alfie's eyes darted to Frankie then back to the barrel of the gun. He stared at Vaughn, seeing his eyes wild and hard, not knowing, not getting what had happened, what he was supposed to say.

He spoke quietly, in a whisper, the gun inches away. 'Vaughn, slow down. You got to slow down.'

'I don't have to do anything. If it ain't escaped your notice *pal*, I'm the one holding the gun, so it's you who has to hurry up and tell us what's going on.'

'I don't know.'

Vaughn bellowed, red-faced. 'Don't fuckin' tell me you don't know. I just heard her, I heard what she said on the phone.'

'Bree. I know, that was Bree.'

The name rang a bell in Vaughn's mind. 'Bree? That bird who came to the house?'

'Yeah, that's the one.'

'And what? You thought you and her would run away? Mug us all off?'

Confused, not understanding his point, Alfie said, 'How would that be mugging you off? I can do what I like, but for your info, I wasn't planning to run away.'

Vaughn, pulling back the trigger which sounded round the car, jammed the gun onto Alfie's forehead, pressing it hard against his skin. 'I must say you have some front. Is it because you don't think I'll do it? Well, is it? Is it!'

Alfie put his hands up, staring at Vaughn directly. 'Mate, this is messed up. So, me and Bree are, I don't know what you'd call us.'

'Bonnie and fucking Clyde that's what . . . Why, Alf? Tell me, why? Did greed get the better of you? Decided you didn't want to take over Reginald's business and you'd do a runner with her instead? What's she getting out of it, or ain't she getting anything out of it apart from sucking your dick? Your cock must taste like candy.'

'You're bang out of order, and I don't know what the fuck you're talking about. And you know I want Reggie's bookies as much as you do, why do you think I'm doing this, putting me arse out there to sell the diamonds?'

Vaughn pushed the gun even harder onto Alfie's forehead. He laughed scornfully. 'Even to the very end, you're larging it. Even with only a few centimetres of metal between you and a bullet in your head, you still think you can play the big man. The mighty Alfie Jennings strikes again, hey?'

'Vaughn, look . . .'

'Don't! I don't want to hear it. You know what the joke is Alf, I knew that something was wrong. I knew it. Like all those times before when you've fucked us over, each time I knew that you were up to something, but each time I never followed me gut. I believed what you said. I *wanted* to believe you, our friendship and our businesses together mattered to me, this chance we've got with the Reynolds mattered. That was our future. All of ours.'

'Nothing's changed.'

'Oh, but it has. The truth's come out. Something you wouldn't know about. Fuck me, I even read them poxy magazines of Lola's on how to communicate successfully. Shame though, cos they're missing a trick, ain't they? Because they should've had an article on how to give a long, slow, painful death to the cunt who fucked you over.'

Frankie, having said nothing so far, touched Vaughn's arm. He spoke cautiously, knowing what he was seeing was the Vaughn Sadler of old. 'Look, just tell me what's going on? Cos I'm lost, Vaughnie.'

Keeping his eyes locked on Alfie, Vaughn said, 'Ask him.'

Frankie turned to look at Alfie. 'Then you better tell me, cos I can't make any sense of it.'

Alfie looked as puzzled as Frankie. 'I dunno Frank. I swear.'

'You're being straight up, aren't you?'

Alfie snarled. 'I've got a gun to me head and me hands stuck in the air, so ask yourself if you think now's a good time for me not to be straight up.'

Frankie frowned. He'd known Alfie for a long time, he'd laughed with him and argued with him, been on the wrong end of one of Alfie's scams, but something told him he was telling the truth.

'Vaughn, I hate to say it, but I reckon he ain't mugging us.'

'Don't let him fool you, he ain't changed. I heard what she said. She was worried because apparently some bloke called Johnny knows all about the diamonds.'

Alfie looked blankly. 'What? Who's Johnny? Who the fuck is Johnny?'

'That's what I want to know.'

Angry, Alfie knocked away the gun. He raised his voice, hissing the words through his teeth. 'I told you, I don't know anything, but what I will say is I can't get me head around why Bree . . .'

Vaughn urged Alfie to continue, his temper subsiding slightly. 'Why Bree did what? And more to the point, why does some bird who you've just hooked up with know about the rocks?'

'Look, I ain't got the answers.'

Vaughn lunged at Alfie, blind rage pushing him on. He grabbed his jacket, swinging the gun against his head, smashing it hard into Alfie's temple. 'Then you need to find them!'

Alfie, not one to back down, struggled with Vaughn in the confines of the car, forcing him back to the rear seat, crushing Frank, who thrashed about, caught underneath.

Alfie brought his fist down into Vaughn's face, blood splattering over the Range Rover's cream seats. With blood bubbling out of his mouth, Vaughn screamed at Alfie as Frankie managed to free himself.

'But you still told Bree, Alf! You betrayed us and now we're fucked because of you, it's always because of you!'

Panting but managing to prise the men apart, Frankie pushed Alfie back into the front seat, his forearm on his throat. He glared at them both as he took control. 'Listen Vaughnie, we don't know if it's fucked up. All it is is a phone call. Maybe this bird just felt bad that she's told some geezer. That's all it might be. And Alf, fuck me son, what did you think you were doing? What possessed you to tell her?'

'I don't know, I just needed to talk.'

'If you'd needed to talk, why didn't you talk about something else? Why didn't you talk to us even? And when did you ever have to talk about some job that you were about to pull off? I don't get it, Alf.'

Vaughn pointed angrily. 'If you've messed this up, I'm going to kill you.'

Embarrassed, angry, confused, Alfie went to spring forward again, but Frankie held him in place.

'Don't make threats Vaughn, you hear me? Don't make threats that you ain't going to follow through on.'

'I'll follow through on them alright!'

Frankie yelled at the top of his voice. 'Shut up! You hear me? Just shut up! This is how it's going to go. We're going to calm down and then Alf, you're going to call this bird, Bree. See what she has to say.'

Vaughn piped in. 'Oh, he don't have to call Bree, because according to her, she's on her way. She'll be here any minute now.'

65

Johnny Dwyer sat in the car with his foot down on the accelerator heading towards Mersea Island. He wanted to get to the island early, make sure there were no mistakes, make sure everything went as it should. Because this would be a turning point for him.

Although he'd made his name around Essex, dealing and trafficking in coke as well as hiring himself and his men out for jacking jobs and to the Mr Bigs when they needed some extra heavies, he still wasn't a main player, but this kind of money could turn it all around.

The other reason he wanted to make sure nothing went wrong was to be certain that Alfie Jennings got what was coming to him, and Christ, he was going to enjoy every second of it. Because all he could see when he closed his eyes was Alfie and Bree. Alfie enjoying himself with his missus, and he was going to make him pay.

He sniffed, feeling the cocaine burning at the back of his nostrils, burning the back of his throat. Looking in the driver's mirror, Johnny said, 'Hey, Eddie, wake up. This ain't a day out you know, so if you're expecting a tray of fucking cockles, forget it. I want you to be on the ball. You hear me? Big Billy Baldwin and the crew are coming down and they're going to be on it, so I don't want any broken links in the chain. You understand me?'

Eddie, sitting in the back seat, looked at Johnny as he stared back at him in the mirror. He really wanted to tell him that this was *his* deal, that they were *his* diamonds, and *he* should fuck right off, but as much as he wanted to, he also knew that it wouldn't be wise, not right now anyway. He would wait until the right time and then, oh God, would he tell him. 'Yeah, I understand you, Johnny. No problem.'

Turning his head away Eddie looked out of the window, watching the A120 whizz by as Johnny continued to talk.

'So, you know exactly what to do? Me and the rest of the boys will round them up, give them the fight of their life. We'll do all the heavy stuff. Have all the fun, so all you'll need to do is make sure you get them diamonds off the island. Like we already discussed, Billy and a couple of his men are going to drive back with me, so you take Billy's car. The minute you get them rocks in your hand, you get away. A couple of the men will be waiting for you on the other side, so no funny business, there's only one way off the island, so don't get any ideas Eddie, and *don't* forget all our cars have got tracking, so if you decide to do a moonlight flit, Johnny will know exactly where you are!'

Johnny screeched with laughter as Eddie gave a nervous laugh, slumping back down in the back seat.

Having given it a few minutes, Eddie took a quick side glance at Johnny who was in the process of reaching over to the passenger seat to dip his finger in the small snuff tin filled with cocaine to rub on his gums as he drove, wired, watching the road with drug-fuelled intensity.

Certain that Johnny wasn't watching, Eddie slid out his phone and scrolled through his contacts. Discreetly he texted a message to Jason Robinson.

ETA half an hour. Drop-off tonight as planned. Make sure you keep down, there'll be eyes everywhere.

He pressed send, then waited for it to deliver before quickly deleting it. He smiled, checking the time. It was still early, but he could wait. Because before the end of the day, he, Eddie Styler, would be a millionaire with Jason and Johnny nowhere to be seen.

66

Alfie Jennings hadn't wanted to kill anybody as much as he wanted to kill Bree. He paced about on the small country lane hidden away off Colchester Road, not feeling the cold, only feeling the anger, the betrayal, the hurt. He was going to make Bree pay.

He should've followed his gut, his doubts, but instead, like a fool, he'd followed his heart, sharing and fucking caring, but not anymore. Not anymore. Whatever she had to say, whatever her excuses, she still betrayed him, she still opened her mouth and told someone else. Whoever this Johnny was, Bree was clearly worried, clearly anxious she'd fucked it up and done something wrong. And of course, that was what all the phone calls were about. That was what she'd wanted to say.

'Alf, let her say her piece, it might be innocent mate. Give her a chance.'

Alfie spun round to look at Frankie, a small puddle splashing his shoes. The hatred clenching and straining his jaw. 'Have a word with yourself, Frank. I ain't going to give her anything than what she deserves. So, if I was you I'd get back in the car and leave it to me.'

'No, not until you tell me you won't do anything stupid.'

'That's right, I won't. Because what I'll do, is kill her.'

'Alfie, listen to yourself. You don't know if she's done anything wrong.'

Alfie stepped in close to Frankie. 'I know she has. She's opened her mouth, hasn't she?'

Frankie stared at Alfie, worried. 'I know you're hurt—'

Jumping in, Alfie pushed Frankie hard against his chest. 'Hurt? Are you having a laugh? I ain't hurt, Frank, I'm angry.'

Frankie shook his head. 'No, Alf. I know you. You may be angry with yourself for being stupid enough to talk, for trusting someone you didn't know, but I know that you're more hurt than anything else. I can see it.'

'Then you should've gone to fucking Specsavers, cos the only thing you should be seeing here is that bitch turning us over.'

'You don't know that. I get it feels like a betrayal. Especially on top of Franny. But you can't do anything that you'll regret just because of the way you're feeling.'

Alfie grabbed hold of Frankie, his powerful, six-foot-plus body rigid with rage. He shook him hard.

'Get it into your fucking head that I ain't hurt. What is it with you and Vaughn and fucking feeling? Cos this is real life, Frank. Right here, right now. Feelings don't come into this game, you know that as well as I do. She wanted to play the big boys' game and know what was going on, and now she does, but instead of keeping her mouth shut, she decided to talk, and that comes with consequences. We both know what happens to grasses in this business.'

Frankie pushed Alfie away. 'But she ain't in this business, is she? So, turn it in until you know exactly what's gone down because I ain't having any blood on my hands. Let's listen to what she has to say.'

Before Alfie had time to say anything, a black car drove down the country lane, pulling up by the men in the entrance to the abandoned farm. It was Bree.

Frankie nodded to Alfie. 'I'll be in the car. But remember what I said.'

As Frankie walked away, Alfie, unable to contain himself, charged up to Bree's 4x4, flinging open the driver's door.

'Get out! Get out! Now!'

He stood watching, trembling, furious as Bree fell out of the car, stumbling, trying to stand up. She looked at him with hazy eyes, her voice slurred. 'Alfie, I'm sorry . . . I'm really sorry.'

He grabbed her, pulling her up, pressing her hard against the car. He shook her, a disgusted look on his face. 'I didn't think it could get any worse, but look at you, you're wasted. You're out of it. Oh my God, how didn't I see it. How didn't I see that you were a stoner. Fuck me, you pulled a good 'un there.'

'Alfie, you . . . got it . . . wrong.'

Alfie's voice soared up into the air. He screamed in her face. 'I ain't though! I ain't got it wrong, have I?'

Trying to get her thoughts straight through the morphine, Bree spoke slowly, concentrating on her every word. 'I ain't on the gear anymore . . .'

Throwing his hands in the air, Alfie stared at her in amazement. 'Oh my God! Fuck me, you're a smackhead now?'

'No, no, I just took some by mistake.'

Alfie's laughter was full of contempt. 'Turn it in, what bag-bitch just takes gear by accident? What happened? You found a bag of brown on the street and you just took it by mistake, did you?'

Bree shook her head but quickly turned away as nausea overwhelmed her. She began to vomit, watery liquid splattering over Alfie's shoes.

Alfie's face screwed up in scorn. 'Oh, fucking hell, and there's me thinking you're a classy bird . . .' He paused for a moment then frowned. He shook his head in disbelief as realisation began to hit. 'Hold on, I remember now, it's all making sense. One of the times I saw you, you were puking all over the place. This is why, innit? Cos you were on the gear.'

Wiping her mouth, Bree stared at Alfie. 'No, I swear, it was down to nerves.'

'Nerves?'

'Because of what I knew was going to happen.'

'What? Are you fucking joking?'

The roar that came from Alfie had Vaughn and Frankie – who were sitting in the car – turning to look. Frankie spoke, his tone full of concern. 'Maybe I should go and see if they're okay. I know what Alfie can be like when he loses it.'

Vaughn shook his head as he rested his eyes on Bree. 'No, leave it. Leave him to sort it out.'

Alfie stood in the cold, his hands on his hips, his mind racing, not able to connect the dots.

'Alfie, please, I need to explain.'

'Don't! Don't give me "please"! It's too late for "please".'

Not giving up, Bree said, 'Look, Johnny asked me—'

Alfie interrupted angrily. 'Hold up. Who the hell is this Johnny?'

'Johnny's my husband, not Mick.'

'What?'

'Johnny *Dwyer* is my husband.'

There was a long pause before Alfie suddenly ran back to his car, opening the passenger door to pull out a gun from the side pocket. He ignored the looks he got from Frankie and Vaughn as he turned to run back to Bree.

Alfie was panting angrily and wiping his mouth, gritting his teeth, sweat was pouring from his brow, his hands were shaking, pointing the gun at Bree, pulling the gun away from Bree, pointing it back to Bree.

'How could you do this! How! Johnny Dwyer? Are you having a fucking laugh?'

'Alfie, please, you don't understand.'

'I told you, don't give me "please"! I understand alright, fucking hell, you proper played me. Well done, Bree. Well done.'

Alfie paced about, not sure what to do with himself.

Frankie came running up to him and held out his hand. 'Give me the gun, Alf. Give me the fucking gun. This is insane.'

Alfie's eyes were wild as he waved the gun towards Bree. 'She's married. But here's the thing, you wanna know who she's married to? Who my little Bree is married to? Johnny Dwyer. Yeah, that's right. That bitch is married to Johnny fuckin' Dwyer.'

Frankie and Vaughn stared open-mouthed at Bree, who shook, crying through her words as she tried to push her dizziness aside. 'I'm sorry, I'm so sorry. He made me do it, but I couldn't go through with it. I couldn't, I care too much about you, Alfie.'

Alfie clenched his fist, charging at Bree, but he stopped in front of her, staring and glaring into her eyes. He raised his fist, smashing it down into Bree's car window. Once. Twice. Over and over again.

Alfie's hand poured with blood, and he stared at Bree who collapsed on the floor. Holding her head in her hands.

'Why Bree, why?'

He crouched down, pushing her hands away, grabbing her chin, forcing her to look at him as his blood smeared across her face.

'I loved you, Bree. You were my family and when you left all them years ago, I looked for you, making sure you were alright. My heart was ripped out. But when I saw you again in that car park, you have no idea how that felt. Me feet never touched the ground. It was like everything was going to be alright because Bree's back in me life. My Bree. Little Bree who'd grown up to be this beautiful, warm, kind woman, but all along you were just a fucking conniving bitch.'

'Don't say that!'

'Why not? It's true. We even slept together, and I thought that meant something, but it was all just so I would trust you and open up. You're no better than a fucking whore!'

'You're wrong, it did mean something. I slept with you because I wanted to, no other reason. That's why I didn't sleep with you *before* you told me about the diamonds. Think about it Alfie, I had all the information I needed by then, so I didn't have to go to bed with you, but I did, because I wanted to be with you.'

'Nice try, Bree. I hate you! You understand that. I hate you!'

Tears streamed down Bree's cheeks as she screamed at Alfie. 'I understand that, but do you understand, do you? Because I loved you too, Alfie. I loved you. You and Sandra. But it was me who was ripped away, not you. Me! You still had your life and I had nothin'! Nothin'! Children's home after children's home, until one day I thought, just for a moment, me life was going to be alright. But it wasn't Alf, it wasn't. You talk about having your heart ripped out? You have no idea. Not about this. Not about my life. You think I wanted to do this? You think if I really wanted to hurt you I'd be here right now? You don't know what I put on the line to do this. But I chose you above everything else. Above the man I thought I was going to be with for the rest of me life, above me own safety, above the fear of Johnny, I came here to warn *you*. So don't talk to me about things you don't know, because I chose you, Alfie. I chose you because I love you, and I always have.'

67

Alfie Jennings sat in the rain on the floor next to Bree. His injured hand was wrapped up in a towel as he listened to her story. He hung his head, unable to look her straight in the eye. Unable to know quite what to say. So, instead he listened, and he hurt for her, for Ryan, for her lost years.

Sighing, she touched his hand. 'I told Eddie and Johnny everything. They are planning to hijack the exchange. I am so sorry.'

Alfie shook his head. 'I should be the one saying sorry. Not you.'

Vaughn, who'd been standing nearby listening, said, 'Are you joking? All of a sudden she gives you the eyes, your cock tingles and it's sweet as. No, mate. No. There's no way I'm trusting her.'

Alfie glared at Vaughn. 'Wind yer neck in. You think what she's just said is a Jackanory?'

'Yeah, frankly I do. Some sob story and you fall for it.'

'Shut up, Vaughn.'

Bree smiled at Alfie. 'Don't be mad at him, he's only watching out for you all. I don't blame him for not trusting me.'

Vaughn turned on Bree. 'I don't need you to fucking smooth things out for me. I should've let Alfie put you in the ground.'

Alfie leapt up, but Bree pulled him back. 'No, don't! I don't want you to fight because of me. Vaughn, I'm telling the truth. If you go to do the drop-off on Mersea Island, you'll be in proper danger.'

Vaughn bent down. 'And why's that, hey? Could that be because you fucked us over?'

'Look, Alfie,' Frankie said. 'Vaughn's right, this could all be a set-up. How do you know that this bird ain't just playing us and is trying to stop us going on the island?'

Alfie looked at Bree, then at Vaughn and Frankie. 'We ain't going to do that. We're going to go through with it.'

Bree looked shocked. 'You can't. You could get killed.'

'And so could you. If they think for a moment that you've tipped us off, well, it'll be curtains. You said yourself that Johnny's paranoid. You're the obvious person to blame. If we don't turn up, he'll think you've given him the wrong information or you've bunged us the heads-up. Whichever way, it'll be safer for you—'

Vaughn interrupted. 'Safer for her? Mate, listen to yourself. I don't care about her. I'm not having me brains blown away for some bird. Let's just call it off with Perry.'

Angrily, Alfie said, 'Nobody's having their brains blown away. That ain't going to happen because we know now, don't we? We're one step ahead. I ain't saying it's going to be easy. And I ain't going to say it won't be dangerous, but it's what we need to do.'

Shielding the flame on his lighter from the weather, Frankie lit a cigar. 'Maybe I'm getting mugged off or I'm too fucking soft, but I can't just turn me back on Bree and what I've just heard. If the bird's telling the truth, then we got to do something.'

Vaughn sneered. 'Hold up! Seriously, Frank, when will you learn? You've always been a patsy when it comes to women, but this takes it to another level, son. Only a few minutes ago she was enemy number one, now you're acting like her shit don't stink.'

Glancing down at Bree and thinking about his own rotten childhood, Frankie blew out a mouthful of smoke. 'I don't think that, but everybody in Essex knows what a psychopath Johnny is.

We've heard the stories of how much he likes to torture people that cross him. I remember having dealings with him years ago when I had a shipment of coke come through, and even then he was a nutter. She don't deserve that. Look, this is just a suggestion but how about we call it off with Perry? Pull him out of the picture because the geezer's carrying two million in cash, and nobody wants that to go walkies if it all goes down.'

Vaughn shrugged, irritated. 'How does that help anyone?'

'We still do as we planned. We'll still go to Mersea, look like we're meeting Perry. Bree says that Johnny isn't interested in going after Perry's money because of the repercussions from Perry if he did. Which is clearly a wise move on his part because otherwise the whole of Perry's syndicate will hunt him down. Johnny's not interested in starting a war with him. He's only interested in us. Us and the diamonds. After all, the diamonds are fair game at the moment, they're up for grabs.'

Alfie nodded. 'But if we postpone Perry so he doesn't show up, won't it look suss?'

'No, why would it? Johnny won't think anything is wrong as long as he eyeballs us, or he'll just think Perry has let us down. But he'll still go after us because he knows *we've* got the diamonds. And *we* want it to look like he's taken us by surprise. We'll go through the motions, turn up on the beach as arranged, but we'll be on our toes to scarper away with the diamonds. Johnny will be spitting feathers that we managed to cut and run, but he *won't* suspect it's anything to do with Bree, which means she'll be safe, which is the most important thing. And then later we'll just set up another meeting with Perry, and that's it. Job done.'

Bree smiled gratefully at Frankie as Vaughn clapped his hands slowly and loudly. His voice dripped with sarcasm. 'Well thanks for that, Frank. And there was me thinking that we'll be walking into danger when all along it's as simple as one, two, fucking three.'

'Vaughnie, you know I'm not saying that. I know it's not ideal, but it's the only way to make sure Bree stays out of trouble.'

'Funny, it sounds *exactly* like that.'

'Then step out of it. Me and Alfie will go ahead. Don't worry, nobody's going to cut you out of the deal, but I understand why you don't want to be involved.'

Vaughn snarled at Frankie. 'You're right, I don't. I don't want to get anywhere near it. I think you're a right bunch of mugs. She's proper turning you over and you lot can't see it. I ain't going to be coming to anyone's funeral. Do what you like, but I'm washing me hands. I'm out of here.'

Alfie called out to him as he walked away. 'Vaughn, come on. Don't do this.'

'Say what you like, but you won't change me mind.'

'Where you going? Vaughn! Vaughn, come on, mate! Come back. You can't walk.'

'Just try me!' he shouted as he continued walking away.

Alfie glanced at Frank, smiling. 'Thanks for staying Frank, I owe you one.'

Frankie winked. 'I'll add that to the list, shall I?'

Alfie turned to Bree, as she got up from the wet gravel. He put out his hand to help her up.

'Look, if you can drive, you need to get back home, and quick. But I need to ask you something, if you could do me a favour.'

'Anything.'

'I'm worried about Sandra. I might be being silly, but I haven't heard anything from her. From what you've said, I have a feeling she might be in trouble though. The thing is with Eddie down here, it's the perfect opportunity to go to her house and have a look around. I know it's a long shot, but it's not like her not to get back to me. What do you say? You in?'

Bree gave a warm smile, relief ebbing from her as she squeezed Alfie's hand. 'Yeah, of course I'm in.'

'And Bree, one way or another, I promise I'll get you and Ryan and the kids out of there. Just give me time to work it out.'

68

Bree took another drink of coffee, trying to clear her head. She was aware she had to get back home, but she still had time if she was quick, and besides Alfie had asked her to check on Sandra, and it was the least she could do. There was no way she was going to let him down. Not again.

Although she was terrified for Alfie and Frankie, she couldn't help feeling grateful for what they'd agreed to do. She was certain now there'd be no way Johnny would suspect anything, at least on that score, she'd be safe.

But everything had changed. Everything that had happened since earlier that morning felt surreal. She felt strange and it wasn't just because of the morphine wearing off. For the first time in more years than she could remember, she didn't know what might happen.

She couldn't go back to her old life, Alfie had said as much, not now her secret was out. Though he hadn't told her exactly what he was going to do or how long it would take. So, for the time being she had to just sit tight and wait.

But as much as the future didn't quite seem so inevitable, so hopeless, so clear cut – and that excited her and scared her in equal measures, allowing her to think about a freedom that only yesterday had seemed so lost, a freedom she wouldn't usually dare to dream – each time she came back to the same question. How? How would she ever be able to leave?

Johnny wouldn't ever let her go anywhere. Not with the kids. Not with Ryan. He'd never let her walk out on him or on Ma. He would hunt her down, find her and bring her back and maybe that would be even worse. And besides, where would she go? She had nothing, she knew no one, and she couldn't go for help, not now, there'd be too many questions, too many accusations, things she wouldn't know how to answer.

So, all she could do was leave it to Alfie. Trust in him like she'd done when she was a kid. When she was a kid, he'd saved her. And maybe, just maybe, the dream she hardly dared to dream – the hope of one day seeing the child she'd never stopped loving but who Ma had so cruelly snatched away and denied her contact ever since – would somehow become a reality.

Draining the last of the coffee, Bree sighed and stared at the imposing double gates belonging to the house Eddie and Sandra lived in, then checked her watch again. She slipped the handgun Alfie has insisted she take into her pocket.

With the effects of the morphine beginning to subside, she took a deep breath and stepped out of the car. She tried the bell first but, getting no answer and not wanting to waste time, Bree punched in the numbers Alfie had given her on the security pad. The gates immediately opened.

She walked down the gravel drive towards the house, looking around but seeing nothing unusual. Everything looked normal, calm and peaceful. Then, smoothing down her clothes, she knocked on the front door, suddenly aware that she was feeling anxious. There was no reply and not wanting to let Alfie down by leaving straight away without having thoroughly checked around, Bree made her way along the side of the house, deciding to look around the grounds first.

'Sandra! Sandra!' She shouted out for her old friend as she

strode down the manicured garden, being careful not to knock the gun in her pocket as she pulled out her phone. She checked the time, working out how long she probably had before Ma began to wake up. There was no way she could risk being late.

Standing by the water fountain, a grey cat purred at her, wrapping its tail around her legs as she began to think that Alfie was worrying over nothing. Perhaps Sandra had just gone away without telling him, after all he had admitted to her that he and his sister hadn't been close of late. Still, at least she'd be able to tell him she'd come to have a look, and maybe that's all it needed to help put his mind at ease.

Striding back to the car, Bree suddenly stopped. She listened carefully, thinking she'd heard a sound. It definitely sounded like banging. Cautiously, she called again.

'Hello?'

There. Yes, she hadn't been mistaken, there was a distinct sound of banging. Edging back along the wall, Bree followed the noise and crouched down at the small basement window she hadn't noticed before.

'Hello? Hello? Is anyone there? . . . Sandra?'

'In here! I'm in here! Hello! Hello!'

Bree scrambled onto her knees, lying down on the wet floor, the gravel digging into her skin. She talked hurriedly through the frosted glass which was covered with bars.

'Oh my God! Sandra! Are you alright? It's me, Bree.'

There was a slight pause before Sandra, said, 'I'm locked in here! Help!'

'What?'

'Just get me out!'

Bree's thoughts raced, she didn't know what to expect but it certainly wasn't this. Trying not to think about the time, or what might happen if she was late, she spoke hurriedly, her voice constricted by the tight knot of panic in her throat.

'What do you want me to do?'

'There's a small black pipe at the back of the house, flush to the wall. It looks like a drain pipe, but if you unscrew the FloPlast cap, you'll find the keys. Hurry up!'

Running around the house Bree saw the pipe, exactly how Sandra had described it, standing no more than a metre tall. Quickly she removed the cap and there attached to a string glued to the inside was a small bunch of keys.

She grabbed them and ran back around to the basement window.

'I've found them!'

'Then what are you waiting for! Get me out of here!'

Rushing around to the front, Bree fumbled with the keys. It took her a moment to open the door, which stuck slightly on its hinges. Then racing through the wooden hallway, Bree spotted a staircase which she assumed led down to the basement.

She switched on the light, taking the stairs two at a time and following the sound of banging, Bree rushed along the beige, seagrass-carpeted hallway and stopped at a large sandblasted wooden door, leaning her head against it.

'Sandra, I'm here!'

Again, there was a slight pause before Sandra spoke. 'On the key ring, there's a grey brushed metal key, that's the one you need.'

With her hands trembling, Bree unlocked the door. She stared at Sandra, breaking into a smile. She couldn't remember how many years it'd been since she'd seen her, and she couldn't put into words how it felt. But it was something like magic.

Overwhelmed, and overcome with emotion, Bree looked at her one-time best friend, she could ask questions later, but for now all she wanted to do was concentrate on this moment. Opening her arms to give Sandra a hug, Bree spoke in a whisper, choking back the tears.

'Hello Sandra, it's so good to see you.'

'Hello Bree.' And with that, Sandra Styler slapped Bree hard across the face. 'Shame the same couldn't be said for you. You little bitch, you fucked over my brother, and that means you fucked with me.'

The shock hit Bree harder than the slap – she was used to those. Tears filled her eyes as she stared at Sandra. 'Please, Sand, let me explain.'

'You ain't explaining anything. What? Did Johnny send you?'

'How . . . how do you know about him?'

'Oh dear, have I spoilt your surprise? If you must know, I heard Eddie talking about how you set Alfie up. How could you do it? After everything he did for you as a kid. He might act the hard man, and sometimes *be* the hard man, but you knew he had a big heart and you played with it. He was falling for you and you used that to get your dirty, grubby hands all over the diamonds.'

'You've got it wrong! It's not like that.'

Sandra screamed at the top of her voice. 'Have I got it wrong? Have I really, Bree? Are you going to tell me that you didn't try to set him up?'

'I did but I . . .'

That was all that Sandra needed to hear. She dived at Bree, grabbing her top, pushing her hard against the wall.

'If anything's happened to him, I'm going to kill you!'

'It hasn't, I swear, that's why I'm here! Please, let me explain.'

Furiously, Sandra shoved Bree again, causing her to stumble, causing her to fall, and as she did, the gun in her pocket came flying out.

For a split second, Sandra stared open-mouthed before running to grab the gun. She picked it up, pointing it at Bree.

'So, you came here to kill me, did you? Finish me off. Go on, tell me who sent you. Was it Johnny? Eddie? Which one?'

Watching Sandra pulling back the trigger, Bree squeezed her eyes tight shut. 'It was Alfie. He sent me.'

'What are you talking about?'

'He was worried about you because you didn't answer the phone, he thought something might've happened.'

'I don't believe you . . . Open your eyes! Look at me!'

Tears continued to run down Bree's face. 'Sandra, I'm so sorry. I'm sorry for everything. I don't blame you for how you feel. I know what I did was wrong, and I swear I tried to make it better, but please, I need to go home . . . I need to go home, it's getting late.'

Sandra stared scornfully at Bree who now had her head in her hands. 'What are you, a fucking kid?'

'No, but it's all going to go wrong. Just let me go.'

'You ain't going anywhere.'

Bree glanced up at Sandra, panic taking over. Her words tumbling out, spilling over each other. 'They'll hurt him if I'm late, if they find out, they'll hurt Ryan, they'll hurt him so badly. Please, you've got to help me, please. I know you don't understand but let me go, just let me go. Call Alfie, do anything but please don't keep me here.'

Without taking either the gun or her eyes off Bree, Sandra gestured to her. 'Phone. Give me your phone.'

Trembling, Bree went into her pocket, passing the mobile to Sandra who snatched it, scrolling through the contacts to get to Alfie's number. She pressed dial. It rang several times before Sandra heard the familiar voice she'd missed.

'Hello? Bree. Are you alright darlin'?'

'It ain't Bree, it's me, Sandra.'

Sandra heard the sigh of relief down the phone and she couldn't help but smile.

'Bree's found you then. I was worried about you, girl.'

'I need to tell you something. I've found out that she's in leagues with Johnny and—'

Alfie interrupted. 'Sweetheart, I know. It's a long story, but I know. Don't be too hard on her, she's had a rough time of it. I'll explain all when I can. But she ain't the enemy here.'

'But—'

'No buts. I know what you're like, so I want you to promise me you won't do anything stupid.'

Sandra glanced down at Bree crumpled up on the floor and at the gun she was pointing at her. 'Come on Alf, what do you take me for? Of course I won't.'

'Thank you, Sand. Look after her for me, and listen, I'll see you soon . . . Oh, and Sand? It's good to hear your voice.'

The phone clicked off and Sandra crouched down, placing the gun gently on the floor. She looked at Bree and slowly said, 'How's about if you and me, we start again?'

Bree's face lit up. 'I'd like that.'

'Me too.'

Sandra leant over and gave Bree a long tight hug. She broke away, looking concerned.

'Look, I don't know what's going on, but if you need to get off home, you better go, we can talk later . . . Don't forget this.' Sandra passed Bree the gun as she stood up.

'I'd rather not take it if you don't mind . . . Anyway, what about you? What are you going to do?'

Sandra smiled, slipping the gun into her pocket as an idea came to her. 'Oh, don't worry about me, I'll be fine. More than fine.'

It was low tide and now evening, and Alfie's Range Rover sped across the half-mile causeway. It was the only access to Mersea Island, a place Alfie had visited as a kid with Connor, eating cockles and listening to the story of the ghost of the roman soldier who still wandered the land, and tales of smugglers with buried treasure.

A long line of weathered fence posts stretched out in front of them as the wheels of the tyres cut through the lapping water, spraying it up and onto the blacked-out windows. Seagulls sat and surveyed, unperturbed by the speeding car.

The evening sun on the horizon crept behind the greying clouds and the sky darkened. A certain melancholy hung in the air as Alfie and Frankie sat in silence, watching the pastel colours of the picture-postcard beach huts flash by.

Driftwood lay on the sand and shingle beach, which spanned for miles, and peeling white-painted ramshackle houseboats sat marooned and abandoned on the mud and peat salt marshes. Small creeks and boardwalks criss-crossed the wetlands, as fresh Mersea oysters piled up in crates outside the small seafood shops, and isolated weatherboard holiday cottages were all closed up.

At speed they turned left, driving down a narrow road heading towards the east of the island, passing rolling grasslands with birds and wildlife on every corner. Seals bobbed their heads up. A group of waders settled on the marshes, merging into the greyness of the evening light.

Seeing the sign for Cudmore Grove Country Park, Alfie stepped on the accelerator, heading towards the drop-off point.

He glanced at Frankie, who sat smoking a cigar. 'So, you ready?

Frankie raised his eyebrows as they neared the forest which sloped down to the vast, expansive shoreline of East Mersea beach where sand dunes hid amongst the trees next to the crumbling sandstone cliffs. 'Yeah. You?

'You mean, am I ready to be bait, a sitting duck?'

As Alfie stopped the car, trying to ignore his own nerves, he turned to look at Frankie.

'It'll be fine, Alf. Perry was sweet about postponing, and we've still got the rocks, so it ain't all bad. All we need to do is show our face, let Johnny and his men see us on the beach where we planned to be. That's it, and then we're out of here before it all kicks off. Johnny ain't got the light brigade behind him you know. What could go wrong?'

Alfie gave a half-smile. 'I just hope we can pull it off for Bree's sake.'

'It's not the cleverest of ideas, I know, but . . .'

Alfie finished his sentence. '. . . but what else can we do, right? Because if we don't show up, she's fucked. The good thing is, Johnny and his men will park their cars on top, we'll park down on the beach. I know a track which takes us down there, only locals really know about it, so we'll be sweet as. And from where Johnny will be, they won't be able to see the car hidden. We'll leave the motor running to make it quicker to get off.'

'How far from the beach will you park?'

'It's less than a minute away. We'll show our faces on the beach, and when they see us, the path they'll have to come down will be on the left of us and totally exposed. Once they're almost on the beach, we'll scarper back to the car and from there we can drive along the track which avoids having to come back up on the top. So, they won't even see which way we'll have gone, and by the time they work it out, we'll be laters. We're already a step ahead. Easy.'

Frankie gave Alfie a wry smile. 'Oh yeah, real easy.'

69

Thankful that no lights were on, Bree crept into the mobile home. It was warm and even from the hallway she could hear the sound of Ryan's cuckoo clock ticking rhythmically away. She could feel herself trembling as she craned her neck round the lounge door, hoping and praying that Ma was still asleep.

She stared at Ma, who still lay with her mouth open and Bree immediately felt relief, the tension in her shoulders disappearing. The only thing she needed to worry about was the car window Alfie had smashed but she was certain she could come up with an excuse for that.

Tiptoeing along the hall, Bree went to check on Ryan. Opening his bedroom door as quietly as she could.

A smile passed her lips as she walked to his bed, whispering to him warmly.

'Ryan, Ryan, wake up, it's me . . . Ryan.'

Reaching down to pull back the covers, Bree suddenly froze, her body going rigid with terror. Under the duvet were pillows shaped to look like a person.

'Hello Bree, been on your travels, have you? I was wondering when you'd get back.'

Shaking, Bree spun around to look at Ma, whose face was a picture of hatred.

'I . . . I . . . I was looking for Ryan.'

'What, in Johnny's car for all these hours?'

'Where is he? Where's Ryan?'

'Oh, Ryan's fine, well, at the moment he is. Though I'm not sure you'll be fine, not when Johnny finds out. I'm looking forward to seeing just what he's got to say . . . Just what he's going to do to Little Miss Muffet.'

And with that, Ma Dwyer slammed and locked the door, leaving Bree alone in the room.

Vaughn Sadler, not for the first time that evening, cursed Alfie's name. He'd been planning to go back to the bed and breakfast and have a nice long bath. And he'd been halfway there, looking forward to doing nothing but relax. He'd sat on a bus, something which he hadn't done for many years, but somewhere between South Green and Wivenhoe it all went wrong because he'd started to think. Thinking about Alfie. About Frankie. About Soho. About everything they'd gone through together. The arguments they'd had, but also the good times, lots of good times, and he'd known right then he couldn't just go home and do nothing.

As Vaughn pulled himself away from his thoughts, he shivered, the pouring rain soaking through his shirt as he sat on the small wooden engine boat he'd stolen from the waterside marina. And whilst the boat chugged through the water in the twilight of the evening, making the short journey from Brightlingsea to East Mersea beach, Vaughn made a promise to himself. He was going to make sure Alfie Jennings owed him big time.

Having parked the car amongst the trees, Frankie and Vaughn stood on the windswept beach with the rain striking down, each holding a machine gun discreetly at their side.

Alfie looked around, it was pitch black and the only sound was lapping water. He knew staying calm was the key to being on the ball, but the longer he waited around for Johnny to show, the harder it was to maintain composure. His mind was racing with everything that could go wrong, as well as what it would mean if they didn't pull this off.

'You alright, Frank?'

Frankie nodded, looking as tense as he felt. He scanned the beach, holding his gun up to his chest, his eyes darting left and right. Alfie, on high alert, walked closer to the shoreline. Watching. Waiting.

'Oh shit! Alf, quick! You know what we were saying about Johnny not having the light brigade behind him, wanna rethink that?'

Alfie spun around to where Frankie was looking. On the top of the cliff, a dozen blacked-out 4x4s appeared. The headlights switched on, lighting up the beach and causing Alfie and Frankie to squint.

'Oh fuck, run!'

Sprinting backwards with his gun held high, Alfie began to fire as he charged towards the edge of the beach, the wind whipping his face as bullets, unremitting, rained down.

On the edge of the deserted beach, Frankie, who'd gone in the other direction, began to run towards the concrete pillbox which was largely buried in sand. Skidding behind it, he knelt down, keeping low, hearing the fire of machine guns through the gusting easterly wind. Further up the beach, Alfie threw himself against a large tree which hung down off the edge of the cliff. He pushed himself into the rocks but there in front were some of Johnny's men. They hadn't seen him yet, but it was only a matter of time before they did.

Drawing a ragged breath, Alfie ran as fast as he could along the bottom of the cliff, his eyes darting round for Frankie as the onslaught of bullets followed him. Seeing a large boulder, he dived behind it, breathing hard as his chest tightened.

Peering around, Alfie fired up at the cliffs.

'Alfie! Over here! Alf! I'm over here.'

Alfie swivelled round and with the lights of the cars shining down, he could see Frankie to the left of him, but he could also see to the right of him, Johnny and his men charging towards them.

Frankie continued to yell, his voice urgent. 'Alf! Come on! Quick! My gun's jammed from the water! I need a gun.'

It was only a short distance between him and Frankie, he wasn't sure if he was going to make it without being seen, but he had no choice. Frankie would be a dead man without a gun.

Then, with a swift look around, Alfie ran, throwing his body onto the cold sand, trying to get under the beams of car lights as the bullets sprayed around them. He crawled along on his stomach, the water lapping over his face as he headed to where Frankie was.

Pulling himself up into a sitting position behind the pillbox, Alfie pressed himself against it. He threw a small handgun to Frankie, shouting over the sound of the gunfire which cracked and popped, splintering and cutting through the air.

'Here, take this. It ain't great, but it's better than nothing. We need to make our way back up to the car and sharpish, before it's too late. You ready?'

Frankie nodded but as they were about to get up he spotted one of Johnny's men creeping up the sand in their direction. He pulled a large knife from his sock. Grasping the tip of his knife he threw it hard, flipping it hard into the air; it landed deep in the man's leg.

'Frank, come on, follow me! Let's go!' Alfie called.

Alfie charged along, aiming his gun either side of him. He ran through the edge of the water, also trying to keep out of the beam of the car headlights. He headed for the bottom of the cliffs, hiding between the sand dunes and behind the sea rocks. Getting to the forest path, Alfie glanced around and whispered to Frank. 'I think we need to go . . .'

Before he could say another word, Alfie saw two of Johnny's men racing down the path towards the beach huts. He backtracked quickly, rushing the other way. 'Frank, scrap that, let's go. Let's just head for the car.'

As he ran, Alfie fired, shooting and taking down one of the men who screamed in agony, his knee blown apart.

Charging towards the car with flashes of gunfire still raining down from the cliffs, Alfie and Frankie ran through the dark shadows of the trees.

'Alfie, behind you! Behind you! There's someone there.'

Alfie twisted round, aiming his gun as he did so.

'Don't shoot! Don't fucking shoot!'

'Vaughn?'

Vaughn stepped out from behind the trees and spoke quickly. 'Don't ask questions, just come on.'

Alfie shook his head, surveying the cliffs for Johnny's men. 'We need to go back to the car to get the diamonds. It's this way. Come on!'

The three men sped through the trees and bracken along the track and, getting to the Range Rover, Vaughn and Frankie kept guard whilst Alfie quickly scrambled into the car. He looked under the front seats, then in the back. Dread beginning to overwhelm him.

Vaughn spotted some lights heading towards them and shouted out. 'Alfie, hurry up, they're coming! They're coming!'

Alfie's voice was panicked. 'They ain't here! The diamonds ain't here!'

'What! They've got to be, look again!'

Frankie held his gun tight and shouted over his shoulder. 'Listen mate, we have to go!'

'No way. No way. They were here! I got to find them. We need them!'

Running up to Alfie, Frankie pulled on Alfie's arm. 'We won't need anything except a body bag if you don't hurry up. Please, Alf, come on.'

Despair peppered Alfie words. 'I can't, this was our chance. We can't just leave them. Give me a couple more minutes.'

Vaughn yelled at him, seeing Johnny's men running through the woods, getting ever closer. 'Alfie, it don't matter, what matters is you, there'll be other chances, but not if we don't go now. We'll never get out if we go by car. We'll have to go by boat.'

Frankie stared in amazement. 'What?'

'Just come on.'

And as the men ran down to the shore, heading towards where Vaughn had left the boat, Eddie Styler slunk out of the shadows, pushing the bag of diamonds into his pocket, running towards where Jason Robinson had parked his car.

70

As Eddie ran, he began to think. And the more he thought, the more the situation frustrated him. They were his diamonds, *his*. Not Johnny's, not Jason's, not Sandra's and certainly not Alfie's. *His*. All his.

He'd been the one who'd been mugged off by Reggie Reynolds. He'd been the one who'd ducked and dived, trying to get the money together, and he'd been the one who'd arranged the transport from Amsterdam to bring them back in the bellies of those horses. The only thing he hadn't been, was the one who had fucked it all up.

But now, through no fault of his own, he was having to run away from Johnny to give Jason a share of *his* diamonds, because otherwise the math just didn't add up. How was he expected not only to give Jason a stake but Johnny too, along with all the people he owed? He'd be left with nothing, and he was sick and tired of having jack shit.

He'd thought about doing it the other way around – give a share to Johnny and not to Jason as payback for the lorry job which had gone wrong – but he didn't trust Johnny not to rip him off and take the whole lot. And besides, it still left him owing Jason a whole lot of money which he wasn't prepared to give.

And the problem was, Jason Robinson certainly wasn't a man to write off any debt, and he certainly wasn't a man to be mugged off either. But he knew if he didn't have the money to get far enough away from Jason and start a new life, he'd have to spend every waking hour looking over his shoulder, which was definitely something he didn't want to do.

But then again, everyone had their nemesis, didn't they? Even Jason Robinson. And every problem had a solution.

As an idea began to form, Eddie smiled, slowing down to a walk and coming to a stop by the large pine trees which gave him cover from the weather. He pulled the bag of diamonds from his pocket then, quickly kneeling, he dug a small hole in the soft wet earth, putting in the precious stones and covering them up.

Checking around, making sure that no one was coming, Eddie picked up a craggy, sharp rock and taking a deep breath, he closed his eyes, before bringing it down hard on his face.

He screamed, dropping the stone and spun around, hopping on the spot as pain ripped through him and blood poured from the deep, fleshy gash on the side of his head.

Breathing hard, he held his face, waiting for the agony to pass, and once it did, Eddie took another deep breath, picking up the stone again, slamming it once more into his face.

The rock caught the corners of his eyes and the centre of his nose and he heard a crunch of cartilage. Hot waves of pain shot through his body and Eddie dropped to the ground; groaning, he rolled around in the muddy earth, trying to catch his breath as he tasted the blood that ran into his mouth and down into the back of his throat.

Taking him well over ten minutes to recover, enough time to get up from the ground. With one of his eyes swollen shut, Eddie squinted at his watch before breaking into a jog following the dirt track round.

At the top of the hill, Eddie saw Jason's car. Bracing himself, gathering up his thoughts, he began to stagger, waving his arms in the air.

'Help! Help! Jason! Jason! Help me! Help!'

Getting to the car, Eddie threw himself against it as the doors of the 4x4 flung open. Jason Robinson stared at Eddie's swollen, bloody face. 'Jesus, what's going on? You look like a fucking monster. Like the walking dead. You could give a man a fright out here in the middle of nowhere. Jesus, Ed.'

'I've been jumped on! Ambushed!'

Jason's face darkened. 'What?'

'I was coming up to you as we arranged and from out of nowhere some geezers jumped on me. I didn't recognise any of them apart from one person. I recognised one bloke.'

'Who?'

'It was Johnny. Johnny Dwyer. He was there.'

Through his good eye, Eddie watched Jason's face turn from anger into a burning rage and he had to fight the desire to smile.

'What the fuck was Johnny Dwyer doing here?'

Eddie, as he so often did, thought how very stupid Jason was, and knowing he knew nothing about his dealings with Johnny, shrugged, his voice feigning bewilderment. 'I dunno, Jase. You're guess is as good as mine. Took me proper by surprise. I ain't told anybody about this drop-off. The only person that knew was you, and the contact that I told you about, the one that was abroad. It was all going so well.'

'Well at least you still got the diamonds, right? That's what matters.'

Eddie shook his head. 'No, Jase. That's the point, I ain't. I ain't got them.'

Jason's face drained of colour, his perma-tanned skin turning pale. 'What? Tell me you are joking.'

'No, I wish I was. That's what I'm trying to tell you. I ain't got them because I was jumped on down in the woods.'

Jason barked out an order at his men. 'Frisk him, check that he ain't got them, cos I can't believe this is really happening.'

Eddie Styler stretched out his arms, letting Jason's men search his body, and watched as Jason paced around as he pointed accusingly.

'How could this happen? How the *fuck* could this happen? Tell me you're not for real.'

'Look at me Jason, look what they done to me. I'm hardly pulling a fast one, am I? Believe me mate, I want to do them some damage.'

'Oh, don't worry about that, Ed. Johnny Dwyer's had it coming for a long time. He is going to pay, and he is going to be buried.'

A hint of a smile touched Eddie's lips. 'Look Jason, I reckon if you're quick, you'll catch them. I heard them say they were heading for Big Billy Baldwin's yard over near Basildon. Anymore than that, I don't know.'

Jason spoke hurriedly. 'How many would you say there were? Did he have a lot of his crew with him? I might have to wait until morning when I can gather up some more of me own men because there's only four of us.'

Picturing the dozen or so cars full of Johnny and Billy's posse, Eddie shook his head. 'Nah, there was only him and three other blokes. Maybe two. If me drop-off contact hadn't left a few minutes before, and Johnny hadn't taken me by surprise, well, I reckon I would've had a chance to take them out. I don't think there's anything to worry about, you'll be fine if you head up to Baldwin's yard now. No need to wait till morning. Tomorrow might be a different scenario, they might have gathered a lot more of his crew. But of course, it's down to you.'

Without saying another word, Jason Robinson nodded to his men as he got back into the car, driving off at speed. Laughing loudly, Eddie raised his hand and waved goodbye before turning back to head towards the beach.

Ten minutes later, Eddie stood by the edge of the cliff as Johnny and his men skidded up in their black 4x4s. The driver's door of the leading car opened and Johnny jumped out.

'Where the fuck have you been? You were supposed to be waiting here.'

'I'm sorry, it took me longer to get across the marshes than I thought.'

In the dark, Johnny peered hard at Eddie. 'What's happened to your face?'

'I was jumped on.'

'What?'

'Jason Robinson.'

Johnny stared at Eddie. 'What are you talking about?'

Enjoying his moment, watching Johnny begin to panic, Eddie put on a sham of distress. 'Jason Robinson and his men, they did this. I thought they were going to kill me. I don't know how they didn't. They jumped me! I wasn't expecting it at all. I'd just watched you guys seeing off Alfie and his men, and when they scarpered I thought it was sweet as. Didn't think there was going to be a problem. Maybe it was my fault, but I had me guard down, so when they nabbed me, I wasn't ready . . . He took the diamonds, Johnny.'

Johnny grabbed hold of Eddie by the throat, squeezing it tightly as he screamed at the top of his voice. 'Jason Robinson! What the fuck is he doing here! How did he know? Have you been talking?'

Trying to get his breath, Eddie whispered his words. 'Not me, I ain't said anything. I know I owe him, but that don't mean I'd tell him about this. Why would I?'

'Someone has, and I want to know who that someone is.'

Eddie coughed and spluttered as Johnny's grip tightened. 'I'd like to know that too because whoever it is needs to be taught a lesson. But as they were leaving, and I was lying on the ground, I did hear something . . .'

Johnny dropped his grip, staring at Eddie with wild eyes. 'What?'

'I heard Jason say that he was heading up to Big Billy's yard. I'm thinking he's planning to take you all out. The element of surprise and all that.'

'You sure?'

'Absolutely. But I warn you, he had a whole heap of men with him, more than I've seen with him before. He meant business. If I was you, I'd take all your men so you can blast him out of the water.'

Eddie watched Johnny's procession of cars speed off before he headed back to get the diamonds and he whistled, knowing that the spider was going to catch the perma-tanned fly, and his problems would cease to exist.

71

Hyperventilating, Bree tried to hold the panic attack at bay. She covered her mouth with a paper bag she'd found in Ryan's bin and exhaled out before slowly inhaling and hoping that she wasn't going to have a full-blown attack.

What had she been thinking? How did she ever believe that she was going to get away with it? Now there was simply no escape. No way out of the situation she'd got herself into.

Her phone was in her jacket, which was back in her mobile home, and Ryan's window was locked tight. She'd also told Alfie she didn't know whether she'd be able to call or not, so he wouldn't be worried when she didn't get in touch. Every option she had was shut.

She was trapped. There was really nothing she could do apart from wait. Wait for Johnny to come back, wait for him to teach her a lesson, but without doubt this would be one of his 'special' lessons, saved for the times when he told her she'd been really bad. And every time she thought of that, her breathing became laboured and her chest became tight, and terror touched every part of her being.

Holding her head, crying, trying to be strong, Bree tried to picture herself anywhere but where she was. But she couldn't, she couldn't, no matter how hard she tried, because there was no getting away from it. She was where she was and not soaring over any trees, not running through any fields, not swimming in any seas, but locked up in Ryan's room, waiting.

Fear ran through her and she could hardly stand as her whole body trembled. She stared at the window. The glass was reinforced, but if she had something solid maybe she could break it and just keep running without turning back. It was a long shot, but what else could she do? She knew it might be her only chance to get out before Johnny came back.

Looking around Ryan's room, Bree's despair become total. There was nothing apart from the wicker wastepaper bin, a few books and a long-forgotten cup of tea. The only other thing in the room besides the cuckoo clock and the bed was the chest of drawers. Perhaps there was something in them she could use to break the window.

Hurriedly, trying not to get up too much hope, she started pulling Ryan's clothes out drawer by drawer. Pants and socks, jumpers and T-shirts, bottle tops and pebbles tucked away at the back, things that he loved collecting, but nothing that might help her.

Kneeling on the soft wool carpet, Bree opened the bottom drawer. She gasped, staring as she saw the rolled-up blue plastic bag she'd hidden in a box in the barn. Ryan must have watched her hiding the bag and taken it for himself as he did so many other things; hoarding bits and pieces and saving them like they were treasure.

She gently pulled out the bag and nervously peeked inside, catching her breath and feeling the same chill she'd felt the first time that she'd seen the tiny bones wrapped up in the dirty knitted shawl.

Pushing the clothes back, Bree's hand brushed against something else. It was a ragged hessian brown cloth. Curiously, she unwrapped it. She blinked – once, twice – staring in horror. It was more bones, looking like tiny skeletal remains wrapped up in a knitted yellow cardigan with white flower-shaped buttons . . . *The* yellow cardigan. The cardigan she had taken from the shop. No . . . No . . . No . . . She shook her head, it couldn't be. It wasn't possible. Surely it wasn't the same. She thought back . . .

She looked down at the beautiful, yellow cardigan and smiled. It was so small and so delicate, with white flower-shaped buttons and a satin hem. She *looked at the price tag. Too much for her to afford. But it was pretty . . . So pretty and she wanted it so much. Then quickly, without really thinking, Bree slipped the cardigan into her bag before hurriedly leaving the shop.*

Dropping the rag cloth and its contents as if they were on fire, Bree scrambled back, trying to get away, pushing herself into the far wall. She didn't want to think about it. She didn't want to look. Oh God. No . . . And then Bree Dwyer opened her mouth and began to scream.

72

Alfie Jennings paced about in the bed and breakfast. He couldn't believe they'd been so close, so near to pulling it all off. He had no idea that Johnny had so many men working for him, or maybe it was more the case, how few men he had himself. But whatever the reason, it was all messed up now, and wherever the diamonds were, he couldn't imagine how they could get them back. And on top of everything else to think about, there was Bree . . .

'Fuck!' He kicked the wall repeatedly, needing to take his anger out on something.

'Can you just stop?'

Janine interrupted Alfie's thoughts. He glared at her furiously.

'Shut up Janine, and start worrying about what we've just lost. Three million pounds' worth of diamonds and the chance of a proper future.'

Furious, and close to tears, Janine threw her hairbrush at him, catching him hard on his nose. 'I blame you, Alfie. You mess everything and everybody up.'

'I was trying to help, Janine. Something you wouldn't know about.'

'Then why are you here?'

Alfie stared at her with hostility as Frankie, Lola and Vaughn watched on. 'What are you talking about?'

'I don't much like what you've done Alf, and I don't know how I'm going to start to forgive you or Franny but I ain't a monster.'

'What's that supposed to mean?'

Janine shook her head. 'You don't get it do you? I feel for that Bree. Me heart goes out to her. She sounds like she's a scheming little mare, but sending her back to the likes of Johnny Dwyer, after she risked everything for you, wasn't one of your cleverest moves.'

'I never sent her back.'

Janine stood up and as was her habit, she poked him hard in the chest. 'No? But ask yourself what choice did you give her? Did any of you give her.'

Angry, Alfie shook his head. 'She couldn't come here anyway, so don't chew off me ear. She had the kids to think of, and this Ryan fella. There was no way she could just walk away because of what Johnny might do.'

'Exactly, but you all still let her go.'

Alfie began to pace, not wanting to admit what Janine was saying had more than a ring of truth to it. He snarled at her. 'It's not like that and you know it.'

Janine looked at each of them in turn. 'You lot need to go round there, and quick.'

Frankie shook his head. 'Come on Janine, we can't just go barging in, we got to think it through. You should've seen the amount of men Johnny had.'

Janine's tone was contemptuous. 'Heroes to the end, you lot. Bleedin' hell if I ever need help, remind me to stick to Superman.'

Alfie raised his voice but the worry, the fear for Bree he'd tried to put aside, began to creep in. 'Just pack it in, will you? Leave it.'

Ignoring Alfie's request, Janine pushed some more. 'Have you even spoken to her? Have you thought about what Johnny will do to her if he finds out that she gave you the heads-up? More to the point, Alfred, how can you be sure she's safe right now?'

Alfie Jennings stared at Janine and then at the others before heading for the door.

'Come on you lot, hurry up, let's go!'

Eddie Styler could hardly contain his excitement as he ran up the stairs of his house. He had to make sure he got a move on, though he was certain by the time Johnny and Jason realised what was happening, he'd be halfway to Scotland. Adios, Essex.

Taking the bag he'd already packed out of the wardrobe, Eddie ran back down the stairs to the kitchen, grabbing a large pink plastic bucket out of the cupboard along with four bottles of water and a family packet of crisps. He checked the time and, seeing it was just past midnight, he charged down the stairs to the basement and unlocked the wooden door.

'Hello Sandra, how it's going?'

Grinning nastily, he threw the bucket at her which she managed to catch.

'I'm afraid darlin,' it looks like you'll have to start pissing in that bucket again because I'm not going to be around. Shame about that, because I know just how much you hated it.'

'What are you talking about, Ed? And what the hell have you done to your face?'

'Never mind about me face sweetheart, because you're finally going to get what you deserve, and so am I.'

Sandra cut her eyes at Eddie, her tone was cold and flat. 'And what is it that you deserve, Eddie? Cos, I can't think of one bleedin' thing.'

'You should start being nice to me, Sandra.'

'And why's that then? How do you work that one out?'

Eddie rattled the keys. 'Because darlin', I hold your future in my hands.'

'You don't make sense, you're talking in riddles.'

Annoyed at his wife's attitude, Eddie snapped, his lips curling up into a sneer. 'The reason you better be nice, Sandra, is that it's down to me whether or not I let anybody know you're in here.' He paused, throwing the crisps and water to the other side of the room. 'It's been a long, miserable time coming Sand, but finally I'm on top. No more shitting on Eddie Styler. And as for what I deserve?'

A grin spread across his face and he chuckled loudly.

'These. These are what I deserve.'

Out of his pocket Eddie pulled a small bag. He waved them about in the air.

Shrugging, Sandra asked, 'What's that supposed to be? I still don't know what you're on about. I'm hardly going to be impressed with a dirty old bag, am I?'

'I'm talking about diamonds, Sandra. Three million pounds' worth of *my* diamonds. Not Johnny's, not Jason's and not your flipping brother's. Mine. In *my* hand. Happy days, darlin'.' He turned to walk away.

'Where are you going, Ed?'

With his back to Sandra, Eddie chortled. Revenge indeed was a sweet thing. He sighed contentedly. 'To start a new life, that's where, but don't worry, in a couple of days I'll let Alfie know you're down here. But for now, it's adios from me.'

'Are you sure about that, Ed?'

Sandra pulled back the trigger on the gun Alfie had given Bree. She pointed it at Eddie, who turned around, shock and horror filling his swollen, battered face in equal measures. She gestured him to move across to the far end of the room. Then, keeping the gun trained on him, Sandra moved to the door, closing and locking it behind her, leaving him in the dark.

'No, Eddie, I think you'll find it's adios from me.'

Deliberately choosing to drive down the country lanes to avoid taking the main roads, Alfie Jennings drove at speed through the village of Great Yeldham, anxiety mixing with adrenaline. At the tiny church, he put his foot down, hitting eighty as he sped on through, the street lights fading as they headed once more into the darkness of the night. As he raced round a corner his phone rang. He hit the answer button on the steering wheel.

'Hello?'

'Alfie, it's me.'

'Sandra, Jesus, where've you been?'

Alfie could hear the urgency in his sister's voice. 'I ain't got time to tell you now, but I've got Eddie . . . and he's got the diamonds.'

'What? Are you serious? How?'

'It's a long story but you need to get here. You need to hurry.'

Driving over a pothole, Alfie swore, and skidded right at a deserted junction. 'Sand, are you sure? I don't want to get me hopes up.'

'I'm certain, there's no mistake. He's in me basement. Can you come, right now?'

'Of course. Listen, we were on our way to see if Bree was alright, but we can do a detour. Where are you now?'

'I'm just near Hornchurch, I needed to get out of the house, go for a walk, Eddie's banging at the door and it's doing me head in.'

'Okay, can you go back to the house? I'll be there in about an hour. See you soon.'

As Alfie cut off the call, Janine, sitting in the passenger seat, glanced across to him. 'Are you sure we shouldn't just go straight to Bree?'

'It'll be fine. It'll just be a quick detour. Stop worrying.'

But as he said it, Alfie Jennings knew that's exactly what he was beginning to do.

73

Bree wanted to make as much noise as she could, so she picked up the bed, turning it over as she yelled at the top of her voice, tears streaming down her face. 'Ma! Ma! Ma!'

She held her stomach as she paced around, her thoughts racing, but they weren't really making any kind of sense.

'Ma! Ma!'

Grabbing hold of the drawers, Bree pushed them over, sending them tumbling and crashing against the wall. She tore Ryan's cuckoo clock off the wall, throwing it as hard as she could at the window. 'Ma!'

She hammered on the door, not caring, not feeling the fear that had crippled her for so many years. The fear that had stopped her walking out. The fear that had caused her to keep all the secrets. Now she had nothing left to lose. 'Ma! Ma! Come here! I want to talk to you, come here!'

The sound of the door being unlocked had Bree swivelling round, her eyes were wild, her face wet with tears. She charged at Ma, her arms flying as she lashed out.

'Murderer! You killed her!'

Bree fought with all her might as Ma clung onto her arms. 'What the hell do you think you're doing? You're going to pay for this. You've gone mad! Just wait till Johnny comes home!'

With hatred burning through her, Bree screamed at Ma. 'Look! Look!'

She pointed to the yellow cardigan lying on the floor and a brief flicker of shock crossed Ma's face.

'How could you do it? How could you?'

Ma, stronger and taller, slapped Bree across the face then gripped hold of her arm again, shaking her hard. 'What are you talking about?'

'You said my baby went to relatives in Ireland, you told me she was fine.'

'She is.'

'Liar! Stop lying! Stop playing your games!'

Bree broke away from Ma, sobbing and shaking, backing away.

'All these years, Ma, all these years. I thought that one day I might have a chance to see her. You told me that one day you'd bring her back to me.'

Full of rage now, Ma's voice turned to scorn as she lunged towards Bree, cornering her in the room, standing inches away. 'Then you're stupid, ain't you. You make Ryan look like he's Bill Gates.'

'But you told me I wasn't well enough to look after her, then you told me it was better for her if she stayed where she was because she was happy, and I believed you! Because that's all I wanted, for her to be happy.'

'It just suited you to think that, eased your conscious. Face it Bree, you didn't care. I did you a favour by telling you that.'

Bree shook her head, gasping for air between sobs. 'That's not true, that's not true!'

'If it's not true, then why did you stop asking? Stop wanting her back?'

'Because it hurt too much.'

'Then you're the fool, ain't you?'

Bree leapt at Ma, her fingernails tearing at her face. She swung her fist, but Ma managed to push her away, sending her backwards to bang her head on the corner of a drawer. With blood running down her face, Bree began to rock. 'You killed her! Why Ma, why?'

Ma's voice sounded puzzled. 'What are you talking about? This ain't my fault, none of it's my fault. It's yours. Nobody asked you to run away that night, but you did. You were pregnant, and you ran off, dragging Ryan with you. What did you expect would happen?'

'Not this!'

'You started to bleed and went into labour too soon, how's that my fault, Bree? We did everything we could to save them. They were weak and underweight. They were ill. It broke my heart to see them born and needing morphine the minute they came into this world. But I blame you for that. If you'd just behaved yourself, just listened like you were supposed to, none of this would've happened. I wouldn't have had to give it you, and them poor little mites wouldn't have been born addicted to the stuff. What chance did they ever have? We buried them up in the woods, and I tell you something Bree, it was one of the worst days of me life. And I'll never forgive you for that because you knew, *you knew*, that nobody leaves Ma.'

Bree stared at her, then glanced down at the yellow cardigan and white knitted shawl. In a whisper she said, 'What do you mean, *them*?'

Nastily, Ma cackled. 'Oh, did I forget to tell you, you had twins.'

Without saying another word, Bree Dwyer leapt up and suddenly bolted for the door, running into the night.

74

'Hello! Hello! Sandra, you've had your joke, now just let me out. I ain't going to be cross but enough is enough. Sandra, I'm talking to you.' Eddie banged on the door as he listened to the footsteps in the house. He couldn't see anything much in the pitch black and he needed to use the bathroom, but there was no way he was going to use the pink plastic bucket, he felt degraded enough as it was. He'd been humiliated and he didn't appreciate what Sandra had done. He certainly wasn't going to let her get away with it. But for now he'd play whatever game he needed to.

'Sandra, I can hear you. Come on, just let me out. Come on darlin'. A joke's a joke. I know you were upset but we can sort this out. Baby . . . Sandra!'

A minute later Eddie heard the door being unlocked, and he sighed, relieved as he pushed down his rising temper. Who the hell did she think she was? Well he would show her.

The door flung open and the light shone in. 'Listen here, Sandra . . .' Eddie trailed off. He stared open-mouthed. Standing in front of him was Johnny Dwyer.

'Johnny . . . I . . . I . . .'

'Wasn't expecting me?'

Trying not to sound nervous, his voice tilted on the edge of hysteria, Eddie said, 'No, but what a nice surprise . . . This is Sandra's idea of a joke. She thinks it's funny to lock me in. Always did have a strange sense of humour that one.'

Johnny held Eddie's nervous stare. 'Is that right?'

'Yeah . . .'

There was silence before Eddie tried to fill the uncomfortable, strained atmosphere. 'So how did you get on with Jason? Or didn't you manage to find him?'

'Oh no, we found him alright. We didn't find the diamonds though.'

Eddie gulped. 'No?'

'No. Odd that, don't you think, but not to worry, I did manage to have a little chat with him. It's amazing what people tell you when they're dying. People's final words can be so revealing, wouldn't you say, Eddie? I reckon you and me need to have a few words.'

Alfie and the others hurried down the gravel driveway following Sandra. About to put the key in the door, she frowned. The door was ajar.

Backing away slightly, she whispered to Alfie. 'Alf, someone's been in here.'

'Are you sure?'

'Well I didn't leave the door open, at least I don't think I did.'

Alfie, Vaughn and Frankie all pulled out their guns but it was Alfie who said, 'Sandra, take Lola and Janine back to the car.'

Janine hissed at the three men. 'I ain't going back anywhere. We came together, we'll stick together.'

Alfie's face darkened. 'This is not the time to argue, Janine.'

'That's right, it ain't, now go on. This is important for us all.'

Knowing he was fighting a losing battle and aware that the clock was ticking away when it came to Bree, Alfie glanced at the two men. 'Come on, we'll go first.'

Familiar with the layout of the hall, Alfie tiptoed along the left-hand wall, gun drawn, finger at the ready. At the top of the basement stairs he waited, listening for any sound, before keeping his voice low as he spoke to Vaughn.

'Vaughnie, why don't you head upstairs, make sure there's nobody about, and Frank, you watch the front door, we don't want anybody coming in and giving us a nasty surprise . . . And girls, do us a favour and stay up top.'

Alfie crept down the stairs, pushing his body against the wall with his gun held close to his body. He tried to concentrate, tried to ignore the fact that, despite his instructions, Janine was following him down the stairs, Lola and Sandra were too, but he was the only one who was armed. He glanced around again, stopping for a moment and checking there was no noise.

Halfway down the stairs, Alfie stopped in his tracks again. He could see a pool of blood seeping from under the wooden door and, breaking into a run, he signalled to the others to stay back.

Slowly and carefully, he crept forward, pointing his gun as he opened the door.

'Jesus!' There on the floor with a single bullet in his head was Eddie Styler. He turned to his sister. 'Sandra, you might not want to see this.'

Sandra, guessing what had happened, opened the door wider. Her voice was embittered as she thought about her lonely, miserable years of marriage life. 'Oh, believe me Alf, I do. There certainly wasn't any love lost between us . . . Are the diamonds still there? He had them in his pocket when I left him.'

Alfie quickly searched Eddie's pockets. He shook his head, anger coursing through him.

'Fuck! Fuck! They've gone.'

Janine, staring at Eddie's lifeless body, asked, 'Who do you reckon is behind this, Alf?'

Alfie spoke knowingly. 'I'll bet me life on it that it was Johnny Dwyer.'

Lola, her voice full of concern, looked at Alfie. 'Then if he can do this to Eddie, what is he going to do to Bree?'

75

Bree could hear Johnny calling her name as she crept into the woodshed. It was dark and she could hardly see anything, but she knew she couldn't put the light on and as silently as she could, terrified to make any noise, Bree looked on the shelves, squinting to see properly in the blackness.

'Bree! Bree, where are you? Johnny's coming!'

Trembling, she pulled some boxes down, taking off the cardboard lids, but there were only screws and tools and nails.

'Bree, you know I'll find you!'

She froze. It sounded to Bree like any moment now, Johnny would come through the door; his voice was getting louder and louder.

Still shaking, she crouched on the floor, pulling more boxes out from underneath the workbench. Some were too heavy to lift and Bree winced at the noise of them scraping along the concrete ground, certain Johnny would hear.

Opening the lid of a large white box, Bree finally saw what she was looking for. Johnny's guns. With no idea how to use the two machine guns, Bree picked out a black, small calibre pistol.

'Bree! Come to Johnny!'

She gasped at his voice, trying to steady herself as panic began to overwhelm her. Her body jolting in spasms of fear as she released the single stack magazine of the pistol, checking it was loaded. Her heart sank as she saw there was only one bullet, and she quickly rummaged at the bottom of the box for more ammunition. There was nothing there.

'Bree!'

Terrified, Bree looked up at the small shed window covered in wire, watching as Johnny stalked past. Wanting to scream, she covered her mouth tight, desperate not to make a sound. Listening, she heard his feet on the gravelled path walking away towards the barn, and quickly she pushed the magazine back into the gun, slipping the pistol into her pocket as she tiptoed to the door, waiting for her chance to run.

Opening the door only a few centimetres, Bree peered through the crack, watching Johnny walk towards Billy's car, which had just driven up with Kieran and Molly in the back. She watched as Johnny bundled them out of the car, making them go into Ma's mobile home, before he angrily began to stalk about the grounds again, looking for her.

Waiting for him to disappear into the darkness, Bree began to run towards the woods. She leant on a tree, crouching down. Somehow she had to go back and get them, as well as trying to find Ryan. From where she was crouching she could now see Ma was looking for her too, calling her name.

'Bree! Bree, come on out,' Johnny shouted. 'You know that I'm going to find you eventually. Make it easy on yourself. Molly and Kieran are waiting for you, Bree. They want to see you! Ma's told me what you did. You've been bad, Bree. Very bad.'

Seeing Johnny walking towards where she was hiding, Bree ran back into the darkness of the woods, stumbling along the path, breathing hard as she made her way down to the outhouses.

'Bree, I can see you.'

Panicked, she spun around, looking all about. Her eyes trying to adjust to the night.

'I'm coming, Bree! Ready or not.'

Johnny's laugh was high and manic as Bree set off running again, tripping over bushes and brambles, stumbling into the ditch, thorns and sticks tearing at her skin. Scrabbling back up covered in mud, Bree sprinted forward, keeping her eye out for Johnny as she slipped and staggered through the trees.

She could still see the mobile site from where she was and if she just stayed put, maybe she could wait and watch out for Ryan. Creeping backwards she suddenly banged into something hard, then she felt someone grab her. She screamed as she began to fight, terrified and trembling, scratching at whoever it was who held her tight.

'Bree.'

She stopped struggling at the warmth of the voice. She turned. 'Ryan?'

He nodded.

'Ryan, what were you doing? You gave me a fright. Come on, quickly, we have to go.'

'Is that right, Bree? You ain't leaving Johnny, *ever*.' She screamed, pulling back as she realised it wasn't Ryan, but Johnny, and in her terror she kicked out, catching Johnny hard in the groin. He doubled up in pain, giving her a chance to escape.

She charged through the woods, banging into trees as she listened to Johnny shout.

'Have it your way, Bree, I ain't going to chase you, I got better things to do. Like have some fun with Ryan.'

She froze, coming to a standstill on the muddy path.

'Bree! I know you can hear me, I know you're out there, so why don't you come and watch the fun, because Ryan's going to be in trouble. *Big trouble*.'

Her eyes filled with tears as the rain battered down and trance-like she turned, walking back towards the mobile site.

At the gravel path she saw them. Ma, Billy Baldwin and Johnny, chains in their hands, dogs at their feet, and Ryan, standing terrified, holding his head in his hands as he rocked back and forth on the spot.

'Here she is. I knew you'd come, Bree. Ryan, look who it is. It's Bree.' Johnny snarled as he laughed.

'Bree, Bree, big trouble, big trouble.' Ryan chanted, his eyes full of tears as he shook, the front of his trousers damp from wetting himself.

Rushing towards Ryan, Bree tried to soothe him. 'It's okay Ryan, Bree's here. I'm here.'

'Bree's here. Bree's here.'

'That's it, baby. Shhh. It's alright.'

Johnny spun the chain in his hand. 'Me and Ma are going to teach you a lesson, Ryan,' he growled menacingly.

'Leave him alone, Johnny. Can't you see he's terrified.'

'And who's fault is that, Bree? You know what happens, if you mess up.'

'Then do it to me, hurt me.'

Holding the barking dog back, Johnny snapped. 'That ain't so much fun though, is it? Look at him. Look at your lover boy now.'

Bree turned to Ryan as he sobbed. She took his trembling hand away from his head, holding it tight.

'Why, Johnny? What did he ever do to you? What did I ever do to you? In all these years of you hating us, I've never understood why any of it had to happen.'

Johnny's voice broke with angry emotion. 'It's your fault. All this. You and Ryan's.'

'I don't understand.'

'Because you were going to leave me.'

'What? What are you talking about?'

'Both of ya, that night, all that time ago. I heard you outside me window. You were planning to leave. You were both going to leave me! You were going to leave me with her! With Ma!'

'Johnny, you could've come with us.'

He screamed out in fury. 'You never asked! You never fucking asked! And now he's going to pay, ain't that right, Ma?'

Ryan began to chant again as Johnny, Billy and Ma walked forward. 'Bree, Bree, Bree, Bree, Bree.'

'It's okay, Ryan. Stay away from him. Leave him alone.' She pulled out the pistol from her pocket, pointing it at them and for just a moment a flicker of unease came over Johnny's face. Then he grinned as he nodded to the gun Billy was holding.

'What are you going to do, Bree. Take us all out? You're forgetting that's my gun, and I know how many bullets there are in there. Just the one!' He laughed nastily as he spun the heavy chain in his hand. Speaking to his brother then, he said, 'I'm coming for you, Ryan. She ain't going to help you.'

Ma laughed, staring at Ryan in disdain.

Ryan turned around in circles on the spot, holding his head in terror. 'Bree, Bree, Bree, Bree.'

Bree, not unkindly, shouted at Ryan. 'Stop! Ryan, stop. Look at me!'

Ryan turned to look at her, his eyes wide and innocent.

With her voice trembling and tears running down her face, Bree softened her voice again. 'You were right Ryan, you were right about having to leave here and that's what you're going to do. I won't let them hurt you anymore. I promise baby, I promise. No one will ever hurt you again. I love you so much. I never stopped loving you, I just couldn't save you. But now you'll be free, like that bird. Fly Ryan, fly.'

And with that, Bree Dwyer pointed the gun at Ryan and pulled the trigger, blowing a hole in his chest, and to the sound of Bree's anguished scream, Ryan slumped to the ground, his eyes rolling back in his head.

Running over to him, Bree cradled Ryan's head in her arms, kissing him gently on his lips as she whispered, 'Come back to me Ryan, come back to me in my dreams.'

76

Hearing a shot, Alfie began to run. 'Bree! Bree!'

His voice called out in the darkness, drowned out by the noise of shots he fired into the air, causing Ma and Johnny and Billy to scatter, trying to see who was shooting.

As Alfie sprinted over to Bree, his expression turned to shock. He crouched down by her side as she buried her face in Ryan's body. 'Bree, come on darlin', we have to go. You got to leave him. It ain't safe. It ain't safe to be here.'

She shook her head. 'I did this.'

He glanced around, checking for any of Johnny's men. 'What?'

'I killed him, Alfie.'

With his eyes darting around anxiously, Alfie said, 'I don't know what's happened here, but Bree, we've got to go. *Please*.'

'I can't leave him. Not here.'

'Bree, please, there's no time. Vaughn and Frankie are down near the barn. We've parked the car along the track and we've got the kids.'

'What?'

'They were playing outside one of the mobile homes, we've put them in the car. Come on!'

He grabbed her by the hand, then taking one last look at Ryan, they ran – back down the path, towards the track. Hearing a noise, they ducked down behind the chicken coop and Alfie watched as Johnny went into the barn.

'Stay here, Bree. Keep down.'

Bree's voice was tight and panicked. Shock of the night sinking in. 'No, Alfie, don't.'

'It's fine, he doesn't look like he's armed.'

'But that's where he keeps some of his guns. It's probably what he's gone in there to get.'

'Trust me. I'll be fine.'

Without waiting for her reply, Alfie crept along to the front, slowly opening the creaking door. Staying low and hiding behind the bales of hay, he held his gun up listening for any noise. Creeping quietly towards the far end of the barn, a sound to the side of him had Alfie spinning around before a hail of bullets blazed down around him.

Alfie aimed his gun, firing back as Johnny ran out of sight. More shots were fired from Johnny, but Alfie couldn't see where they were coming from, so he sprinted along the wooden wall and took cover behind several large bags of feed. Alfie threw himself down, raising his gun and craning his head round the feed bags.

He was breathing hard, unable to see properly in the dim light, then suddenly a shadow loomed above him. Alfie pulled the trigger, just as he felt the searing pain as a bullet ripped through his shoulder.

Yelling in anguish, Alfie dived to the side, gritting his teeth as he pushed on his shoulder with his hand, trying to stop the flow of blood. He heard the barn door swing open, and just caught sight of Johnny running out.

With the storm getting up, Johnny charged across to his mobile home, looking to see if Billy was about. Banging open the door, he rushed into his bedroom, stuffing his clothes into a bag. He didn't know how many of Alfie's men were about and he didn't want to wait and see. And besides, he wanted out.

Hurrying back down the hallway, Johnny stopped to grab the picture off the wall of him and Ryan when they were little boys, then running out into the stormy night he came to an abrupt halt as Ma stood in the driveway, a gun tucked under her arm.

'Where's Billy?' Johnny asked.

'He's been shot. One of them men took him out in the woods.'

'Fuck. Fuck.' Johnny began to walk again, picking up his pace as he glanced around and headed for his car.

'Where are you going, Johnny?'

He shouted through the wind. 'I'm leaving, Ma. I'm out of here. I ain't doing this anymore. I can't do it.'

'What are you talking about.'

He spun round, staring at her in contempt. 'I'm talking about this. Here. I should've left you ages ago. Me and Ryan should've gone, but now look what's happened. It's all a mess. A fucking mess and the noise in me head don't get any quieter.'

Ma sounded distressed. 'You can't leave me. What am I going to do without you? Johnny, I love you.'

'I don't care anymore.'

Ma's face screwed up in fury. 'You will care, even if I have to make you! If I tell you to stay here, you'll stay here!'

'No, Ma. I ain't Ryan, and you ain't going to tell me what to do ever again. Now get out of me way.'

'But you can't go.'

'Just watch me, Ma. Watch me go.'

Johnny headed towards his car, throwing his bag in the back. He grabbed his coat from the hook in the corner then he turned around to get into the driver's seat, and standing there, smiling, was Ma.

'Please son, won't you change your mind?'

'Never.'

Her faced darkened and she shoved the barrel of her gun into her son's abdomen. 'Johnny, when will you learn, son, that nobody leaves Ma.'

And at that, Ma Dwyer pulled the trigger.

Bree was traumatised and scared. She stared at Frankie, terror on her face as they stood at the end of the road. 'Where are the kids? Are they alright?'

'It's fine, Bree. They're in the car. They're okay, don't panic.'

As Bree ran to the car, Frankie turned to Alfie who was holding his shoulder, grimacing in pain.

'I don't know if it's the right time to tell you, but Johnny's dead.'

'What?'

'I was heading to where he parked his car, and saw his ma shoot him. Blew him clean away. Saved us a job anyway.'

Alfie shook his head. 'Jesus Christ.'

'I didn't want to sound insensitive in front of Bree, but just before Johnny and Ma got to the car, I grabbed his bag. We've got the diamonds.'

Unable to muster up any sort of enthusiasm, Alfie watched Bree smile as she opened the back door of the car to greet her children. But her face instantly froze.

'Molly, where's Kieran?'

Molly shrugged as she held onto her teddy bear.

'Please sweetheart, tell Mummy where he is.'

'He went back to the caravan.'

'What's the matter?' Alfie walked up behind her.

'Kieran, he's gone back to Ma.'

Without waiting for his reply, Bree began to run, racing down the muddy, potholed track towards the mobile home.

Catching up with her, trying to ignore the agony in his shoulder, Alfie grabbed hold of her with his good arm. 'Bree, hold up. Think about this. Just wait. It's dangerous.'

She shook her head, pulling herself free, fighting to get away from Alfie's grip. 'I can't wait. I can't!'

She turned and began to run again, charging along the road and ignoring Alfie as he called her back.

'Bree! Bree, stop!'

Running up to the caravan, Bree banged on it hard. She yelled at the top of her voice, crying, angry, waves of emotion overwhelming her.

'Open the door! Ma, open the door. Where is he? Where's Kieran?'

The door flung open, and there, standing in her dressing gown, was Ma. A shot gun held tightly under her arm. She stared at Bree. 'You've got some fucking front coming here. You killed my boy. You're lucky I don't kill you.'

Shaking, Bree stood her ground. 'I want him. I want Kieran to come with me.'

Ma grinned, hissing with angry laughter. 'How dare you, after everything you've done. You've got the nerve to come here and ask for Kieran?'

Still not backing down, Bree's voice was firm. 'I want him, Ma. He needs to come with me.'

'I don't think so.'

'I love him, Ma.'

'Point is, I don't think he loves you, and he doesn't want to leave Ma.'

Bree trembled. 'Ask him then.'

'Oh, I will. I will.' Ma's eyes narrowed. Keeping her focus on Bree, she called over her shoulder. 'Kieran! Kieran! Come here, boy.'

Kieran Dwyer walked down the hallway, his features darkening as he saw Bree standing by the door. Speaking softly to him, Ma pulled him gently towards her.

'Now Kieran, this is important, the question I'm going to ask you. You need to tell me where you want to be. You want to be here with me? Or do you want to be with her and Molly? Tell me the truth, Ma ain't going to be cross.'

Bree smiled at Kieran. 'Why don't you come with me, sweetheart. You and me and Molly, we could go and live somewhere else. Somewhere nice.'

'This is my home. I was here before you. So why don't you leave. I don't want you here anymore.' He glanced at Ma and then pulled himself loose from her hold and stepping away he turned his back and said, 'I want to be with you, Ma. No one should ever leave Ma.'

'There's your answer, Bree.' And with that, Ma Dwyer slammed the door leaving Bree, standing frozen to the spot, pain etched on her face.

Alfie came up to her. 'I'll go and get him.'

'No.'

'It's fine, she don't bother me.'

'I said, no.'

Alfie looked bemused. 'You can't let her do this, Bree. You can't leave him with her.'

Ignoring Alfie once again, Bree walked away, back towards the car, tears running down her face. He moved in front of her, blocking her way. 'What the hell are you playing at? Just take him.'

'You heard him, Alfie, he don't want to be with me.'

'He's only a kid, his mind's a bit messed up that's all. Just take him.'

Bree looked at Alfie, pain and hurt pouring from her. 'You don't understand, do you?'

'I understand that you're leaving your boy.'

'But that's just it, Alf. That's the point. He ain't my boy, he ain't my son. God, how I wish he was.'

'What? I don't understand, who are his real parents then?'

'Alfie, Kieran is *Ma*'s son. Ma and Johnny's biological son.'

TWO MONTHS LATER

Alfie, Frankie and Vaughn sat around Janine's kitchen table along with Reenie Reynolds and two of her late husband's henchmen. Alfie winked at Reenie, who sat dressed head to toe in black designer clothes, playing the grieving widow, though most of Essex knew she'd already set up with her toy boy. He nodded to the piles of money on the table.

'It's all there Reenie, all two million quid, in untraceable notes.'

Reenie sniffed, her face caked with foundation and her dyed black, hairsprayed beehive not moving an inch as she shook her head. Her cockney accent was even thicker than Alfie's. 'It bleedin' better be, Alf. For a moment there, I thought you were going to fuck this up. Mess it up like most things you do.'

Alfie gave a tight smile, glancing at Lola and Janine who stood by the sink watching.

'You've got to be joking. There was no way this was going to go wrong.'

Janine coughed loudly, and Alfie gave her a hostile glare.

'Well I'm glad, cos I like you boys. Reginald wanted to hand over the business to somebody he respected and would know how to handle things. I'm just happy that things have worked out like they have. I'm not interested in trying to keep the business running, it's too much of a headache if you ain't got a clue. So just show me the money.'

Alfie grinned. 'And that's exactly what we're doing, darlin'. Two million pounds of showing you.'

'And you're getting a touch at that,' Reenie said haughtily.

'I know, and we appreciate it Reen. We're looking forward to getting the business back up and running. We've already sorted out the on-course bookies' licences from the gambling commission, so we can set up the pitches at Newmarket and Chelmsford. Though we had to give a proper bung to those in charge to get everybody's name on the licence, but what can you do? We could hardly go in front of local magistrates for them to assess whether we was fit and proper people to carry out the activity, could we?'

Reenie laughed loudly, as did the others. 'And what about the betting shops?'

'They'll take a bit longer to reopen but, Lola, Janine and me sister, Sandra, will oversee the recruiting side. Like Reginald, we'll use the shops for legal gambling but also, we'll be able to launder money through them, which will be sweet. And then of course, there's the betting rings and the racetrack protection he had. Me, Frank and Vaughnie will be running that once we've sorted out the men we want to work for us. We don't just want anybody, obviously.'

Taking a bite from the egg cress sandwich that Lola had made, Reenie said, 'Some of Reggie's men were good, trustworthy. Apart from that runt, Eddie. But most of them had been with him for years, and they'd be happy to work for you guys, I'm sure. Why don't we set up a meeting with them next week, and you can take it from there?'

'That's sounds like a good idea. I think this would be a good moment for us to have a toast to the future. Janine get the champagne, I'm just going to find Bree. She should be part of this too.'

Upstairs in one of the bathrooms, Bree stared at the pregnancy test. It read positive. She closed her eyes, opening them quickly as the image of Ryan lying dead in her arms filled her head as it so often did. The past couple of months she'd struggled to cope with the guilt of what she'd done. It consumed her like a hungry wolf. If it hadn't been for Molly, and Alfie's kindness in letting her stay at the house, treating her so beautifully, so passionately, holding her tight in his arms at night, she didn't know what she would've done. And even though it was only early days with Alfie, perhaps she would've been excited to be pregnant if it wasn't for the fact that she didn't know if it was Alfie's or Johnny's baby she was carrying.

'Bree, you okay, darlin'? We're just about to do a toast.' Alfie knocked on the grand, wooden door.

'Yeah, I'm fine. I'll be out in a minute. Just give me a second.'

'Okay.'

As Alfie Jennings waited by the door, his phone buzzed in his pocket. He pulled it out and read the text.

> Alfie, I know you're probably angry with me, but like I said b4, I had something I needed to do, which I couldn't tell you about. But I want to explain now. But I'm going to come and do it face to face. I'll be home next week . . . And Alfie, I love you. I hope you can forgive me. Fran x

'All ready. Are you okay?' Bree spoke as she opened the bathroom door.

'Yeah, you?' Alfie replied, quickly shoving his phone back in his pocket.

Bree nodded, not quite meeting his eye. 'Yeah.'

'Good, come on then. If we're not careful, Janine will have drunk all the champers.'

They smiled at each other, neither one noticing the tension that lurked behind their eyes. As Alfie followed Bree down the stairs, he knew that Franny coming home could only mean one thing – trouble. Big, big trouble.

THE END

If you loved *Toxic*, turn the page for a sneak peek from Jacqui's thrilling new book *Fatal* coming soon . . .

Adesso

Now

Cabhan Morton, a man with trouble on his mind, stepped out from the luxury private wooden lodge into the chill of the summer evening. Shivering, he stood dressed in a white linen shirt, watching the shimmering waters of Grand Lake which nestled at the bottom of the Rocky Mountain National Park, Colorado.

He let out a long sigh as he walked across the deserted glazed timber boardwalk against the backdrop of the snow-tipped mountains. The town of Grand Lake – a tiny community of about five hundred people – was the perfect place, away from prying eyes and ears, for the annual meet up of the Russo brothers and the extended family.

Pulling out his phone and dialling a familiar number, Cabhan listened as Franny Doyle's voicemail clicked in straightaway. He needed to speak to her urgently. Scrolling down his contacts, he tried another number. This time it rang twice before he heard Alfie Jennings chirpily inviting him to leave a message.

Frustrated, Cabhan cut off the call as a burst of loud laughter made him glance around. From the shadows he watched Bobby and Salvatore Russo walking down the stairs of the luxury hideout, deep in conversation.

He'd been here too long. When he'd needed it, leaving England to come and work for the Russo brothers had been the perfect solution to his problems and the painful memories. But now he wanted out. And the quicker the better.

He wanted to go back home, maybe not to Ireland, but at least to England. Take his beautiful daughter, Alice Rose – the daughter he didn't know he had until four years ago – away from this life. Because apart from Franny, who he loved like his own, and her father, Patrick, Alice with her gentleness and innocence was simply the best thing that had ever happened to him, and by far the best part of him, and he was determined to take her back home to family. To Franny. To Alfie. To everything which made him feel safe. Though trying to get the Russo brothers to let him go was another thing entirely. He knew it'd be at a price, but the problem was he wasn't sure what that price would be.

Salvatore's loud, coarse New Jersey drawl, cut through the air.

'Hey Cabhan, hey Cabhan, what the hell are you doing out here? We've got guests.'

'Just making a call.'

Shrugging, Salvatore looked at his brother, Bobby, as he continued to speak to Cabhan.

'You can't make the call inside? I thought we were all friends here? Family. What's so goddamn secret you need to hide out here?'

The cold stare from Salvatore made Cabhan feel uneasy. Since he'd told the brothers he'd wanted to leave, the suspicion and paranoia had set in, especially with Salvatore who ran the main branch of the family business along the East Coast.

Cabhan replied, his soft Irish lilt coated his words, 'No, not at all, I didn't want to be rude. I thought I'd just check in with Franny and Alfie, see how they are. It's been awhile since I've spoken to them. The time difference doesn't help. Apologies if I was out of line.'

Salvatore, his steroid-pumped muscular frame blocking out the light from the lodge door way, continued to stare. 'Give me your phone.'

'What?'

'I said, give it me.'

Hesitantly, Cabhan – his face strained, with his black velvet skin paling slightly – walked across to where Salvatore stood, placing the phone in his outstretched hand.

He spoke evenly. 'Like I say, Sal, I was just calling home. See for yourself.'

Salvatore, holding eye contact before breaking it to scroll through Cabhan's call log, pressed last number redial. Staying silent, he put the phone to his ear, listening as the voicemail clicked in.

'*This is Alfie, I can't answer right . . .*'

Salvatore's laugh startled the old man standing by the door. Loud and menacing. He grabbed hold of Cabhan's shoulders, shaking him hard, pressing his flushed face into Cabhan's. His breath sweet and sickly, stinking of cigars. 'See what you've done to me Cabhan, you've made me a bag of nerves. All this talk of you wanting to leave makes me edgy. Can't understand what the problem is. Why the big change. Maybe I should start looking over my shoulder.'

Cabhan, feeling the hard bone of Salvatore's forehead pushing on the bridge of his nose, knew better than to try to pull away. 'It's not personal, Salvatore. You know that. I just miss home.'

Salvatore stepped back, looking up into the night sky. 'Not personal?

'That's right, Sal. I appreciate everything you've done for me. Giving me a job and welcoming me as part of the family, but that's the point, I miss *my* family. Franny. Alfie. Like I say, it's not personal.'

Salvatore nodded, closing his eyes before whipping out a pistol from his pocket, banging it and pressing it hard into Cabhan's face. 'And neither is this.'

Cabhan's hands shot up in the air. 'Sal, please.'

'Get on your knees. I said get on your fucking knees unless you want me to put a hole in you now.'

'Sal, please, Jesus Christ, you and me, we go back a long way. *Ti rispetto, ti amo Salvatore, tu e la tua famiglia.*'

Another burst of laughter came from Salvatore. 'You say you respect me? You love me and my family?'

'I do.'

Salvatore flicked off the safety catch of the gun. 'Yet you want to leave and go back home. To me that doesn't sound like a man who loves and has loyalty to his friends. And a man that doesn't have loyalty is a dangerous enemy.'

Bobby Russo, his temper as violent and as volatile as his brother's, yet with the ability to recognise discretion was sometimes needed, spoke as he kept his eye on the door of the lodge as more and more guests, curious at the commotion, began to come outside.

'Sal, why don't we sort this out tomorrow? We're celebrating. We've all had a good year. Put the gun away. Cabhan was only calling Franny and Alfie. That's all. *Nessun danno fatto*. No harm done . . . Good? *Bene*?' Bobby kissed his brother on both cheeks. '*Bene?*'

Salvatore, stared at Bobby, slowly nodding, his face showing a thousand thoughts. He answered slowly. '*Si. Bene.*'

A grin spread across Bobby's pockmarked face, the handsome Russo genes not having passed down to him. 'That's right, Sal. All good. No harm! *Nessun problema.* No problem!' He broke his hold, grinning at the guests. 'Nothing to see here, ladies and gentlemen! Please, continue to enjoy, we've talked business too long. Now we celebrate.'

Helping Cabhan to his feet, Salvatore slapped him hard on the back as he pulled out a gold cigarette case from his pocket. He snapped it open, revealing several grams of finely cut up cocaine along with an engraved toot. 'Have a line with me, Cabhan.'

'No, I'm fine.'

The ice ran back into Salvatore's words. 'I said, have one.'

Cabhan, realising he had no other choice, took the toot, bending over the cigarette case as Salvatore watched him snort a line.

'Again . . . Have another.'

It was just a glance from Cabhan, a slight hesitation, but enough for Salvatore to again think to himself how he didn't trust Cabhan's motives anymore.

'Cabhan!' Alexandra Russo, Salvatore's, spoilt, seventeen-year-old niece, shouted loudly as she swayed her curvaceous body down the stairs.

'Cabhan, I want a lift home, I'm tired! In fact give me the fucking keys, I'll drive, and you can keep me company.'

Looking at Alexandra, Cabhan hid his disdain whilst attempting to sound courteous. 'Ally, I'm happy to take you home, you know I am, but it's probably best if I drive.'

Ally licked her lips seductively before her face screwed up in anger. She poked Cabhan hard in his chest. 'Don't ever try to fucking tell me what's best, *especially* in public, or I might have to get Uncle Sal to teach you about respect. *Capisci?*'

Evenly, Cabhan answered, remembering the last occasion Salvatore on Alexandra's orders had paid him a visit to remind him of the Russos' definition of respect. That particular visit had landed him two weeks in the lower Manhattan hospital. 'Oh I understand, Ally. You've made your point very clear . . . as you always do.'

A large smile spread across Ally's face. 'Then what are we waiting for, let's go.'

And as Salvatore Russo watched them drive away, he smiled to himself, because although he'd been outvoted by the rest of the Russo family on permanently disposing of Cabhan, he was sure, once he'd spoken to Nico, that might change. After all, Cabhan had been privy to the family business and there was no guarantee he wouldn't start shooting his mouth off once he'd left. And the one certainty about dead men was that they couldn't talk.

Acknowledgements

Firstly, I'd like to thank the beyond fantastic, amazeball Avon team who've welcomed me back with open arms and unbounding enthusiasm. I couldn't be happier if I tried. Also, a big huge shout out of thanks to Victoria, my editor, who not only is full of genius ideas but gives me constant encouragement and inspiration. You rock. And a thank you to Sabah, who I'm so excited to be working with so we can think up ways to take over the world! And of course, there's my wonderful agent, Darley, who just continues to be in my corner no matter what new idea I decide to come up with. A big thanks to the rest of the agency team but especially, Darley's awesome assistant, Pippa, who puts up with my constant emails with such kindness and helpfulness. Thank you as always to my family and friends who are just incredible. And lastly to my loyal and wonderful readers who are simply the best. It's good to be back x